DARKNESS UNDER HEAVEN

WILLIAM CHRISTIE

ROUGH
EDGES
PRESS

Darkness Under Heaven
Paperback Edition
© Copyright 2022 (As Revised) William Christie

Rough Edges Press
An Imprint of Wolfpack Publishing
5130 S. Fort Apache Rd. 215-380
Las Vegas, NV 89148

roughedgespress.com

Paperback ISBN 978-1-68549-113-0

DARKNESS UNDER HEAVEN

Tianxia (pinyin: Tiānxià):

UNDER HEAVEN

This term is usually used in the context of civil wars or periods of division, in which whoever ends up reunifying China is said to have ruled Tianxia, or everything under heaven. This fits with the traditional Chinese theory of rulership in which the emperor was nominally the political leader of the entire world and not merely the leader of a nation-state within the world.

"Wars spring from unseen and generally insignificant causes."
—Thucydides, **The Peloponnesian War**, c. 404 BC.

"War is an act of force, and there is no logical limit to the application of that force. Each side, therefore, compels its opponent to follow suit; a reciprocal action is started which must lead, in theory, to extremes."
—Carl von Clausewitz, **On War**, 1832.

A Note on Chinese Police Ranks

China's Ministry of Public Security, which controls the Public Security Police or national police force, has a rank structure of 5 grades with 12 levels that roughly correspond to their equivalents in the People's Liberation Army. The system was adopted in 1992 according to People's Police Regulations 1992. They are:

Police
General Commissioner
Deputy General Commissioner
Commissioner 1st Grade
Commissioner 2nd Grade
Commissioner 3rd Grade
Inspector 1st Grade
Inspector 2nd Grade
Inspector 3rd Grade
Sergeant 1st Grade
Sergeant 2nd Grade
Sergeant 3rd Grade
Officer 1st Grade
Officer 2nd Grade

Army

Lieutenant General
Major General
Senior Colonel
Colonel
Lieutenant Colonel
Major
Captain
Lieutenant
Sergeant 1st Class
Sergeant
Corporal
Private 1st Class
Private 2nd

There are 6 noncommissioned officer (NCO) classes in the People's Liberation Army, from Corporal to Sergeant Major. So, I have simplified the Army ranks listed above.

The People's Armed Police is a paramilitary force organized along Army infantry lines, though without heavy supporting weapons, under the control of the Ministry of Public Security (Police) rather than the Army. Having been created from existing Army units, they wear an Army-style uniform with their own branch insignia and use the Army rank structure.

The Ministry of State Security, China's intelligence organization, is highly secretive about its rank structure, as are the Western agencies that study it. So, I have arbitrarily decided to use military ranks for their personnel.

There is little agreement among sources as to correct terminology used when translating police ranks into English. So, these tend to vary according to the police terms the individual translator finds most familiar. For example, "Constable" for Officer or "Superintendent" for Inspector among English sources in Australia and Britain.

Therefore, I've chosen, again totally arbitrarily, to use terms most familiar to American readers.

Chapter One

DUCK IN BEIJING was a lot like pizza in New York. Voice an opinion on who made the best and you were guaranteed an argument, if not a brawl.

Peter Avakian had never been to Liqun Roast Duck Restaurant because he'd heard wildly varying opinions on it. Either the best in town, or at least the top five, or an unsanitary dump that served a greasy duck. But tonight wasn't his choice. He was having dinner with the Chinese police. Or, more precisely, the Ministry of Public Security.

He wasn't surprised by the invitation. After two months of negotiating with various Chinese agencies over security arrangements for the 2010 Association of Asian Nations Ministerial Meeting, it was past time they took a run at him.

The restaurant was located in the south-central part of Beijing. A very old part of the city, one of the *hutong* neighborhoods that were rapidly becoming endangered species as they fell to the wrecking ball of runaway real estate development.

The taxi let him off at a *zhaimen*, or residential gate. More like a triumphal arch than the entrance to a gated community—a massive brick structure about twenty feet high. Once these gates had led into a series of walled quadrangle courtyards that belonged to very large, very rich households. But the Manchus were gone, and Communism meant that those princes' places had been subdivided into housing for the masses. Sometimes even the courtyards were filled in to provide more shelter. They were all linked together by the *hutong* alleyways.

Avakian could see through the gate that the *hutong* lane was too narrow for a car. And because of this, as soon as he paid off the cab he was mobbed by a crowd of very aggressive "tour guides" and rickshaw drivers.

"Liqun Roast Duck?"

"I take you there!"

"You never find!"

"You get lost!"

One of the disadvantages of not being tall was that people felt less restraint about putting their hands on you. And Avakian barely reached 5' 7" on days when his spine wasn't compressed by a lot of heavy clothing. Normal human instinct was to shove back. But in his travels around the world, he'd witnessed enough confrontations where the belligerent natives both outnumbered the foreigner and spoke the same language as the authorities. He just shook his head, no.

Some frustrated entrepreneur shouted, "*Da Bizi!*"

Big nose. A traditional Chinese insult for Caucasians. Which brought a faint smile to Avakian's face. That just happened to be the first thing everyone noticed about him. The powerful, curving scimitar he'd inherited from his ancestors in Armenia's Vardenis mountains appeared to take up most of his face. It was brought into even sharper relief by the deep middle-age lines that ran from the sides of each nostril down to the corners of his mouth, two crevasses that seemed to have been cut by its great weight.

But he acted as if he couldn't hear. He made no eye contact and walked through them, nudging out his own path, his hands covering his wallet and passport, letting his momentum pull him free from all the fingers tugging at his sleeves.

The evening temperature had barely dropped below 90°, and it was correspondingly humid. The air was full of the Gobi Desert dust the prevailing winds carried into Beijing in the summer. Not to mention plain brown smog. Smog as bad as the Los Angeles basin in the days before catalytic converters. Avakian was wearing one of the dark, conservative, yet extremely lightweight suits he'd had the foresight to have cut for himself in Hong Kong, with a white shirt and equally conservative tie. He also had on a straw dress hat that matched his suit. He shaved his head, and a bald head was not something to be casually exposed to the Beijing summer sun.

The *hutong* alleys were warrens of twists and turns, the doorways in the crumbling brick walls offering little glimpses into other lives. Avakian greeted everyone he saw in Chinese bad enough to make a few of them titter. A mother trying to hurry a stubborn little boy along pointed at him, and he knew she was telling the kid to mind or she'd let the foreign devil get him. A few rickshaws pedaled by, the drivers glancing over at him smugly.

Every so often there were restaurant signs in English on the walls and hanging from the lamp posts, so even if he didn't get to Liqun Roast Duck he felt he could find his way out. Otherwise, he might be wandering around those concrete alleys until dawn.

He glanced at his watch. He was supposed to be there at 8:00, and the Chinese considered lack of punctuality disrespectful. He was still okay. But something else bothered him. All the local pedestrians had vanished.

Anywhere else in the world that might not be too worrying. But in China there was never no one around. Twenty years ago, his first team sergeant, a philosopher-poet masquerading as a tobacco-spitting *Tejano* master sergeant, used to say that millions of years of humans narrowly escaping being eaten by wild animals had given us that almost extra-sensory warning of impending danger, which you ought to ignore only if you didn't mind being one of the runners-up in the natural selection sweepstakes.

He stopped and listened. Nothing. Telling himself he was being at least halfway stupid, Avakian turned the corner and continued down the deserted alley. He walked quietly, still feeling uneasy.

But after only a few steps he was halted again by a woman's cry, a sharp one of surprise and panic, from around the next turn. Avakian thought it over for a moment, then moved forward lightly on the balls of his feet. He got in close to the wall and listened, but other than the fact that there were at least two men, and one woman in distress, the voices told him nothing.

He crept to the corner and dropped down low, his head nearly touching the ground. People watching corners always expected heads to appear at head level, so no one ever looked near the ground. He exposed one eyeball, just for an instant.

A well-dressed couple that looked Japanese was being held at knifepoint by three Chinese men.

Oh, great. Avakian sprang to his feet and quietly retreated to the last turn, pulling out his cellphone and dialing the number of his dinner host, Commissioner Zhou Deming of the Ministry of Public Security. A much better idea than calling the 110 police emergency number with his limited command of Mandarin.

The connection clicked. "Colonel Avakian, are you having trouble finding the restaurant?"

"Commissioner, I'm in the *hutong* lane and there's a mugging in progress. Three Chinese men robbing a couple at knifepoint."

A short pause while the commissioner digested that unexpected bit of news. "I will have officers there as soon as possible, Colonel. Do not attempt to become involved."

"Don't worry about that," Avakian replied. Before he could pass a description of the three Commissioner Zhou broke the connection. No doubt to call the cavalry. Avakian made sure he switched off the ring tone on his phone. He'd stay there to point the cops in the right direction and make sure no one else stumbled onto the scene.

It was a fine plan, and it only took a few seconds for it to fall completely apart. Suddenly the woman screamed much louder, a scream of pain that was abruptly silenced before its natural conclusion.

Ah, shit. Avakian ducked into the nearest courtyard entrance and looked around for something useful. He grabbed a rake propped up against the wall and snapped off the handle.

As he ran toward the corner, he fished the key ring from his pocket and threw it over the wall so it would land farther down the lane.

When the keys clattered on the paving stones Avakian sprinted around the corner. The three Chinese were all looking the other way down the lane, where the keys had landed.

The nearest man turned sharply at the sound of Avakian's footsteps, but not fast enough. Avakian swung the rake handle in a two-handed stroke over his shoulder. He was aiming for the line of the eyes, but the stick caught the Chinese across the nose. The rake handle broke and the Chinese let out a hard grunt. Avakian followed that up with a blood-curdling yell, which combined with the surprise and shock to send the other two thieves into flight.

But one man wasn't quick enough. Avakian still had a couple of feet of wood in his hand, and as the Chinese turned to bolt Avakian caught him on the back of the head. The Chinese went down, and the rest of the rake handle cracked in half.

The third thief was long gone, so Avakian whirled around to see what the first was up to. He was halfway up off the ground, with blood on his face, and probably some in his eyes because he was feeling around for his knife—it was hard to hurt someone when the adrenaline was pumping.

Avakian grabbed him by the hair and yanked the head right onto his knee. Once, twice. Avakian kept putting the boot in. There was a loud crack that had to be bone. It wasn't Avakian's knee, so it had to be either skull or neck. The thief went limp, and Avakian let go of his hair.

That was it. The street fighter's rule: you didn't put them down, step back, and see what they wanted to do next. You put them down so they didn't get back up.

The Japanese woman was on her knees sobbing away; the man was trying to comfort her.

Footsteps from the other side. Avakian swung around, and there was Commissioner Zhou with his pistol in his hand.

"These two?" Commissioner Zhou said in his excellent English, checking the first one who was splayed across the pavement and moaning softly.

"One got away," said Avakian, breathing hard from his exertions. As soon as it came out, he felt embarrassed by his I'm-cool-and-you're-not pose.

The commissioner was now spitting Mandarin into his cellphone. You wouldn't want to be those two muggers, Avakian thought. Big loss of face tonight for the Public Security Ministry, and they were definitely going to pay for it. If they were lucky, they'd only get the standard Chinese criminal penalty of one shot from an SKS rifle in the back of the head and their organs sold off to wealthy foreign transplant patients.

It actually hadn't been such a bad scheme. Pick off

the rich tourist diners on their way to or from the restaurant. Say the victims somehow managed to surmount the language barrier and call the cops. Well, with a lookout and local knowledge of all the alleyways an easy getaway wouldn't be any problem at all.

Even with a commissioner summoning them, it still took the police a while to make their way down the lanes. Unlike a Western investigation, which would have kept them there answering questions all night long, Commissioner Zhou translated Avakian's statement into the notebook of the first sergeant to appear on the scene and then turned everything over to him. Bad face for commissioners to deal with something so mundane.

Then he turned back to Avakian. "Are you injured?"

"No, Commissioner. I'm fine."

"Then perhaps you misunderstood my request not to become involved."

Avakian wasn't really in the mood for an ass-chewing. He knew how reckless he'd been. "No, I didn't. But the woman started screaming like they were hurting her, and I didn't feel as if I had a choice."

The Commissioner stared at him sharply, then seemed to accept it. "You were courageous but foolhardy. And now you must accept my apologies. What happened was unfortunate and inexcusable."

Avakian knew that Chinese apologies were exquisitely judged things. "Every nation has street crime, Commissioner. No apologies necessary."

"I would imagine you have lost your appetite."

"No, not at all," Avakian said, peeling off his suit jacket because he'd sweated through his shirt.

The Commissioner was staring again, as if trying to get a handle on him. Avakian couldn't really blame him. "Then let us proceed to the restaurant."

"I'll be with you in a moment." Avakian walked back and left some money under the tines of the broken rake.

The loss of any possession wasn't a small thing if you were poor.

The next courtyard was only a short way down the lane. This one had a particularly ramshackle building added to it. Seemingly room by room whenever the owners could afford it, based on the wide range of construction materials and dimensions. There were a couple of parked rickshaws and an enormous pile of split firewood stacked against a brick wall. Two red lanterns hanging over a doorway. And, on the rough projecting concrete block wall of an addition that looked like a large outhouse, a six-foot-high sign of red letters on white. On top, in English, LI QUN ROAST DUCK RESTAURANT. Then three lines of Chinese characters. And again, in English, WELCOME OVERSEAS GUESTS ENJOYING TRADITIONAL CUISINE IN OLD CHINESE COURTYARD.

Avakian's first impression: he could see where some might call it a dump.

Passing through the narrow entrance they stepped into a blast of wood smoke and roasting meat. It smelled good. And it sounded like a New York restaurant with a raucous din of diners' voices, cooks yelling, and woks clanging. The place was packed, and the décor looked like it hadn't changed in 20 years. He liked it.

The hostess recognized the commissioner, and after a brief exchange of Mandarin led them inside. They had to pass through the kitchen to get into the restaurant. The ducks were hanging up inside a wood-burning brick oven, roasting away nicely. A chef was blowing one up as if giving it mouth-to-mouth resuscitation, a traditional technique to separate the skin from the fat. Avakian grinned. There was your bad restaurant review right there.

They were ushered into a private dining room. Wood paneling halfway up the wall and framed Chinese prints on the white plaster above it.

The commissioner gestured toward a seat. "If you please, Colonel."

It always amused Avakian when Commissioner Zhou insisted on using his former military rank. But the Chinese were all about face, and face was all about relative social status, and this put them on somewhat of an equal footing. Though no Chinese would ever accept a non-Chinese as his exact equal. This was confirmed when the commissioner took the traditional chair facing the door. By doing so he designated himself the highest status person at the table.

Commissioner Zhou was a thin, angular man, with an equally angular face—all brow and cheekbones. He'd had extensive dental work somewhere along the line. Not good dental work, but extensive.

The waiter brought tea. Just what Avakian didn't want after his little workout.

But the commissioner took care of that. "I prefer to drink beer with duck," he said. "The red wine, I regret, is not good. But they also have *Beiju*. What would you prefer?"

Beiju was a traditional rice wine, over 50% alcohol. No way, Avakian thought. Not the way the Chinese toasted. "I'll join you in a beer, thank you."

"Menu?"

"I'll have what you're having, Commissioner. Please order for me."

Commissioner Zhou snapped out a string of orders to the waiter who returned a few minutes later with two huge .75-liter bottles of cold Yanjing beer.

After the pouring, Commissioner Zhou raised his glass and smiled. "Despite all the difficulties, thank you for joining me tonight. To friendship."

That was a good one. Avakian thought that the Chinese, contrary to their reputation, were the least inscrutable people he had ever met. All you really had to do was recognize how they were trying to play you and you'd see what they were after. "Oh, of course. Absolutely."

Most Chinese weren't receptive to irony, but Commissioner Zhou gave him a sardonic smile and a, "*Kan Pei*." Bottoms up.

"*Peng Pei*," Avakian replied emphatically. Cheers. Which meant only a sip or two. It was breaking protocol —he ought to have followed Zhou's toast. But he wasn't about to slam beers all night long. Especially since with the Chinese you didn't just sip your drink whenever you wanted. Every time you picked up your glass you had to make a toast, and everyone was expected to drink with you.

Commissioner Zhou acceded to that with, "*Peng Pei*," and that same sardonic smile. "Colonel Avakian, we Chinese usually prefer not to discuss serious subjects over dinner. I hope you will excuse me if I violate this custom."

Avakian was wiping his hands with the hot towels the waiter had brought for that purpose. "As you know, Commissioner, we Americans definitely don't follow that." He liked that Zhou didn't feel the need to display the stone-face stoicism that most Chinese officials seemed to spend their day rehearsing. It was a Chinese thing to regard those who smiled gratuitously as either silly or devious. Maybe the commissioner didn't mind being thought of as devious.

"Then I will begin with a compliment. I have learned a great deal from you this past month. You have a most excellent technique of negotiating by making us extremely uncomfortable. And, since you leave it unclear whether that is your intention, you do so without being insulting."

As the Chinese became more powerful and assertive, they'd become correspondingly harder to deal with. Avakian had been hired to negotiate the security arrangements for the upcoming Foreign Ministers' conference because it was the trend in U.S. government circles to hire private contractors to do what government employees had always done. Not because it was more efficient or less expensive, but for two reasons. It was a nifty way of funneling public money to political contributors, and if anything went wrong the government employee could now blame the contractor. "There must be some cultural misunderstanding then, Commissioner, because I would never want anyone to feel uncomfortable. *Peng Pei.*"

"*Peng Pei.*" Commissioner Zhou sat his glass down. "Thank you for making my point."

Avakian only smiled.

The waiter laid down some plates of appetizers. The Chinese enjoyed all parts of the duck. All parts.

"Please," said Commissioner Zhou, following custom by taking charge of the plate and offering the best to his guest. "Try the liver."

"Thank you," said Avakian, reaching for a piece with his chopsticks. He'd ignored the knife and fork set at the table only for him. "Excellent." The liver was fried, and it really was excellent.

"These ducks are force-fed, the same as those raised for fois gras."

"I didn't know that."

"We are not all provincial."

The Chinese combined an overwhelming sense of racial superiority with a centuries-old inferiority complex that came from being stepped on by the big powers. Something that economic success and becoming a world power themselves hadn't quite cured. "I can't recall ever using the word provincial, Commissioner, or even implying that anyone was provincial."

"Of course, you didn't, Colonel Avakian. My apologies."

"In any case," said Avakian, "if anyone's a provincial here, it's me."

"How is this?"

"Because I come from the provinces."

"But you are a graduate of the United States Military Academy. Forgive me, but I will not pretend that I am ignorant of your biography."

"That's a relief," said Avakian. "Yes, I went to West Point. But I grew up in Bethlehem, Pennsylvania, and I couldn't afford to go to college otherwise."

"And this Bethlehem…?"

"Not like the one in Palestine. A mostly working-class steel town. And when I was a teenager, steel was dying. Other countries were making it cheaper. One day you'll have to worry about that. So, it was West Point for me."

"Your father was a steel worker?"

"Until he got laid off."

Commissioner Zhou was quiet for a moment, then he pointed to one of the plates. "Now that I have started you on something familiar, I must ask if you have ever eaten boiled duck tongue?"

"Not to my immediate recollection." Avakian popped one into his mouth. Kind of rubbery. "Obviously, this duck never said an unkind word to anyone."

"Very good. When you make another toast to clean your mouth, I will know you did not like something." And then, "My father was an engineer, here in Beijing. He was always pleased that we shared the surname of Premier Zhou Enlai. He said that Mao was a tiger who would frighten our enemies but also devour China whenever he became hungry. But Zhou was always for the people. When Mao began the Cultural Revolution, the Red Guards threw my father from the roof of his factory."

"You were sent to the countryside," Avakian said. It wasn't really a question.

"Shanxi. I became a student in shoveling all types of animal dung. Mostly pig. My older brother cut his arm and died of blood poisoning because the village barefoot doctor was afraid to treat a class enemy. My mother killed herself. I was not permitted to go to school, but the teacher left the door open at night and I would go in and read all the textbooks and do the problems on the blackboard. Over and over."

Avakian wondered how many people had made it thanks to a heroic teacher. He raised his glass. "To survival. *Kan Pei*."

"*Kan Pei*. How do you do that, drink the glass down without moving your throat?"

"Just a little trick." Somehow it didn't seem right to tell Commissioner Zhou that while he'd been shoveling pig shit, the teenage Avakian had been mastering the art of chugging beer. "How did you get out of Shanxi?"

"After Mao died and the Gang of Four were overthrown, my sister and I were rehabilitated. She is a doctor now."

"I'm glad to hear it," said Avakian.

"How ironic that the American is from the rural proletariat, while the Chinese is from the urban intelligentsia."

"It is, isn't it? Did you attend the Police University?"

"No, I passed the examinations for the Beijing University of Science and Technology. What were you doing in 1989?"

Avakian had to think for a moment. "I was a captain with the 7th Special Forces Group. In...South America."

"Ah, yes. Panama. I did not recall. And you fought in the invasion of that country in December of that year."

Avakian was hardly surprised that Chinese dossiers were much more comprehensive than American. "It's not much of an invasion if you were already in the country, Commissioner."

"Your modesty does you credit. In 1989 I was in Tiananmen Square. Protesting."

Avakian never expected to run into a police commissioner with that kind of history. But the world was a funny old place. "You don't say?"

"Yes. We were young and naïve. We wanted democracy, and an end to corruption, but we did not want to overthrow the government. Others did, however, and eventually I grew sick of it and went home. On my way I watched a battle on the streets between soldiers and a mob, and I knew China could not withstand any more turmoil. I joined the police."

It was a good story. And since it seemed tailor-made to gain an American's sympathies Avakian couldn't help but wonder how much of it, if any, was true. But just then their duck arrived on a metal tray, burnished brown, almost maroon, with the glossy lacquer of the molasses rub. Head still attached, of course. It was sliced up before them and the meat arrayed on a platter for serving. At other places Avakian had seen the skin removed and presented separately, but Liqun chopped the meat and the skin together.

More plates were set down. Small, thin flour pancakes that weren't quite as dense as tortillas. Chinese broccoli. Bamboo shoots. Cucumber spears. Slivered scallions. A brown sauce.

The deal, as Commissioner Zhou demonstrated, was to place your choice of duck meat and crispy skin in the pancake, add whatever extras suited your fancy, roll it up, and dip it into the sauce. The broccoli and shoots were the side dishes.

But before he tried rolling his own Avakian plucked a chunk of duck meat with his chopsticks and tasted it. Juicy, tender, and great flavor. Not at all greasy. "This is excellent."

"I am very happy you enjoy it."

They both ate with silent dedication. Always a sign of those who'd known what it was like to not just miss a meal but be truly hungry and learned the hard way that the next meal was a promise not always kept.

Then, after the pancakes had been replenished once, and the pile of duck whittled down to the point where it would have been impolite to snatch any of the few remaining pieces, Commissioner Zhou wiped his mouth and said, "What are your plans, after the conference is concluded?"

"I usually take some time off after a contract. Then I get bored and start looking for another job."

"Perhaps you would be interested in consulting with us?"

Avakian considered stringing that along to see what they had in mind. Then just as quickly dismissed the idea. Either the word would get around that he'd been interested, or the CIA would try to run him as an agent—and those idiots would put you up a tree and then saw the branch off behind you. "I don't want there to be any misunderstanding between us, Commissioner."

"Then if I do not understand, I will ask you to explain."

"That won't be necessary. I intend to speak frankly."

"And after you have spent these past months being as subtle as a Chinese? Then I will prepare myself for you to speak as an American."

"As you please. I don't work for any country, or any company, that's a potential adversary of the United States." Though there were more than a few in the security trade who only cared about the size of the quote.

"Since you have paid me the compliment of such honesty, I will not insult you by mentioning the value of the consulting offer."

"I appreciate that. It wouldn't change my mind, but it would almost certainly depress me."

Commissioner Zhou was giving him that look again. And then said softly, "I would have expected nothing else." As he was about to go on, the waiter arrived with two bowls of duck soup. As the final disposition of the duck's remains, it signaled the meal's impending conclusion.

Avakian sipped his soup. "You were going to say something, Commissioner?"

"Only that I appreciated your answer. And I received it as a compliment. Rather than put on a false face and pretend to be the friends we are not, we can be what we are: adversaries, but with a common goal at the present, who can respect each other and enjoy a meal together."

Avakian raised his glass. "That sounded like a toast to me, Commissioner."

They both drained their beers, and Commissioner Zhou refilled the glasses. "Tell me, why did you attack those thieves?"

Avakian knew what was behind the question. For a Chinese, the idea of sticking your neck out if it wasn't a matter of personal or family advantage, or the requirement of your job, was totally inexplicable. "The only reason in the world, Commissioner. It was easier to do it than live with myself if I'd stepped aside and someone had gotten hurt."

Commissioner Zhou was clearly baffled by that. But he let the issue drop, bringing his soup bowl up to his lips and slurping away.

They finished that course in silence, and when the soup bowls were empty the waiter brought a plate of plums and sliced apples.

"This has been a most memorable meal, Commissioner. I can't thank you enough for your hospitality." Avakian raided the last of his beer. "*Kan Pei.*"

"*Kan Pei*. It has been most pleasurable. But there is something else."

There always was, at the end. That's why you didn't spend the evening slamming drinks. "I'm all ears, Commissioner."

Unaccountably, Commissioner Zhou giggled. "I have always enjoyed that expression. Such things make learning a language so challenging. I am directed to share certain information with you. It was thought best that it be passed along in a more...informal setting."

Avakian just sat back and devoured another plum. He had a feeling this was going to be good.

"It concerns the island to the south," said Commissioner Zhou.

The Chinese even got jumpy when it came time to *say* Taiwan. No subject was more radioactive among Chinese officialdom.

"Oh?" was all Avakian said.

"There will be a visit," said Commissioner Zhou. "While the Foreign Ministers' meeting is in progress. From that island."

This was very big. So big that it made it hard to maintain the required pose of detachment, though Avakian still managed it. "On what level will this visit take place?"

Commissioner Zhou did everything but melodramatically swivel his head from side to side to check who might be listening. "The highest."

In 1949, after being beaten in the civil war with Mao and the Communists, Chiang Kai-shek and his Kuomintang, or Nationalist, party fled the mainland for Taiwan.

The Communist People's Republic of China regarded Taiwan as a renegade breakaway province that had to be restored. And they would have tried, but the U.S. Navy kept them from coming across the Taiwan Straits.

For their part, the Republic of China on Taiwan always felt that one day *they* would be going back across the Straits to take back all of China.

So, with both sides considering themselves to be the true representatives of the Chinese people, there was never any question of Taiwan declaring itself an independent nation. Which worked out fine for everyone. Until the opposition Democratic Progressive Party took power in Taiwan in 2000 and promptly threatened to declare independence. China threatened to invade if that ever happened, backing it up by test-firing ballistic missiles across the Straits whenever they felt they needed to make the point.

The U.S government was equally displeased by the prospect of the country they'd pledged to defend from attack dragging them into a shooting war with China.

So, this visit was huge. Nothing like it had happened in over sixty years. Chiang and Mao had met briefly in 1945, smiling through their teeth as they toasted the defeat of the Japanese, while simultaneously plotting to kill each other.

Now that the Nationalists were back in power Taiwan must have decided that extending the olive branch was their best policy. The mainland was apparently ready to accept it, at least for now. And why not, with a roaring economy, the military balance completely in their favor, and time on their side?

"An official visit, on the Presidential level?" said Avakian, not quite believing it.

"Not official," Commissioner Zhou said firmly. "But a visit."

Ah, Chinese subtlety at work again. "But Presidential."

"Yes. A visit to Beijing."

That just happened to be at the same time as the conference. Okay. It was to give everyone political cover and save everyone's face. And while all the Asian foreign ministers, including the U.S. Secretary of State, were together in one place. Maybe to put the stamp on a China—Taiwan détente. This was huge. Like Sadat going to Jerusalem. Secret negotiations must have been going on for a long, long time. "Just a visit. By the President of Taiwan."

"Exactly," said Commissioner Zhou, either missing or ignoring the irony. "And, as the United States security representative, it is necessary to inform you that the visitor will also be attending the women's gymnastic competition all the foreign ministers have been invited to.

At that time the United States competitors will also be greeted and congratulated. So, I have been directed to inform you."

If, as Avakian suspected, both the embassy here and the American Institute in Taiwan, the de facto embassy there, were in the dark about this little visit, Washington was going to go ballistic. But why the hell were they telling *him*?

Commissioner Zhou was now munching on an apple slice.

"Anything else?" Avakian asked.

"Not at this time."

Okay, so it was a trial balloon. If the U.S. was somehow opposed to the visit, both sides wanted to know before any official announcement, so no one lost face. That's why Taiwan was letting China take the lead on it, and that's why the Chinese were laying it on their security liaison unofficially over a duck dinner. "I assume more details will be forthcoming."

"I am told this will be so." Commissioner Zhou stood up. "Please excuse me for a moment."

Avakian guessed that he was going to have a chat with the proprietor, assuring him of continued police protection in exchange for the free meal. Hopefully it would be cooler outside. The kitchen was breaking down for the night. He thanked them on his way through, and they bowed him out.

The Beijing night was still hot, with only a faint smell of duck and wood smoke in the air. Along with cabbage that the light breeze had carried in from somewhere else in the neighborhood. Just a faint buzzing of insects, and the skittering sound of rats hunting in the darkness.

The lanterns over the door were out, but so were the stars. There was just the faintest halo of light from the nearby windows, and he paused to allow his eyes to adjust to the darkness. A clicking of feet on the pavement signaled the commissioner's return. "It is a pleasant evening, is it not?"

"It is," said Avakian.

They walked back down the *hutong*, which was repopulated with locals now that the stick-up artists were gone. The neighborhood always knew what was going on, Avakian thought.

The commissioner's car was waiting on the street at the *zhaimen* gate. "May I drop you at your hotel?"

"No, thank you, Commissioner. I'm going to walk for a while."

"Yes, you are well known for this."

First, he and Commissioner Zhou weren't friends, and now the concession that he was actually being followed around. Who knew what other illusions of international relations were going to be shattered next? "Good night, Commissioner. You'll probably be getting some feedback on our discussion very soon."

"I anticipate so. Good night to you, Colonel."

Zhou got into his car and drove off. Avakian took out his phone and called his boss Russell Marquand, the State Department Diplomatic Security Service Regional Security Officer at the embassy.

Before he could say a word, Marquand said, "What now?"

"Meet me in your office," said Avakian.

"When?"

"Right now."

"Oh, shit," Marquand moaned. "You can't tell me over the phone?"

"No." Not that the Chinese didn't have the embassy bugged, but a cell call was a gift to everyone.

"Oh, shit."

"Don't worry," said Avakian. "It's nothing you're going to take a hit on. But you do need to get to the office ASAP."

He stuck the phone back on his belt. The Taiwan

news couldn't keep until morning. Not with a 13-hour time difference between Beijing and Washington. Waiting until morning would push the information back 24 working hours. Too long. Marquand was going to have to talk to the ambassador tonight.

He passed a construction site where, even at that hour, they were demolishing an old building under portable floodlights with nothing but wheelbarrows and crowbars. A couple of teenagers were sorting out the recyclables near the street, and that gave Avakian an idea. That rake handle had been a lot better than trading punches. Some hand gestures and 10 yuan persuaded the workers to cut him an 8-inch-long piece of $\frac{1}{4}$ inch diameter steel reinforcing rod. A bike shop on the way sold him a roll of leather handlebar tape that, later that night, in his swanky room at the St. Regis Hotel, he wrapped the pipe in. Just a little something to stick in his waistband when out on the town. Just in case.

Chapter Two

IT WAS two years after the Olympics and compared to the rest of the crowded city Beijing's Olympic Green might as well have been a ghost town. There were some people enjoying lunch on the grassy expanses, a few more using the grounds as a shortcut to get somewhere else in northeast Beijing, and Pete Avakian.

He walked past the National Outdoor Stadium the Chinese called the birdcage for its open top and the outer frame that consisted of a crazy-quilt lattice of steel girders like interwoven twigs. Continuing north along the avenue-sized pedestrian walkway there was the Aquatic Center on his left, then the Indoor Stadium just beyond. That was what he wanted to take a look at.

The Association of Asian Nations was brand new. The Chinese had formed it in the hope of both assembling a regional power bloc, with themselves leading, of course, and splitting the other Pacific countries away from the U.S. and Japan. They modeled it after ASEAN, the Association of Southeast Asian Nations, and had very little trouble attracting members. The smaller countries rushed to join in anticipation of more Chinese foreign aid and trade deals. The bigger powers like Japan, South Korea, and Australia took seats at the table as a way to keep an eye on the Chinese and if possible, put the brakes on their influence. All of which the Chinese had counted on. And, just like ASEAN, the Foreign Ministers' meeting being held now was the preparation for a presidential level summit later in the year.

The Chinese had a lot of face tied up in everything going well and were taking their security arrangements as seriously as they had the Olympics. But Commissioner Zhou's mention of a gymnastics competition had piqued Avakian's interest. It was the kind of extracurricular event they always laid for the delegates at these conferences, along with the opera.

When doing a security survey, he always liked to begin with how he would attack the target himself. He'd be leery of the well-guarded downtown hotels and conference locations. But he might be tempted to take a run at some peripheral site like the gymnastics venue.

The National Indoor Stadium was all polished steel and glass that looked deceptively see-through from a distance. The roof undulated like a wave from one side to the other. At the turn toward the building the walkway widened into the size of a double avenue, big enough to handle a capacity crowd leaving all at once.

Avakian took out his little 4-inch-long pair of Zeiss pocket binoculars. Perfect for watching sporting events. And other things.

No Chinese plainclothesmen around. The haircuts and clothes always made them easy to spot. Two uniforms were gossiping near the south corner of the building. Most of the video cameras were concealed—the architect had screamed long and loud about them ruining the lines of his masterpiece. But there were a couple of visible ones, mainly for deterrence, tucked away in the corners. They weren't panning. Avakian really wanted to see how long he could stand out there in plain sight, looking through his binos, before he was challenged. No risk involved. When it happened, he'd just flash his credentials.

But it didn't seem like it was going to be happening anytime soon. The dirty little Chinese secret was that their number one security priority wasn't terrorism but embarrassing political demonstrations. Human rights groups in general, but particularly the banned Falun Gong religious movement. Avakian knew that all he'd have to do was unfurl a banner and they'd be dropping onto him from the skies.

He glanced at his watch to keep track of the response time, then went back to the binoculars. The stadium was getting boring, so he glassed around the area. No good-looking women in the general vicinity.

He twisted at the hips to sweep through the green belt of grass and trees surrounding the stadium.

And he would have missed it but for a little flash of sunlight on either glass or metal. Avakian halted his sweep and went back. A man sitting under a tree with a camera up to his face. A single lens reflex with a big tele-photo lens attached.

Interested now, Avakian kept watching him. And the guy kept working that camera, snapping photo after photo. It didn't take long for Avakian to start feeling that drumbeat thump of adrenaline. A tourist would have taken a couple of snaps and moved on. Even someone doing an architectural study wouldn't have taken that many. Or at least would have changed lenses or moved to another vantage point. But this guy stayed there and doggedly kept at it.

You couldn't do an attack without a reconnaissance of the target. So, any good security officer wondering whether an attack was being planned always kept an eye out for the reconnaissance.

Avakian took out his cellphone and flipped it open. He held the phone right up to his face so the camera lens was positioned directly over his right eye. Then he brought up the binoculars again, so the left eyepiece was over his left eye, and the right was over the camera lens.

Focusing the binoculars on the photographer, Avakian snapped a picture and immediately checked the screen. It worked. The binoculars acted just like a telephoto lens. But the guy's camera was blocking his face.

Now Avakian stopped and thought through his moves, because he might not get a second chance. It was worth a try. And if he flushed the quarry, that might not necessarily be a bad thing. He set his cellphone camera to video and began walking parallel to the shutterbug.

He thought he'd be noticed, but the photographer was engrossed in his work. When he was almost directly opposite, he got the cellphone and binoculars ready. No, still snapping away. Avakian took a step. Nothing. He took another. He had to be in the line of sight. One more step. Then a little start from the photographer, and the telephoto swept up toward Avakian's face. Avakian focused in and tripped the shutter.

At the count of two the camera came down, revealing a startled Oriental face. Probably Chinese, but that wasn't definite. Avakian kept shooting.

Then the camera came back up again, and Avakian was looking down the barrel of the telephoto. But his own face was still obscured by the binoculars and cellphone. He offered the other party a big toothy grin. Just to see what that would do.

The photographer sprang to his feet and headed in the opposite direction. Fast. Someone had a guilty conscience.

Avakian followed. Trying to attract the attention of the Chinese police wouldn't be any use, not with his language skills. And the pair who usually followed him around weren't likely to come running over if he waved for them. He decided to trail the photographer from about 30 yards away, outside effective pistol range, and see what happened.

But he did get on the phone to Commissioner Zhou, imagining how his second call of this kind would go over.

"Colonel Avakian, how are you this morning?"

"Commissioner, I'm at the Olympic Green. And I'm following someone who was scouting the Indoor Stadium."

Another pause at the other end of the phone. "Are you certain of this?"

"He took so many photos of the building that if he wasn't doing reconnaissance, he's planning on building a replica in his backyard. And now he's fleeing the scene just like he stole something."

Another pause to digest that, then Commissioner Zhou was back to business. "Where are you?"

"Heading south past the eastern side of the Aquatic Center. I'm following a male, Asian, mid-twenties, about..." —Avakian strained to do the math— "...175 centimeters tall, about 63 kilograms. Brown hair. Red short-sleeve shirt, blue jeans, running shoes." Then he thought better of it. "You might want to give your people my description, I'm a little more distinctive."

"Wait, please."

Avakian could hear him issuing orders into another phone. He did some calculations. A call to a radio dispatcher. Ordering some cops to the right place. The cops getting to the right place. It would take time.

Commissioner Zhou came back on the phone. "I have people on the way to you. Where are you now?"

"Just took the turn heading west along the southern side of the Aquatic Center. I think he's heading for the Beisihuan Zhonglu ring road." Then something else occurred to him. "If anything should happen, Commissioner, I've got his photo on my cellphone."

"Assistance is on the way to you, Colonel."

Avakian was looking through his binoculars again. The photographer was on his own cellphone. Maybe summoning his own help. A fine reminder to not get fixated on the target and keep an eye out for an ambush.

A siren started wailing in the distance, then another. Wonderful, Avakian thought. They just had to announce their arrival. That was the trouble with police states—they never had to walk softly.

The sirens goaded the photographer into a flat-out run. Which confirmed to Avakian that he was definitely following the right guy. He jammed the binoculars into his jacket pocket and matched the stride. "We're running now," he informed Commissioner Zhou. "Heading west, almost past the Aquatic Center." And almost at the edge of the Olympic Green. Running in dress shoes wasn't the easiest thing in the world. The situation was going to become problematic once they got out into Beijing traffic.

In the distance Avakian could see a group of about six Chinese on the walkway. The photographer ran right through them. As he did, they blocked him from sight, and Avakian kept leaping up as he ran to try and see over them.

But the Chinese were spread across the walkway, and Avakian couldn't see a damn thing.

As he ran up on them, they all had their hands outstretched. Two women and four men all carrying their lunch bags. He thought they were trying to warn him about something, so he slowed down. But one look at their faces as they closed in around him told him just how wrong he'd been.

One of the women started yelling at him. That kicked things off and the rest joined in. This wasn't good. Avakian glanced around them, but the photographer had disappeared from sight. As his own anger flared up, he almost automatically took the kind of action he would have in Latin America. But in China, and with his quarry gone, it wouldn't be worth all the trouble it would cause. Though the sight of those snarling faces had him clenching his fist. Trying to talk to them or showing any subservient posture at all would only encourage them. Instead, he spoke quickly into his cellphone. "Commissioner, right now I find myself surrounded by a group of your countrymen. They seem very upset with me, and I'm going to put you on speaker."

Avakian hit the button, set the volume all the way up, and held the phone out in front of him. An action that by its very strangeness took some of the edge off the rapidly developing hysteria. A couple of them were still shouting, but the rest had paused to see what was going to happen next. And as the intensity of their yelling died down it became easier for everyone to hear Commissioner Zhou yelling through the phone.

Which now made them all shut up and edge nearer to listen to what the voice was saying. A couple actually bent over and presented one ear so they could hear better. Avakian really had to restrain himself from kicking the nearest one in the head.

But Commissioner Zhou kept yelling, and the mood definitely changed. Everyone started looking uneasy, as if *they* might be the ones in trouble now.

The sirens were louder, and then a couple of cops came running across the grass from the Aquatic Center. Blue uniforms, ties blowing back over their shoulders, walkie-talkies to their ears. They rushed up on the little gathering, eyes wide, buzzing on the same adrenaline everyone else was.

The difficulty with the angry citizenry now solved, Avakian's new problem was to calm the police and cut them off from that particular source of information before it led to any snap judgments everyone would regret later. So, he calmly handed his phone to the nearest cop, who was nearly as unhinged by that move as everyone else had just been. Automatically he put it up to his ear and barked out a question. Then he was just listening, and Avakian and everyone else could see the steady change in his posture. He didn't quite come to attention and click his heels, but he definitely straightened up.

Now all the Chinese were looking both sheepish and worried. One of them at the outer edge of the circle started backing away, as if to slip off while everyone was otherwise occupied. But the other cop ran around the circle and pushed him back into the group.

The first cop handed Avakian back his phone with a little bow. Then he abruptly shifted gears and exploded all over the crowd, shouting and slapping everyone within reach. His partner took the cue and joined in.

The Chinese now reminded Avakian of nothing more than a bunch of poodles who'd yapped, snapped, and lunged trying to establish dominance. And when that had only gotten them a crack across the muzzle, they were all whining and submissive. After all, he thought, we weren't that far away from the pack ourselves.

He got back on the phone. "Here I am, Commissioner. I'm afraid the man I was following got away."

"I surmised this. Regrettably, we have lost him also. We had been following you both on closed circuit camera, but he scaled a fence to leave the Olympic complex and entered a dead spot in the surveillance zone."

"There is one thing," said Avakian. "He left his camera bag outside the Indoor Stadium."

That brought some excitement back into Commissioner Zhou's voice. "Then please once again give your phone to the officer. I will have a car bring you to the stadium, and I will meet you there."

"Hold on," Avakian said. The two cops now had the group all sitting down on the pavement. The bulk of the slapping around was done, but the haranguing was still going on, though they were still dealing out a few shots every now and then for good measure. He had to give a little whistle between his teeth to get their attention. They turned around quickly, and he handed the phone to the one who'd had it before.

The squad car took a little longer. The cops kept the group sitting there, probably waiting to be dragged off for questioning and some more slapping. They were now all regarding Avakian with considerable bitterness, as the source of their misfortune.

Avakian was picked up by a white Volkswagen Santana sedan with black POLICE lettering in both Chinese characters and English script along each side, and an American-style red and blue flashing lightbar across the roof. Just like every other police car he'd ever been in, the back seat smelled vaguely of vomit.

They let him out in the plaza in front of the indoor stadium. A few minutes later, another squad car dropped off Commissioner Zhou.

"Are you all right, Colonel?" Zhou asked him.

"Oh, I'm fine," said Avakian.

"I am relieved to hear this. Were you able to determine this person's nationality?"

Avakian knew the Chinese would love it if the guy turned out to be Japanese or Korean. He flipped open his phone and brought the picture up on the screen.

Commissioner Zhou examined it closely. "It seems this person is Chinese." Then he looked from the phone up at Avakian. "You were rash to approach him so closely."

Avakian took out the binoculars and showed him how he'd used them with the phone. And immediately regretted it once he saw the expression on Commissioner Zhou's face. Now the spy issue was going to be on everyone's mind.

"An interesting technique," Commissioner Zhou said. "I must remember this."

The cops had obviously found the camera bag, because there was a little knot of them standing around on the grass right where Avakian had last seen it. "I think the camera bag is over there," he said, pointing.

As they both walked up, the ring of police parted, revealing the bag. The contents had all been removed and laid neatly out on the grass.

The cops were smiling proudly. Avakian fought to stifle his own grin. Commissioner Zhou finished acknowledging his patrolmen's salutes, looked down at the bag, blinked in disbelief, and then exploded himself.

So much for fingerprints or DNA, Avakian thought. No doubt everyone had pitched in to make the display look nice for the brass. And it really did. It reminded him of inspection day at Fort Benning, everything all perfectly covered and aligned.

It took Commissioner Zhou a while to wind up his tantrum. Whether it was for mishandling evidence, or making him lose face before the foreign devil, or both, Avakian was pretty sure he'd never know.

In the interim he bent down to take a closer look at the gear. Professional quality Nikon digital setup. Couple of extra lenses, couple of extra memory cards, lens cleaning gear. And a notebook. That he had no intention of touching. But there might just be something there.

Chapter Three

"NO WAY," said Avakian.

Russell Marquand seemed to take the rejection in stride. "I think you're forgetting that I am, in fact, your employer."

"Check the job description in my contract," Avakian replied. "You won't find it there. A contract that, by the way, has a week left to run. So, feel free to fire me."

If that wasn't the usual employer—employee banter, that was because they had known each other since 1997, when Avakian was still in the Army and both of them had been trying to keep the U.S. Embassy in Freetown, Sierra Leone, from being overrun during the civil war there.

"I figured that would be coming next," said Marquand. He was a man who had crossed the Rubicon of age 50. The comb had more hair in it every morning, and the suits didn't fit so good anymore because he spent too much time in an office chair. "I have to deal with the Chinese every day, and now I have to take crap from you?"

"Oh, you're breaking my heart," said Avakian. "You saying this plum posting isn't so plum? The Chinese been mean to you?"

"Just once I'd like to know what it feels like to come to work in the morning and find out that they *haven't* tried to pull a fast one, *aren't* being obstructive for no other reason than the sheer unmitigated bitching joy of being obstructive. I don't think that's too much to ask, do you?"

"In your job it is," Avakian replied. "They're letting you know they're for real. They're letting you know it's their town, they're running the show, and they're not going to lay down for the big, powerful U.S. of A. They're making sure you never take their cooperation for granted."

Marquand just stared at him for a second. "So basically, you're saying the Chinese are my wife, and I need to send them flowers?"

Avakian burst out laughing. "Not exactly, but it's not a bad way of looking at it. But I don't think flowers would do you any good." Then he paused, still grinning appreciatively. "Might not hurt, though."

"Okay, that was a nice little amusing interlude," said Marquand. "Now I need you to help me out on this."

"I feel your pain, I really do. But the answer is still no."

"I don't understand why you're having such a problem with this."

"Probably because it's a job for one of the Citizen Services Consuls. Or whatever young sprout you've got hanging around here who just passed the foreign service exam."

"Oh, so it's beneath you. You never got anyone out of jail before?"

"Plenty of times. About 23 years ago when I was a lieutenant. Wait a minute. I did it once when I was a major. But that was just so I could fire a dumbass staff sergeant personally. Because if you're not smart enough to keep your ass out of jail, you're too dumb to wear a green beret."

"A heartwarming tale."

"And the moral of it is, I am not getting some bitch-kitten Paris Hilton girl gymnast out of jail for you. It's a simple chore. Send one of your large-necked security people to do it."

"The Chinese are making an issue of it."

"I'm not surprised."

"And they asked for you. Personally."

Avakian's expression was pure exasperation. "You couldn't have told me that at the beginning? You don't have enough heartburn you have to manufacture your own?"

"I appreciate you absolving yourself of responsibility for my heartburn. Why would the Chinese ask for you?"

"Because we're like this now," Avakian said, holding up two crossed fingers. "*Hermanos*."

"Seriously."

"They're killing two birds with one stone. They release the notorious girl gymnast whose release everyone is screaming for, and they're going to release her to me personally, so I get the credit and I'm obligated to them."

"Will you be?"

Avakian shook his head. "You're only obligated if you acknowledge the obligation."

"I'm not even going to pretend I understand that."

"You should try to get more sleep."

"So, will you do it?"

"Sure."

"You'll do it," said Marquand.

"You might want to get your hearing checked the same time you deal with that learning disability," Avakian observed.

"What makes the Chinese asking for you enough to change your mind?"

"Because whenever the Chinese have an ulterior motive it's worth finding out what it is. Maybe they have some information on my little chase they want to share with me."

"By the way, the CIA decided that stadium recon was nothing to be worried about."

"They would," said Avakian. "Do yourself a favor—put your money on the CIA. After all, it's not like they've blown the call on every major crisis of the last 50 years or anything."

Marquand paused to give that some thought, then decided not to comment. "You really think the Chinese want to pass you something else? Washington went nuts on the Taiwan thing. I really don't need my life any more complicated right now."

"Oh, don't worry, I understand perfectly. We'll forget all about the Taiwan question maybe getting resolved after 60 years of tension. I'll make sure I let the Chinese know this is all about you."

"Thanks, I appreciate it. And USA Gymnastics is also grateful. By the way, they want you to take someone along with you."

"Forget about it. Deal breaker. No mothers, no coaches, no suits, no reality TV crews. Dealing with the Chinese on this is going to be hard enough."

"They want you to take a doctor."

"A *doctor*? Did the Chinese work her over?"

"No idea," said Marquand. "Same as I have no idea why they want to send a doctor with you. Just that they do. Are you going to argue about that, too?"

Avakian rolled his eyes. "Okay. How long am I going to have to wait around for this doctor to show up?"

"You mean the lady sitting outside? The one you walked right past."

"*Her*? She's a doctor?"

"Yeah, one of the team physicians. Doctor Rose."

"*Really*? Interesting. I'm kind of relieved to hear she's a doctor."

"Now what the hell are you talking about?"

"Well, I saw her at the embassy party. The one to

welcome the team to China? She just struck me as a little…well, severe."

Now Marquand was amused. "What?"

"I pictured her as some kind of no-nonsense, tightly-wound coach. Very focused, with that low-maintenance hairstyle—essential makeup only look. You know, puts on sun block to get the mail? Makes little girl gymnasts cry, runs ultra marathons for fun, vegan, every conversation's a lecture. Wouldn't crack a smile if Robin Williams spent the weekend at her house. Drives a car that runs on used French fry oil, writes an angry letter to the editor every time the circus comes to town. That's just what I thought. But being a doctor puts a whole different spin on it."

"Do you do this for everyone you meet?"

"I just noticed her, that's all."

"Then it's good you're not into making snap judgments about people. By the way, the team is very anxious to have this taken care of."

"I'm pretty sure I got that part," Avakian said. "What did our gymnast do, anyway? I've heard about five different stories."

"Shoplifting. Got caught, pitched a tantrum, started throwing stuff. Then slapped a cop."

"That'll do it," said Avakian. "Contempt of cop is the one offense that *always* lands you in jail. So, there's face involved. Anything else? Want me to wash your car while I'm at it?"

"No, thanks. I think this ought to cover it for now."

Marquand opened his door and disappeared into the outer office. Avakian was glad he'd at least smiled and said hello to her on his way in.

Marquand returned with the doctor. "Doctor Rose, Pete Avakian."

She extended her hand. "Judith Rose."

Judith, Avakian thought. Any tighter and her ass would squeak when she walked. So much for snap judgments. He looked up into the brown eyes that were about two inches higher than his and took the hand lightly. "Nice to meet you, Doc." She was most certainly the palest white girl on the face of the earth. But she had really big eyes.

"I'll leave you to it," said Marquand. "Call me when it's done."

"Almost forgot," said Avakian. "Where's she being held?"

"The Beijing Bureau of Public Security downtown."

"Oh, then they *are* pissed," said Avakian. "The one just south of the national ministry building, right?"

"Yeah, the city police headquarters."

"Have somebody call and tell them we're on our way over."

"You think that'll make the wait any shorter?" said Marquand.

"May make it longer," said Avakian. "Depends on what kind of mood they're in. But we can always hope for shorter." He motioned toward the door. "Doc?"

On the way through the outer office, she grabbed a leather medical bag that had been sitting on the sofa.

"Now, I haven't seen one of those in a long time," Avakian said.

"My Marcus Welby bag?" said Doctor Rose. "Let's hope the American Medical Association doesn't hear about me making a house call."

What do you know, Avakian thought. Maybe it wasn't so tight after all. "I was going to say, the last time I saw one of those was when Doctor Crowley made house calls when I was a kid."

"Mine was Doctor McGee. He was a chain-smoker."

Avakian chuckled. "Mine, too. We've just dated ourselves, I'm afraid."

She looked at him and smiled. "It's nothing to be afraid of."

I'll bet you aren't, either, Avakian thought.

"It's basically sat in my closet since medical school. But in this job, I carry it all the time, and lately I've been thinking about moving everything over to one of those knock-off Prada bags I see everywhere around here. What do you think?"

"Well, I've got to come down on the side of old school," said Avakian. "You see that bag you've got right now? You're reassured. If Wyatt Earp had carried his six-gun in a Prada bag, he'd still be Wyatt Earp. But would everyone have respected the law the same way?"

There was a moment of silence, then Doctor Rose said, "Now, am I Wyatt Earp in this, or are you saying I need to carry a gun in my bag?"

It didn't happen often, but against his will a wide grin spread itself across Avakian's face. "Clearly, I have no gift for analogy."

"My mistake may have been thinking fashion instead of psychology," she said.

"That always trips everyone up," said Avakian. "Besides, you'd probably be leaving a trail of medical supplies behind you when the seams let go. All the best counterfeits go overseas."

"Is that true?"

"Actually, yes. The middle class here gets bigger every year, but the export machine still takes the lion's share of everything."

"That's interesting. It must explain why everyone's been complaining about the shopping."

"It's kind of like South Korea in the '80s. Back then tourists went shopping for mink blankets, $20 leather jackets, and $2 Ralph Lauren polo shirts. Now all that stuff is over here in China and the Koreans are fighting the Japanese over high-end consumer electronics."

They emerged from the elevator.

"I came in Mr. Marquand's car," said Doctor Rose.

"We'll go in mine," said Avakian. "If we took his and got stuck there, I'd be hearing about it all day tomorrow."

"Is there anything I need to know?" she said abruptly.

"Sorry, but I don't have any medical information. Her name is Brandi something, right?"

"Oh, yes," the doctor said dryly. "Definitely Brandi. Brandi Pressley."

"Any relation to The King?"

"Not that I'm aware of. But just to backtrack for a moment, I wasn't asking about medical information. I was thinking about protocol. I have no idea what I should be doing."

"Oh, there won't be much of that," said Avakian. "Everyone we'll deal with will either speak English or have a translator. I'll give you a few tips, though. If you already know any of this, stop me. For a greeting, a slight bow and say *Ni Hao*."

"*Ni Hao*."

"Perfect."

"What does that mean?"

"In Mandarin, literally: you good? Don't offer a handshake unless they do first. Most everyone follows the Western way now, but a few traditionalists and more than a few rabid nationalists with attitude problems don't. If they do want to shake, throw in another little bow along with it. Slight, not deep. Bow deep and you're conceding you don't have status. If someone wants to exchange business cards, offer yours with both hands. One handed is considered rude. If you're used to talking with your hands, try not to. It's considered arrogant. That's about it."

"I've heard some of this, but I've always been afraid of messing up."

"Better to make the effort rather than come off as arrogant or oblivious."

"You mean a typical American?"

"Yeah, basically," said Avakian. "Okay, other than

that, when we get there, I might have to leave you alone for a bit. But you won't be alone for long. Some pleasant English-speaking Chinese is going to show up and be absolutely fascinated by everything about you. Good rule of thumb is to be polite, but never tell them anything you wouldn't want to have in your permanent Chinese intelligence file."

"Seriously?"

"Seriously," said Avakian. "The Chinese will sock it all away on the oft chance you might be of some use to them two days or twenty years from now."

"Wow."

"Americans never think about stuff like that. But these are serious people. You make a new friend, they ask you for an official gymnastics team handbook or something. You get it for them, and they give you a nice gift in return. You keep doing back and forth favors, thinking nothing of it. Then one day they ask you for some confidential team document, because it's going to help them out with their boss. You think: what's the harm? So you hand it over, and this time they give you money in return. You don't know the ways of the East, you're feeling awkward, but you don't want to offend anyone, so you take it. Next time you meet they show you a photo from a hidden camera of you handing over the document and taking money. And guess what? You're now a Chinese spy."

She was looking at him with a definite sparkle of excitement in her eyes. "That's how it happens?"

"Just that easy. Americans in particular walk right into it—they're the innocents abroad."

"This is my first experience with international intrigue."

"I may have raised your expectations a little too high," Avakian said. "I doubt it will be all that intriguing."

His car was waiting right outside the back entrance.

He held the door open for her. "Doctor Rose, my driver Kangmei."

"*Ni Hao*," said the doctor.

"Good day, missus," Kangmei said gruffly.

"What did I tell you about smoking in here with the windows up and the air on?" Avakian demanded as he ran the windows down to let some fresh polluted Beijing air into the car.

Kangmei only grunted.

"Every day that goes by, my parting gift to Kangmei keeps getting smaller and smaller." Avakian directed those words to Doctor Rose, but loud enough for his driver to hear. "He's working on a nice firm goodbye handshake right now."

Kangmei grunted again.

The doctor leaned in toward him and whispered, "Is Kangmei his first or last name?"

That was some really nice perfume, Avakian thought. "First. But in China it goes in the opposite direction. He's Sun Kangmei. Which would be Mr. Sun, if I ever had reason to call him that."

"So Yao Ming?"

"Mr. Yao."

"Yao Ming?" Kangmei demanded, leaning over the seat toward them with rare enthusiasm. The Houston Rockets center had a fanatical fan following in China.

"Drive," Avakian ordered. "Beijing Public Security Bureau, not the ministry headquarters." Then to the doctor, "Believe me, you don't want to get him started on Yao."

"Sorry," she said. Then, in another whisper. "Does his name mean anything?"

"Yao Ming?"

"Kangmei."

"It means Anti-American," Avakian replied, not in a whisper.

Doctor Rose laughed nervously. "Really?"

"Very popular Cold War name, back in the day. Bit of a business liability now. But don't worry about it. Kangmei's rude to everyone, not just Americans."

"I take it you didn't hire him."

"No, and I can't fire him, either." She had a very delicate, fine-boned face. That was probably what made her eyes look so big. "Are you buckled in?"

"Is that the law here?"

That tweaked Avakian's funny bone. "No. You'll see people dangling out windows like they were in clown cars rolling down the street. Seatbelts are your only faint hope of surviving Chinese driving."

"That I've seen."

"Fifteen years ago, you could have put all the cars in Beijing into an average American high school parking lot. Everyone was riding bikes."

"They do have driving tests, don't they?"

"Have you seen those cellphone numbers painted on walls all over the city?" Avakian asked.

"Yes, I have."

"Those are the numbers of forgers. And from what I understand, the preferred method for getting a driver's license in Beijing is to have a forger knock one off for you. Next is to bribe someone at the Motor Vehicle Administration. I hear you take the driving test only if you don't have the cash for either of those options."

"That does explain a lot of what I've seen so far."

"Never drive in China. And if at all possible, try not to watch while it's being done for you."

It took over an hour to get across town, even with traffic relatively light and Kangmei hitting all his favorite shortcuts.

"Something else I forgot," said Avakian. "Do you have your team credentials with you?"

"Yes."

"Good. You'll have to show them. I've been in the

national ministry building, but never the city office before."

But the guards apparently knew Avakian by sight and were expecting him. They were bowed through without a document check.

"Impressive," said Doctor Rose.

"Somebody ordered that," said Avakian. "By the way, they're very interested in you."

"Are they?"

"They are. Don't be offended if I don't introduce you at first."

On the other side of the security desk was a tall Chinese inspector Avakian was pretty sure he'd met before. "Colonel Avakian, how good to see you again."

Avakian shook the hand. "Likewise, Inspector."

The inspector turned to Doctor Rose and awaited an introduction, but none was forthcoming.

"Lead the way, Inspector," said Avakian.

The inspector smiled tightly and led them through the building.

Doctor Rose took a step closer to Avakian and whispered, "Will be we taken to the cells?"

"You can depend on one thing," Avakian whispered back. "We won't be seeing any cells."

The inspector led them deeper into the building, then down a couple of floors and through a wing of administrative offices. Then into a sort of waiting room. "Please make yourselves comfortable. Would you like some tea?"

The doctor glanced over at Avakian, who gave her a "go ahead" look. "That would be nice. Thank you."

The inspector left them.

Doctor Rose took in the nondescript room. Plain white walls, carpeting so thin it almost wasn't there, padded vinyl furniture, and the usual faint smell of body odor. She was a little disappointed that there weren't any revolutionary posters hanging on the walls. It could have been a waiting room anywhere. "How long are we going to be here?"

"There's only one answer to that," said Avakian. "As long as the Chinese feel like it."

A moment later, the door opened and Commissioner Zhou walked in.

Avakian stifled a smile and stood to shake his hand. "Commissioner Zhou, what an unexpected pleasure."

"Colonel Avakian, I hope you are well."

"As we observe the nations of Asian gather together in an expression of peace and understanding, how can I be otherwise?"

Commissioner Zhou chuckled softly and turned expectantly to Doctor Rose.

Avakian said, "Doctor Rose, allow me to introduce Commissioner Zhou Deming of the Ministry of Public Security of the People's Republic of China. Commissioner Zhou, Doctor Judith Rose of the United States Women's Gymnastics Team."

Commissioner Zhou bent over her chair and took her hand. "My pleasure, Doctor."

"*Ni Hao*," she said.

Commissioner Zhou beamed. "*Ni Hao*. How charming. You are a physician, Doctor Rose?"

"Yes, I am. An orthopedic surgeon."

"I congratulate you. My sister is what I believe you would call a general surgeon. Do you come from a family of physicians?"

"No, I'm the first."

"As is my sister. Would it be an imposition if I spoke with Colonel Avakian in private for a few moments?"

"Not at all. Would you like me to leave?"

"Certainly not. May I offer you something while you wait?"

"I believe there's some tea on the way, thank you."

As Avakian went out the door he hoped he hadn't laid the spy stuff on so thick she'd think the tea contained truth serum or something. And pour it into the plants. Except there were no plants in the waiting room. This was why he always liked working alone.

Commissioner Zhou led him into a nearby office.

"I hope I'm not taking you away from your duties," Avakian said. He always liked to begin by reminding the Chinese it wasn't his first time in the big city.

"You are not. I have been requested to convey my government's strong concern over the seriousness of this incident."

"My government shares this concern and expresses its thanks to the Chinese government for the speedy resolution of this regrettable matter." But that was it—it didn't apologize for the actions of spoiled brat athletes.

"Usually our legal process would take much longer than this. But as a firm advocate of sportsmanship, the Chinese government could not permit an athlete to miss an event, no matter the grave provocation. And I must say that this speedy release is also an expression of our great regard for you. We hope the United States government appreciates this."

Commissioner Zhou didn't need to put that little drone in his voice to make it clear he was reading off a script. But he also gave Avakian a good idea how to nip the whole favor issue in the bud. "I'm very flattered," he said. "But the U.S. government only cares about you holding one of its citizens. Not about her missing a meet. I know I certainly don't."

"Yet you are here to retrieve her."

"I do my job, Commissioner. Just like you. I get the same paycheck whether you decide to keep her or let her go."

Commissioner Zhou was now giving him that familiar faint little smile. "Tell me, Colonel Avakian, have you ever played the board game Go? It is our chess."

"I've seen it, but I've never played it."

"I suspect you would be good at it."

"I understand studying doesn't help much. You have to play the game to get good at it."

"This is correct."

"Sounds like fun."

Now came that moment when the official business was done, and everyone had questions of their own they wanted to ask. Something Avakian stubbornly refused to do. He sat patiently, not moving a muscle or changing expression, until the silence had run way past the awkward stage.

Commissioner Zhou had been matching him silence for silence until he finally sighed and said, "Our…people do not believe there was a reconnaissance of the Indoor Stadium."

"Our spooks think the same thing," said Avakian. "And in my personal experience, whenever the intelligence community reaches unanimity on any issue you can be absolutely sure they're wrong."

"Unfortunately," Commissioner Zhou replied, "that belief alone is not likely to persuade any who have made up their minds. They feel convinced by the clumsiness of the individual involved. The inability to detect any other accomplices upon review of the closed-circuit television. And the absence of any other indications of a reconnaissance."

"Nothing in his notebook?" said Avakian.

"No, nothing."

"All those conclusions you mentioned happen to be the exact same ones our side reached," said Avakian. "But as for myself, if I needed to work something on the inside of a building that was under pretty effective visual and video surveillance, I might hire myself some half-criminal fool who knew nothing about my team or plans, feed him a cover story in case he gets caught, and tell him to take a hundred pictures of the outside of the building and run away if he's spotted."

"And the purpose of this?"

"If no one notices him and the work inside gets done, all the better. If he's noticed and chased off, everyone's attention is focused on the outside of the building and my inside people get away. And, if we're lucky, everyone thinks that because the amateur reconnaissance was blown the plotters were scared off. If he gets caught, he doesn't know anything except the cover story."

Commissioner Zhou mulled that over for a while. "I do not say your theory is not interesting. But there is less evidence to support it than that a Chinese taking photographs was frightened by a foreigner and ran away."

"I really didn't expect to convince anyone whose mind was already made up," said Avakian. "Anything on those people who got in my way?"

Now Commissioner Zhou looked embarrassed. "You must understand, Colonel, that for many decades the Chinese people were taught to both fear and hate all foreigners. These were just simple people…"

"Who saw a foreigner chasing a Chinese man." That was just about what Avakian had thought. He understood the ugly side of nationalism. Particularly the Chinese variety.

"Even though my country has joined the outside world, many of my countrymen still fear the outside world. I must apologize."

"Not necessary, Commissioner. This is also not unique to China."

That was all the face Commissioner Zhou was prepared to give up. "We will search the inside of the stadium again."

"Bomb dogs?" said Avakian, though he knew there were a million places to hide something in that kind of building.

"With bomb dogs," said Commissioner Zhou.

"I'd consider planting a few cellphone jammers inside. The spectators will only think they can't get a signal. If you can't command-detonate an explosive from a distance, someone's going to have to try and get in close."

Commissioner Zhou did not reply to that. Avakian was pretty sure Zhou could order a search on his own authority, but the jammers would require higher permission. So, being Chinese, he probably wouldn't ask.

"You will be attending the gymnastics competition?" said Commissioner Zhou.

"I was thinking about it. If the Chinese government has no objections."

"I doubt this."

"Then I wouldn't miss it."

Commissioner Zhou looked at his watch. "Allow me to take you to your fellow citizen."

Avakian followed the commissioner down another hallway and into an elevator that brought them even lower in the building and let them out into what he imagined was the Chinese version of a holding slash release area. It was much louder, and the walls were tiled about halfway up to the ceiling. For easier hosing down, he guessed.

The sound of plaintive female weeping echoed down the hall.

"I believe your countrywoman is ready to be released," said Commissioner Zhou.

Well, if anything was going to scare the shit out of you, Avakian thought, it was an overnight stay in a Chinese jail. With any luck it had tightened the kid up. Hopefully it had, because when he was on the job nobody ever did anything the easy way.

They went around a corner and through an open door into what looked like some kind of hearing room. Heavy wood benches facing a big, raised desk with a commissioner 3rd Grade in uniform behind it. A bunch of Chinese in plainclothes, higher authority, milling around the edges of the room. They weren't making any bones about both their personal distaste and lack of patience. There was one older gent with a snow-white crew cut who everyone was taking their cues from.

The gymnast and shoplifter in question was an elfin blonde holding her hands over her beet red face and blubbering away in the center of the room, flanked by two stone-faced policewomen. She must have been a teenager except she looked like she went to Munchkinland Elementary School. Doctor Rose was alongside looking like she had no idea what to do about the young girl's histrionics.

Avakian ignored Commissioner Zhou beside him. Without a word, he walked up to the kid and said, "Have a seat on the bench over there and don't say anything."

The weeping clicked off and she looked up over her hands at him. "Who are you?"

Oh, she was slick, Avakian thought. "The guy who got sent to get you out."

The mouth opened and Avakian knew he was about to receive a stream of teenage consciousness, without commas or periods. "Not a word," he said. "No matter what happens. You're not out of here yet."

The mouth screwed up into an angry little pout, but he had to give her credit. She sat down and shut up. Most teenagers didn't have instincts that good. Avakian glanced over at Doctor Rose. She got it instantly and went over to sit down beside the girl.

Without looking back at them, Avakian took a few steps closer to the desk. That the officer was the equivalent of a lieutenant colonel was another subtle Chinese message. Making him deal with a supposed inferior in rank. Which would only be an issue to someone who cared. Looking at the desk officer but directing his voice toward everyone, he said, "Gentlemen, shall we take care of business?"

The desk officer looked over Avakian's shoulder. Avakian didn't have to see the older party's nod to know it had happened. The officer slid a sheaf of papers across the desk and said in English, "Please sign the release form."

Avakian picked them up, wet a thumb and forefinger, and leafed through them. Everything was written in Chinese characters. "I would like to see the English translation of this document, please."

"I will translate for you," the desk officer said.

"Thank you," Avakian replied. "But I will wait for a printed English translation." He heard an inrush of breath from the kid behind him and took that as his signal to move across the room and take a seat on the bench beside her. "Relax and keep quiet," he muttered. "You kick up any fuss and they'll drag you back to your cell." He leaned forward and spoke to Doctor Rose on the other side. "Did you get your tea?"

"Yes, I did," she said. And then in a whisper, "How long will it take them to translate that?"

"Oh, it's already done," Avakian replied under his breath. "Only question is how long they make us wait before they pull it out."

"I *have* to get out of here," the girl whimpered.

"Keep your mouth shut and you will," Avakian muttered back.

There was face involved now, and because of that Avakian knew they wouldn't give anything up easily. The only thing he had going in his favor was that the authority in the room didn't want to leave in case the American barbarian Avakian made a scene or otherwise embarrassed himself, but they also weren't willing to wait around all day. He settled back, crossed his legs, and refused to look at his watch.

Finally, another uniformed cop came in with papers and handed them to the desk officer. Who motioned Avakian back up.

With one elbow on the desk and cupping his chin in his hand, Avakian read every word. Then he flipped back to the front page and pulled a black Sharpie from his jacket pocket. And carefully blacked out all the propaganda. That is, all the admissions of guilt and responsibility, all the promises that the United States would never allow such a thing to happen again, and all the groveling thanks to the Chinese people for their forbearance. "I understand the shopkeeper has been compensated?" he said to the desk officer.

The commissioner nodded.

Avakian crumbled up the page dealing with that and dropped it into the wastebasket next to the desk. The only sound in the room was his marker squeaking across the paper. He initialed the beginning and end of each blacked-out section and signed and hand-numbered each page before affixing his signature at the end. He walked the paper over to the bench and handed Brandi the pen. "Sign it."

"I can't sign anything without my lawyer," she said in a too-loud little girl whisper.

Avakian bobbed down until they were mouth to ear and hissed, "Sign the damn thing!" She signed.

Avakian took it back to the desk. "I will wait for a photocopy of *this* particular document," he said, pointing down at it.

The desk officer again looked over Avakian's shoulder, then barked out an order. One of the enlisted cops grabbed the papers and ran off with them. "You must sign these," he said, sliding the Chinese version across again.

Avakian pushed it back. "You can sign that you witnessed me put my signature to the English version."

Another look over the shoulder. The Chinese document was withdrawn.

The cop returned with the copy. Avakian flipped through it again. "There seems to be two pages missing."

For the sake of form, the uniform was dressed down

for his carelessness. He dashed off again and returned with the two pages.

Avakian checked them, too. "Are we finished, gentlemen? If so, we'll let you all get back to work."

A bag of personal effects was turned over.

One of the cops held a hand to the door. Avakian gave Commissioner Zhou a small bow. Wouldn't do to act too buddy-buddy in front of all his people—someone might get the wrong idea. He nodded to the rest of them. "Thank you, gentlemen."

The car just happened to be waiting outside that particular exit.

Doctor Rose looked at it and said, "How did that happen?"

"Chinese efficiency," Avakian said.

Once they were in the car Brandi took a deep breath and said, "Am I out now?"

"Well, you're out. For now," Avakian replied from the front seat.

She took another deep breath, and it came out at just shy of a scream, "I want to know why the FUCK it took so long to get me out of there!"

Avakian glanced over at Doctor Rose, whose eyelids were at half staff and who gave him a weary little nod, like this was exactly what she'd been expecting.

Avakian was only amused. The kid was quite a piece of work. "It didn't take us this long to get you out. It took the Chinese this long to let you go."

"What the *fuck* does that mean?"

"It means they were sending the message they didn't want anything like this happening again," Avakian said, still calmly. "And just so you know, if this was a major competition, and the Chinese thought you were in the running for a medal, you'd still be behind bars."

"How the fuck am I supposed to compete after this?"

"Was that a question for me?" Avakian inquired.

"Yeah, I'm still taking to you..." Avakian gave her his

warning look and she held up before she said motherfucker.

"If you really cared, you would have paid for your
shopping instead of trying to lift it. Now, you want to go
to the hospital or the team hotel?"

"Just take me to the fucking hotel." And then a lapse
into sullen silence.

Avakian had been leaning over the seat. The bang
and squeal of skidding tires turned him back around even
before the car started swerving. Avakian instinctively
braced his feet against the floorboard, though for all the
good that would do.

The pileup began down the street, the collisions in
neat succession as each driver jammed on their brakes
too late. Avakian was pretty sure that any advice he might
offer Kangmei would be counterproductive at this stage.

The car in front of them spun out, and Kangmei cut
the wheel before they smashed into it broadside. The two
cars swapped paint side by side, which was probably a
good thing since it slowed them down as they approached
the sidewalk. Little Brandi let out a scream so impressive
that it felt like someone had forcibly rammed their
thumbs into Avakian's ear canals.

Even with Kangmei standing on the brakes, they
punched between two parked cars, knocking them both
out of the way, and went up over the curb and onto the
sidewalk. Avakian prepared himself for impact with the
upcoming storefront, but the front end only lightly tapped
the building as they came to a stop. He let out the breath
he'd been holding in and checked the backseats.
"Everyone all right?"

The two women, eyes wide, only nodded. Kangmei,
ashen faced, still gripped the steering wheel. Avakian
reached over to shift into park for him and turned the key
off. "Sit tight," he said. "I'm going to see what
happened."

He was able to get out his door but had to climb over

the hood to make his way up the sidewalk. It was about an eight-car pileup, but most of the drivers were already out on the street and shaking it off by screaming at each other. No one seemed badly hurt.

Up ahead on the sidewalk a China-sized crowd had gathered, and Avakian pushed his way through. The spectators had formed themselves into a neat ring around a young Chinese guy lying in the street. The impact with the pavement had left his exposed skin looking like it had been run through a cheese grater, and the handlebar of his scooter was sticking right through his left leg, just above the knee. He was moaning and thrashing, breathing hard, and rapidly slipping into shock.

This was going to require the doctor and her bag. As Avakian turned around to get her, he heard her voice on the outer edges of the crowd saying, "Let me through, please, I'm a doctor."

That wasn't cutting any ice with a Chinese crowd, even if anyone did understand what she was saying. Avakian shoved his way through to her, then shoved his way back with her in his wake. They burst into the miniscule open space surrounding the casualty.

Doctor Rose knelt to evaluate the injury and immediately saw that every time the agonized young man moved, the wound around the scooter handlebar opened and arterial blood pumped out. "Keep him still!" she ordered Avakian.

Who felt carefully to make sure the pelvis wasn't broken before pinning down the guy's hips. If they weren't moving, the legs weren't.

Doctor Rose already had her medical bag open and a pair of latex gloves on. She ripped the sterile packaging off a hemostat clamp and slid it into the wound along the path of the handlebar, trying to locate the ruptured vessel.

The patient howled like a banshee. Feeling the hot breath of a hundred Chinese spectators on the back of his neck, Avakian fervently hoped that the kid wouldn't die out here on the street.

Doctor Rose located the bleeder and clamped it. She packed gauze into the wound and started a bag of Ringer's intravenous solution. Shining a light into the young man's pupils, she checked their reactivity before examining the nose and ears for signs of blood or cerebral fluid. Satisfied that there wasn't a brain injury, she prepared a syringe of five milligrams of morphine and injected it into the IV line.

The patient's color had already improved, and he was much calmer.

"Is there some way you can get the handlebar off that scooter?" the doctor asked Avakian.

He took a quick look at it, then disappeared into the crowd.

Doctor Rose couldn't understand why an ambulance hadn't arrived yet. She took her patient's hand and said, "Don't worry, you're going to be all right."

Reacting more to her tone, the young man gave her an anxious smile. The doctor looked up at the ring of spectators. They regarded her impassively, neighbor commenting to neighbor on her every move. Doctor Rose busied herself in adjusting the IV flow.

Peter Avakian suddenly reappeared, carrying a hacksaw. He leaned over the scooter and steadied the blade against the handlebar, about six inches from where it entered the leg.

"Wait a minute," said Doctor Rose. "Let me push five more milligrams of morphine before you start."

After giving that shot a chance to work, she tapped the handlebar with her finger. The patient didn't make a sound. "Try not to move it too much," she told Avakian.

He nodded and began sawing. About twenty strokes and he was through. Just then the sound of sirens filled the air. Of course, Avakian thought.

Doctor Rose placed an inflatable splint on the leg and

pumped it up. That section of handlebar was going to have to stay in his leg until surgery. "I should go with him to the hospital," she said.

"Not a good idea," Avakian replied. "And not just because of the language barrier."

"Then how am I going to tell them about the morphine?" she demanded. "If they give him more, they could kill him."

Avakian reflected that Kangmei would have been helpful just then, for translation purposes. Too bad he wasn't around. "Does anyone speak English?" he asked the crowd.

They discussed him in Chinese, but no one answered in the affirmative.

Avakian sighed and thought it over. "What's the abbreviation for morphine?" he asked the doctor.

"MSO4," she said. "Morphine sulfate."

"How much did you give him?"

"Ten milligrams."

Avakian took the Sharpie from his pocket and wrote across the patient's forehead: .01 MSO4. "That ought to cover it."

A policeman pushed his way through the crowd and began interrogating Avakian and Doctor Rose in excited, rapid-fire Chinese. Avakian just held out his hands in a questioning motion.

The spectators immediately began telling the cop what had happened.

Not good, Avakian thought. It looked like another call to Commissioner Zhou was going to be in order.

Two ambulance attendants pushed through the ring with a stretcher. Doctor Rose, using pantomime, showed them the clamped artery. They remarked to each other over the lightweight inflatable splint.

The cop said something, and the two attendants began arguing with him. Then a couple of firemen rolled in and joined the argument.

Avakian just stood there, waiting for some resolution, when he received a tap on the shoulder. He turned around and a few of the spectators were gesturing for him to get out of there.

When in Rome, Avakian thought. He bent down and picked up the doctor's bag and, with the argument still raging, wrapped one arm around the doctor's waist and pulled her into the crowd. Which closed in around them, a couple of Chinese patting him on the back.

"Should we be leaving the scene of the accident like that?" Doctor Rose asked him.

"If they want us, they can come get us," Avakian replied. "Otherwise, why bother them?"

They were now free of the crowd and heading down the sidewalk.

"Why didn't any of those people help that man?" Doctor Rose asked.

"You're incurring an obligation," said Avakian. "Which can be a very serious thing. Besides, you open yourself up to all kinds of potential official hassles, as our case proves."

"At least someone gave you that hacksaw."

"Are you kidding? This is China. I had to buy it."

"I still don't feel right about leaving."

"You did good, Doc," Avakian said. "Besides, it was time for the locals to do their job."

"But they could be arguing for the next fifteen minutes, while that man needs to be in the hospital."

"Yeah, but they were going to do that whether you were standing there or not."

Back at the car Kangmei was arguing with a group of other drivers over potential liability.

Avakian stuck his head in the window. "C'mon, Brandi, we're going to walk a few blocks and catch a cab."

"It's about fucking time," she said.

There were press and photographers waiting on the

curb in front of the hotel, along with a whole herd of gymnastic team suits. Little Brandi bounced out with a brave smile on her face and was embraced by her mother before they were all engulfed by the media scrum.

Doctor Rose stayed in the cab.

Avakian had a feeling he was about to receive a sensitivity lecture. Whatever. "You're not going with her?"

"It'll be a while before we get a chance to check her out. I wanted to ask, are the Chinese going to do anything else about this?"

"Depends on how much she embarrasses them with the press. They may let it go. But they're just as capable of picking her up for spitting on the sidewalk and either deporting her or putting her on trial."

"Why didn't you tell her that?"

"I may have been wrong, but she just didn't seem prepared to listen."

"I wanted to tell you that I did get quizzed by the Chinese once you were gone."

"You didn't tell them anything, did you?" Avakian demanded, mock-sternly.

"Just name, rank, and serial number…I want to thank you. This turned out to be *very* intriguing."

She seemed about to say something else but didn't. So Avakian did. "Tell me, Doctor…"

"Please call me Judy."

"As long as you call me Pete. Tell me, Judy, do you like dumplings?"

"As in chicken and?"

"As in Chinese."

"My knowledge of Chinese food doesn't extend much beyond General Tso's chicken, I'm embarrassed to say."

"Then maybe you'd like to join me for dinner? I know the best dumplings in Beijing."

She favored him with a sunny smile. "I'd like that."

The smile worked its magic on Avakian. "I'm going to be busy during the gymnastics."

"You're going to it?" she asked, surprised.

"Business. But dinner right after that?"

"Great."

They sealed it with the modern ritual of entering each other's cellphone numbers into each other's cellphone address books. Then he opened the cab door for her, and she left.

"United States Embassy," Avakian told the driver.

———

"THAT'S GOOD," said Marquand. "Another diplomatic incident averted. The ambassador will be ecstatic." He was checking through the release document. "Did you really cross out all this stuff right in front of the Chinese?"

"You'd better believe it. And good thing, too, otherwise you would have been delivering the formal apology from the middle of Tiananmen Square, dressed in nothing but a Chinese flag jockstrap."

"Just as well, then. Red and gold really aren't my colors. Did you hit on the doctor?"

"I have to admit," Avakian said. "She's not the tight-ass I thought she was. She could have blown the whole deal any number of times, but she kept her head and kept her mouth shut when she needed to. Then we ran into that road accident, and she saved a guy's life, just as cool as you please."

"So you did hit on her."

"We're having dinner," Avakian said grudgingly.

"Do you good. Your mother probably always wanted you to meet a nice Jewish doctor. And the Chinese don't think the Indoor Stadium recon is any big whoop either?"

"Not officially."

"Well, look, don't worry about it. With the Taiwan president in there, they're going to have that place hermetically sealed anyway. CIA station chief is practically living with his Chinese counterpart over this. All the big eyes and big ears are tuned this way."

"I hope so," said Avakian.

———

"HE LOOKS LIKE TELLY SAVALAS," said Doctor Judith Rose.

Doctor Regine Toussaint, her partner on the team, looked up from her coffee. "And who is Telly Savalas?"

"You're kidding. *Kojak*?"

"If you make me guess, I have to say a TV show."

"Now you're pretending you're too young to remember *Kojak*."

"And I must be doing a very fine job of it. What else was this Telly Savalas in?"

Doctor Rose had to stop and think. "*The Dirty Dozen*!"

"This time, I'm going to guess that was a movie."

"You've never seen *The Dirty Dozen*?"

"M'dear, why on earth would I have ever seen a movie called *The Dirty Dozen*?" Doctor Toussaint's family had rowed from Haiti to Miami when she was a little girl, and she still had the Creole lilt to her voice.

"It's a classic."

"What is this Telly Savalas doing now?"

Doctor Rose sighed. "He's dead."

"You don't say."

Doctor Rose paused to try and calculate how old Doctor Toussaint had been when *Kojak* was on the air, then abandoned the effort when it began to depress her. She wracked her brain for an age-appropriate alternative. "Vin Diesel!"

"He looks like Vin Diesel?" said Doctor Toussaint, without an enormous amount of enthusiasm.

"No, not really. He's short, and bald, with very strong kind of ethnic features." That made her pause again. "I'm not making him sound very attractive, am I?"

"Come to think of it, I seem to remember your new friend from that party. With the shaved head? The craggy face?"

"Weathered," Doctor Rose countered. "A distinguished face."

"And the large nose?"

"It's not that large."

"Darlin', it's not Cyrano, but it's not small."

"Oh, all right."

Doctor Toussaint unleashed a triumphant smile. "Now I see what you're getting at. He's a sexy ugly man."

"He's not ugly, Regine. He's just not…conventionally attractive. How about that?"

"I always say you can tell a lot about a man by how he deals with male pattern baldness."

"You have to admit he's a striking looking man."

"M'dear, I don't have to admit anything."

"He can also pull off wearing a hat with a suit."

"Like a Kangol cap?"

"No, no, I hate those. Dress hat, matching the suit. Just right."

"I never look good in hats," Doctor Toussaint mentioned sadly.

"You should have seen it, Regine. They led me all the way into the basement of police headquarters, and it sounds like a cliché to say it felt menacing, but it did. There was a room filled with Chinese policemen, all with their arms crossed and refusing to say a *word*. They gave new meaning to the word hostile. They brought Brandi into this room, and as soon as she saw me, she started the pathetic wailing act she does so well to get her way. Now, I do not know what to do. I can't examine her in this room full of policemen, and she won't stop crying. Am I supposed to say something to the Chinese? I'm the surgeon, right? There isn't a stressful situation I can't handle, and I was petrified."

"Don't blame yourself. It sounds scary."

"My knees were literally knocking together. And then this burly little guy strolled in and took complete control of the situation. Unbelievably cool. He quieted Brandi down in about ten seconds flat. The Chinese were trying to pressure him into one thing after another. And he just *deflected* it, without a hint of anger or even annoyance. In five minutes' time, he had *them* fidgeting around. I would have signed anything, just to get out of there. And everyone knew he was ready to spend the night to get what he wanted. Not only did he insist on an English translation of all the documents, he spent fifteen minutes *amending* them before he signed them."

"It sounds like I need him to negotiate my next contract."

"You'd be the highest paid doctor in the country. It was amazing. And then when we left Brandi started acting up again in the car."

"The same diva act?"

"Well, she was a little tired, so she wasn't on the top of her game. But the volume was right up there. But then this man Avakian took control again, just by telling her the facts of life as if he could care less one way or the other. Never raised his voice. Brandi didn't know what to do. And listen to this. When she asked how she was going to compete after this, this is what he said: if you really cared, you would have paid for your shopping instead of trying to lift it."

Doctor Toussaint laughed uproariously. "Oh, I wish I had said that! This is the problem with being a doctor instead of a…what on earth is he, anyway?"

"Something to do with security."

"A spy? Darlin', no wonder he got you so excited."

"I don't think so. One of the Chinese officers called him colonel. And he did not get me excited, Regine."

"We always succumb to the man of mystery."

"Oh, please. At least I got to practice some medicine so he wouldn't think I was completely useless."

"Did you ask him out?"

"I was going to, but I froze again. But he asked me. We're having dinner."

"Let's hope he's not married."

Doctor Rose sat up in her chair, suddenly concerned. And then, "I didn't see a ring."

"Child, that doesn't necessarily mean a thing."

Chapter Four

OH, you should have known better than to go to the gymnastics competition, Avakian told himself. You should have known that hanging around the stadium with nothing to do was first going to drive you crazy, and then make you want to start running around correcting things. That would be great. You could be the kind of old fart colonel you always despised, sticking your nose into everything and giving the young 'uns the benefit of your wisdom. Stay in your lane, he kept telling himself. You'd rip the lips off anyone who poked his nose in *your* job. Oh, it was going to be a great day.

At least the Chinese were doing everything right. They'd taken a page out of the U.S. Secret Service book and issued special color-coded lapel pins to anyone who had access beyond the regular seating: the media, coaches and trainers, and the security personnel of all the teams. Right when they'd arrived at the Indoor Stadium that morning, everyone's face cross-checked against the database. That way it wouldn't matter if someone had managed to steal or forge a set of the laminated credentials they all wore around their necks. No lapel pin and they'd be exiting the hard way. Very important, because security personnel didn't go through the metal detectors. It was expected that they were armed.

The President of Taiwan was sitting ringside, or whatever it was called in gymnastics, with the President of the Beijing Gymnastics on one side and the minister in charge of sports on the other. A nice way for the Chinese government to finesse how to be seen in public with him. Not such a high level that it would imply any present or future relationship, but not insulting either. And everyone sitting beside, in front, and behind them were Chinese security, both male and female.

The U.S. Secretary of State was on the other side of the floor, and probably grateful for that. Boxed in by Marquand and his Diplomatic Security people.

So, for now, at least, there was nothing to do but watch the gymnastics. And watch the lapel pins.

Though he would never, ever admit it to anyone, Avakian found the whole thing almost unbearably sad. On TV you only saw the top ten girls competing to see who was going to win the medal and be on the cereal box. But there were a hundred of them here. Every last one having given up their adolescence to be trained like cute little poodles for the circus. Except Avakian suspected that circus dogs were treated better by their trainers and parents. Watching a coach snap at a limping girl to stand up straight and then hug her once he knew the cameras were on them was enough to incite him to violence. Or catching a glimpse of another kid throwing up in a bucket offstage while another coach looked impatiently at his watch. He had to restrain himself from hitting them. He was glad he didn't have a daughter.

And then when the scores came up there was only one example of joy through sport to be seen, and that was on the face of the winner. Everyone else didn't take it very well. A little girl shattered by failure was enough to break his heart.

Avakian decided to continue his habit of keeping an

eye on the spot that was away from the center of attention. As he went through the tunnel leading into backstage two Chinese cops on either side nodded him through.

With the teams still out on the floor, there wasn't much traffic. The venue had been designed for other uses, like expositions, so there were a few smaller public spaces in addition to the 19,000-seat main floor and dressing/locker room areas. The reason why Avakian was checking the seals on all the doors he walked past.

Then something made him stop. Two Chinese photographers were leaning against the tunnel wall, chatting. Avakian had to ask himself why they were there instead of out photographing the awards ceremony. He stared at them, probing for a reaction. One of them finally noticed and nudged the other. They both stared back at him and continued talking.

Avakian was wary of crying wolf. But if something did go down it was always the guy like him who got shot by mistake. He walked back down the tunnel and caught the eye of one of the Chinese cops, cocking his head in the direction of the photographers and firing off a questioning look. The cop got it immediately. With his partner watching with one hand on his sidearm and the other on his radio, he went over, checked their pins and credentials, and rooted around in the camera bags. When he finished, he said something to them, and as he passed Avakian gave an almost imperceptible shake of the head. Okay, Avakian thought, so much for instinct.

Loud applause rose from the other end of the tunnel, and the photographers came flooding in. A few minutes later, a parade of girl gymnasts in their warm-up suits, trailed by coaches and trainers. The ones with the medals around their necks were prancing and smiling. The rest were not. A few were still red-eyed, sniffling, and wiping their faces on their sleeves. Avakian positioned himself out of the way of the rush, off to the side near one of the sealed doors.

Camera flashes popped wildly. Then the teams were through, but the photographers stayed where they were, muttering impatiently.

A few minutes later, the noise rose again from the tunnel entrance. Avakian knew what was coming next. In the trade they called it "riding the diamond". The security men in the point sweeping everyone out of their way like a human snowplow. The seal on the sides, all facing outward, pushing everyone toward the walls, carefully watching hands. Cocooned in the middle of the diamond formation were the VIPs, the Taiwanese President and the two Chinese sports bigwigs. More security men closed off the rear. The four points of the diamond meant that the whole formation could change direction instantly.

It was a common sight on TV, but what the viewing public couldn't see on the other side of those cameras looked like a cross between a bread riot and a goal line stand in the Super Bowl. The gentle members of the press were elbowing and kicking each other for position with an abandon that explained why, other than terrorism, they had all been searched for weapons at the door. When the flashes and TV lights went off again Avakian kept seeing white spots before his eyes. And they were all screaming questions, literally screaming, all at the same time. Why, he had no idea, since it was impossible to pick out a single word they were saying. The effect inside the tunnel was like unfolding your lawn chair next to a jackhammer. Avakian was afraid his eardrums were going to burst. He pressed a finger to each ear canal to try and reduce that awful pressure. And in the eye of that hurricane the VIPs strolled along as if nothing was happening, waving casually and wearing steady, pleasant, pasted-on smiles for the cameras. It gave Avakian something he thought he'd never have: respect for politicians. To hang tough in the middle of all that was an achievement.

The diamond passed by him, sucking along the rear security and more photographers. Then it was like the storm had passed and the ocean was calm. The noise diminished only slightly as the crowd moved a little farther down the tunnel.

Just then the door in front of Avakian opened, the tape seal twanging off. A Chinese in a maintenance uniform emerged, credentials dangling around his neck and a little walkie-talkie clipped to his belt. Avakian relaxed. Just another dope taking the wrong door at the wrong time. But then the right hand came out of the pants pocket clutching something, and the left hand swung over to yank the pin from a hand grenade.

Avakian froze for a second out of sheer disbelief, took another second to reprocess the whole image to confirm what he was really seeing, then burst forward, the adrenaline tunneling his vision and seeming to slow everything down. He swept his jacket back, clawing for the homemade anti-mugger blackjack stuck in his waistband at the small of his back.

The maintenance man was standing sideways so the rear security couldn't see his hand. His body tensed and his right shoulder dropped as he started into his pitching motion.

Avakian had the tape-wrapped steel rod out, but the arm was coming up and he was still a good two steps away. Everyone was naturally looking toward the front, and the assassin was obviously planning on letting his grenade fly and being back through the door before it even went off.

Avakian dove forward, swinging his arm over his head like a tennis serve. He caught the maintenance man a solid shot on the back of the head, and they both went down together. Avakian landed across the back of the man's legs. His knee hit the floor hard and sent an electric jab of pain up his leg and into his groin.

When his mind finished processing that he looked up

and saw the grenade finish a short bounce and land back down on the floor in front of him. It was Russian, looking like a green soup can with the shiny metal detonator housing sticking out from the body like a pencil. Only Russian grenades had that feature. Didn't get the pin out, Avakian thought desperately, more in the form of a prayer than an observation.

But as the grenade spun on the floor it suddenly twitched with a sharp, clearly audible pop. Another unique feature of Russian grenades. Other countries developed primers that initiated silently to start a grenade's fuse burning. But the Russians never believed in going to all that fuss and expense.

So, the pop told Avakian he had less than four seconds. If he picked it up, there were people in every direction he could possibly throw it. Screaming, "Grenade!" he bounced up and grabbed the maintenance man's belt, then lunged forward to get ahold of the back of his collar. With one foot underneath him and one knee still on the ground, and a powerlifter's scream, he jerked the Chinese up off the floor as if he were a 150-pound barbell instead of the equivalent in human dead weight. Avakian lifted him about two feet in the air and, still screaming from the exertion, thrust the body forward onto the grenade. His shoulder popped like the primer with another hot poker of pain, but he didn't release his grip, landing on top of the maintenance man to tamp him onto the explosive.

He waited there all tensed up, eyes screwed shut, for what seemed a very long time. It might just be a dud, he thought. And in the midst of a muffled roar, he was launched into the air with enough force to snap his neck back and his teeth together.

He landed hard on the floor with another shooting pain, in his elbow this time. That, and the stink of explosives in his nostrils told him he was still alive. He was in the midst of a cloud of black grenade smoke and couldn't see a thing. And then someone jumped on top of him, pointed knees stabbing into his back. Jesus. His arm was wrenched behind his back, and if the pain in his shoulder had been a little less intense, he might have screamed before all the air went out of his lungs. He was just about to spaz out and start fighting when he realized he was being frisked. It had to be the Chinese cops. Just relax, he told himself. We'll get this straightened out. That is, if he wasn't bleeding to death—something he couldn't tell at the moment. Just don't resist and make it worse.

Something clicked in his head, and it was like the first time he'd heard sound in a while. The screaming echoing through that tunnel was ungodly. As his head was pulled up off the floor a bunch of pistol shots, like a string of firecrackers, went off down in the direction of the VIPs. And an instant later an absolute roar of more gunfire, too many rounds to count. Avakian's head cracked nose-first onto the floor as whoever had his arms let go and jumped back on top of him to try and get closer to the ground. Christ that hurt. Avakian could feel the warm liquid tickling of his nose bleeding, and as he turned his head to the side to try and get some air, all he could see and feel was feet stampeding past. The screaming was even worse now, something he would not have thought possible.

Eventually whoever was lying on him got up, very cautiously. His arms were twisted back once again, and cold metal handcuffs snapped on. He was grabbed and thrown with his back up against the wall, though still sitting on the floor. There was nothing he could do about the blood streaming from his nose onto his shirt front. On the bright side, it was actually the least painful position he'd been in for a while. Every photographer in Asia stopped to take his picture as the cops pushed them down the tunnel toward the arena floor.

Once his vision cleared from the flashes, he managed a look up at the two cops standing above him with their pistols drawn, preening like heroes. And then over at the maintenance man face down on the floor, seemingly intact but lying in a literal lake of spreading blood. It wasn't going to be pretty when someone tried to roll him over. That triggered a thought that struck Avakian as incredibly funny. If anyone was ever going to die of an untreated nosebleed, it would be him. He'd always suspected it would be his karma to go out in the least dignified way possible.

Casualties on stretchers, he couldn't tell who, went rolling by. In the midst of all that bedlam, Avakian couldn't make heads or tails of what had happened. Then a female Chinese photographer came running up, flanked by two cops of her own, super agitated. She was screaming, too. Pointing down at Avakian and screaming, pointing over at the body of the maintenance man and screaming. Look, take me out and shoot me, Avakian thought desperately. Give me People's Justice. Just tell her to shut the hell up.

But it got worse, because the cops started yelling back at her. Then she screamed some more. For the sake of his sanity Avakian tried to find his happy place and tune it all out, which wasn't easy with his knee, shoulder, and elbow killing him, and blood continuing to pour from his nose.

But something happened, because suddenly he was pulled to his feet and the handcuffs came off. The cops were brushing him off and patting him on the back. Maybe she was on his side after all.

Avakian pointed to his jacket, asking permission to open it. The cops nodded, and he pulled out his handkerchief and pinched his nose shut and dropped his chin to his chest. The woman photographer tugged his sleeve and gave him the thumbs up. Avakian nodded gratefully, still clutching his nose.

Once he got the bleeding stopped, they led him down to the dressing rooms. There were at least half a dozen bodies covered with sheets and jackets, smears of blood all over the floor, dropped handguns, and expended shell casings. The Chinese police were busy taking photos of everything.

All the gymnasts and coaches were still under guard in the dressing rooms. Avakian got a look at himself in a mirror, and damn he was grim. You could barely tell his shirt had been white. He definitely looked like he'd lost the title bout.

As he came limping in, one of the trainers from the Polish team came over, took him by the arm, and shooed some girls off a massage table so he could sit down. A blonde Viking in braids, a pocket battleship of a woman who looked like she could have pressed that grenade thrower right over her head. She got his jacket and shirt off and began cleaning him up with a bottle of water and a handful of gauze pads.

All he knew were the languages of former enemies. He almost spoke to her in Russian, but that would only work on a Pole his own age. Someone in her 20s wouldn't even remember the Berlin Wall coming down. "Do you speak German?" he asked in German. His German wasn't as fluent as his Spanish, but he could hold his own with it. As a more senior officer he'd done tours with the 10th Special Forces Group in Germany.

"A little," she replied, now half-wary and half-suspicious. "You German?"

"No, American," said Avakian.

Now a smile came over her face. "Then why not did you say so?" she demanded in somewhat better English than her German.

"I wanted to thank you," said Avakian.

"Then thank me," she said gruffly.

"Thank you," Avakian said softly.

She blushed red as she smiled. Then turned gruff again, as if embarrassed. "Where hurt?"

Avakian pointed to his knee, elbow, and shoulder. The knee was already nicely swollen, and the elbow and shoulder were as sore as a toothache.

She poked and prodded him relatively gently. One of the other trainers came over and said something to her in Polish. She laughed and told Avakian, "She say, coach on Russia team. Look same as you. Could be brother."

"No Russian brothers," Avakian said.

"I no think so. Russian bad teeth. Smell bad." She pinched Avakian's cheeks together with thumb and fore-finger until his mouth opened involuntarily. "You, good teeth. Smell good."

Lying flat on a table with two Polish Amazons peering at his teeth, Avakian could come up with no adequate response.

She finished her examination and told him, "Be strong man now."

Oh, that didn't foreshadow anything good. Before Avakian could reply, she grabbed him by the upper arm, pulled back, moved it around, and slammed the heel of her other hand into his shoulder. Which he felt click back into place.

It hurt so bad he almost bit his tongue through. He hoped he'd been at least outwardly stoic, since he got the impression she might beat him out of sheer disgust if he started whimpering.

But he must have done all right, because she patted him on the head like, well, a circus dog, before strapping ice packs onto him with Ace bandages.

"What is your name?" Avakian asked.

"Jozefa."

"Piotr. Thank you, Jozefa."

She gave him another smile, and two enormous brown pills that he hoped were anti-inflammatories. No matter, as he was too afraid of her not to take them. Then she made him lay down on the table, creating a pillow and shoulder support from some towels. Avakian almost proposed to her right then and there.

The pills were the real deal, because in short order he was pain free and a nice warmth had replaced the chill of the ice. Despite the noise of a room packed full of excited people all talking in twelve different languages, he drifted off to sleep.

He was awakened by someone tugging on his uninjured arm. He opened his eyes and there was a pair of Chinese, a man in plainclothes and a female sergeant in police uniform, with Jozefa hovering protectively behind them.

The man asked the questions and the woman translated. "Please, sir," the policewoman said in English. "I must interview you now. Are you able to speak?"

Avakian almost said no, but that would only be postponing the inevitable. "I can speak."

Her English was British-accented, which for some reason was a little jarring coming from a Chinese uniform. She had a palm-sized digital voice recorder, but also took careful notes in a regular paper notebook.

As he told them what had happened everyone else in the room shut up and listened in. He could hear whispered translations going on in multiple languages.

After hearing the story, the one question the Chinese asked him was, "Had you ever see this man before?"

"Never," said Avakian. "Tell me, what happened with all the shooting?"

She closed her notebook and translated primly, "You will be informed at the appropriate time, sir. Do you need to go to hospital?"

Until that moment Avakian had almost forgotten he was in China. But that brought him back. He could only imagine what the nearest hospital must be like if there had been as many casualties as he thought. He'd be on a gurney out in a hall the rest of the night. "No, thank you. I do not need to go to the hospital."

The guy in plainclothes, who might have been either a cop or State Security, now held up a plastic bag containing Avakian's blackjack. And the translator asked, "This is yours?"

Ah, the Inspector Columbo moment: wait until the end, then spring the evidence on them. Avakian had mentioned hitting the maintenance man from behind. He hadn't mentioned with what. "Yes," he replied, since it wasn't really a question.

"What is it, please?"

"A back scratcher," Avakian said.

This provoked a conference in Chinese. "This is what?"

"A back scratcher. I suffer from dry skin."

"This is a weapon."

He almost said: then why did you ask me what it was. But what he actually said was, "Of course not. It's not a knife or a gun. How can it be a weapon?"

Another conference. "This is a serious matter."

"I know," said Avakian. "My back is itching right now."

More discussion. "This will not be returned to you."

Avakian had been talking to the policewoman. Now he fixed his gaze on the plainclothesman. "You should be glad I had it with me."

No more questions. The plainclothesman just turned around abruptly and left now that he was done. The policewoman didn't seem to know quite what to do, so she gave him a little bow before trotting after her boss. Jozefa gave him two more pills that he downed eagerly and kissed him on both cheeks.

Avakian thought he was doing surprisingly well with the ladies lately. Getting wounded with women around was obviously the way to go. Then he crashed again.

He had no idea how much time had passed when he was awakened again from a dreamless, drug-induced sleep by the voice of Russell Marquand. He opened his eyes, and it really was Marquand. Jozefa was gone. As a matter of fact, everyone was gone. They were all alone in the dressing room. Him, Marquand, and Dave Kinney, the second in command of the Secretary of

State's bodyguard detail. "Have you been watching me sleep long?"

"To be honest, no," said Marquand. "We pretty much just came in here and woke your ass up. How you doing?"

"I can't believe this week I'm having," Avakian groaned.

"Neither can anyone else," said Marquand. "But I was really asking how you're feeling."

"I was a hurtin' cowboy," said Avakian. "But I'm better." A Polish warm-up jacket was spread over him like a blanket. As he moved, he heard the rattle and squeezed the pocket. There was a large bottle of pills in there. And something else. He pulled out a piece of paper with a phone number written on it. Well, he owed Jozefa flowers and chocolate, minimum. Though anything else would definitely have to wait until he healed up. And maybe did some serious training.

The ice packs were gone, and his right arm was in a sling strapped tightly to his torso, immobilizing the shoulder. It was hard to believe he hadn't woken up for that. Good drugs. He raised his arm to look at his watch, but the crystal was shattered. "What time is it?"

"8:15," said Marquand.

"I hope that's PM," Avakian said.

"Yeah, you slept through all the excitement," said Marquand.

"No, I didn't," said Avakian. "If I had, I wouldn't be this messed up."

"Well, at least you didn't jump on the grenade yourself," said Marquand.

"That was a little farther down on my list of courses of action," said Avakian. "Give me a hand up."

They pulled him up into the sitting position. Avakian grabbed the side of the table as the room swirled around on him. His sinuses ached, and his nose felt like it was packed full of dried blood, but he didn't want to blow it and risk bleeding again.

"Still a nice call in four seconds or less," said Marquand.

"Necessity is the mother of invention," said Avakian.

"I hear that," said Marquand. "Witnesses said the guy you were on top of never came off the floor when the grenade went off. But you went about three feet in the air."

"It felt higher," said Avakian. "And I didn't nail the landing."

"Nobody got blown up, though," Kinney broke in. "Except the guy who needed to."

"Yeah, let's all just forget about me," said Avakian. Kinney always reminded him of a blond California surfer boy 20 years down the road. Still bright-eyed and bushy-tailed but battered by too much sun and salt.

"How did you make him?" Marquand asked.

"I didn't," Avakian said.

"You didn't?"

"It would probably boost my street cred if I said I did. But the truth is he stepped out of a door right in front of me. The Avakian luck. If there's some shit, I'll step in it. Now what was the deal with all the gunfire?"

"You don't know?" said Marquand.

"I hardly would have asked it I did," said Avakian. "I've been a little out of the loop."

"The grenade went off," said Marquand. "Everyone, and I do mean everyone, went for their guns. The exact details are a little hazy, but it seems that a couple of the Taiwanese security men started shooting. And they shot their own guy."

"The President?" said Avakian, amazed.

"Dead," said Marquand.

"No shit?" said Avakian.

"He goes down," said Marquand. "Then the Chinese security detail opens up on them, and it's *Reservoir Dogs* all over again. You've got both details shooting at each other point blank. Twelve dead so far, over twenty wounded. There was lead ricocheting all over that tunnel. Turns out you were in about the safest place, down on the deck."

"Yeah, it sure felt like that," said Avakian.

"Everyone's trying to figure out whether the president got shot accidentally or on purpose," said Marquand. "And all the people who could answer that for sure happen to be dead."

"This is going to make the Kennedy assassination look cut and dried," said Kinney. "The conspiracy theorists will get off on it forever."

"Panicking and shooting into the crowd is easy," said Avakian, groaning again as he shifted position on the table. "Panicking and shooting the principle you're there to protect is hard. So, I'm guessing some part of the Taiwan security establishment decided they didn't like snuggling up to Beijing, and decided to have themselves a little coup. And decided that here was the perfect place for it—let your traditional enemy take the rap and get stuck with the clean-up. Maybe they even had a little help from some Chinese."

"I was saying a few prayers that wouldn't turn out to be the case," said Marquand. "Once again they're not answered. You haven't mentioned your little theory to anyone, have you?"

"Are you kidding?" said Avakian. "And I won't, either."

"But what about the grenade?" said Kinney. "You throw a grenade that might take out your own assassins? I don't get it."

"It was a concussion grenade," said Avakian.

"Okay," said Marquand.

"You mean a stun grenade?" said Kinney.

"No," said Avakian. "Our good old American hand grenade you're thinking about is one size fits all. Kills you within 5 meters, wounds you within 15, and beyond that the fragments slow down to where they're not lethal. Other parts of the world they issue an offensive grenade and a defensive grenade. Defensive sends fragments out a good long way, so you throw that from behind solid cover. Offensive is just explosive. So, you can throw it while you're rushing forward in the assault without fragging yourself. It has to land right next to you to be lethal, but the blast knocks everyone off their pins until you can close in and finish them off. It was an old Russian RG-42 concussion, or the Chinese copy. Just TNT in a tin can. Literally."

"You sure about that?" said Marquand.

"Believe me, I got a real close look at it," said Avakian. "And we used to see them in El Salvador all the time."

"You tell anyone about *that*?" said Marquand.

"That I told them about," said Avakian.

"So, they plan on throwing the grenade," said Kinney. "Toss it maybe in the middle of all the press. It goes off, lots of blast and smoke. All the cameras swing in that direction. And in the confusion the Taiwan security guys shoot their own president."

"And maybe even get away with it," said Marquand. "If they're carrying a couple of throwaway pistols they can drop on the ground."

"But the grenade doesn't go off the way it's supposed to," said Kinney.

"Thanks to our boy here," said Marquand.

"But they start shooting anyway?" said Kinney, as if he couldn't quite believe that part.

"I suppose you've got to admire having the balls to stick to the plan no matter what," said Marquand.

"Face," said Avakian.

They both looked at him.

"You're given the plan by your superiors," said Avakian. "Something unexpected happens, you still stick to it. Because it was the plan given to you by your superiors. How do you think we beat the Japanese? Face."

"This is going to be such a fucking mess," Marquand breathed. He looked up at the ceiling. "Thank you, God, for not dropping this one in *my* lap."

"All your clean living finally pays off," Avakian said dryly. He gingerly slid off the edge of the massage table and tested his ability to stand. So far so good. Unless he missed his guess, his jacket, tie, and shirt were in the plastic bag under the table, thanks to Jozefa. So, the Polish warm-up jacket was going to have to do. Nice souvenir anyway. "Can we get out of here?"

"*We* can," said Marquand. "Chinese are holding the whole damn stadium incommunicado until they're sure they're not letting any co-conspirators go. But that's not my problem. The Secretary of State's back at the embassy already."

"If it's not your problem," said Avakian, "it's certainly not mine. Besides, I'm starving."

"The embassy cafeteria can cure that," said Marquand. "I'll even buy."

"The embassy cafeteria?" Avakian said, without any enthusiasm whatsoever. "I was thinking more along the lines of some Korean barbecue. I know a good place, and you can still buy."

"Keep thinking," said Marquand. "But you're going back to the embassy. I don't think the shit is done hitting the fan for a good long while yet."

Chapter Five

"THIS IS REALLY GOOD," said Kinney, digging into a container.

The three of them were seated around Marquand's desk, cartons of food spread across the top. Traumatized by the thought of the embassy cafeteria, Avakian had talked them into stopping along the way. Unfortunately, Korean barbecue didn't lend itself to takeout, since the meat was traditionally brought to your table raw, and you grilled it yourself over a brazier. But a Xinjiang restaurant was the next best thing. They roasted their meat on skewers. No pork though—it was the Muslim part of China.

They'd sent Marquand's driver in for it, which was funny because in China Chinese takeout wasn't all that common. You either went out to eat or you cooked at home. So, the driver had to be persuasive and show them the color of Marquand's money.

Marquand was eyeing the meat on the end of his fork suspiciously. "You sure this is lamb?"

Avakian had to finish chewing the steamed sesame bun impaled on the end of his chopsticks before he could reply. "Of course, it's lamb. You're just not used to the cumin. Or having your lamb barbecued."

"It's really good," Kinney offered, popping another kebab-sized chunk of meat into his mouth.

Marquand shot him a dirty look and nibbled a microscopic bit off the end of his lamb. "What if it's rat?"

"That all depends on whether they're free-range or cage-raised," said Avakian.

Marquand returned his meat to the plate and moved over to the thin hand-pulled noodles.

Avakian shook his head. "I'm sure the cafeteria would be happy to whip you up a grilled cheese on white bread, with some nice orange processed American cheese flown in from the States at government expense."

"Should you be mixing that with those meds?" Marquand asked, now turning his eye to the bottle of dark Xinjiang beer Avakian was drinking.

"After the day I had?" Avakian said. "I need all the muscle relaxant I can get."

"What did the Poles give you, anyway?"

"No idea. But whatever the stuff is, it works. And I'm willing to bet it doesn't even show up on a urine test."

"Here we go," said Kinney, watching the TV. "Something's coming up."

Marquand's TV was turned to CNN International. It was no accident they were watching that instead of reading the Top-Secret message traffic off the printer. Even the CIA relied on CNN for breaking news rather than their people on the ground.

There were tanks on the streets of Taiwan's capital, Taipei. "Uh, oh," said Avakian. "Nothing says coup like tanks."

The reporter was an English-speaking Chinese. Obviously, Taiwan hadn't been considered a news hotspot. Until today.

"Did I hear that right?" said Kinney. "Taiwan is accusing the Chinese of assassinating their president?"

"Not looking to defuse the situation, are they?" said Marquand. "Looking to start something is more like it."

"They're playing with fire," said Kinney. And then after a short pause for further reflection, "And they think they can get away with it because the Chinese won't do anything to screw up their economic boom."

"Taiwan wouldn't be that stupid," said Marquand. Then he had his own short pause. "What am I saying? They arranged to kill their own president in Beijing."

He was clutching his stomach, and Avakian didn't think it was the lamb. "History, my friends, is the story of human miscalculation."

The CNN anchor broke in to report that Taiwan's National Defense Minister had just announced he was forming a provisional government.

"They seem to have misplaced their vice president somewhere," said Marquand.

"Nothing like sitting at ground zero while history is being made," said Avakian. "I'm starting to get an idea what it must have been like in Sarajevo."

"The Winter Olympics?" said Kinney.

Avakian almost spit his food out laughing, and Marquand leaned forward and mock-slammed his forehead into the desktop. "You had to have been a phys ed major," he told Kinney. "Not Sarajevo 1984, you idiot. Sarajevo 1914."

"Sorry, but I'm still drawing a blank," said Kinney.

"The assassination of Franz Ferdinand?" said Avakian. "Archduke of Austria-Hungary? The kickoff for World War I?"

"Oh," said Kinney.

"I guess that's what they did in 1914," said Avakian. "Sit there with their mouths open and say, *oh*."

"I think I had better start putting together an evacuation plan," said Marquand. "Just in case." He turned to Avakian. "What are you doing tonight?"

"Besides helping you with the plan? Probably wondering what's going to happen next."

Chapter Six

"ARE you sure you want to go out to eat?" Avakian asked.

"You mean it would be a lot safer to have dinner in the Olympic Village," said Doctor Rose.

"That's a definite consideration."

"No one's moved from in front of a TV since Taiwan declared independence this morning. Half the people around here say there's going to be a real war, the other half that there'll only be a war of words. What do you think?"

"The Chinese are hard to predict," said Avakian.

"I appreciate your concern. But I'd really like to go out. As long as you think it's safe."

Avakian did think about it. He'd wanted to give her an out in case she was scared but was actually kind of interested to see what Beijing would be like. He doubted there'd be any problems. "Let's go."

It had been raining on and off all day, and every time it did the water turned to steam on the hot pavement. It was just misting now as they walked out of the Continental Grand Hotel with the last of the sun slipping away. The overcast made the evening less hot but much more humid. Avakian was carrying an umbrella. Because a gentleman didn't let his date get rained on, of course, but if the weather report said rain, he always carried one. He'd been rained on all over the world and didn't care to be wet again without a very good reason.

Doctor Rose was wearing a dark dress suit with a simple blouse and string of pearls. Her usual brown pageboy was looking a little fluffier than usual, a little less businesslike. Avakian was pleased to see her skirt end just above her knees. He hated it when women were neurotic about their legs and wore skirts so long even their ankles weren't visible—he'd never seen a woman who looked good in a floor-length skirt. Evening gown, yes; skirt, no. The doctor had great legs, too. With those calves she must be a runner. And she was wearing flats for him. A sweet gesture but standing next to taller women didn't bother him. Nonetheless, all the omens seemed favorable. "You look lovely tonight."

"Thank you. I've been admiring your hats. Where do you get them?"

"Hong Kong."

"Your suits the same?"

"They know how to make hot weather clothing that doesn't look like it's cut from crinkly tissue paper."

"They're very nice."

"Thank you."

She noticed him limping slightly. "Are you all right?"

"A little bruised up, but otherwise fine."

"You should come by and let the staff take a look at you."

"Never on a first date."

That got a laugh out of her. "You're the talk of the town."

Avakian had spent the past few days dodging the world press. "Take my word for it, it's exaggerated."

"Sounded heroic to me."

"Heroism is having to do something drastic to keep from getting killed." He opened the car door for her.

"*Ni Hao*, Kangmei," Doctor Rose exclaimed.

"*Ni Hao*, Doctor," Kangmei replied with a smile that revealed several missing teeth.

Avakian just shook his head. "You're a positive influence on my driver. That's a role I never thought anyone would play."

The restaurant was located in the northeastern corner of central Beijing. For some reason all the traffic seemed to be going in the opposite direction. Then they drove past hordes of people on the sidewalks. They seemed pretty fired up and were all walking in the same direction, some carrying flags and rolled up banners, like a crowd heading home after a football game.

"This must be the tail end of the anti-Taiwan demonstration they had this afternoon at Worker's Stadium," said Avakian.

"On TV it said it was a spontaneous demonstration by tens of thousand of people."

Avakian snorted. "There are no spontaneous demonstrations in China. Especially not at Workers Stadium. The government's trying to make propaganda points and at the same time let everyone blow off some steam so there *won't* be any spontaneous demonstrations. Note that Worker's Stadium is far away from Tiananmen Square."

Up in the front seat Kangmei was muttering quietly to himself. Doctor Rose smiled at that. "I was talking to a few people who'd been downtown, and they said the streets were pretty empty today. That seems funny, doesn't it? Even if you're where something is happening, you have to watch TV to know what's going on."

"Same as if you were in Washington during the Cuban Missile Crisis. Or London during The Blitz. You knew the Germans were bombing you, but other than that you had to listen to the radio."

"You don't think the Chinese are going to sit still for this, do you?"

Avakian leaned over and whispered in her ear. "Let's wait until we're out of the car to talk about that."

He had Kangmei drop them off near the Yuyang Hotel. It meant a short walk to the restaurant, but that would give them a chance to look at the Liangma River. And talk out in the open.

"Not discussing things in the car is very intriguing," said Doctor Rose. "Is it bugged?"

"No idea," said Avakian. "Could be. But Kangmei's definitely reporting on all our conversations. That's just the way it's done."

"And we don't want to talk about certain things because...?"

"Well, we really don't care that the Chinese know what we're talking about. What we care about is them using the topic of our conversation to make assumptions that aren't based on reality. Not that they won't do that anyway, but the less complicated I can keep my life here in China, the better."

"So they might think you're a spy."

She was quick. "Oh, they halfway think that already."

"*Are* you a spy?"

"No," said Avakian.

"But if you were a spy, you'd assure me that you weren't a spy."

"Correct," said Avakian.

"I seem to have lost my train of thought."

"The Chinese think everyone is a spy. Mainly because all their academics and businessmen traveling outside the country, even the ones who aren't actual intelligence officers, are expected to do favors for the Ministry of State Security."

"Or else?"

"That's how they work. The Chinese are only subtle when they have to be. But I'm just a retired Army colonel who got hired to be the conference security liaison between the Chinese and the State Department."

"A spy would say that, though, wouldn't he?" Doctor Rose said mischievously.

"Correct," said Avakian, another grin spreading across his face. "But—and this is the crucial point—if they ever became totally convinced I was a spy, I'd be followed around by a whole platoon instead of the couple of guys doing the job now."

Doctor Rose suddenly spun around in a full circle. "We're being followed right now?"

"Sure," said Avakian. "When I first got here, there was the two I was supposed to see, and then the pair who were really following me. Just to see if I'd try to give the first pair the slip."

"And that would mean you really were a spy."

"Well, sort of. But since all real spies are aware of this little detail, they rarely try to give their surveillance the slip."

"Now am I supposed to be able to see them, or not?"

"The pair trailing us? Well, it's kind of like they're minor leaguers trying to get promoted to the majors so they can follow CIA officers around, so for the most part they practice staying out of sight. The manpower Chinese security has is amazing. They've got eight guys just on me—four shifts a day. And I'm not even a spy."

"So you say. I don't know whether this is more exciting or confusing. But I'm leaning toward exciting."

"Not for the poor schnooks who have to follow us around all over the place."

"Maybe we can send them out some hors d'oeuvres or something? Isn't that what they'd do in the movies?"

"We're not that fond of them," said Avakian. "Besides, they're like working dogs. It's not good to spoil them."

"I think I understand now. No spy talk, no war talk, in the car."

"And, unfortunately, no jokes about it," said Avakian. "Better to be safe than sorry. The Chinese don't handle irony well."

Occasionally the moon poked through the overcast,

giving the low clouds a purplish hue. The rain had freshened the air a bit, but as they drew closer to the restaurant the hanging humidity made the smell of food equally heavy. But not unpleasant. It was doing wonders for Avakian's appetite.

"What's the name of this restaurant?" Doctor Rose asked.

"Din Tai Fung," Avakian replied.

"And that means?"

"I haven't the faintest idea."

"Funny name for a restaurant."

Avakian looked over at her.

"Sorry," she said. "Couldn't resist it."

"It's okay," Avakian said. "You timed that perfectly."

Concrete planters sprouting small trees were situated every twenty feet or so down the length of the sidewalk. The restaurant was in a two-story building with metal lattices running horizontally every couple of feet down a glass front. The evening lighting made the glass frames appear blue and the lattices green.

Avakian held the door open for her, then stepped around and presented the card with his name on it in Chinese characters to the hostess. He'd had his hotel concierge make a reservation because it was usually full, with a crowd waiting. Tonight, there were many empty tables.

A smiling waitress started to lead them to a table near the front windows, but Avakian pointed to one in the back while at the same time surreptitiously slipping a few bills into her hand. A quick look down at them made her smile even harder and guide them to the back. They passed by one of the attractions, a window into the kitchen. Cooks in whites, including baseball caps and surgical masks, were whipping up dumplings at a long table and loading them into bamboo steamers.

"They look like they're making microchips instead of food," Doctor Rose mentioned to Avakian.

"The typical Beijing restaurant kitchen isn't anywhere near this fastidious."

At the table they were presented with menus printed in Chinese, English, and Japanese. Very short, only two pages.

"What would you like to drink?" he asked her.

"I'm sort of on call."

"Tea?"

She nodded. So did the waitress who rushed off.

"What should I have?" Doctor Rose asked.

"The dumplings are the reason to be here," said Avakian. "The fillings depend on your taste. Are you a vegetarian?"

"No."

Another misconception sorted out. "Maybe we should have a little of everything, then. The dumplings are about the size of a meatball and come ten to a steamer, so you can eat quite a few of them."

"Sounds great." She picked up the black lacquered chopsticks and admired the gold inlay at the end. "I love these. Will I get pounced on if I try and walk out with them?"

"I won't rat you out," said Avakian.

The waitress returned with the tea and stood behind Avakian's shoulder as he pointed to their choices on the menu.

When she left, Doctor Rose said, "I love this tea set, too." It was simple white porcelain with the restaurant name in red characters.

"I don't think your purse is big enough," said Avakian. "Maybe I steered you wrong on the Prada bag."

"I'll try not to be resentful about it. Why did you have her seat us back here?"

"When we walked in, I noticed there aren't any Chinese diners in here tonight. Then I remembered that even though they serve Shanghai-style dumplings this group of restaurants is based in Taiwan."

Doctor Rose looked around the room. "You're right, there aren't any Chinese in here."

"The way feelings are running in town, if by some chance someone threw something through the window, we can step out through the kitchen door over there."

"You mean something like a rock?"

"Something like that."

"Or a Molotov cocktail?"

Avakian shrugged.

She just looked at him.

"This is what I do for a living," he said.

"Better to be safe than sorry?"

"Better to be safe than sorry."

"I'd never have thought of that in a million years."

"Well, I wouldn't try to repair someone's ACL," said Avakian.

"Now tell me what you think is going to happen now that Taiwan's declared independence."

"Are you sure that's the dinner conversation you want?"

"Since we *are* here in Beijing, it's a matter of some interest to me."

"Whatever you say," Avakian replied.

"And please give it to me straight, as opposed to tactfully not mentioning Molotov cocktails flying through the window."

"Okay, unless Taiwan backs down, or some face-saving arrangement is reached, I think China's going to war."

"Even if it wrecks their economic boom?"

"That's what Taiwan's counting on. And I think they've miscalculated. Nobody in China believes in Communism anymore, but it's still a Communist dictatorship. You can make money, but you can't challenge the government or mess around in politics. Other than bribing politicians, that is. Communism used to keep a big, chaotic country with a lot of different regions, ethnic groups, and interests in line. The government turned to nationalism to fill that void. They don't teach the dictatorship of the proletariat anymore, they teach a unified China as a great power, China's rightful place in the world, and traditional grievances about being oppressed by the other great powers throughout history. The government made everyone happy by getting Hong Kong back from Britain and Macao back from Portugal. Taiwan's the last piece of the puzzle. They can't back down and lose face over this. Nationalism's a powerful thing."

"Powerful enough not to care about wrecking everything they've built?"

"I went to Armenian summer camp when I was a kid. Swimming, archery, and hating the Turks."

"Did you?"

"Swim?"

"Hate the Turks?"

"Even as a kid, those ancient grievances never appealed to me. I have a rule. I don't hate anyone I don't know personally. But it gave me a little insight into what I'd have to deal with later on in the Army."

"The Army has ancient grievances?"

Avakian chuckled. "That was good. Not as many as you'd think, but Central American Indians, Kurds, and Pashtuns have a lot more. The Chinese have their share, too. Their economy's booming, but there's practically no economic security. The social safety net is gone. The law only works for the powerful. Any morning you might wake up to the tanks rolling in like Tiananmen Square, or the whole fabric of society could get torn to pieces like during the Cultural Revolution. Lot of fear out there. And I get a sense of barely contained hysteria."

"Hysteria as a symptom of repression?" said Doctor Rose.

"Sure. And the Chinese are pretty high strung to begin with. The leadership doesn't mind using that as long as it's directed outward at the Japanese, or Americans, or whatever, but they've been very careful about reeling everyone back in before they get out of control. So far. The only thing they care about more than the economy and trade is power. They'll do whatever it takes to hold onto power. Which is why I think they'll have no choice but to go to war."

"You mean invade Taiwan?"

"Now that I'm not so sure about. If you asked me before, I'd have said that the Taiwanese were too rich and too soft, that all China would have to do is fire a few salvos of missiles at them and they'd surrender rather than see their way of life go down the tubes. But I think this new group in charge in Taiwan would fight. They'd lose, of course—their military is equipped mainly for parades. And that's not a good thing."

"For Taiwan?"

"For us."

"What do you mean?"

"We've promised to defend Taiwan from invasion. If they just gave up before we could get involved, I think everyone would prefer that. But if our 7th Fleet gets close enough to make the Chinese nervous, that means real trouble."

"You mean someone starts shooting."

"We'll try to bluff the Chinese out of it, the way we have before. But if they have decided to invade, they've already made up their minds to fight us. And that means our fleet will get hit without warning. Our style is a big show of force. Chinese military strategy is based on deception."

"Could our navy stop them?"

"In my opinion?"

"In your opinion."

"I'm in the minority, but I say no. The Chinese don't have to defeat the 7th Fleet to keep us from interfering with their plans. They just have to engage it far enough out to sea. They don't have satellites like ours to locate our ships, but they have a lot of fishing boats with radios. They don't have aircraft carriers, but they have a few hundred of the latest Russian supersonic anti-ship cruise missiles specifically designed to kill aircraft carriers. They can fire those from their brand-new Russian submarines or destroyers, their brand-new Russian Sukhoi fighters or their old 1950's-era Badger bombers, or even from launcher tubes strapped on the decks of fishing boats. It's easier to shoot off a hundred missiles than it is to keep from getting hit by a hundred missiles. Quiet diesel-electric submarines get through to aircraft carriers all the time in exercises. No carriers, no fleet."

"Do we have a defense against them?"

"The supersonic missiles? Yeah, our defense is the Navy acting like they don't exist because they don't have a defense that works."

"You're giving me chills now. Would the Chinese throw us all out of the country?"

"No," Avakian said.

"Why not?"

"Because they're smart enough to realize that tens of thousands of foreigners in your capital city is the best defense against air attack ever devised."

Now she was staring at him again.

Avakian told himself to snap out of it. You just had to show off by running off at the mouth, didn't you? "Pay me no mind. In case you hadn't noticed, I'm kind of addicted to the worst-case scenario. Thankfully, our waitress is bringing food."

She delivered the first course, cold cucumbers with chili oil and garlic.

"The longer you let the cucumbers sit in the chili oil, the spicier they're going to be," said Avakian.

"Are you married?" the doctor blurted out.

Avakian grinned. "Did I lose focus and miss the preamble to that question?"

Doctor Rose's coloration turned deeper by several shades. "Sorry, I sort of skipped over that. I apologize."

In Avakian's experience, not answering a woman's personal question only meant that she'd find 30 new and different ways of asking it in the immediate future. "I was, but I'm divorced."

"How long?"

"Fifteen years."

"I'm sorry. I'm starting to interrogate you. It's a bad habit women and doctors have."

"If you want to know, I'll tell you. But I warn you, it'll be even more of a buzz kill than my war lecture."

"For the record, I freely acknowledge I was the one who asked both of those questions."

"We fell in love in high school. I had a rough time at home, and she was my refuge. We got married after I graduated from West Point. She was a sweet naïve girl from Bethlehem, Pennsylvania who thought she was going to see the world and ended up seeing Fayetteville, North Carolina and Savannah, Georgia instead."

"Savannah is nice," Doctor Rose offered.

"For a week's vacation. I was just as naïve, but totally wrapped up in the Army. Always off either training or deployed, and I was too stupid to see what she was going through. It's the one thing in my life I feel guilty about, and I still feel that way fifteen years later." He held up a hand. "Here I go again."

"No, not at all. Do you have children?"

"One son. I was in South America when he was born. He's 23."

"What does he do?"

Avakian shook his head again. "The Army."

"Did he go to West Point, too?"

"No. I tried so hard to steer him away from the Army so of course that's what he went for. He dropped out of college and joined up. He's a sergeant in South Korea. His mother didn't deserve that, either."

"It doesn't sound like your fault."

"Thanks for saying so. Change of subject?"

"These cucumbers are excellent."

The waitress rescued him again by arriving with a stack of steamer baskets. She arranged them on the table and removed the lids with a flourish and a puff of live steam. The white dumplings were closed with a swirling crimp at the top and sat on a circle of rice paper.

"Any tips?" the doctor asked.

"The wrapping is super thin," said Avakian. "And there's juice inside. So, you've got real problems if you punch a hole in one with your chopsticks. Same if you try to nibble at it. The expert technique is to bring it up to your mouth, bite a little hole in the wrapping, drink the juice, then dip it in sauce and eat. But if you try that, you're flirting with disaster. The only safe play is to eat like a foreign devil." He reached for a spoon, scooped up a dumpling, and slid it into his mouth intact. Pressed against the roof of his mouth, the dumpling exploded in a burst of pork, spices, vegetables, and savory meat juice. Rich pork, unlike American pork, which had all the flavor and consistency of a hockey puck. He chewed slowly, aware that he must have a beatific expression on his face. "These are *really* good."

Doctor Rose duplicated his technique. "Oh, my God. How do they keep the juice inside a wrapping that thin?"

"Witchcraft. What was yours?"

"Shrimp and pork."

"Mine was the green vegetable and pork. I encourage you to switch between baskets."

"If I wrap my arms around the steamer and say: mine, mine, just ignore me. Can we keep eating these all night?"

"I don't see why not," said Avakian. "But you'll have to tell me how you ended up with USA Gymnastics."

"Is this just a ploy to keep me talking so you can eat more dumplings?"

"You see through me like I'm made of glass," said Avakian.

"I'm not married," said Doctor Rose. "Never have been."

Avakian cocked his head at her and narrowed his eyes. "Was that some clever way of avoiding my original question?"

"No, I just think it's only fair to cover the same ground you did. Grew up in Hibbing, Minnesota. University of Minnesota, Harvard Medical School."

"Very impressive," said Avakian.

"Did my residency in Denver and stayed there. Orthopedists love ski country. I never had time for anything except building my practice and skiing. Wow, what are these dumplings here?"

"Crab roe and pork," said Avakian.

"They're amazing. Where was I?"

"Building your practice."

"One day I woke up and I was bored. So, I said: Judy, why don't you go see about one of the sports teams? That was because I knew a few people. My first choice was joining the circus."

"High wire or animal act?" Avakian asked.

"I'm not good with heights and I'm afraid of tigers. And do you have any idea how few openings there are for circus doctors?"

"From your tone, I'm guessing not many." Now he knew why he'd thought she was kind of severe. It was part of being the doctor. Don't look at me—listen to what I'm telling you. Because of that she wasn't into display, not a flirty woman by any stretch of the imagination. But when he made her laugh, she opened up like a flower and it all came out. It made him want to keep doing it.

"I suppose it's not really a life-changing adventure if you have more than enough money in the bank to cushion the life change."

"Don't expect me to comment on that. The Army pays me my pension every month."

"How long were you in the Army? I'm switching this back to you, but you've noticed how I do that."

"Pardon?"

"You've been reading me, the same way you read all those Chinese the other day."

Avakian paused at the brink of eating another dumpling, not wanting to risk choking. He'd never been caught at it before. Or at least never been called on it. "I'm not following you," he said innocently.

"Kinesics. The study of body language."

"Never heard of it," said Avakian. "Sounds interesting, though."

"So how easy am I to read?"

"I'm drawing a blank. You should join the professional poker circuit."

"A likely story."

"Twenty-three years in the Army. There, see how I learned that from you?"

"You're a quick study. And what did you do in the Army?"

"Started off as a paratrooper. But spent most of my career in Special Forces."

"Really? And this is how you became…?"

"Security liaison. Really, just a glorified negotiator. I moved into security consulting after I retired. I tell you how to keep your executives in Colombia from getting kidnapped, that sort of thing. Do security surveys, risk assessments. Compared to government service, the money is pretty incredible. I knew a few of the people here. The Chinese drove everyone crazy, so they hired me."

"And the Chinese don't drive you crazy?"

"No. When you don't have a career dependent on the results there's no anxiety. I've tried to evolve beyond being the little guy with the chip on his shoulder. He shows up every now and then, but for the most part I follow the wisdom of Elvis Costello: I used to be disgusted, but now I try to be amused."

"And the angels want to wear your red shoes?"

That gave Avakian more of a jolt than if he'd found out she was heavily into body piercing, except this was a turn on. "I warn you, don't toy with me by quoting Elvis."

Her complexion darkened again, and she made a point of ignoring that. "So, the more you cared about getting little Brandi out of Chinese custody, the worse the Chinese would have made it for you?"

Avakian refilled her tea and saluted her with the pot. "Exactly. The more you *seem* to care, the more they have you over a barrel."

"So, you have to develop a don't give a crap attitude?"

"It's something I've honed through many years of hard work."

The waitress reappeared with two dishes.

"Oh, my God," Doctor Rose groaned. "What's this?"

"Unless I miss my guess, fried rice with egg, scallion, and pink prawns."

"I don't think I can eat another bite," she said. Then, after sampling it, "I can eat another bite. I have never had fried rice this good. What's in the other one?"

Avakian slid the bowl over to her. "Hot noodles with peanuts and sesame sauce."

"That doesn't sound like my kind of dish. Okay, I want all of that, too. This is totally undignified, isn't it? I should be picking at my food and pretending I'm never hungry."

"Actually, it's refreshing. You know what I'm going to say next, don't you?"

"You're going to express your regrets on my eating disorder?"

"No. Ask what you want for dessert."

"No, no. Not another bite. At least not after some more fried rice."

"Whatever you say."

Outside they did what everyone does upon leaving a restaurant in a good mood: stop, look around, stretch a bit, smile in satisfaction, taste the change in air, and be reluctant to move on.

"That was wonderful, Pete," Doctor Rose said. "One of the best meals I've ever had. Thank you."

"You're more than welcome, Judy."

"You're quite the gourmand, aren't you?"

"I never can understand why people go to all the trouble of traveling only to eat room service or look for the nearest McDonald's."

"Would you mind walking a bit?"

"A walk sounds great, but we're really not near anything." Avakian took out his phone. "Let me get Kangmei over here. We can take a walk around Houhai Lake. It's just north of the Forbidden City. For me, it's China in a nutshell."

A half hour later, as they stood on the edge of the lake, Doctor Rose had to ask, "Now tell me why this is China in a nutshell."

"I wanted to start you out on the northern shore here because it's the quietest part." Avakian stood beside her and pointed down the bank, at the silhouettes of fishermen sitting with their long poles, lit by the red dots of their cigarettes. "Forget them, and don't look into the distance." Now he was pointing toward the opposite shore, a shimmering wave of multi-colored neon from all the bars and restaurants. "Look at the middle distance, the water. Half a million years ago, Peking Man drank here. This was nothing but scattered pools and ponds that formed in the spring when the Yongding River overflowed."

"Homo Erectus dazzled by the moon reflecting on the water," said Doctor Rose. "That's a nice image."

Avakian offered her his arm. She hooked her hand in the crook of his elbow and they began walking.

"Three thousand years ago they started planting crops on these banks," he said. "In the 13th century Kublai Khan built his winter palace here. His engineers dug out all the little ponds, connected them, and turned them into these three lakes. Fed them with aqueducts, so they wouldn't dry up in the summer. Barges came up and down the river systems and let off their trade right here. Financed the Mongol Empire. During the Ming Dynasty the waterfront and a short commute into the Forbidden City made this prime real estate for the Imperial eunuchs."

He smiled over at Doctor Rose, and she said, "Tell me, would you rather administer the empire and wield all that power, or… or not be a eunuch?"

"Power is overrated," said Avakian. "I've never heard anyone make that claim about sex."

They both laughed, and he said, "This was a very popular place in the daytime. Everyone in the city came here when the lotus was in bloom. But it was deserted at night."

"Why at night? Crime?"

"It was also a popular place to commit suicide by drowning. The Chinese believed that the spirit of a suicide could only be freed if someone else took its place. So, if you walked the shore after dark, ghosts might tempt you into the water."

Doctor Rose chuckled. Tonight, the lakeshore walk was filled with sightseers, vendors, pub crawlers, restaurant goers, and knee-hugging drunks. "The ghosts are going to have to fight for you."

The shoreline was now filled with neon bars. Most with al fresco terraces overlooking the lake, pounding music you could feel in your fillings even from outside, and desperate barkers out front trying to drag in business.

"See that?" said Avakian, pointing at one of the few

ancient looking buildings they'd come across. A real triple-arched stone structure, as opposed to the bars and cafes with pseudo-ancient facades.

"What is it?"

"The Guangfuguan Daoist Temple."

"Can we go inside?"

"Sure. It's a bar now."

"I think I'm getting an idea of your nutshell view of China," said Doctor Rose. "Lotus blossoms to bar district. Was that your point?"

"Well, I suppose my point is whatever you thought it was after my little presentation," said Avakian. "But I might have been sort of aiming in the general direction of implying that there aren't many spots on this earth where you can stand on half a million years of continuous human history."

"And have a nice walk."

"I'm glad you feel that way. How about some coffee, or a cold drink, or some dessert?"

"Now you're talking. Maybe not dessert, but we doctors can drink coffee in any climate."

"Coffee it is. Keep your fingers crossed—it's not as consistently reliable here as tea."

"And maybe some place where we won't be risking permanent auditory damage."

"I hear you on that," said Avakian.

"Very funny."

"Just trying to keep up with you."

They found a small café in the midst of a sea of bars. There seemed to be more of an older crowd there, probably due to the relative quiet. It was hard to see anything through the cigarette smoke inside, so they walked around to the outside deck.

A waiter was clearing off a small two-person table and motioned them over. As they stood there waiting for him to finish, two Chinese, a man and a woman, stepped right in front of them and began to sit down.

Doctor Rose was so stunned by that she didn't know what to do. She looked over at Avakian.

Who, without a word, grabbed the man by the shoulders, picked him up, and spun him around behind them. Doctor Rose had her mouth open. The Chinese woman had already scampered off.

Avakian held the chair for her. The doctor checked around the area, but no one seemed to be paying any attention. The waiter was laughing and patting Avakian on the back.

"How do you like your coffee?" Avakian asked her.

"Uh, black. Please."

"*Hei kafei*," Avakian told the waiter, holding up two fingers.

The waiter smiled and nodded.

"I always choke on numbers," he told her.

She was staring at him again.

"For the most part, one-on-one the Chinese are really nice, really polite people," he said. "But out in public if you're not family or friend they're the rudest swine on earth. It's every man for himself. Whether this is a fact of city life, or the legacy of the Cultural Revolution, when I first came here, I'd be standing in a line and I'd never get anywhere because Chinese kept cutting in front of me. At first you go, look at that chutzpah, no wonder they're doing so well in business. And then you realize you're never going to get anywhere. So, I asked a Chinese what to do. And he said to grab them by the shoulders and throw them out. So that's what I do. When in Rome…"

"And this works?"

"Consult the evidence of your own eyes."

The waiter returned with two tall glasses containing a milky brown liquid and what seemed to be either whipped cream or ice cream on top.

Avakian held out his hand as if to say: what the hell?

The waiter just pointed to the glasses as if to say: trust me on this.

"In case you're wondering, I can order coffee in Mandarin," said Avakian. "Evidently he's positive he knows what we need better than we do. You game?"

"Why not?"

"If it's too weird we just won't drink it. I'll go first. That way you can treat me if I go down."

"That would be an interesting finale to the evening."

Avakian took a sip. "Hmmm. It's kind of like really strong ice coffee with some type of Chinese spice twist and not quite whipped cream but lightly beaten sweet cream on top. It's not like any ice coffee I've ever had, but it's good." He nodded to the waiter, who was hanging around for the verdict.

Doctor Rose sipped hers cautiously. She rolled her eyes up, as if making a decision. "It's not like anything I've ever had, either. But it's interesting. And good." Now she nodded to the waiter, who broke into a big grin.

"*Xiexie*," Avakian told him.

The waiter gave them the thumbs up.

After he left, Doctor Rose said, "What did you say?"

"Just thank you," said Avakian. "Not what you were thinking—I wasn't calling the drink something naughty."

The doctor began coughing over her ice coffee.

"Not that it wouldn't be funny," said Avakian. "But my Chinese isn't muscular enough for it. I've been trying to get the verbs down, but the tones keep kicking my butt."

"That was our euphemism for poop when I was a kid."

They sipped their drinks and watched the lights from the opposite shore dance across the water. The lake was only a few hundred yards wide at that point. The rest of the overcast had blown away, and the moon and all the stars were out.

"This is nice," said Doctor Rose.

That relieved Avakian of a massive amount of date

anxiety. He knew she'd liked the restaurant but wasn't sure about the lake.

The inside of the café erupted in a solid roar of cheers. People were jumping up and down and standing on their chairs.

"Somebody's team must have won," said Avakian.

Doctor Rose looked at her watch. "At this time of night?"

"Some sports program showing replays? Maybe there's a soccer game on TV?"

Everyone out on the deck was looking just as puzzled. Then someone crashed out the door and yelled something in Chinese. And everyone around them started cheering too.

Avakian dug into his pocket and started tossing cash onto the table. "I'm getting one of those feelings."

"It's contagious," she said.

Two Caucasian men in their 20s emerged from the café door, looking plenty worried. "Either of you guys speak English?" Avakian called out.

"Yeah, mate," one said in an Australian accent.

"What's going on?" Avakian asked.

"Bloody Chinese are shooting missiles at Taiwan. Premier was on the TV. Looks like war."

"Oh, shit," Avakian said.

"Too bloody right," the Aussie replied. "Time to get back to the hotel before the fucking Chinks start turning all xenophobe and anti-foreigner. Later."

"Thanks," Avakian called out after them. And then to the doctor, "Politically incorrect but factually correct. His instincts are on the money."

"My instinct is to be scared to death."

"That's okay. Just don't look worried. Smile and act like you're as pleased with this as everyone else."

"Are you kidding?" she said as he took her arm.

Avakian was congratulating everyone they pushed past. "One time I turned a corner in Rome and stumbled

right into the middle of a Communist street demonstration. Joined the parade to keep from getting my ass
kicked. Screamed for the downfall of capitalism louder
than anyone. Got bought a lot of drinks afterward. Nice
people. For Commies."

"That's not making me feel better."

"Best I can do. Keep smiling."

They made it back out to the lakeshore walk without
any problems.

"Every drunk in Beijing is going to come pouring out
of these bars looking to whoop it up," said Avakian. "We
need to move inland, into the city. Find a place where
Kangmei can pick us up. If he isn't out whooping it up,
too." He pulled the city map from his jacket pocket and
studied it by the light of his key ring flashlight. He was
aware of shouting Chinese running past them, and
Doctor Rose clutching his arm tightly.

"Should we be standing out in plain sight while you're
doing that?" she asked, her voice cracking slightly.

"I think we'd attract a lot more attention hiding
under a bench doing this. It's dark, we look like we're part
of the local scenery."

"I really think we need to get out of here."

"We just need to stay calm," he said soothingly. "It's
never as bad as your imagination tells you it is." He
jammed the map back into his pocket. "Too many *hutongs*
around here. Too many people on the main drags, and
too easy to get lost in the *hutongs*. Okay, let's go. Nice and
easy—no rushing."

Out in the street the cars were all blowing their horns,
people hanging out of them and pounding on the sides
of the doors. Avakian had no intention of mentioning
just how dangerous he thought it was. One of those
moments when a spontaneous eruption of emotion put
perfect strangers all on the same frequency and made
them look around and realize that there were too many
for any authority to stop. Every really good riot had

gotten started just that way. You never knew, and they never knew, in what direction people's emotions were going to carry them.

That the traffic was more concerned with making noise than moving made it easy to cross the usually quite busy Dianmen Waidajie as they headed east. Once across, they ducked into a side street. Doctor Rose was moving so fast she kept threatening to break into a trot, so Avakian kept a braking hand on her arm. Heads were bobbing from apartment windows and shouting to their neighbors across the street. Beijing streets were never really empty, and now even the side streets were full as people spilled out of their homes to discuss what was going on.

A string of shots went off behind them. Doctor Rose jumped a foot into the air. Avakian whirled about to confront the danger, but it was only firecrackers. And once that first string went off everyone must have decided it was a great idea and rushed to start lighting up their stash.

Avakian was trying to reach Kangmei on the phone but couldn't get a signal. System was probably over-loaded. Not that the Chinese weren't capable of doing anything in the name of censorship, but you didn't shut down the cellular networks of a major city if you didn't want chaos. And he was certain they didn't.

He was now leading the way down the street, holding the doctor's hand as they weaved through the Chinese. The crowd thinned out at the next turn into a narrower street. Avakian stepped into the entrance of an alley to consult his map again and give them a chance to catch their breath.

He was still reading it when they heard feet pounding on pavement. Three Chinese boys went running past the alley. Then the sound Avakian didn't want to hear—shoes skidding to a stop. And, "Hey, hey, hey," which meant the same thing in almost every language.

The boys reappeared at the alley entrance. Avakian grabbed Doctor Rose and pulled her behind him.

They were teenagers, or maybe 20-something since Chinese always looked younger, out on the town with their mullet haircuts and jacket sleeves pulled up their bare arms like Don Johnson in the original *Miami Vice*. The leader danced into the alley, shouting and waving his arms. The other two, spread out on either side of him, laughed loudly. One was on his cellphone. Avakian wouldn't have been surprised if it was surgically implanted into his head.

He calmly put his map away and slid his hand under his jacket. Even though the Chinese police had relieved him of his original homemade blackjack, he'd acquired another at the very next construction site he'd passed by. He pulled the steel rod from his waistband and fed it through his fingers into his right sleeve. And smiled his coldest smile.

Anyone with any sense, seeing that smile instead of fear, would have turned around and kept going. They didn't have any sense. The leader kept waving his arms and dancing about, from his tone quite clearly mocking them.

Avakian was thinking that they must have lost their official Chinese tail in the crowds. Of course, it would have to happen the first time he really could have used them.

Then the Chinese kid dropped into a kung fu stance, one arm forward and the other cocked back into a striking claw hand. He charged into the alley to within a foot of Avakian, screaming a ki-ya to see if he'd run.

Avakian was flashing on Central America again, just as he had during his previous difficulty with the Olympic spectators. A favorite Latin game was to draw a crowd, accuse someone of a crime, whip the spectators up into a nice little frenzy, and then watch the other guy get gunned down or beaten to death in the heat of the moment. In 1988 a Salvadoran captain he'd known was running drugs had tried it on him in downtown San Vincente. A total setup. They were in the market when all of a sudden, the Salvo turned and started screaming at him. No fun being the foreigner then. He'd reflexively pulled the .45 automatic from under his shirt, laid it on the captain's skull, and gotten the hell out there before anything else could happen. No .45 this time, but the important thing was quick action before things got out of hand. Because unlike the Olympic Green there was no help on the way here.

Still smiling, and with his hands down at his sides, Avakian let the tape-wrapped rod drop into his palm. No one saw it.

When the Chinese kid turned his head to make sure his homies weren't missing any of his act, Avakian swung his arm and swung the steel rod down onto that outstretched forearm with all his might. The blow landed with a pop as loud as a firecracker, and a second later there was a shrill piercing scream as the kid went down to his knees.

With a growl, Avakian took three steps in the direction of the other two and they bolted down the street. He turned back and the kid was still down on the ground, sobbing and hunched over his broken arm, tears running down his cheeks. As Avakian drew nearer he commenced a tearful pleading. Doctor Rose was standing off to one side as if she were paralyzed. Avakian walked right by the kid on the ground and took her by the arm. "Let's get moving."

He'd been half expecting shock, outrage, perhaps a reproach, or maybe a request to follow the Hippocratic Oath and go back and take a look at the kid. But all she said was, "The little punk. I hope you broke his arm."

"Wish granted," said Avakian. "We've got to get clear of here as quick as we can. Without running."

There was only one street they could take to get out

of the area. Avakian wasn't willing to risk trying any *hutong* lanes. They passed quite a number of Chinese celebrants, but the streetlights weren't much, and everyone remained anonymous. Fireworks were exploding everywhere now, not just firecrackers but skyrockets, too. Whenever one of those went off it really lit up the street.

Nothing like a little adrenaline, Avakian thought, because Doctor Rose wasn't holding him back at all. As a matter of fact, he'd never seen anyone in dress shoes maintain a pace like that.

He had the street layout in his head, and the next turn was right where he expected it to be. One more side street and they'd be out on a main drag. He'd try his phone again then.

In between the detonations of the fireworks, he thought he heard heavy feet running behind them. A quick look around told him there was nowhere else to go. And running only meant that people ought to be chasing you. "Slow down," he muttered under his breath, and they dropped back to a regular walk.

After the next few booms, it was even clearer. There *were* heavy feet behind them, louder now on the damp pavement. Closer, and then a shout.

Avakian turned around slowly, facing a sight that made his stomach clench up so hard it ached. Two Chinese in full battledress, carrying rifles. With one of the kids who'd run off from the alley. And the kid was pointing at him and shouting exultantly.

As they drew closer, he could see they were definitely soldiers, not police or the paramilitary People's Armed Police. Which wasn't good. Soldiers were taught to fight, not deal with the public. There were two entire army groups stationed around Beijing, all on alert for the foreign ministers' conference. They'd either been sent out onto the streets to make their presence felt, or things had already gotten out of hand, and it was worse than he thought.

The soldiers had their rifles leveled at him. They were wearing camouflaged uniforms like the U.S. Army's old woodland pattern. Now he could finally see the epaulets. A corporal and a second class private. That was even worse. The more junior the troops, the more trouble you were going to have. They were never quite sure of either themselves or what to do in any given situation.

The corporal shouted at them. Again, that was bad. Shouting meant nervous. Avakian had no idea what he was saying. Then more shouting and an upward gesture with the rifle, which had been pointed at his heart, to put his hands up.

Avakian raised them slowly. The steel rod was still tucked away in his sleeve, which was probably going to prove embarrassing. The corporal jammed the rifle barrel into his stomach, grabbled him by the jacket lapel, and ran him up against the nearest wall. His torso, but not his sleeve, was patted for weapons very perfunctorily. He turned his head to see what was happening to Judy and the corporal slapped his face.

It took every last bit of self-control to hold himself in check. Everyone was yelling now, he couldn't understand what they were saying, and all his usual Chinese phrases like nice to meet you and good evening didn't quite seem equal to the situation.

The corporal was still digging that barrel into his stomach. The corporal's finger was on the trigger, too, which wasn't good. The corporal was also barking questions at him and getting progressively more upset when there were no answers forthcoming.

It was funny what your eyes locked onto. The corporal's helmet was almost identical to the U.S. model, with a fabric cover that matched his uniform camouflage. But centered right on the front was a big gold Chinese Army crest, complete with red star. Which kind of defeated the purpose of camouflage.

Avakian tried, "*Wo bu hui shuo hanyu.*" I can't speak Chinese.

The rifle barrel pulled back, and then came driving up under his ribcage. Avakian bent over as the air went out of his lungs. Okay, he told himself as he gasped for breath. Just think happy thoughts, enjoy the taste of the pavement once you get down there, and take your beating like a man. They'd get dragged off to jail, eventually. And it would all get sorted out. Eventually. After the war was over. God-damn.

Still bent over and still trying to get his wind back, he snuck another look off to the side. The private had Judy pushed against the wall with one hand. The hand that was squeezing her breast. He had that wild, knowing smile on his face, like he knew he was getting away with something. It reminded Avakian of Africa. And not in any good way.

The rifle butt cracked Avakian under the jaw and brought him upright and eyes forward. There was the sound of a slap on skin, then of clothes ripping, and a scream from Judy.

Another rifle jab in the stomach. That made Avakian snap, and he snapped his body sideways, the rifle barrel sliding right off his torso toward the wall. In the same motion he swung his forearm, and the steel rod hidden in his sleeve caught the corporal in the side of the neck, the only place that wasn't covered by helmet and gear.

The rifle fired with an explosive report and a shower of brick chips from the wall. As the corporal went down, Avakian got his left hand on the rifle stock and twisted it away. It fired again and the blackjack slipped out of his sleeve and clattered on the pavement. He kept twisting, and got both hands on the rifle, ripping it free. At least he knew the safety was off. Momentum was already carrying him down, so he dropped to one knee and brought the rifle up to his shoulder. It took him a second to find the sights.

The private was standing there with his mouth open and his eyes wide. First time frozen, Avakian told himself. Buck fever. Avakian fired and kept squeezing the trigger until the private hit the ground.

The Chinese civilian kid had been just as shocked, but now he was off and running again. Without even thinking about it, Avakian dropped from the knee onto his butt for a more stable sitting position. It was one of the brand-new Chinese bullpup rifles with the magazine and action behind the pistol grip, and unlike his old friend the good old-fashioned AK-47, he had absolutely no idea where the selector switch for full automatic fire was located. And since he had no idea if the sights had even been zeroed, he held his breath and kept shifting his aim point all the way across the kid's body as he squeezed off round after round. Five shots downrange to no effect —if the kid got away, they were as good as dead—then at the sixth the kid stumbled and started to go down.

Avakian sprang to his feet and ran down the street. Fireworks were still going off all over the place, and if there had been people around, they'd cleared out. The kid was crawling across the pavement, still trying to get away, a single dark entry wound in the light-colored jacket just above his ass. Avakian aimed the rifle at the base of his skull and blew his brains out onto the pavement.

Judy Rose was sitting against the brick wall, arms crossed tightly over her chest, holding the two halves of her torn blouse together. She watched Peter Avakian run up, lift the corporal's helmet with the rifle barrel, and shoot him in the head. The sound of the shot and the sight of the head bouncing gruesomely made her flinch. Then there was some kind of disconnect because he had her by the shoulders and was shaking her.

"Are you hurt?"

"No," she said. And then thinking to herself: what did he mean by that?

Then he was pulling the belts with the pouches off the Chinese soldiers. He threw his suit jacket onto the ground and laid the rifle and belts on top, wrapping the fabric over them and tying the sleeves together to make a bundle.

After that he was back in front of her, and she couldn't believe how gently he was speaking. "You have to get up. We're in an unbelievable amount of trouble."

Chapter Seven

JUDY ROSE FELT herself being pulled to her feet. She stood unsteadily while Pete Avakian tucked his bundle under one arm and her under the other.

Then they were walking. Streets and cars and people flashed by. She knew she was walking, but she couldn't feel herself walking. It was like she was watching herself walking. And it felt maddening to not be in control yet at the same time fully aware that she wasn't in control. The doctor knew she was having a classic dissociative reaction, but she couldn't do anything about it.

It started raining and she heard Pete Avakian mutter, "Finally we catch a break." Though she had no idea why the rain was a break.

It came down harder, and even though the air was hot, and the rain was warm, it felt clammy cold on her skin. She began to shiver and felt as if she couldn't catch her breath. She managed to gasp out, "I have to stop."

Then she was sitting down, and her head gently but firmly pressed down to the level of her knees. And Pete Avakian's voice saying, "If you feel sick, go ahead. Don't try and hold it back."

But she didn't feel sick. She was shaking. Her whole body. She tried to stop, but it was uncontrollable.

"Don't fight it," Avakian said. "Ride it out. It's just your nervous system discharging on you. This is a good thing."

Now she was angry at him. Shaking like an aspen in the wind and furious because he was right and so calm, and it *was* a reaction of her overloaded central nervous system and for the life of her she couldn't stop shaking.

It felt like it would never stop, but it finally did. She didn't think she even had the strength to lift her body off her knees.

"I know you feel wiped out," Avakian said. "But we can't stay here. I want you to tense and relax each of your major muscle groups in succession. Start with your hands."

She tried to ignore him, but he wouldn't leave her alone. It seemed silly, but she tried it and did feel some of her strength coming back.

"Get mad," he said. "At me, at anything. Just get mad."

That wasn't hard. Especially when he pulled her to her feet once more. Except this time, she felt everything, and her legs were so weak they were wobbling. It was the same sense of absolute fatigue after a high fever had broken.

He was still at her. "You can always move even when you think you can't. Just put your mind to it, because we've got to go. Get mad at me—I'm the one making you walk."

How did he know she was angry? But soon she discovered that there were worse things than not being in control of yourself. Like being dragged through Beijing in pouring rain when you could barely move your legs. She was hoping they'd go numb, but they never did.

The only rest she got was whenever they passed by an ATM, because Avakian always stopped to draw out money. Either Bank of China or Industrial and Commercial Bank of China. There were only a few Chinese banks that accepted foreign ATM cards, and those two had the only ATMs you could actually find. A third of the time Avakian ended up muttering darkly when the machine either declined the transaction or was out of cash. Both common occurrences at Chinese ATMs.

There wasn't that same sense of danger on the streets as before. It was like New York City on New Year's Eve. Except in this case everyone was celebrating a war. You were wary, but you weren't scared. It took so much effort to just put one foot in front of the other that she took no notice of where they were going until they were off the street and standing at the rear door of a modern apartment building. Avakian started digging in his wallet by the light of the flashlight held in his teeth. After some effort, he produced two keys tied together with a twist of wire.

"Let's hold a good thought that this works so we don't have to go past the doorman," he said. He slid a key into the door lock. It didn't turn.

Judy Rose was leaning against the building wall, too tired to think positively. She wanted very badly to sit down on the concrete walk, but the thought of having to get up again was too much to bear.

Avakian put the second key in the lock. "C'mon baby," he told it. The key turned and the door opened. "That's what I'm talking about." He held the door open with a flourish.

She was still leaning against the wall, only able to manage a weak smile.

Avakian held the door open with his foot, pressed the very heavy bundle into her hands, and swept her up into his arms.

And he wasn't even trying to look for an elevator. The door to a stairwell was right nearby, and he charged up without any hesitation.

"This is so embarrassing," she said. "I've run four marathons."

"But not under the present conditions," Avakian replied.

She couldn't believe how strong he was. He went up seven flights without even pausing to catch his breath.

And set her down in front of apartment 707. Brandishing the keys once again, he said, "Same good thought."

When the door opened the relief was so great Judy Rose felt like crying.

The lights popped on to reveal a small studio apartment, simply furnished and neat. It was hot and smelled stale, like every place that had been shut up tight and not lived in for a while.

He tucked his arm around her waist and guided her over to the couch. "Put your feet up. I'm going to have a look around."

He hadn't needed to say that. The couch felt so good she did in fact shed a few tears. Then the air conditioning came on and she started to feel cold again in her soaked clothes.

But there was Avakian again. He thrust a plastic bottle of water into her hand. "Drink up."

She knew she had to replace fluids. But had a terrible time getting the bottle up to her mouth. God, she was in terrible shape. He put his hands over hers and helped her drink, and she felt humiliated all over again.

"Now, unfortunately," said Avakian, "you have to get up."

She was gripped by utter despair. "We're not leaving…"

"No, just a short walk." He half-dragged her down a hall into a small bathroom with the shower running. The room was already filling up with steam. He slid her sodden jacket off and dropped it with a plop onto the tile floor. Then sat her down on the edge of the tub. "Towels, bathrobe, soap, shampoo," he recited, ticking the items off.

She kicked off her shoes, reveling in the hot steamy air hitting her back.

"Can you handle the shower yourself?" he asked.

She looked up at him looming over her and felt a cold jet of fear hit her stomach. "Yes."

"That's the worst news of the night," he said, smiling now. And then he was gone, and the door clicked shut behind him.

Judy Rose sat on the edge of the tub and laughed so hard she started crying again.

She came out wearing the white terrycloth robe, her hair wet and brushed back. He was sitting in a living room chair, wearing a T-shirt and shorts that were much too big for him. Eyes closed. Not asleep—deep in thought.

The eyes opened and he said, "You look a lot better."

"I feel a lot better." She sat back down on the couch with a little gasp of pleasure. The temperature in the apartment seemed to be just right now.

She had a million questions, most of which she hoped she had sense enough not to start blurting out. Like how a smart, kind, and funny man, with manners impeccable enough to reduce her mother to tears if he ever came to dinner, could suddenly turn into a cold-blooded killer right before her eyes. It would be one thing if he'd just flown into a murderous rage, but it seemed to her that he'd quite rationally decided that the situation had escalated to the point where there was no alternative to taking the loaded gun away from the soldier and then methodically executing all three Chinese so there wouldn't be any witnesses.

She would have thought she'd be repelled, but she wasn't. There had to be some biological basis for what she was feeling. Something to do with an evolutionary requirement to be predisposed toward a male's ability to protect the family group. A few hours ago, she would have told herself that we weren't Peking Man anymore. Now she wasn't so sure.

"You're quite the clinician," she said. "This wasn't your first experience with emotional shock."

"No," was all he said.

But she noticed his eyes drop down to her robe several times. "What are you looking at?"

"What do you mean?" he said.

"Tell me."

He let out a breath. "I'm seeing how even though your robe is tied tight you're holding the front of it shut with one hand, without realizing you're doing it. And I'm hoping I'm not making you feel unsafe."

She looked down at her hand and let go of the robe as if it was on fire. "You're not, I promise." She made an angry noise. "I've never been so humiliated in my life."

"Why?" he demanded. "Because you're a doctor?"

"That's a big part of it. I did everything tonight except throw up."

"Our reactions have everything to do with what we're used to," Avakian said calmly. "If you'd come across someone with a shattered femur sticking up out of their leg, you wouldn't have batted an eye. This was something totally outside your experience."

"But not yours."

He let out another breath. "No. Even though I've run into more stuff this last week than in the last ten years."

"Would they have tried to rape me?"

Avakian just raised his eyebrows.

"Tell me that, too."

He definitely didn't want to answer, but she kept staring at him until he did. "I don't know," he said finally. "Maybe not, but that's really not the point."

"What's the point?"

"How far they were going to go."

That was one theory confirmed. "So, if I hadn't been there, you would have handled it differently?"

"That's *definitely* not the point. If you weren't there it would have been easier for me to wait and see what was going to happen. I'm being honest with you, now."

"I appreciate that."

"But that's all irrelevant. You were there. And by the time I knew how far they were going to go it would have been too late."

"That feels like my fault."

"You're the only one whose fault it wasn't. It was their fault. And my fault. The bottom line is that I didn't feel like sitting in a Chinese prison cell until this war is over. You do not want to be a prisoner of the Chinese under the best of circumstances, which this most definitely is not. With my luck this would be the next Thirty Years War."

"Are you saying that to make me feel better?"

"It's the truth. If you feel better, all the better." He passed her another bottle. "More water."

"Doctor's orders?"

"Doctor's orders."

She uncapped it and took a sip. At least her hands were working again. "I went right by the book, didn't I? Traumatic shock followed by physiological response to stress—you bet. Disorientation in time, place, and person —all of the above. Another extreme physiological response when the central nervous system discharged from being overstressed—oh, yeah. Followed by exhaustion. What's next, doctor?"

He was watching her with that focus that could be a little unnerving. "You may feel agitated and easily irritated. You may feel fearful and depressed. You may have trouble sleeping, and nightmares when you do. Whatever you do feel, it's normal and it will pass."

"Good advice."

"You may also experience dry mouth, increased sweating, skin rash, abdominal pain, sensitivity to light, uncontrolled diarrhea, or liver failure."

"Thanks, I'll keep an eye out for those symptoms."

"That was probably in poor taste."

"In my experience, something's in bad taste only when it's not funny."

"And the verdict is…?"

"Oh, it was funny. Not as funny as it would have been if I hadn't just walked for miles across downtown Beijing in the pouring rain in a state of emotional shock. But funny nonetheless."

"Good point. I'll remember that next time."

"The worst part was knowing that it was all happening to me and not being able to stop it."

"When you get that far out on the edge, you sometimes become the prisoner of your body."

"Do you have any formal training?"

"School of life."

She took another swig of water. "A lot different from the one I attended." Then it just slipped out of her mouth. "They were so young." Both panicked and embarrassed, she straightened up off the couch. "I did *not* mean it that way! You were *totally* justified in how you acted."

But Avakian was just smiling at her. "Relax. I know what you meant."

"It was a terrible thing to say. I know he was going to hurt me, and you saved my life."

He held up a hand to stop her.

She had to give it to him. It took a lot to get him upset. Just how much she'd seen. But the embarrassment still burned. "My God, what a cliché. Bad movie dialog if I ever heard it."

Avakian was still unperturbed. "Ironically, if they'd been a couple of older soldiers, we wouldn't have had that kind of trouble. Teenagers with guns and uniforms and power. And, most important, nobody watching them. Bad things happen then."

"Are all Chinese soldiers like that?"

He got up, walked across the room, and sat down on the couch beside her. "Judy, all armies have soldiers like that. You think what happened to us didn't happen somewhere in Iraq every week?"

She knew she was staring at him again, but she had no idea how to respond to that. Not for the first time that night. But he just matter-of-factly came out and said what other people were usually careful to only think about.

He continued along those lines by saying, "And, no, at the risk of freaking you out, it didn't bother me. And it doesn't now."

She wanted to, but she couldn't hold his gaze. "Okay, I was going to ask you that."

"It's the question no one can ever resist. It makes people feel better to hear that the men you killed torment your soul. But they don't."

"I'm going to change the subject now."

"Well, that's up to you," Avakian said.

"Is this your apartment?"

"No. The government pays…or should I say they paid for my room at the St. Regis."

"I remember you told me that."

"This belongs to a friend of mine. Works for the World Bank—they pay his rent. He makes sure he's out of Beijing in the summertime. He gave me his keys, and I stuck them in my wallet and forgot all about them until now. Good thing he didn't want me to feed his goldfish. I'd never involve anyone I know in something like this, but I have a feeling he won't be back in China for a good long time. If ever."

"Nice robe," she said.

Avakian grinned. "We've got multiple robes and a whole drawer of toothbrushes. Clearly, my boy is a player."

Okay, Judy, she told herself. Time for the big question. "What do we do now?"

"Lay low tonight, let the city calm down. Then

tomorrow I get you back to your hotel like nothing happened. You went out to dinner, got caught up in all the ruckus, and we waited it out in a bar or something. There'll be world opinion and propaganda points to make. Eventually the Chinese will let all the gymnastics teams fly home. Even the American."

"What about you?"

"That's a little different. I really don't feel like being interned along with the rest of the U.S. diplomats. So, I'll see what happens, maybe try and make my way out of the country on my own."

"You're going to try to get out of China? In the middle of all this? On your own?"

Avakian shrugged.

"That's why you took the rifle and all their equipment, isn't it?"

"You're a smart lady."

She was momentarily in awe that he'd been thinking that far in advance in the midst of everything last night. "I'm staying with you."

Avakian shook his head slowly. "Now *that's* bad movie dialog. And no, you're not."

"If those two kids went to the police like their friend went to the soldiers, they're going to be looking for me as well as you. Especially with Kangmei dropping us off at the lake and never picking us up. It's not going to be that hard to figure out it was us."

"The odds on that are better than hanging with me. With everything that must have gone on last night those soldiers and the kid could have been killed by anyone. If the cops do come for you, the three kids attacked us, and you watched me break that one's arm. But you don't know anything about any soldiers getting shot. You never saw them. And now," he said, picking a folded bed sheet up off the coffee table and snapping it open, "I'm evicting you from the couch. The bedroom is yours. I'm going to get some sleep."

He stacked the cushions up at one end and motioned her off. She got up grudgingly. "We'll talk about this more in the morning."

"That remains to be seen," he replied, tucking the sheet around his feet. "Please be good enough to turn the lights off on your way out of the room."

She stood before the couch, stubbornly unwilling to let it go, but just as unwilling to start an argument after all that had transpired. "Thank you for taking care of me tonight, Pete. Thank you for saving my life."

His voice was already drowsy. "Let's hope I didn't ruin it."

She opened her mouth to say something, but his breathing had already changed. He was actually asleep. Unbelievable.

Chapter Eight

AVAKIAN WOKE to thin cracks of intense sunlight highlighting the edges of the window drapes. He could tell all those old instincts were coming back because he woke up instantly, alert and not wondering where he was. The only problem was that he thought he might be having a heart attack. Then he realized why he could barely move his left arm. He'd been carrying that bundle of rifle and equipment in it all night long.

Judy Rose was sitting in front of the TV, watching it with the sound off. The light from it haloed her hair in the dark room. She was wearing a man's dress shirt and too-big sweatpants. Avakian wondered if she'd gotten any sleep at all.

He checked his watch. "Good morning."

She looked over her shoulder and smiled at him. "Good morning."

At least she was smiling. Avakian sat up and flexed his fist to try and work some blood back into that dead arm. "Any news?"

"All the non-Chinese channels are black," she reported. "No CNN."

"They don't want anyone getting any unapproved news."

"They can just turn it off like that?"

"The Chinese are the world's experts at censorship. And all the Western companies who sold them their hardware and software built in everything they need to flip the switch. Anything for a buck. That is, if the Chinese haven't jammed the satellites or even blown them out of orbit. Satellites are something they can live without. We can't."

"The channels that are on have been showing nothing except people giving speeches, soldiers singing, and the same video of missiles being fired all morning."

Chinese news anchors came from a much geekier prep school than their Western counterparts. The reader was speaking rapid-fire Mandarin, much too rapid for Avakian to follow reliably. He could only catch a word here and there. "I'm going to take a shower." He'd wanted to last night but held off because he wanted to bring the debate to a close. And now, sensing another one in the offing, it was time to scamper away.

He always did his best thinking in the shower. Not knowing exactly what was going on was really complicating the decision making. And there was no place to call for the real scoop. The Chinese would definitely have an electronic monitoring blanket around the U.S. Embassy.

He stepped under the water and reminded himself not to make assumptions. So, what do you know for sure? Not much. The Chinese might be firing missiles at Taiwan's cities while they prepared for an invasion, or they might be firing them onto military bases or unpopulated areas to pressure them into surrendering. A full-blown war, including the U.S., might be in progress right now. Or it might not.

As he soaped himself down, he felt the rough stubble on his head. Time to stop shaving the old grape and start changing the appearance. And the way he grew hair, facial at least, a couple of days max for a good start on a beard. Maybe just a goatee.

He began mentally assembling a shopping list. Not a good idea to be walking around in the daytime. Everything would have to be done at night from now on. No cabs. Definitely no subway—every station had surveillance cameras. Which meant that if the Chinese happened to pick up on one of his movements some good old-fashioned detective shoe leather and pattern analysis would probably get them to within maybe a square mile of this apartment. Then they could flood the zone with manpower. He'd have to move every two days, max.

As soon as he got her back to her hotel he could get started. The Chinese would probably take her in but at least she'd be alive. He'd tell her to give them anything they wanted to know. It was the only way. The two of them would never be able to make it out of Beijing. She might get roughed up a bit, but they wouldn't kill her. And if she stayed with him, she was going to get killed. That was not something he wanted to deal with.

He felt better then. His gut always told him when he'd made the right call. Get her out, and then he could start moving.

He was toweling himself off when she yelled, "Pete!"

That wasn't the news—there was some real panic in her voice. Avakian cursed himself for leaving the rifle out in the living room. He whipped on the shorts and dashed out, ready for combat.

But she was just pointing at the TV. That really ticked him off. He was going to have to restrict TV hours around here. Then he immediately felt like a jerk. She was still dealing with what happened last night. He focused on the screen. The talking head was still babbling Mandarin way too fast. "What?"

"Wait for it," she said.

An insert appeared over the anchor's shoulder. Photos

of the two dead soldiers. Record book ID shots. Well, that was inevitable, Avakian thought. The heroic soldiers giving their lives for the preservation of order. Now they were doing an interview with an Army officer in dress uniform. The camera angle was such that he couldn't see the rank on the shoulder boards. Then another insert, of the kid he'd shot. School picture this time. Much younger. Grieving family. If they'd kept the little bastard on a tighter leash, it never would have happened. And finally, another interview, from the hospital, of the punk with his broken arm in a cast. Looking a lot more innocent than he had last night.

That wasn't good, Avakian thought. That they'd put two and two together that fast.

The talking head again, speaking gravely now. And an abrupt transition to a grainy black and white photo of the alley where he'd broken the kid's arm. A cellphone camera shot. Shit. There he was, just a dark blob with his face obscured by shadows and his hat. But Judy Rose standing behind him as clear as day, caught by a street-light or whatever.

Total silence in the apartment, for quite some time. Then Avakian broke it. "I hate cellphones."

"Right now, I'm not feeling so hot about them myself," said Doctor Rose.

Avakian sat down. She started to say something, but he cut her off. "Hold that thought for a few minutes."

They watched the TV in silence, but he didn't see what he'd been waiting for. "No photo of me."

"Maybe they still don't know who we are?"

"Maybe."

"Maybe they don't have a photo of you?"

"Sure, they do. On file from my credentials." He quickly let that go as irrelevant. "No matter. It's always a mistake to assume that police states are unfailingly effi-cient. We know what happened, and we're looking at it from that perspective. They may not and could be appealing to the public for help in putting it together. Where's your phone?"

The abrupt transition threw her. "What?"

"Your phone."

"In my purse."

"Could I see it, please?"

She rooted around in her bag and handed it over. "I turned it off last night to save the battery."

"I'm very glad to hear that." He cupped the phone in his large hand and then slammed it onto the wooden arm of the couch. Still holding the pieces, he twisted the battery pack loose and ripped the wires free.

"So much for checking my voicemail," she said.

"Whenever you turn on a cellphone it pings the nearest tower, indicates it's ready to receive calls, and identifies itself by number for billing purposes. Which means you can track any phone to a general area. How close depends on how close the towers are to each other."

"Okay. Are you going to break your phone, too?"

"As soon as I get far away from here and make one call."

"What now?"

She was regarding him quite calmly, he thought. "Now everything's changed. I can't take you back to your hotel, so it looks like you're stuck with me. If that's all right with you?"

"I wasn't all that thrilled about going back anyway. But I repeat: what now?"

"Well, I'm going to spend the day thinking this through. And then tonight I'll go out and call my former boss at the embassy and see what's really going on. And then it'll be decision time."

"So, what you're telling me, is: you don't know what to do."

Avakian was not offended. "Actually, I have a whole bunch of ideas. But I'm not going to act on any of them until I know exactly where we stand. Nothing wrong with bouncing off the walls, you understand, but you don't want to do it until it's *time* to bounce off the walls."

"Okay."

"Just as an exploratory question, how do you feel about changing your appearance?"

"My appearance?"

"Since they have your picture. We can't make you look Chinese, but we can make you look less like that photo on TV. How do you feel about becoming a blonde?"

"I hear they have more fun."

Chapter Nine

THE MEETING WAS HELD at the People's Liberation Army offices northwest of the Forbidden City because the troops from the Beijing Military Region now outnumbered both the Police and People's Armed Police on the streets. Though the leadership had sent in the Army they'd been careful not to declare martial law, since this was linked in the people's minds with the crushing of the Tiananmen student demonstrations in 1989. Now the official line was that *caiqui jieyan cuoshi*, or short-term limited use of martial law measures—as opposed to a formal declaration of martial law—was necessary to protect the people from foreign attack.

In Communist Party jargon a small-group meeting, or *xiaofanwei huiyi*, was an ad-hoc working group of ranking officials. In this case, the general mood among them was relief, and, as usual in any bureaucratic setting, self-congratulation was the order of the day.

"Latest reports are that the streets are quiet," said Major General Liang Guang of the People's Liberation Army. The only warlike aspect of the General's appearance was a face like a chow dog—jowly and turned down in perpetual disapproval. Other than that, he was shaped like a pear and had a habit of compulsively beating his burning cigarette on the edge of the ashtray. If he hadn't been a general this would have made it hard for the others to concentrate on what he was saying. But generals were never assigned to the Beijing Military Region staff without demonstrating both high-level political influence and absolute ideological reliability. And it was widely known that General Liang had risen through the ranks not as a fighting soldier, but as a political commissar. "It is now clear that the majority of events last night were merely the masses expressing their joy."

So that was the line. Colonel Ma Bai of the People's Armed Police, a paramilitary force under the control of the Public Security Ministry—more heavily armed than the Police but less so than the Army—eagerly took it up. "There were a few instances of beating, smashing, and robbing by a tiny minority of troublemakers."

The rest of the group shifted uneasily. Since no official would ever directly voice what was on their mind, terminology was everything in Chinese dialog. It was common practice for everyone to minutely dissect every statement for the speaker's true meaning. *Jishaoshu*, or "tiny minority," was a stock phrase used to belittle and isolate one's enemy. But *da za qiang*, or "beat, smash, and rob," was a set phrase used to describe Red Guard violence during the Cultural Revolution and therefore had strong negative connotations. Even if Colonel Ma had only misspoken, his choice of phrase would now mark him down for even closer scrutiny.

But Colonel Ma went on as if nothing had happened, lending credence to the theory that he had not misspoken but was, in fact, a fool. "Fortunately, the presence of Army, Armed Police, and Police forces deterred many problems, and these unruly elements were swiftly dealt with. The numbers were so small that it was not necessary to activate emergency detention camps outside the city," he continued.

"And Chaowai and Sanlitun?" Until that moment

Deputy Minister Wei Chongan had been sitting silently. Where the general was fat and angry the politician was fat and delicate. That, however, did not mean that he was less of a shark than the rest. He was in that room because senior officers of the Army and security services would never be allowed to meet without a Party representative present. Otherwise, it might be thought that a coup was being contemplated. He would be reporting back to the Party Central Military Commission.

The others in the room were colonels, because generals and deputy ministers gave orders and colonels made sure they were carried out. The colonels were leaner because they were still hungry. A Chinese officer or official had to reach the rank of major general in order to retire with a house and office and car and driver and all the other perks.

"The foreign embassy areas are completely calm," replied Colonel Shen Li of the Ministry of State Security, which unlike the spy agencies of most other countries also had the mission of counterintelligence. "Some small demonstrations by members of nations who would be expected to oppose our interests. They were encouraged to disperse peacefully and did not achieve the provocations they had hoped for."

Deputy Minister Wei laid down the Party line. "Many delegations to the conference have been confused by events. We are working hard to explain to them that our country is exercising its legitimate right of self defense. We hope to persuade the world community of this, and that this matter is an internal Chinese question. This is a high national priority. Taiwan's aggression must not be allowed to ruin things. Our success in this area will be greatly helped by a stable security situation in the capital."

This thinly veiled threat was recognized and noted by all.

Colonel Shen of State Security said, "Though the

streets are calmed, our work in this area is complicated by the large number of foreign tourists. They are simply too many to contain without drastic measures."

"It is the decision of the Standing Committee that no such measures be taken," said Comrade Wei. "No matter the provocation or difficulty, we will continue to fulfill our duties as a friendly host to all visitors. It is the task of all security forces to maintain the calm and circumvent all problems. It is the judgment of the Standing Committee that Project 137 be put into effect."

Project 137 was a wartime contingency plan. The Chinese had absorbed the lessons of Saddam Hussein and the U.S. strategic bombing of both Iraq and Serbia. After Saddam invaded Kuwait, he rounded up Americans and other Westerners and detained them in strategic locations throughout Iraq. Those areas were not bombed as long as the hostages remained there. As soon as the detainees were released, Iraq was bombed. NATO's air war against Serbia had provided the Chinese with more lessons learned. They had sold the Serbs a great deal of military equipment and intelligence assistance and felt that the bombing of their embassy in Belgrade during the NATO air campaign had been an intentional message, not an accident as NATO claimed.

Project 137 was a perfect example of Chinese pragmatism and Chinese ruthlessness. The security forces were under strict orders not to disrupt hotels or businesses or engage in any public roundups. But every American who attempted to leave the country through an airport or border crossing was quietly taken aside for what was ostensibly a security check and then secretly transported to facilities for indefinite detention. These prisoners could always be released later, but a good supply of American bargaining chips was valuable insurance.

"The Party's main worry now is that foreign agents will engage in acts of sabotage," Comrade Wei continued.

"Known foreign agents have been located, detained, and returned to their embassies, in accordance with orders," said Colonel Shen of State Security. "Doubtless more will appear. But they will be deterred by our efforts."

"By the Army presence on the streets," said General Liang. "And the protection of key persons and facilities by the Central Guard Unit and Garrison Divisions."

The Garrison Divisions were the only Army units to be stationed in Beijing proper and were therefore under the control of the Party Central Military Commission rather than the Army Military Region headquarters. As was the Central Guard Unit, an elite force responsible for the personal security of senior government, party, and military leaders.

"That is all good," said Comrade Wei, raising smiles around the table. "And what of the foreign agents who killed two of our soldiers?"

The smiles vanished, and everyone looked to the general. Which was one of the disadvantages of being a general. "Through the media, we have encouraged the masses to expose the criminals," he said.

"This was perhaps hasty," said Commissioner Zhou Deming of the Ministry of Public Security, speaking for the first time. He turned a clear plastic bag over in his hands. Inside were two steel rods wrapped in bicycle tape. Peter Avakian's two homemade blackjacks, that he had immediately recognized.

No one had been expecting that, least of all the general. "Two soldiers are dead!" he boomed. "Revolutionary Martyrs!"

Now all eyes turned to Commissioner Zhou, expecting him to show proper contrition and engage in self-criticism. "This is indisputable," he replied. Though his tone left the question as to what exactly was indisputable, that the soldiers were dead or that they were revolutionary martyrs. However neutral the statement, that he had not begun with an apology was a not-so-subtle challenge to the general. The next sentence was a shot directly across his bow. "But these news broadcasts have only served to warn the American that he has been identified and is being sought."

The general looked fit to explode.

"Will this speed or delay his apprehension?" Comrade Wei asked.

State Security had also opposed releasing the information to the media. But if Public Security wished to oppose the Army, Colonel Shen would allow them to do so alone.

"These American spies will never be able to leave the city or return to their embassy," said the general. "If Public and State Security resolutely accomplish their work, the apprehension of these spies should not prove difficult."

Having the gauntlet thrown down before State Security was another matter, and it roused Colonel Shen to action. "Now that the American has been alerted, our work will prove more difficult. He will find it easy to hide among the sea of foreigners in Beijing."

The other colonels were impressed. Blame thrown back on the Army, and the necessary groundwork laid to explain away the possibility of failure.

But one did not reach the rank of general by being a stranger to this game. "Was this American not under surveillance by State Security?" General Liang demanded.

"Yes," Colonel Shen replied. "He was lost in the confusion of last night. So, it was doubly unfortunate that, using only the handmade club Commissioner Zhou is now holding in his hands, he was able to overpower two armed soldiers and turn their weapons against them."

The Party, in the person of Comrade Wei, stepped in before any more words were exchanged. "It is imperative that our relations with other foreign governments not be strained during these difficult hours. Their citizens who are our guests must be handled with utmost care. There is agreement on this?"

Everyone received the message that the bickering must cease. There was a chorus of: "Of course, Comrade Deputy Minister."

"Eventually this sea of foreigners will be drained, and the Americans found," the general added.

"I believe it is crucial to our understanding of the situation to recognize that this man Avakian is a subtle, clever, and dangerous operative," said Commissioner Zhou. "An experienced Special Forces officer. Skilled in sabotage and terrorism."

"All the more reason to catch him quickly," said the general.

No visible reaction from the room, but nothing but contempt for the general's loss of face in retreating from Commissioner Zhou's challenge. They all now marked Zhou out as a man to watch, but for entirely different reasons. To be unafraid to challenge the general he must have political support at the highest levels.

As for Commissioner Zhou, who in reality had no high-level supporter, he was thanking his adversary, Peter Avakian. First, for teaching him that acting unexpectedly with the confidence of power was equivalent to actually possessing the reality of power. And second, for becoming the means by which he would advance himself. If the American did cause them problems, everyone at this table would remember his words.

"The Standing Committee desires to know whether this American was involved in the assassination," said Deputy Minister Wei. "Is there a link between America and Taiwan in this matter? Colonel Shen?"

Commissioner Zhou particularly enjoyed this. He knew Avakian had not been involved but would say nothing—if the leadership wished to believe it, then the greater the reward for the one who captured him. State Security undoubtedly knew the same thing, but in China that made no difference. If the Party believed in an America-Taiwan conspiracy, then a conspiracy existed. But at that moment Colonel Shen of State Security was on the horns of a possibly career-ending dilemma, because with the Party line unclear, he had no idea which position to take.

"As of now there are no firm conclusions," Colonel Shen replied. "The discovery of further evidence and the interrogation of the American will provide definitive answers."

Masterfully evasive, Zhou thought. Shen was clearly destined for general's stars.

"All the more reason to work together and take concrete action," said Comrade Wei. "I emphasize that harmless Western visitors must be treated correctly. Anti-social elements must not be encouraged. And any threats to social stability must not be permitted, particularly at the present time. I hope that we are all in agreement, and you join me in resolutely supporting these principles."

An encore chorus of: "Of course, Comrade Deputy Minister."

"Excellent. Then the Ministries of State Security and Public Security will take the lead in this effort, working in harmony, with the Army rendering every assistance."

The Army being taken down a notch did not leave the general looking pleased. But he joined them in a finale of: "Of course, Comrade Deputy Minister."

As they packed up their files, Colonel Shen came around the table to Commissioner Zhou. "I wish you success."

"I thank you," Commissioner Zhou replied.

Shen vowed to find out who was behind Zhou. "In light of your friendly relations with the American, I am certain it will not be noticed if you are not successful."

"If he does cause any further damage," said Commissioner Zhou, "I am certain it will be forgotten that your men lost him."

"Have no fear. State Security will find him."

"I have no fear. I am confident he will be found."

INSPECTOR 1ST GRADE Yong Cheng sat patiently, fighting the impulse to examine the papers atop Commissioner Zhou's desk. He heard the hand on the door and stood up as the commissioner entered. The inspector was over six feet tall, with the musculature of a weightlifter—not typical of the average Chinese policeman. Though his name was Han Chinese, he had the Vietnamese facial features of the Jing ethnic minority of the Guangxi region. This had not made his path through the ranks easier since the majority of Han were not particularly broadminded about the national minorities, let alone their traditional adversaries the Vietnamese. Cheng had no idea that Commissioner Zhou had chosen him for this very characteristic, knowing that as a minority he would be dependent for advancement on Zhou alone, not the organization, and his loyalty therefore assured.

"Sit, sit," said Commissioner Zhou, tossing a thick file folder onto his desk. His chair squeaked as he sat down. "I have just come from the minister. I am in charge of the search for the American Avakian. You will be my deputy for this task."

"I am honored."

"You may be. But only if we are successful."

Inspector Cheng was used to this. Commissioner Zhou was not the typical senior officer. Since he never had any idea when the man was joking, he always worked under the assumption that he was not. And recently the commissioner had been acting with unheard-of boldness. It could only mean that he had acquired a powerful patron. All the more reason to remain a valued part of his circle. "The team leaders are assembled."

"All the best investigators?"

"Yes, Commissioner. But there will be few available for other investigations."

"This has the highest priority. And they will all be needed. This American is not a spy, contrary to the belief of State Security. He is much more dangerous. I think that, rather than surrender himself, this Avakian will seek to fight us."

"Fight us? How?"

"In any way he can. I saw this man defeat three robbers with only a piece of wood. He subdued one of the Indoor Stadium assassins and threw the man onto his own hand grenade before it detonated. And as you know he killed two armed soldiers—with only a club."

"He killed them to obtain their weapons?"

"Of course not. Speak the official line to others but by no means allow it to affect your thinking. He was accosted by youthful troublemakers and fought one. I interrogated the two survivors myself. The one who did not survive sought out the two soldiers and must have told them some fanciful tale. The soldiers found Avakian and, I surmise, treated him harshly as a bad element and paid with their lives for this. But this is not the official line." Commissioner Zhou did not even mention the woman with Avakian. For a Chinese male the woman was irrelevant.

"I understand," said Inspector Cheng. It would not be wise to mention to others anything that was not the official line. "Will we be working with State Security?"

"The natural inclination of the Center is to always place our organizations in competition. State Security desires the credit for catching the American. But they do not know who they are dealing with. They will seek him as they would a CIA agent. But a CIA agent would only attempt to escape. The American Special Forces learn to fight terrorists and would therefore not find it difficult to become one."

"I understand, Commissioner."

"When we capture him there will be much credit, not only from our superiors but the Center also. If we fail and State Security succeeds, then we are policemen and not counterintelligence specialists. If we both fail, the blame is shared. This is for your ears only."

"Yes, Commissioner." Inspector Cheng wondered if Commissioner Zhou had not somehow arranged that. Of course, he would never ask. Not that the commissioner would ever answer.

"I will address the work group now." Commissioner Zhou picked up the plastic bag with the blackjacks and they walked down the hall to a conference room. Everyone rose and bowed as they entered. Twenty junior inspectors from the Bureau of Criminal Investigation who each led their own 10-man teams.

"Be seated," said Commissioner Zhou. "You have read the dossiers?"

They all nodded.

He took them through the history, then passed the plastic bag around the table. "This is how we identified him. He has made and used two of these so far. He may again, but that is doubtful as he is now armed. You must be aware that this Avakian has knowledge of our security arrangements. He will not show many vulnerabilities. I see three. He must seek shelter. All hotels are now prohibited from accepting new registrations from foreigners. If he makes the attempt, we will be aware of it. He has been in Beijing for some time and is an engaging personality, so I feel he may seek shelter with someone he has previously come in contact with. You will examine his dossier and surveillance record carefully and visit and interview every person listed."

He paused, but only to drink some water. Chinese would never ask questions in a room filled with their peers, for fear of losing face. If there were questions, they would be broached privately and obliquely, if at all. Commissioner Zhou set his glass down and continued. "Next, transportation. I doubt he will risk public transportation. So, we must make ourselves aware of all stolen vehicles within the city. Particularly those large enough to sleep inside, with tinted windows. Third, the woman. Contrary to the belief of State Security, she is a physician, not a spy. If he keeps her with him, he will become more vulnerable, and together they will be more identifiable. In any event, apprehending her alone will provide valuable information. I have told you this is a dangerous man. He is now armed with a Type 95 assault rifle and two basic units of ammunition. There will be great credit in capturing this man, but not if in attempting to take him without assistance he kills you and escapes. He is not a young man, but he has extensive combat experience with American Special Forces in wars all over the world and you have not seen his like. Do not be hasty and do not be careless. You are here in tribute to my confidence in your skills. Now, we will discuss each group's work assignment. We will proceed methodically but quickly. I am certain that if we allow this man freedom of action, he will cause us to regret it."

Chapter Ten

AVAKIAN WAS THREADING his way through South Beijing, skirting the inner ring road. No interior lights on in the small, nondescript white van. He was driving with one hand and dialing his cellphone with the other.

It was a hot, muggy night in Beijing. For some reason it reminded him of the same kind of night in Philadelphia when he was a teenager. Nothing was more lonely or more exciting than a big city on a muggy summer night, the darkness filled up with lights. And though nothing at all like Philly, wartime Beijing was still all lit up—business as usual.

The phone was ringing.

"Hello?" Russell Marquand sounded cautious, as if he were expecting a different voice to be calling him from that familiar number.

"It's me," Avakian said.

"I assume you realize we're not the only parties to this conversation," Marquand said.

"Doesn't matter," said Avakian.

"You know they're looking for you."

"I'm on my way out of town even as we speak. How about telling me what's going on?"

"Okay, but nothing the Chinese don't already know.

They're still shooting missiles at Taiwan. Concentrating on the ports and airfields. They haven't made any move to invade. Yet."

Avakian understood immediately. "I got it. Are we involved?"

"Not at the present. The Secretary of State tried to talk to the Chinese, but they're refusing all offers of mediation. They say it's an internal Chinese matter."

"Secretary still there?"

"No. Snubbed and left. We're restricted to the embassy. Chinese say it's for our own safety, considering the mood on the streets."

"Right," said Avakian.

"There's reports of Americans being detained at the airports. People calling because relatives supposed to fly out never showed back up in the States."

"What do the Chinese say?"

"They don't know anything about it."

"Human shields?" said Avakian.

"We're not going to speculate right now."

"Anything else?"

"I don't want to add to your problems, but the Chinese are moving a lot of men into North Korea. Though they haven't crossed the DMZ."

"Yet," said Avakian.

"I'm sorry, man."

Marquand knew about his son being stationed in South Korea. "Are they moving on anyone else?"

"Not so far."

"Then is anyone else involved in this thing?"

"You mean like Europe?"

"Please. And have to back up their lofty principles with anything besides talk?" Avakian scoffed. "That I could figure out for myself."

"No one else right now. Everyone's sitting on the sidelines, hoping they don't get rained on."

"Is Annie with you?" Avakian asked. It was time to wrap up the call.

"Yeah, she's here."

"Give her my love. Good luck to you, bro."

"Feel like saying I'm sorry I brought you over here."

"We're all grownups."

"Stay lucky."

Avakian broke the connection and turned off his phone. At least Marquand's kids were both back in the States.

———

ALL NIGHT long Judy Rose felt like she was going to throw up. She understood why she couldn't go out on the streets, not with her picture all over the TV. But that little piece of logic was irrelevant compared to being trapped in an apartment in a foreign country in the middle of a war with the police looking for her and the one person with any idea of what to do out gallivanting around town. If he got himself killed or arrested, her only alternatives seemed to be staying in the apartment until she starved to death or walking outside and turning herself in to the nearest policeman.

The TV had gone way past irritating. There wasn't anything on except propaganda war movies where everyone periodically broke into song, and news she couldn't understand.

She had been pacing around the apartment until she suddenly realized it was past midnight and at any moment an aggrieved downstairs neighbor might begin pounding at the door. The shock of that little realization almost had her clinging to the ceiling fan.

Sleep? That was a laugh. And to cap it all off the leaseholder of the apartment definitely wasn't a reader. Unless you counted a closet filled with back copies of Maxim and FHM.

And there wasn't even any chocolate to get her through it.

She wound up sitting on the floor with her back to the door. Listening for footsteps in the hallway.

The first time she heard the elevator door open she jumped to her feet. But right after the ding there were loud drunken voices speaking Chinese going down the hall.

The second time there were heavy footsteps but no voices.

Stop driving yourself crazy, Judy.

A half hour later, the fire door at the end of the hallway opened very quietly and then closed even quieter. No footsteps in the hall but then just the slightest jingle of keys in front of the door.

Doctor Rose sprang up and put her eye to the peephole. It was Avakian. Thank God. A key scraped in the lock, and she yanked the door open, almost dragging him into the apartment.

He recovered his footing and said, "Hi," as he fed bulky shopping bags into the entryway. "Hold the door open a crack. I've got a bunch more of these stacked up in the stairwell."

It took him six more trips, arms fully loaded. Groceries, clothes, cardboard boxes. Even, incongruously enough, a big bundle of metal pipes all strapped together. When he'd brought the last of it inside, he locked the door, turned around, and gave her a double take. "You cut your hair."

Honestly, she was surprised. "How very un-male of you to notice."

"Every now and again I drop in on my feminine side, just to keep in touch." He eyed her anew. "You did a good job. It looks nice."

"Thanks."

"A lot better than I could have done, which is why I guess you took matters into your own hands. Good call, but I'm always astounded by how women can cut their own hair."

"Well, you cut yours."

"That would be like me complimenting you on how well you shave your legs."

She began surveying the purchases. "What is all this stuff for?"

"We'll talk about that in just a second." He was poking through the bags, looking for something. "I know it wasn't easy sitting here twiddling your thumbs, wondering if I was ever coming back. Here's your reward." He handed her a thin brown box. "As far as the treatment of stress goes, chocolate is the non-prescription Valium, am I right?"

She stared at the box in her hand, well and truly creeped out by that.

"Yeah, I know," he said. "Got in touch with my feminine side again. Don't tell me you're the only woman in the world who doesn't like chocolate."

After a moment of contemplation, she said, "I admit I was thinking about fibbing to you. But when I took this into the bathroom with me, you'd know, wouldn't you?"

"I'd have my suspicions. Sorry, but I couldn't find any plain chocolate bars."

"I love Toblerone. Wait a minute, how did you know...?"

"Plain chocolate? You really want Snickers, you really want peanut butter cups, but with a plain bar or maybe some kisses or even baking bits it's easier to convince yourself you're not doing anything naughty."

"That is entirely irrational," Doctor Rose informed him, while at the same time blushing red.

"Don't I know it."

"You *were* married, weren't you?"

"I wouldn't lie about something like that. Why don't you sit down? We have some things to talk over."

"Oh, one of those."

"Yeah, pretty much." Avakian got himself a bottle of water and settled onto the couch. "This is the situation. China's launching missiles on Taiwan's airports and shipping ports. In effect, blockading the island. It's a pretty shrewd strategy. Taiwan's an industrial exporter. They're not self-sufficient in food or energy or damn near anything else except computer chips. So, the Chinese figure that if they can keep everyone and everything from going in or coming out, Taiwan's going to have to cry uncle sooner or later. Without them having to invade. And if they don't invade, they don't give the U.S. a clear-cut reason to intervene. The Chinese are betting that, after Iraq, we're not in the mood for any more trouble. Especially war with a major power. Then you've got the possibility of war between two nuclear powers, which has never happened before. So, we're going to be very careful what we get ourselves into, and the Chinese are deliberately making it difficult for us to make a decision. Very smart. That's the big picture."

"And the little picture?" Doctor Rose said.

"The Chinese are apparently detaining Americans trying to leave the country. Remember what I said back in the restaurant about foreign civilians being the best defense against air attack?"

"I remember."

"This brings us to the problem of what we're going to do." Avakian sat back and closed his eyes. It was a much tougher proposition now, being responsible for her life too. He had to ask himself whether he'd be doing it for his own ego, or because it was the right thing to do. Trying to get out of the city was going to be a one-time, one-shot deal. No opportunities for multiple attempts. Okay, maybe a little ego involved. But there were larger issues at stake. His original plan was still the best. And might just be their only option. "Before I tell you my plan, I've got to lay it on the line. We're probably not going to make it out of the city. By which I mean we're probably going to get ourselves killed. So anytime you think surrendering to the Chinese is a better option, you let me know."

She was still regarding him very calmly. "You don't strike me as suicidal, so I don't think you're going to go out of your way to get us killed. And since I think what happened to me last night would happen all over again, and worse, if I turned myself in to the Chinese, I don't think I'd want to do that. So, I'll say it one more time: what now?"

Okay, Avakian thought. "First, I'm going to create some chaos. And then we're going to try and escape from Beijing."

"I'm assuming there's a lot more detail than that. Let's start with the chaos."

"We can't fly. The train stations and bus terminals will be totally covered. So, it'll have to be by vehicle. And there are only ten roads leading out of the entire city. You see, being a security consultant, you learn these things."

"That's lucky, at least."

"Luck is relative. Knowing all that, under ordinary conditions we'd have no expectation of making it out without being caught. So, we'll need to do it under the cover of a substantial amount of chaos. I intend to cause that. And I want to be honest with you about the reasons."

"Okay."

"I thought my fighting days were over. Other than the odd street punk or two. I've seen too many wars and the stupid reasons they're fought to think there's anything noble in them or that appeals to patriotism aren't just another form of marketing. I spent my professional life watching patriots get screwed by opportunists. But the Chinese declared war on me last night, and that made it a matter of personal survival. We, *us*, we're at war. If we don't fight, we go under. And I don't intend to go under just yet."

"And what can two people do to a city of sixteen million?"

"If I told you the damage one person can do to a modern city, you'd never believe me."

She seemed to be trying to properly phrase something. "And this would involve killing…"

"No. You'll be happy to hear that I don't intend to kill anyone. On 9/11 Al Qaeda killed thousands of Americans, and what did that accomplish? Put every American, regardless of political persuasion, right behind their government. So, for strictly practical, if not moral reasons, we don't want to do that. Besides, it wouldn't bother the Chinese leadership if I killed ten thousand of their people. But what they really fear is chaos. So that's what I'm going to give them."

"You keep using that word."

"What happened when New Orleans went under water? Chaos. And who did Americans blame? Their government."

"I admit it's a relief you're not going to be killing people. I was picturing us as the Washington D.C. snipers."

"Well, kind of keep that overall idea in your head. Those two lunatics pretty much shut down the entire East Coast."

"You're not going to kill people. But you're going to replicate a hurricane?"

"In a way. You know anything about systems disruption?"

"Sorry. I was carrying a full course load that semester, and it was only an elective."

Avakian grinned at that. Welcome back, Doctor Rose. A few hours away from molestation, three killings, and a near-meltdown—and now she was actually getting all jazzed up by the prospect of mortal danger. He'd never understand women. "We're on a really tight timeline, and I need to get a few things in motion." He was up off the couch and dumping the first shopping bag out on the kitchen table. He handed her a box. "Here's your hair color."

She looked first at him and then at the box, brow furrowed. Agreeing in principle was one thing. Staring at the reality quite another.

Avakian knew that changing hair color when it wasn't your idea was a major, major minefield. One that, if he was going to have to walk through, had better be done both quickly and lightly. "There are actually directions in English inside. Well, sort of English."

Her expression had now changed to one of pure skepticism. She opened the box.

"I made a judgment call on the shade," he said. "After weighing a number of different factors."

"You just walked down the aisle and grabbed one, didn't you?"

"I'll have you know that there was a great deal of careful consideration, one might even say personal anxiety, involved in making that choice."

"You picked the box with the best-looking model, didn't you?"

Avakian shook his head sadly. "I would have thought that a doctor, of all people, would be above sexist slander."

One more look, and a raised eyebrow from her.

"Okay," Avakian conceded. "The box was a factor."

Now she gave him a crooked grin. "How did you get all this stuff around?"

"Stole a car. Actually, a van."

"Have you broken your cellphone yet?"

"After I made my call, I happened to pull up next to a bus at a stoplight. That gave me an idea. The phone's turned on and taped to the side of a westbound bus right now. So even if the Chinese don't pick up the signal and track it down, I still amused myself."

"It's better than being disgusted. Am I allowed to know who you called?"

"Sure. My former boss Russell Marquand at the U.S. Embassy. The Chinese have all our diplomats locked in there. He gave me the news."

"Anything besides what you told me?"

"The Chinese are moving troops into North Korea. They haven't attacked the South yet, but they probably will if we get involved and any real shooting starts."

Judy Rose put her hand over her mouth. "Your son."

Avakian's face was impassive. "He'll have to take his chances like any other soldier."

"Why would the Chinese invade South Korea?"

"It's our only base, and our only troops, on the Asian landmass. Bounce us out of there and we're never coming back. Not with a 10 division Army. And I don't think the Chinese would be sad about eliminating South Korea as a peer competitor."

Doctor Rose clenched her fists in frustration. "And millions of people's lives will be completely shattered."

"You could say that, by definition, the people who start wars don't much care about such things," Avakian replied.

She broke off a piece of chocolate and popped it into her mouth. "Now that we're trapped together in this apartment, can I ask you what is it with men?"

"We really don't have that kind of time," Avakian said, theatrically looking at his watch. "Unless you'd like to narrow down the scope of that question."

"What is it with men and war?"

Quite aware that he was walking the tightrope over Niagara Falls, Avakian kept a smile on his face. "Well, do you want to talk about ingrained aggression that comes from being both a predator and a prey species, that still governs our brains and hormones? The survival imperative to acquire, expand, and defend hunting grounds and agricultural lands? Or that there could never be war and killing if women ran the show like, say, Eleanor of Aquitaine, Elizabeth I, Golda Meir, Margaret Thatcher, and Benazir Bhutto?"

"I'm going to withdraw into bitter silence now."

Avakian most definitely did not try to get the last word in by saying that was something women so rarely do. Instead, he shut up and breathed a sigh of relief over having made a narrow escape. And busied himself in the bags.

"What's on the agenda now?" she asked, the bitter silence officially over.

"I'm going to finish unpacking and get organized. You could start on your hair, if you like."

"What are you going to do?" she asked.

"Nothing, really."

She broke off another piece of chocolate and popped it into her mouth. Chewing hard, hands on hips, not budging an inch.

"Okay," said Avakian. "I'm going to make some explosives."

"And I'm supposed to color my hair while you're doing that?"

"Well, that was sort of my motive in not mentioning it. But of course, another set of hands would be very welcome."

They cleared off the kitchen table and unpacked all the ingredients. Doctor Rose was checking out all the bottles of hair lightener. "I don't know what you have in mind here. But I have no intention of being *that* blonde."

"Have no fear," said Avakian. "It's not for you. We need hydrogen peroxide in a concentration of 6% or stronger, and the first aid products are only 3%. Check out the main ingredient in that hair bleach. I got the strongest they had, and the nice thing about beauty supply shops is that every day they deal with people who want to dye their hair green. No one gets suspicious about anything."

She read the back of the bottle. "H²O². I didn't major in chemistry, but that sounds like hydrogen peroxide. And strong enough to turn me into Edgar Winter."

"Just what the doctor ordered," said Avakian.

"Very funny."

"If you would, please open this box of hexamine tablets and pull each one out of the foil wrapping. Just put them on that kitchen towel."

"And these are?"

"Solid fuel tablets. For camping. Light one and heat up your morning coffee."

Avakian measured hydrogen peroxide into a glass bowl. When she was finished, he wrapped the towel around the fuel tablets and smashed them into powder. Using a teaspoon measure, he dissolved crushed hexamine into the peroxide.

"What now?" she said.

Avakian was setting the kitchen timer. "We wait 30 minutes."

When the timer went off, he dissolved powdered citric acid, what the Chinese called "sour salt", into the solution. After mixing, he slid the bowl into the refrigerator.

"We let this stand until solid particles form in the bottom," he said. "About 8 hours for precipitation to take place. Pour the liquid through a coffee filter to collect the solids. Let the filter dry and remove the particles. Carefully. They're *very* sensitive explosive. We'll use it to make a blasting cap to set off less-sensitive explosive."

"That was actually pretty easy."

"Yeah, well, handling that dry powder isn't going to be. It goes boom at the drop of a hat. Now we make the stuff it's going to set off."

"I assume that's what all the granulated swimming pool cleaner is for."

"You assume right." Avakian measured the pool cleaner into big glass storage jars. China wasn't big on environmental protection, and you could buy benzene at any paint store. He poured the liquid into the pool cleaner and stirred. "That's it."

"Even easier."

"This is not the hard part about being an urban guerrilla. It's a low velocity explosive, but we're not going to be blowing up any bridges. Now we come to the initiators."

With the jars of explosive lined up on the kitchen counter like baking ingredients, Avakian methodically cleared the table of all the leftovers. He threw the packaging into the rapidly filling trash bag and sprayed the table with cleanser. "Just in case there's any explosive residue," he told her as he wiped it down.

"You're very careful," she said.

"You can always tell a careful demo man by whether he still has all ten fingers." He presented the full complement for her inspection. "So far so good. You have to stay focused, but it's not like surgery."

"Patients don't blow up during surgery. I was nervous enough watching. If you gave me the job, I'd be so scared I'd have to be sitting on a bedpan while I did it."

Avakian grinned and said, "It's always a good rule of thumb not to make the bomb-maker laugh."

"Sorry."

Still chuckling, he unboxed the soldering iron and plugged it in. While it heated up, he dismantled the bag full of flashlights he'd purchased, keeping the bulb housings and discarding the rest. Prying off the battery contact plates, he lined them all up on the table. Soon followed by another corresponding row of battery-powered digital kitchen clocks, with the back plates removed and the circuit boards exposed. A number of different models bought in different places—you didn't walk into one kitchen store and ask for 30 timers.

Next Judy held the two reels of blue and white insulated electric wire while he cut 6-inch lengths and stripped the ends, making two piles.

The iron was hot. Avakian went down the row and soldered positive and negative wires onto the battery housings and the buzzer contacts of the timers.

While the solder cooled, he used a file to cut two grooves for the wires in the plastic back plates of the clocks and screwed them on again. "Let's see if it works," he said. He twisted the blue wires together for a bulb and a timer. Then the white. Setting the timer for 10 seconds he pushed the button to start it. "Keep your fingers crossed."

The seconds ticked down to zero, and when the buzzer went off the bulb lit up. "Eureka," Avakian exclaimed. He went down the line and checked every one. Two didn't work, and rather than fool around he threw them away.

After that he unhooked the wires and moved the bulbs down to the other end of the table.

China was the land of fireworks. And unlike America they still made and sold the original cherry bomb. Avakian cut a couple of the round firecrackers open to harvest the propellant. Which was not black powder, but flash powder.

With the file, he carefully cut a hole in the top of each bulb. And filled the insides with flash powder, sealing it back up with epoxy.

"So that's what sets it off," she said.

"It's kind of a 3-stage process," Avakian replied. "I've got some ¾-inch diameter brass tubing, and we'll cut that into 3, 3½-inch lengths and seal one end with the epoxy. I'll fill that with the sensitive explosive and fit the bulb on the open end. The bulb sets off the sensitive explosive, which produces enough detonation velocity to fire the main charge. But first comes the grunt work. We have to cut that steel pipe into about foot and a half lengths and thread both ends for a cap."

"With our teeth?" she asked.

"Well, if you want. But I'll be using the pipe cutter and the threader I bought."

"Won't a saw wake up the neighbors?"

Avakian showed her the pipe cutter. "It's like a clamp with a blade. You just tighten it onto the pipe, turn, and it cuts a groove. Screw it down a little tighter and keep going until the pipe comes apart. You'd have to drop it on the floor to make any noise. After that I spoon the explosive into the pipes, fit in the detonator, run the wires out, screw on the end cap, and tape the timer to the outside. Your basic pipe bomb. With a little more kick."

"And you're sure it will work."

"There are only three sure things in this world," Avakian told her. "Death, taxes, and the fact that any white guy who wears dreadlocks does not use deodorant."

Chapter Eleven

"FROM THE PATTERN of the cellphone signals it is certain that he was inside a vehicle," said Inspector Cheng.

Commissioner Zhou was peering at the clear acetate overlay that covered the large wall map where the clerk had marked the location of the signals received by the cellular base stations. He traced a line with his finger and tapped the acetate with his fingernail. "State Security discovered his cellphone on a bus in Yanch. What does this mean to you?"

"That he did not flee west," Inspector Cheng replied.

"It means nothing. He may have fled in any direction. He may not have fled at all. I think not at all, so we will allow State Security to spend their resources searching for him outside the city. Avakian enjoys his cleverness, but there will always be a plan. We must discover the plan behind his cleverness. Join me at the map."

Inspector Cheng moved up beside him. "I could assemble all this information on the computer for you."

Commissioner Zhou turned his head briefly to look up and over at him. "And then I would be straining to see detail on a small computer screen, and doubtless miss something important."

"I am sorry, Commissioner."

"One should always endeavor to not say anything which will require an apology. Now, observe the map. From the location where he killed the soldiers, we see his path move roughly eastward through the automatic banking machine transactions he made. He is clever and does not move in a straight line, constantly changing direction. Then near the city center he stops withdrawing money. No taxi or bus picked them up, and there is no video from the subway. They were both on foot. And could have proceeded in any direction. But I think not to retrace his steps. So north, south, or continuing east. Which narrows the area we must search."

The phone rang, and the inspector answered. He hung up and announced excitedly, "A white man of Avakian's description purchased five flashlights from a shop in the Dongzhimen district last night."

"Dongzhimen?" Commissioner Zhou tapped the map once again. "How did we gain this information?"

"From the local officer on patrol. Why would he purchase so many flashlights?"

"That is not the relevant point, however interesting. Send an immediate alert to all local bureaus in the city. Particularly the small foot stations. They must make inquiries at every shop in their localities with Avakian's photograph. We must know immediately of any shop that has seen him."

A Chinese officer would never willingly lose face by saying he did not understand. So, Inspector Cheng instead asked, "And what he has purchased?"

"Yes, but that is still less relevant than us being aware of every location he has been seen. These we will mark on the map."

"To seek a pattern?"

"No. The absence of a pattern. When we plot every location where he has left an identifiable trace, we will see that he has been all over the city. Except for one area.

That area is where he is hiding. And when we discover which of his friends and contacts lives within that area, then we will have found him."

Commissioner Zhou picked up a marker and began shading in sections of the city. "We must make significant progress this day. I suspect he will be stationary in daylight, and active at night. If everyone completes their work assignments satisfactorily, we will find him tomorrow."

Chapter Twelve

"ANY SECOND THOUGHTS?" said Avakian. "I can still take you back to the apartment, no problem."

"No thank you," said Doctor Rose.

"Just so you understand this means you have to go where I go. You don't want to be sitting here alone in the van if someone stops by and wants to know what you're doing. And where I'm going tonight won't be all that pleasant."

That combination of what she considered to be condescension veiled as consideration was really starting to annoy her. "No matter how many times you tell me, I still understand. Even the way I'm feeling now, it's better than staying behind in that apartment."

"Everyone feels that way the first time they do something like this. I feel tight right now myself."

She didn't buy it. He looked like he'd just scored free tickets to the hottest show in town. Having the time of his life. While as soon as she heard what she'd agreed to do she had to go to the bathroom. Every time she went, she felt like she had to go again a minute later. "I doubt that anyone ever felt like this."

"Your stomach's squeezed down to about the size of a raisin, right? If your hands aren't shaking, your knees are.

And if you haven't sweated through your shirt yet, you will."

She looked over at him as they weaved through the evening traffic. "You described all my symptoms perfectly. At first, I thought I was starting menopause. Which was just what I needed right now."

Avakian chuckled. Menopause.

"*You* felt this way?" she said.

"You'd better believe it."

"Doing what?"

"Parachuting into Grenada."

"Okay," she said. "That beats med school finals, or my first surgical procedure."

"But having done those, you know the anticipation is always worse than the execution."

"I'm not so sure this time. You know, the only symptom you didn't describe was…"

"You feel like you could shit through a screen door without touching the wire, right?"

Doctor Rose burst into laughter. Rocking back and forth, straining against her seatbelt. Wiping her eyes, she said, "Oh, I feel much better now. Thanks, Pete."

"One strong emotion always counteracts another." Avakian took the exit off the West Third Ring Road. "We're getting close."

"If you don't want me talking, tell me to shut up."

In his experience, there was no way that keeping a woman from talking was ever going to make her less nervous. "Doesn't bother me. Go right ahead."

"Why haven't I ever heard of something like this?"

"Well, two reasons," said Avakian. "First of all, terrorists are mainly concerned with making a big media impact. Their attacks aren't military operations, they're armed propaganda operations. The second reason is not politically correct."

She smiled in the darkness. Then it was probably going to be good. "Go ahead."

"Okay. The vast majority of today's terrorism is Muslim, with Arab origins. And the only thing Arabs are really any good at is murder."

"I thought you said you didn't hate anyone you didn't know personally."

"I did a security contract in Saudi Arabia. For the first and last time. And the less said about that, the better."

"Sounds like they didn't make much of an impression on you."

"They didn't. Now, what were we talking about?"

"Terrorism."

"Right. Critical system vulnerabilities aren't spectaculars that lend themselves to great TV. Beijing had major water supply problems even after they expanded their infrastructure for the Olympics. And I just happen to know that they've got 11 treatment plants in the city, most of them in a circle between the 4th and 3rd Ring Roads, and 6 in the suburbs." The map was taped to the dashboard. "There's probably a battalion of troops guarding each one. Which, since we don't have a thousand rangers hanging around, means we won't be getting anywhere near those plants. But we don't have to. Okay, here we go. A likely looking spot."

Main water and sewer lines always followed main roads into cities. Avakian had picked a location that wasn't residential, with no businesses that were open at night. Traffic of course—it was Beijing after all. But you couldn't have everything.

He pulled over near the curb and activated his 4-way flashers. Reaching under the seat, he pulled out the magnetized revolving red light. Turning it on, he leaned out the window and stuck it on the roof of the van.

"You remember the routine," he said.

"You made me practice it enough."

As soon as they'd gotten into the van, they'd changed into cheap 1-piece white Tyvek plastic coveralls, with hoods. Splash suits. With high rubber boots. And since those suits were damnably hot, nothing but underwear underneath. The suits not only looked right, but they were going to make cleanup a lot easier.

And before they exited, they donned full-face respirators, the industrial type with filter canisters on each side. They were a good disguise against non-Oriental features, and Avakian was worried about toxic gases. Rubber gloves were also going to be necessary. And, strictly for camouflage, yellow plastic construction hard hats and reflective safety vests.

Opening the back door Avakian saw that he had in fact stopped right in front of one of Beijing's attractively ornate steel manhole covers. Perfect.

He stuck another revolving light on the back roof. They looked official enough, and no one was likely to be checking for vehicle logos in the middle of the night.

With the traffic whipping by, Avakian unloaded the construction barriers he'd stolen from an unattended site, arranging them around the manhole. Cheap yellow and black plastic sawhorses with solar-powered yellow blinking lights. Then farther down the road a line of reflective red plastic traffic cones.

"Should we be calling this much attention to ourselves?" Doctor Rose asked, her voice muffled by the respirator.

"Sneak around and people get suspicious," Avakian replied. "Look and act like you're supposed to be there, no one pays any attention."

With a narrow pry bar in one hand and a crowbar hook in the other, he wedged the manhole cover up and dragged it clear. Clicking on the big 12-volt lantern, he shined it down into the hole. Good news and bad news. Good news: it wasn't a sewer. Water lines didn't run down sewers—only flowing streams of sewage did. Bad news: it wasn't a sewer, but it still looked pretty bad. He glanced over at the good doctor. And foresaw problems.

Avakian pulled the sliding metal ladder out of the

back of the van, extending it to full length as he ran it down into the hole. At least it hit bottom. That had been a major concern.

Now he returned to the van and unlocked one of the three large metal toolboxes. Removing the top tray revealed shiny pipe bombs swaddled in bubble wrapping. He took out two and completed the connections, wrapping the bare wire in electrical tape. Then he tucked them back into their bubble wrap and carefully zipped the package into the nylon duffel bag he slung across his back. "Check your respirator."

She clapped her hands over the filter canisters and took a breath. The rubber sealed to her face, and no air leaked in. "It's working," she reported.

"Okay, follow me."

He started down the ladder. From the look of the walls in the lantern beam the respirator was going to be a godsend. Because there seemed to be about a thousand years of grossness down there. He stepped off into a few inches of liquid. Oh, this was not going to go over well at all.

But on the bright side it wasn't like a manhole—there was actually a tunnel continuing down a ways. Though relatively narrow and only slightly higher than himself.

There was a big pipe that had to be a conduit into the sewers. It actually looked like it was made out of…he gave it a knock to confirm. It really was made out of clay. And running right above it a smaller diameter cast iron water pipe. And was that a gas line? It sure looked like it. An added benefit.

Doctor Rose was coming down now. Seriously stressed, if the indications were correct. She was breathing through her respirator like Darth Vader. He began war gaming what to do if she freaked out on him down here.

It started for Judy Rose as she came down the ladder into the tunnel. She couldn't take her eyes off the walls, from which were hanging mini stalactites of filth. Just what kind of filth she tried hard not to speculate about. Her stomach was rolling around enough as it was.

The bottom of the tunnel held a liquid that only an optimist would have guessed to be water. She hadn't thought it would be that small. She also hadn't thought she was claustrophobic. But she was definitely feeling claustrophobic.

Her lantern barely penetrated the gloom farther down the tunnel. Oh my God.

Without realizing it, but she'd said it out loud. When the hand grabbed her arm, she almost leaped all the way up the ladder.

"You need to slow and shallow your breathing," Avakian was saying. "You're breathing harder than those filters can give you air. You'll get hypoxic."

So that was the source of the headache. God, she couldn't even diagnose a medical condition now. Come on, Judy. This wasn't as bad as…okay, as her first human dissection. She looked around the tunnel again. No, this was worse.

"Why don't you wait here," he suggested. "Just lean against the ladder and look up. I'll be back in a few minutes."

"Back from where?" she demanded. Oh, now even she could hear the panic in her own voice.

"Farther down."

"Why can't you put them here?"

"Because the tunnel goes farther down," he explained patiently. "We want to make this hard to locate and repair."

He started down the tunnel. But when the darkness swallowed up his light and she couldn't see him another wave of panic hit her. It was scarier to stay. She hurried after him, but the sewer pipe took up so much space she could only walk sideways. The top of the pipe was at low chest height.

Avakian saw her light coming. He shined his down at her and waited. Wonderful. Just wonderful. If they were all going to be like this, he might get one more done before dawn.

"Sorry," she said. "Too scary to wait."

"Okay, let's get moving," he said.

She thought it would be cooler underground, but it wasn't. The pipes probably conducted a lot of heat. The humidity was incredible, with water—or whatever it was —dripping off everything. And the plastic suit definitely didn't help. Salt sweat was pouring into her eyes, out of reach inside the respirator. She could feel the perspiration running down her legs and squishing inside her boots every time she took a step. It was actually easier to think about dying of heat stroke than thinking about the tunnel closing in on her.

When she'd been rushing to catch up, she'd focused her light down the tunnel and ignored everything else. Now as they moved, she played the beam over the tunnel wall. And the wall seemed to be moving. The light, which had been steady a moment before, now began to shake along with the hand that held it. The moving wall was a mass of cockroaches, disturbed by the light.

Avakian heard a sound like moaning behind him. He turned around quickly and saw what the light was focused at. He grabbed both her shoulders. "If you feel sick do *not* take off your respirator, no matter what. Breathe through your nose, head back to the ladder, and climb up."

"I'm okay," came the muffled reply.

She had guts, all right. They'd probably gone far enough. He'd been watching the lengths of pipe to see how often there was a joint.

He finished examining one of those joints and swung the light back down the tunnel. Two small, narrowly spaced reflections flashed back at nearly head height. Just as Avakian registered the fact that they were eyes, the rat ran straight at them down the top of the sewer pipe and skittered past at impressive speed. He'd been keeping his hand on the pipe for balance. He pulled it off and reared back with his light, ready to take a swing as the rat passed by within a couple of feet.

There was a shriek from Doctor Rose, and before he could turn around, she'd jumped onto his back.

From a distance it probably looked like one of those great old Warner Brothers cartoons, Sylvester the Cat and Porky Pig. But Avakian had other things on his mind just then. He had one hand on his respirator to keep it from coming off under the assault, but otherwise hadn't moved a muscle. He tamped it all down, forcing himself not to yell. Nothing to add to the general panic. Instead, he said calmly, "Judy, everything's all right now. Very carefully, without a lot of bouncing around, I need you to climb down off my back. Right now."

It was that calm voice that awakened Judy's sense of shame and caused her to realize just how profoundly humiliating it was to be clinging to the poor man's back with both arms wrapped around his neck, probably choking him to death. If he'd thrown her off or something it would have been easier to deal with, but he just stood there as if she wasn't actually clinging to him like a barnacle. There was little dignity to be salvaged from the situation, but with what she could muster she extended her feet until they touched ground again and then released her death grip on his neck. And managed to get out, "I am so very sorry."

"No one likes rats," Avakian replied, as if he were ordering lunch. "It's just that I'm carrying two live bombs strapped to my back."

She took two very fast, very involuntary steps back. That happened to be a little piece of information she'd totally forgotten in the crush of events. And also forgetting all about rats for the moment, she put her hand on the sewer pipe to steady herself. Well, if she hadn't passed out by now, she probably wasn't going to.

Now that she'd given him a little room, Avakian took off the duffel bag and set it atop the sewer pipe. He also set his light on the pipe and aimed the lens down. "If you could shine your light over here too, that would be great," he said, unzipping the bag.

First of all, the timer buttons hadn't been hit and the timers weren't running. He'd picked ones without any prominent front-mounted buttons, and that was looking like a really good call right now. Now that priority had been dealt with, he checked everything else out. He'd taped the wires down so they couldn't be pulled out, and the taped connections were intact. "Everything's okay," he reported.

She hadn't realized she'd been holding her breath until he said that. And she started to breathe again. Now she felt so hot, sweaty, and exhausted that she'd forgotten how disgusting she'd felt just a moment before. "Don't worry. If I see a hundred rats come screaming down this tunnel, I will *not* do that again. I may try to knock myself unconscious with the flashlight so I don't have to see it, but I will not do that."

"Well, try to do none of those things," Avakian replied. He flashed his light back down the tunnel. It looked like it ended just up ahead. "Let's go just a little farther."

The tunnel did stop, which was probably why the rat had run toward them. The pipes branched out in a T connection. One kept going straight ahead, the other two at 90° angles. All vanishing into the earth. A major stroke of luck. "I think the universe has delivered the message that this is the place. Light?"

She'd been looking for more rats, and irrationally wondering if there were anything like alligators in Chinese sewers. But now quickly swung her light back to the bomb.

Avakian checked the clock on the timer by his watch, then switched it from clock mode to alarm. He double-checked that setting, and that the AM and PM were correct. Then said, "May I borrow your finger?" Taking her gloved index finger, he pressed it against the button to activate the alarm, which happened with a surprisingly loud beep.

"Is it on?" she asked.

"You just started it." Said in a very preoccupied way, because he'd just realized that he couldn't reach the top of the water pipe with the bomb in his hand. "You're going to have to hold this for a second."

She just stood there. Too much thinking, Avakian decided. He was offering too many choices, too much information. He grabbed her hand and wrapped it around the pipe bomb. "Don't move."

He pulled himself up on the sewer pipe and grabbed the overhead water pipe with one hand. "Okay, give it to me."

She extended her arm up, and that bomb was shaking all over the place. Nothing she could do about it, because everything she had was going into the death grip to keep it from slipping out of her hand.

Avakian took the bomb, and she was still hanging on. "You can let go now."

She actually had to will herself into doing that, finally releasing the steel casing before he had to pry her fingers off.

The water pipe ran right against the wall of the tunnel. And the crevice where the two came in contact was where Avakian placed the bomb. Perfect. It couldn't be seen, and the tunnel wall would focus the force of the blast into the pipe. No patch or collar was going to be able to handle that. They'd have to break ground to make repairs. And no bomb dog was going to be working down there, so the only thing that could go wrong was the bomb not going off.

Which was why he placed the second device on the other branch of the T connection. So more than one section of replacement would be necessary. And because, as they said in the demo trade: two is one and one is none. The odds were a lot better that at least one of two bombs would go off. If he hadn't screwed up somehow in making them.

"Lead us back to the ladder," he told Doctor Rose.

She proceeded to shatter the world record for moving sideways down a sewer tunnel.

Back aboveground the hot summer night air felt positively arctic by comparison.

"You can take off your respirator," Avakian said. "Unzip the suit and open it up to get some air. Push the hood back, but don't take the suit off, whatever you do."

Judy removed her respirator. The pooled sweat actually poured from the rubber face piece. She took a few cautious whiffs. "Whew. Not as bad as I thought it would be, but still bad. You sure about the suits? We'll stink up the van."

"That's why I covered the seats with those garbage bags," Avakian said. "The van is going away tonight, but if we take the suits on and off, we'll never get the smell off ourselves. Go have a seat and pound some water down. I'll pack up."

No way. She had to redeem herself somehow. "I'll help you," she said, trotting off to retrieve the traffic cones.

Avakian grabbed the ladder and pulled it out of the hole. He was going to have to figure out a way to get her to actually follow some simple instructions without an hour of negotiations. Otherwise, this I'm-a-doctor-and-I don't-have-to-listen-to-anyone shit was going to get them both killed.

They drove south with all the windows down, and after a while the smell either dissipated or they got used to it.

Avakian had planned on maybe nine more manhole trips as they traversed the ring road around the city. Time permitting, of course. And it wouldn't if they ran the rest of them like that one.

As he was driving around looking for the right spot to do the next one, he said, "What about staying by the ladder this time?"

She didn't like that one bit. It was like giving up. Something she acknowledged she had real issues with. But then she also had to acknowledge newly discovered issues with claustrophobia and…what the hell did they call fear of rats? Not to mention fear of sewers. And… well, it was past time to swallow her pride and say it. Because if she didn't, he was probably going to. "You'd be justified in pointing out that I've done everything wrong tonight. All the while you tried to tell me the right way. I was dead wrong, and pigheaded to boot."

That was the breakthrough he'd been hoping for. But he just said, "It was a route we had to take."

That definitely rubbed her the wrong way. "What are you saying?"

He almost told her to calm down, but a man saying that to a woman was like waving a red flag at a bull. "I'm saying that if we were in the Army, if we'd met for the first time and had to do something dangerous, I'd give you orders and you'd carry them out, because I outranked you. Then after a while you'd see that I knew what I was doing, and you'd follow me willingly. Here, I couldn't just give you orders."

She was torn between knowing she wasn't going to like the answer and dying to know the answer. "Why not?"

"You wouldn't be a surgeon if you weren't very smart. And if you didn't have an ego, you wouldn't be a good surgeon. So, if I told you that you needed to follow my lead because your lack of experience with this kind of work made it impossible for you to make the right decisions on your own, that wouldn't go over all that well, would it?"

This was going to be harder than she thought. But once again, Judy, you brought it up. "No, it wouldn't."

"Even though it would be like me trying to make surgical decisions against *your* advice."

Once again, it stuck in her craw, but she had to admit it. She was the surgeon and he'd just been a soldier. Well, she'd learned her lesson about the skill set involved in just being a soldier. "You're right."

"Okay, we've worked it all out and you realize I know what I'm doing. We managed not to get hurt during the learning process, and we're still friends. Right?"

She had to give him credit. Compared to the arrogant and abusive way doctors were educated—especially women doctors—he was like the laid-back uncle who taught you to drive because your father made you cry. Especially considering that she could have blown them both up or had a full-blown panic attack in the middle of a Chinese sewer. "Right."

He stuck his hand across the cab, and for a moment she didn't know why. Then she got it and shook it. "I'll stick by the ladder." That was still very hard to get out. "I thought the military was all about yelling and screaming."

"Only in the beginning, when they're teaching you to function under pressure. Otherwise, it's usually counter-productive. The trick, of course, is to keep yourself from yelling and screaming."

"Do you have an ulcer?"

He laughed. "No."

"High blood pressure?"

"No. At West Point they called me Tas."

"Tas?"

"Short for Tasmanian Devil. Remember I told you about the little guy with the chip on his shoulder? It's been a lifelong project."

She smiled as she thought about the cartoon. She would have liked to have seen that young guy. Now—well, maybe with the Chinese soldiers. But even then, he switched it on and off like she never would have believed possible.

At the next two manholes their new agreement made everything go a lot faster. That and practice really cut the equipment setup time. They did number two in twenty minutes, and three in under fifteen.

After that they'd finished the trip west and were driving north. Avakian suddenly pulled over. Carefully, because it seemed that sometimes the Chinese considered highway breakdown lanes to be a waste of expensive asphalt.

"There's a sewer around here?" Judy said.

"No, a railway bridge," Avakian replied, pointing ahead. "That's the Beijing-Qinhuangdao line below. Bring your flashlight and wear your helmet."

He turned on the revolving lights and set the traffic cones out behind them. Opening the back door, he grabbed one of the toolboxes. He already had the duffel back slung across his back. "Follow me. Use your flashlight." He headed down the hill.

Standing on the edge of the highway embankment, nostrils assaulted by the transition between leaded gasoline exhaust and newly cut sun-scorched brown grass, Judy Rose felt like her legs were made from stone. Every step had to be consciously forced. She'd thought being out in the open would be easier than underground with the rats. But she was wrong. Even though it was pitch dark, it still felt like walking naked across the Rose Bowl field on New Year's Day. But Avakian's light disappeared down the hill and she was not going to be left there alone.

Avakian waited at the bottom of the hill for her to catch up. They reached the tracks and followed them under the bridge. He half expected to find a vagabond or two camping out there, but they were alone. Picking his spot, he opened the toolbox. "Light, please."

Judy was practically hopping up and down from the sheer tension. What made it even worse was the fact that they were standing under a bridge in downtown Beijing about to put a bomb on a railroad track, and he was acting like he was only sorry he'd forgotten his lawn chair, tiki torches, and margarita. Not only that, but she was wearing reflective clothing and holding a flashlight on him while he was doing it. She felt like digging her own manhole just for someplace to hide.

Focused on the job at hand, Avakian was oblivious to her mood. He'd made up a few bombs with an entirely different firing mechanism. The one he was holding had its wires soldered to two thin sheets of copper. Positive and negative circuits, the sheets were held apart by only a few non-conductive pencil erasers. He slipped that in a narrow gap between the steel track and a tie. The weight of a train would squeeze the plates together and complete the circuit. But there was also a clock attached to the system. Until the timer went off there would be no power running through the circuit, so any number of trains could pass over harmlessly until then. He used the roll of duct tape in the toolbox to secure the bomb to the track channel. Then the can of black spray paint to camouflage the shiny metal pipe, and a couple of handfuls of dirt thrown onto the wet paint for good measure.

"We're done," he said. It hadn't taken more than a few minutes. He put his hand to the track. "Train coming. Don't worry, that's not a problem. We've got plenty of time to get out from under the bridge."

The train arrived just as they were preparing to re-climb the hill. The engineer was leaning out of the cab, wondering if there was a problem. Avakian flashed his light and waved. There was a friendly blast from the train whistle.

She couldn't believe it.

The trip up was a little harder with rubber boots on dew-covered grass. Avakian set the toolbox back in the van. "I'll get the cones."

Judy was standing behind the open back door when a police car coming up the highway changed lanes twice to get into the right hand one and headed toward them, slowing down.

Avakian just kept walking down the line, stacking up cones. Bending over to pick one up, his face turned away from the headlights, he gave the police car an everything is okay wave.

The police car blinked its lights and swerved back into the center lane.

Judy was afraid she'd peed in her plastic suit. Avakian just tossed the cones in the back and shut the door.

After he pulled back onto the highway she said, "I nearly had a heart attack when you waved to that police car."

"Well, running away pretty much confirms to everyone that you need to be chased. Which is why you don't sneak around wearing a black ski cap. I've gotten into more places just by walking in the door like I was supposed to be there than I have crawling around in the mud with a pair of wire cutters."

"Tell me, how is blowing up a train not killing people?"

"That little shot?" Avakian scoffed. "Someone might spill some hot tea on their lap, and the engineer might bite his tongue, but otherwise it'll just knock the engine off the tracks and tie up the line for a while. Inconvenience ticks people off worse than mayhem."

It was back underground after that. In northeast Beijing near the Bahe River it was just a plain old manhole. Barely big enough to turn around in. The bottom was flooded with water, so Avakian had to place the bombs half-hanging off the ladder over the water. This wouldn't have been that much of a problem until he happened to shine his light down and saw that boiling up in the water was a writhing ball of snakes. He almost lost it and launched himself up through the manhole like a rocket before tamping his own panic down and realizing they were just water snakes. No kraits or cobras in downtown Beijing. Good thing Judy was higher up the ladder.

After completing four more sewer visits, they were rounding the clubhouse turn. Avakian put another of his railway bombs on the Number 13 subway line that swung around the northern suburbs of Beijing and didn't disappear underground until closer to the city.

The next manhole in the Shuangyushu district in northwest Beijing was comfortably bigger and much dryer. Avakian should have known that everything was going too well. As he was getting ready to set the timer on the second bomb Judy nearly came flying into his lap. She was so close he could feel her shaking and she whispered harshly into his ear, "Someone's walking up to the manhole! I hear them talking."

Avakian was straddling a sewer pipe with a bomb in his hand. "What are they saying?" he whispered back through the respirator. And watched her eyes go wide.

Judy almost yelled at him then. The only thing that held her back was the fact that someone was up on the street walking up to the manhole. She actually had that realization when she thought about yelling, then realized she wasn't panicked any more. How the hell did he know how to hit her with something just off-center enough to distract her from the latest cardiac event-level situation? And then that preternatural calm of his made getting upset seem totally inappropriate. Even when it was totally appropriate, like now. It was maddening because that was exactly how she was in surgery. The more serious the emergency, the calmer you had to be. She was a surgeon, for crying out loud. And just how many times was she going to have to keep telling herself that? Probably as long as she kept crawling around setting bombs in sewers instead of doing surgery in operating theaters. She took another deep breath and vowed not to be out-cooled by him again. "I don't know," she whispered. "Something in Chinese."

"Did they see you?"

"No. There's at least two of them. I heard them talking as they came near, so I moved back from the hole."

Avakian tried to remember if he'd locked the toolbox with the remaining bombs. Yes, he had. And there was still the matter of the one in his hand. He set the timer and placed the bomb behind the pipe. Then checked that everything he might need was at hand in the duffel bag. "Not a sound, no matter what," he whispered, shinnying down the pipe a bit so he could get in front of her. "Okay?"

She just nodded. The learning curve was high, but she was learning.

Avakian made sure he wasn't standing in the shaft of streetlight pouring down through the manhole. There was somebody up there all right. Nothing to do but take the bull by the horns. He shifted the duffel bag, so it hung under his right armpit, opening the zipper about halfway. Concentrating on a good Chinese accent, he called out, "*Qing wen?*" Excuse me, but in the form to gain attention rather than beg pardon.

"*Jingcha!*" the gruff voice of authority called out. Police.

Then Avakian saw the head with the police cap, followed by a lot more Chinese he didn't understand. He turned back to Judy and pointed: stay here.

Unconsciously, Judy crossed her arms across her chest, grabbing her upper arms. The term getting a grip on yourself didn't just come from nowhere. She had to pee so bad she squatted down, holding it in like a little kid.

The voice from above was ordering him to do something. No matter what it was, Avakian started up the ladder, keeping his head down to conceal his round eyes.

Two cops. The senior guy firing cop questions at him while the other watched. Avakian just grunted from the effort required to get up the ladder. As his body poked up from the hole the cop did some noisy sniffing and made a comment that probably had something to do with the smell. Must have been funny, because the other one laughed.

As Avakian swung his leg onto the pavement and stepped off the ladder, head still down, his right hand fell casually into the duffel bag. His fist closed around the plastic handgrip of the rifle, flicking the safety off. The range was point blank.

He straightened up and swung around so the end of the duffel bag was pointed at the cop's torso. The two cracks were barely muffled, and as the recoil made the bag jump the muzzle gasses puffed the end up like a balloon. The cop crumpled to the ground.

He pivoted toward the second one; who was going for his pistol. Two more shots and he was sprawled out on the pavement. And the end of the duffel bag was on fire from the muzzle blast. Avakian slapped at the bag with his gloved hand to put it out. It was all over in three seconds. And like every good ambush the other side never had a chance.

He looked around for witnesses. None. And no traffic on the street at that hour of the morning. The cruiser was parked behind them on the other side of the manhole opening.

Keeping one eye on the cops, Avakian leaned his head down toward the hole and called out, "Judy! Come up quick!"

The ladder clattered as she pounded up it.

The yellow helmet popped out of the hole and looked around.

Judy's first thought at seeing two bodies on the

ground and Pete Avakian bent over one was indescribable relief. Something she then had some very conflicting emotions about.

He said, "Go check and see if the keys are in that police car."

As she went clomping off in her rubber boots, he stripped the cops of their pistol belts and turned out their pockets.

She came back and reported, "The keys are in the ignition." Then, looking down at one of the policemen, "This man is still alive."

Avakian handed her the pistol belts. "Go wait in the van. Driver's seat."

She opened her mouth to say something, then turned and went to the van. Stuffing the pistol belts under the seat, she peeked out through the open back door.

Avakian pulled the ladder up just far enough to disengage the locking hooks, then dropped it back into the hole. It collapsed and disappeared from sight. The plastic sawhorses of the construction barrier got kicked apart and tossed down into the hole too.

She watched as he dragged one body over, and, picking up the legs, dumped it into the manhole like garbage down a chute.

The next was the one who was only wounded. Avakian pulled him by the arms and kept going by straddling the hole, dropping the arms when just the head dangled over. Judy saw him lift his leg and deliver a savage kick onto the back of the neck.

She recoiled and turned back to the windshield. And only heard and felt the back door slam, and the ringing clank as he set the manhole cover back into place.

"Follow me," said the sudden voice in the window that made her jump right out of her seat.

"Sorry," Avakian said. "You okay to follow me?"

"I'm fine." She started the engine by turning the screwdriver stuck into the steering column.

The police car pulled out in front of her, and she stepped on the gas. Avakian kept making turns onto side streets. With no idea where they were she hung on his fender, terrified of losing him and being lost.

He turned into an alley and waved at her not to follow. She parked across the entrance. A minute later, he came trotting out with a green metal can and two cloth bags in his arms.

She slid over to the passenger side as he threw his burden in the back. "What are those?"

"An ammo can full of tear gas grenades and two gas masks I found in the trunk. As Chairman Mao said, let the enemy be your quartermaster."

"You're not keeping the car?"

"I'd love to," he said, shifting and accelerating out. "But when those guys don't show up at the end of their shift—or sooner if they made a radio call when they stopped—every cop in Beijing is going to be looking for that cruiser."

"Then what now?"

"Hop into the back and change into your street clothes. Throw the suit, gloves, and boots into the garbage bag along with your seat plastic."

"Don't we have more sewers to crawl through?"

"No more sewers tonight. No sense pushing it."

She had to admit it, he had a surgeon's attention to detail. Sitting atop her clothes in the plastic shopping bag was a neatly folded towel. Which was a necessity because she was so bathed in sweat the plastic suit stuck to her body. And a big bottle of waterless hand sanitizer. Which was a godsend.

Whenever Avakian made a turn, he gave her fair warning. "Right turn coming up." And then he snuck a look in the rearview mirror, when she was too busy holding on to catch him at it. Nice body.

Freshened up, and with dry new underwear, blouse, and jeans on she swung back into the passenger seat, pulling on her sneakers and feeling a million times better.

"Water?" she said, opening one of the bottles.

"Now we've cleared the area, I think I'm going to pull over and change first."

He parked unnoticed among all the late-night deliveries at Zhongguancun Agricultural Products Market. Doctor Rose had the same idea he did but was not positioned to use the rearview mirror. He changed much faster than she had.

"Did I take too long?" she said.

"We just need to get rid of this van in case they called in the plate. I'll have that water now." He chugged the whole bottle down. "Ah, that's good. That Tyvek is worse than an NBC suit."

"NBC?"

"Nuclear, biological, and chemical. Very unpleasant."

"What kind of vehicle are we looking for?"

"A car, not a van or a truck. Something common and nondescript. Luxury models are too hard to get into without leaving visible damage. We're not going to look anywhere around here, though."

He got back on the West 4th Ring Road and headed south, exiting the highway near the Fengtai Sports Center.

They cruised around a bit, Avakian keeping well away from the nearby railway station.

"What about that one?" said Judy, pointing.

"It's nondescript all right," he said. The car was a beige Xiali Vela, a compact 4-door Toyota licensed copy. He double-parked beside it and killed the headlights. The Vela alarm gave a little chirp.

"Should we look for something else?" she asked.

"Not a problem," said Avakian. He was examining one of the cops' pistols, a Type 92 9mm. Which looked like a close but much cheaper and unlicensed copy of the German Heckler & Koch USP. Except for the communist star on the grips. Double action, 15-round magazine. A little too big to be easily concealed in the belt. Maybe he could rig something with one of the holsters. He checked the chamber. There was a round in it. "Hop behind the wheel and be ready to get us out of here if anything goes wrong."

He exited without slamming his door, carrying the pistol, three tools, and a flashlight. Ducking underneath the car without touching the body, he easily located the Achilles' heel of car alarms—the power wire leading away from the battery. And yanked it out. Not that anyone in the world paid any attention to a car alarm, but now he could work in peace.

While he was down there, he checked for a magnetic key box. Someone who was anal about an alarm usually stashed a spare key. No luck. It would have to be the hard way.

A screwdriver jammed in between the driver's window and the weather-stripping opened a gap. Into which went a thin but stiff metal rod that he'd given a hook on one end and strategically kinked with a pair of pliers. He got it in behind the door lock lever and pushed to open. Now that he was inside, he twisted the metal shaft of the auto body dent puller to jam the pulling screw into the ignition keyhole, nice and tight. The weighted slide hammer that rode on the shaft looked like a barbell. Getting a good grip, he pushed the hammer forward on the shaft and yanked it back against the handle. One bang, two bangs, and on the third the ignition popped out like a wine cork. He inserted his screwdriver into the hole and started the engine. He leaned out the window and called over to the van, "Follow me. We'll be driving for a while."

Avakian turned back on the 4th Ring Road and headed south, then west, joining the steady flow of trucks and vans off to make early morning deliveries. He kept his speed down and didn't change lanes, though that really didn't matter. There would be no losing Judy. That van couldn't have been locked onto his bumper any tighter if he were towing it.

Crossing the breadth of Beijing he finally turned north and exited near Beijing Polytechnic University. But not on campus. Always feared as hotbeds of potential unrest, Chinese universities were ringed with cameras and surveillance. He parked on the street for the same reason, not wanting to take a chance on any store or parking lot surveillance cameras.

Judy tucked the van into the space he'd left behind. He popped the trunk open, and they quickly transferred the four big gas cans and the cases of bottled water from the van. The bags of food and clothes went into the back seat of the car. And the one toolbox with the remaining bombs on the floorboard between the front and back seats.

Avakian had filled an empty water bottle with gasoline, and in the back of the van inserted one of the extra flashbulb initiators into the neck just above the liquid. Screwing the cap on over the wires kept the bulb suspended there. Leaving the bottle upright in the back of the van, he set the timer for thirty minutes.

"I'm not going to tell you that drive was the scariest part of the night," Judy said as he got back on the Ring Road and continued north. "But it wasn't all that great not knowing how far we were going to go."

"If we dumped the van anywhere near where we stole the car it wouldn't be hard to put two and two together," he replied.

Dawn was breaking over Beijing. First a sooty grey through the haze and dust, then the sun announced its presence with a rich, angry red pollution-assisted sky.

"Sailor take warning," said Judy, reading his mind. "Where are we headed?"

"Back indoors," said Avakian.

Chapter Thirteen

COMMISSIONER ZHOU WAS TRYING to make time for a very late lunch at his desk. His morning had been consumed by two missing police officers; their vehicle discovered in an alley. But no trace of the men at all. And that was what had attracted his interest. Officers had been killed by criminals before. They had deserted and joined criminal gangs. But they had never simply disappeared, leaving their vehicle behind but otherwise untouched. A thorough search of the area had uncovered nothing.

He had just begun tucking into his noodles when Inspector Cheng dashed into the office without either a knock or a word of apology.

"We have found him!"

Commissioner Zhou set down his chopsticks, preparing himself for the information to be incorrect, as it had been before. The hunger for recognition had led two of his inspectors to be overly hasty, to their subsequent regret. "Where?"

"Chongwai. An apartment near the New World Plaza."

Directly in the area predicted by the pattern of Avakian's movements. And not more than two kilometers from his office. Commissioner Zhou almost laughed at the effrontery of the man. "And the details?"

"The apartment is rented by a Mark Strauss."

Inspector Cheng had a great deal of trouble pronouncing the name, and the Commissioner did not correct him. "The one employed by the World Bank." Commissioner Zhou always relied on a mastery of detail to impress his superiors and keep his subordinates vigilant. He had examined Avakian's dossier many times.

"Yes, Comrade Commissioner. In the search area you determined."

"You may appeal to my vanity when time is less pressing. I now require the details of how he was found."

"Inspector He's team was checking the address and made inquiries with the manager before proceeding to the apartment. This Mark Strauss is out of the country, but the apartment is occupied. There were complaints from other residents about noise at night. The manager assumed that the occupants were guests of the tenant."

"Did the manager go to the apartment?"

"No. Inspector He felt the manager was afraid of a confrontation with a strange foreigner."

"What is Inspector He's status?"

"Awaiting orders."

"Did he radio the information?" This would have been a grave error, and contrary to his specific orders. Other agencies also monitored the police radio nets.

"No, Comrade Commissioner. He attempted to call your cellphone but only reached the voicemail. He then called me."

Commissioner Zhou angrily snapped open his phone. It must have occurred during his last call. He punched in Inspector He's number. "He? What is your situation? Have you approached the apartment? Good. Do not. That is correct—do not enter that floor. Seal off the building exits and do not alert the residents. Keep the manager under your control. No, no evacuation of residents. It is imperative that we not warn him in any way, so do not display your weapons. By phone, notify the rest of your team and have them join you at once. I will also send additional forces to you, and you will assume tactical command until I arrive. Your orders are to cover all exits and stairs, including the roof and the floor above. Immobilize the elevators but take no action unless he attempts to leave. Yes, capture is preferable, but do not unduly risk the lives of your team. Accept no orders from anyone else without contacting me first. Communicate by radio only within your team. No transmissions through the municipal dispatcher. I will arrive there presently. Yes." He took the phone from his ear and motioned for Inspector Cheng to follow as he went through the door dialing a new number.

"Alert the Special Force?" Inspector Cheng asked.

"No, not yet. I want no marked police vehicles, no uniforms, no brandished weapons to attract gawking crowds and attention from other agencies. I must be sure we have him first. And have him contained."

"Shall I call in all the teams?"

"And have 200 men converge on this apartment building?" Commissioner Zhou said impatiently. "No. I will call in two more teams. The others remain at their work."

INSPECTOR 2ND GRADE He was waiting in the building lobby when they walked in. Unlike most police, who were generally well fed, he was a slight man who almost disappeared inside his civilian clothes. But he had an intensity that gave him natural authority, and his competence had won the loyalty of his investigators.

Commissioner Zhou only nodded in response to the salute. "Report."

"All exits and the roof are under observation,

Comrade Commissioner. The apartment is number 707. The majority of our men are in the stairways and on the floors above and below. The residents on those floors have been ordered to remain in their apartments. The elevator cars remain here." He motioned toward the two open doors.

"Very good, Inspector," said Commissioner Zhou. "Now, is the apartment occupied?"

"We cannot tell, Comrade Commissioner. With your permission we will enter the apartments above and below and attempt to determine this."

Commissioner Zhou thought that over. "You have my permission. But He, the apartment above. One man, not an entire team tramping across the floor to alert him that something is amiss."

"Yes, Comrade Commissioner. With your permission I will accomplish this task myself."

"Proceed." Commissioner Zhou turned to Inspector Cheng. "By phone, order a small technical support team with listening equipment to this location. No uniforms, and an unmarked car. No sirens."

Cheng plucked the phone from his belt. "Yes, Comrade Commissioner."

The sound of sirens in the distance, loud enough to be heard through the glass lobby front. More than one and drawing nearer.

Commissioner Zhou was furious. "What is this?" he demanded.

No response from any of the policemen around him. All of whom began making strenuous efforts to avoid catching his eye.

Several blue police trucks, lights flashing and sirens wailing, pulled up in front of the entrance. And disgorged a company of the Special Force of the Beijing Municipal Public Security Bureau in their dark blue jumpsuits, body armor vests, blue fabric-covered military helmets, and submachineguns.

Commissioner Zhou grimly realized that he had an informer within his ranks. Thinking of what he would do when he discovered their identity helped channel some of his anger. He turned to the nearest sergeant with a radio and snapped, "All teams on high alert. Our presence has been revealed."

"Yes, Comrade Commissioner!" The sergeant made the announcement.

The Special Force were led into the building by their commander, a Commissioner 1st Grade named Kuo. The force was nearly a thousand men, so they had a brigade-level commander. And how unusual that he should arrive personally at the scene of such a minor incident that required only a small part of his unit. Outranked, Commissioner Zhou saluted. "Greetings, Comrade Commissioner. What brings you here?"

"The orders of the Central Military Commission," came the reply from a familiar voice behind a group of the Special Force, who immediately cleared out of the way. Revealed were Major General Liang and Colonel Shen of State Security.

All together, Commissioner Zhou observed. For an idle moment he wondered whether they had spent the day assembled in a limousine in order to be ready when one of their spies called. The Central Military Commission was very high, and by comparison, they were very low. And just who had issued any order would be impossible to determine. Intentionally so.

"Our congratulations on locating the enemy spy so quickly," said the general.

Commissioner Zhou's first instinct was to begin fighting for control of the operation. But seeing Colonel Shen's happy face changed his mind. They would be more than pleased to saddle him with none of the authority and all the responsibility. "Thank you, Comrade General. But your praise is perhaps premature. We know only that some person who is not the registered foreign tenant has been using this apartment."

"Commissioner Zhou is too modest about his investigative skills," Colonel Shen replied for the benefit of the rest. "He is aware that the American Avakian is a known associate of the American who rents this apartment."

Mocking him with his knowledge, Zhou thought. "Since, as the colonel has stated, my skills are primarily investigative, I feel I must now stand aside in favor of comrades whose skills are more suited to the task at hand." A formal bow to the Special Force commander, who was perhaps beginning to grasp the power dynamics at work. And looking somewhat uneasy about it. Commissioner Zhou wondered what promises they had made him.

"You do not wish to remain in operational command?" said Colonel Shen.

"How can I command the Special Force?" Commissioner Zhou asked rhetorically. He turned to the Special Force commander. "Comrade Commissioner, when your men are in position, I will withdraw mine. They are only investigators, after all."

"You have not determined how many people are in the apartment?" said Commissioner Kuo.

"Not yet," Commissioner Zhou replied.

"What difference does that make?" the general growled. "When in doubt, attack."

Commissioner Zhou was reasonably certain that the only thing the general had ever attacked was many courses of dim sum. "My inspector will meet with your commanders on floor 6 and brief them on the situation," he told the Special Force commander.

As the force began filing into the elevators Commissioner Zhou took the radio from his sergeant and ordered Inspector He to meet and brief them on the 6th floor. And then to immediately withdraw all his people down to the lobby.

Inspector He merely acknowledged the order. But then the radio net crackled with pleas from the two other team leaders to remain in place. Commissioner Zhou curtly repeated his order.

And then he stepped outside and called the Public Security Minister directly. The minister was in a meeting, but Zhou related the events of the past hour to the minister's chief administrative aide, stressing that he had turned the scene over to the Special Force.

The aide, a very experienced and politically influential Deputy General Commissioner, had one main question. And it was the one Zhou hoped he would ask. "Who exactly ordered the Special Force to the scene?"

"I do not know," Zhou replied. "I had intended to confirm that they were actually needed before I requested them."

"And they arrived at the same time as General Liang and Colonel Shen?"

"That is correct."

"The minister will be informed," was all the aide said.

Doubtless the Special Force commander would have to explain to the Public Security minister why he had placed himself under the authority of the Army and State Security. Pleased with the way that had turned out, Commissioner Zhou returned to the lobby. All his teams were waiting. He kept Inspector He with him and sent the rest off to continue their original assignments.

"But Comrade Commissioner," said one of the other inspectors, "has the man not been found?"

"I do not recall asking you if the work had been completed to your full satisfaction," Commissioner Zhou replied witheringly. "Follow your orders."

"My apologies, Comrade Commissioner," the inspector sputtered out.

Though angry, Commissioner Zhou knew they would not continue to work diligently without an explanation. "The American may have other associates, perhaps some of them Chinese, and other ties we are not aware of. These we must uncover or satisfy ourselves and the leadership that they do not exist. Do you understand?" he said.

"Yes, Comrade Commissioner," the team leaders replied quickly, the mention of the leadership invoking the fear he had intended.

"Then carry on," he ordered.

They left the lobby very quickly.

Leading Inspector He off to a private corner, Zhou asked, "Is the apartment occupied?"

"The television is on, Comrade Commissioner. There was no opportunity to listen for other voices."

"Well done, Inspector. If it were my decision, you would have remained."

"Thank you, Comrade Commissioner."

"Place your men at ease and await further orders."

Commissioner Zhou felt calmer now that he had protected himself from all sides. No matter what, the credit for locating this place would be his.

He looked back over his shoulder. The parking lot was filling with spectators. Pickpockets would soon begin working the crowd. An argument would turn into a flight. Uniformed police should be called for. It would be unfortunate if someone had not thought of this.

"You have stayed to observe?" Colonel Shen inquired.

"Who knows what I may learn from such experts?" Commissioner Zhou replied.

A moment later, everyone heard the general shout, "Listen at keyholes? Why? For two people, one of them a woman? Ridiculous. Insulting."

Commissioner Zhou could imagine the Special Force commander's frustration. Realizing that tales of his personal timidity would be circulating the corridors of power in short order, he barked orders into his radio.

Both Chinese face and foreign reluctance to be associated with a unit that might be breaking the heads of dissidents as well as rescuing hostages from terrorists meant that the Special Force did not have direct access to state-of-the-art equipment and tactics. But according to Chinese manufacturing practice they had good but lower-cost copies. They looked like a SWAT team, right down to the blue fatigues and the embroidered white public security crests on their left shoulders. If their kneepads and drop holsters were rougher, and their vests did not look as if they would stop a bullet of any substance, then at least they were Chinese.

And they did not use explosives or shotguns to breach the apartment door. They used their feet.

Receiving the signal to go, the breach man reared back and delivered a kung fu kick to the door. Which cracked but did not open. A second kick, and more face lost. At the third, slightly more frantic one, the lock came loose, and the door flew open. Though not much surprise remained.

A stun grenade was tossed in. And when it blew, the entry team poured into the apartment, though the Chinese stun grenade threw off more smoke than a Western model and consequently made it harder to see. The point man took three steps and ran into an ankle-high wire that blended perfectly into the white wall, falling flat on his face.

As he hit the floor the ones behind him watched with alarm as something dropped from the ceiling fan and bounced in midair. They all dove to the floor.

After an uneventful few seconds, they lifted their heads up and observed a shiny piece of pipe, capped at both ends, dangling from an electrical wire in the air above them.

The team leader shouted, "Bomb!" They grabbed the feet of the man who had tripped and dragged him back into the hall, diving for the floor again once they reached it.

When everyone in the hall saw that happening, they went down in succession, like dominos.

Word that there was a bomb passed over the radio net and was heard in the lobby. With impressive decisiveness, and a speed that belied his bulk, General Liang dashed out the front door long before anyone else could make up their minds what to do.

Commissioner Zhou had taken the time to read up on the American Special Forces and did not doubt that Avakian was capable of constructing explosives from commonly available ingredients. But he did doubt that Avakian could have constructed enough to destroy an entire apartment building, let alone a single floor. "The general seems to have left," he said to Colonel Shen. "If you require a lift back to your office later, I am at your service."

Having lost quite enough face, Colonel Shen did not add to it by replying.

The Special Force commander was shouting on the radio, trying to determine what was going on.

"I hope someone is watching the apartment balcony during this confusion," Commissioner Zhou mentioned.

Colonel Shen quickly moved over to the Special Force commander and said something to him. The commander nodded. And Commissioner Zhou chuckled under his breath.

The apparent bomb dangling from the ceiling placed the commander in something of a tactical quandary. If he sent his bomb disposal technicians into the apartment without clearing the other rooms, they might be shot by the American. And if he sent his men in to clear the rooms without the bomb techs checking first, they might hit another bomb that might explode instantly.

Where other units might have sent in a dog, the Chinese resolved the question in classic military style. By calling for patriotic volunteers. Who would of course lose face if they did not volunteer patriotically.

First an ultimatum was delivered to the apartment. By megaphone, of course, though the entire apartment could not have been more than 50 feet long. "*Mr. A-vi-kan, exit the apartment with your hands up and you will not be harmed.*"

There was no response from within the apartment.

The two 3-man teams tiptoed through the living room, giving the dangling pipe a wide berth. Both the bedroom and bathroom doors were closed. But rather than kicking them in the point men instead twisted the knobs and opened the doors a crack, shining a flashlight to check for trip wires. Only then were the doors pushed open and the flashlights played across the floor to detect other wires.

Rather than taking a chance on snapping on light switches the teams used the flashlights mounted on their JS submachineguns. They entered the room very gingerly, covering the corners and under the bed. But there was the closet. And opening that a crack wouldn't work if someone was hiding in there. So, one officer took hold of the knob, looked down at the floor so the top of his helmet and not his face would take the brunt of any blast or gunshot, and yanked it open.

The dancing flashlight beams revealed an empty closet.

The bathroom was equally empty.

When the word made it down to the lobby, Colonel Shen said, "Another regrettable investigative failure."

"Perhaps," Commissioner Zhou replied. "Whomever called out the Special Force will have much to answer for. Yet someone apparently planted a bomb in this apartment, and I doubt it was an economist for the World Bank. Perhaps we may yet recover valuable evidence." He turned once again to Inspector Cheng. "Cancel the listening team and summon a scientific team."

Upstairs the entry team had pulled back and turned the apartment over to a bomb disposal technician, who was waiting in the hallway in his padded Kevlar blast suit.

The tech waddled inside and examined the hanging pipe. The end of the wire wrapped around the ceiling fan dangled free. He thought about cutting it and bringing the bomb down to the street in the steel bomb bucket. But inside this outwardly crude device there might be a mercury switch on a timer, and any movement after it had hung stationary would set it off.

Instead, he reached in a suit pocket and peeled the adhesive off a small disruptor charge, about the size of a spool of sewing thread. Holding the pipe motionless with one hand, he carefully attached the charge and spliced the two contacts to the spool of wire that hung from his belt, paying it out as he backed toward the door.

The tenants had finally been removed from their apartments, and firemen were standing by. The bomb tech ran his wire all the way down the stairwell. Hooking it up to a blasting machine, he paused to radio, "Stand by for explosion." And pressed the firing button.

A small pop, not much louder than a firecracker, that could not even be heard a floor away.

The bomb tech waited fifteen minutes and took the elevator back up to the 7th floor. And a few minutes later, took it down to the lobby. He presented his commander with the pipe, split down the middle from the disruptor charge. Which would have scattered any bomb mechanism before it could ignite a charge. But this particular pipe had nothing inside but a rolled piece of paper.

Colonel Shen reached for it.

"Wait," said Commissioner Zhou. He handed Shen a pair of latex gloves.

Shen yanked them on and unrolled the paper, which was quite scorched from the disruptor charge. Everyone leaned over to see what it was. It was a sheet of plain white paper. And written in large capital letters, in English, was the word BOOM. With an exclamation mark.

Chapter Fourteen

JUDY ROSE HAD CRAWLED underneath a side table she was particularly taken with, examining its provenance. "You really found this place on Craigslist?"

"Craigslist Beijing," said Avakian. "I knew about a couple of apartments rented by American companies that never got used. Except to entertain the occasional call girl, that is."

"Great," came the droll voice from under the table.

"But I figured the Chinese would know about them, too. Then I remembered someone at a party saying they'd found their apartment on Craigslist. And after I gave it some thought, I kind of came to the conclusion that any furnished luxury apartment advertised in English wouldn't be getting a lot of renter interest right about now, so why not let ourselves in?"

"So, in a nutshell, we're squatters."

"On the bright side, it's probably the least serious crime we've committed in a while."

"Always looking on the bright side, aren't you?"

"It keeps my morale up."

"So, following your theory to its logical conclusion, it *is* the last thing anyone would expect anyone to do."

"Why, thank you. With the added benefit that

furnished luxury apartments on the market always have the utilities turned on. People like playing with the faucets and appliances."

"Very clever. But what if the leasing agent does happen to show up with someone who wants to view the apartment?"

"We'll just have to cross that bridge if we come to it." Avakian actually had his pry bar wedged into the door-frame, to give them a little warning if that occurred.

The southwest exposure from the big sliding glass window provided a dramatic though somewhat hazy view of downtown Beijing. The living room walls were a very subtle gold, with a marble gas fireplace mantle, and the furniture, as shown by the doctor's interest, was top of the line. And even arranged according to the principles of fengshui.

"There was something I wanted to ask," she said, still under the furniture. "Were you some kind of juvenile delinquent?"

"What do you mean?"

"You seem to have some definite skills in the areas of lock picking and car theft."

"Oh, that. When I was in high school, we only stole street signs with interesting names. But lock picking and car theft are actually on the curriculum at the U.S. Army Special Warfare School."

"You're kidding."

"Nobody sleeps in that class. Great practical application portion, too. Your tax dollars at work."

"They don't teach good stuff like that in med school."

"I guess they don't expect you to personally seize your patients' cars for nonpayment of bills."

"Funny."

She didn't seem to be any worse for wear after the night's activities. As a matter of fact, she still seemed tweaked on the adrenaline. He didn't think she'd be crawling around checking to see who made the furniture otherwise. "I don't want to put a crimp in your antiquing, but we're out of here this afternoon. And if you don't take a shower before the water goes off, and hopefully the water *will* go off, you're going to be bathing from a pail."

Her head emerged from under the table. "You had me at pail."

"I boosted my probably no-longer buddy Mark's robes, so we can also put on a wash."

"We are still carrying around a faint suggestion of l'air de sewer, aren't we? Or is the smell just stuck in my sense memory?"

"If it is, it's also in mine. Toss your clothes out the bathroom door and I'll load up the washer."

"You bought laundry detergent, too?"

"Sure."

"Unbelievable."

"You say that because you've never lived for six months in a small, rented space in a foreign country with 11 other guys who worked out every day."

"And I never imagined there were those gaps in my life experience until I met you."

"Just be glad we're not doing laundry in the afore-mentioned pail."

"I will be giving thanks for that later."

"Though sticking your clothes in a garbage bag, adding water and soap, throwing it in the back of a Jeep, and driving over rutted 3rd World roads for an hour or two also works pretty well."

"What do you dry them with, a flame thrower?"

"You know, nobody really uses those anymore," Avakian said, with a definite note of regret in his voice. "They kind of went out of fashion. Maybe it was carrying thirty pounds of pressurized napalm around on your back."

"More's the pity. There's nothing like that dryer-fresh napalm smell."

"Yeah, it smells like victory."

"That's your commercial jingle, right there."

While she was in the bathroom Avakian went through the bags and got everything ready for their next evolution. And he really didn't know what he was more worried about. That she wouldn't go along—or that she would.

So far so good. Avakian didn't believe in luck. Luck was as much a factor in events as examining the entrails of a goat was in predicting the future. Luck was what happened when your preparation was meticulous and your execution aggressive but flexible.

"I'm done," came the call from the hallway.

He enjoyed his shower. Even if that filmy feel of sewer on his skin was more psychological than vestigial, it was still good to get it off. While he scrubbed himself the rifle lay propped against the toilet, and the pistol on the tank. But he didn't linger under the water. Too much imagination about what might happen during those moments of vulnerability.

Toweling off, he wiped the steam from the mirror and examined himself. The new beard was coming in, though right now he looked like a French actor. It was the first time he'd seen his hairline in years. And damn it had gotten high.

As he opened the door and turned off the fan, he heard Judy say, "Pete, can you come in here?"

"Where are you?" he called back.

"First bedroom."

He took a step toward it, then held up and leaned the rifle against the wall. No sense walking around like G.I. Joe. He stuck the pistol in the front pocket of the robe.

Avakian really didn't stroll anywhere. It was too ingrained. Move with a purpose, as they always used to bellow at West Point. And as he breezed through the bedroom doorway the curtains were closed and only the bedside lamp was on, so it took a second for his eyes to adjust. What he saw brought him to an abrupt stop. Because Doctor Rose was standing there naked.

He was suddenly terrified of saying anything that might kill the moment.

So, it was left to her to say, "Well?"

He managed to squeeze out, "You're a very beautiful woman." Then, after an equally long pause, "Sorry, but I'm drawing a blank on anything else right now."

"Then take off your robe and come over here and kiss me."

"Okay." If he'd known this would happen when you turned a respectable surgeon in the throes of a midlife crisis into an urban guerrilla, he might have considered the career change earlier.

She'd been hoping he wasn't too hairy, and he wasn't. And it really was true what they said about short men with big hands.

The now-forgotten pistol thumped on the floor when he dropped the robe, making him cringe. He did of course waste no time in going over and kissing her.

And if he'd been capable of more abstract thought at that moment, he might have realized that sex was making him act the same way she had the previous night. While she was the one moving with confident calm.

He wrapped his arms around her shoulders, holding her as close as he could because she felt spectacular. While this was happening, she grabbed both his buttocks and he nearly swallowed her tongue.

He broke their kiss, smiled, and said, "Be gentle with me."

"Where's the fun in that?" she replied.

Chapter Fifteen

COMMISSIONER ZHOU WAS NOT sure which he found more amusing: the sign in Colonel Shen's hands or the look on Colonel Shen's face.

"What does this say?" Shen demanded, shaking the paper.

Commissioner Zhou had to pause in order to keep his composure. "It is the English word for the sound made by an explosion." He noticed Shen's arms tense and said, "Please refrain from damaging this evidence."

Colonel Shen dropped the paper on the floor. Zhou motioned for one of his sergeants to retrieve and bag it.

"Perhaps you will salvage something from this investigative failure," said Colonel Shen.

Commissioner Zhou was not only amused, he also decided to show it. "Do you truly believe you will persuade people you did not create this carnival if only you accuse me enough times?"

What made the moment so fulfilling was that everyone in the lobby had heard it.

Commissioner Zhou said to the Special Force Commander, "Comrade Commissioner, if your men are finished with their work, I will examine the apartment for additional evidence."

Commissioner Kuo nodded and moved in closer to say, "I am confident you will be able to salvage something."

Commissioner Zhou replied, "I assure you that I strongly share your hope, Comrade Commissioner." Which was enough to acknowledge that the Special Force Commander was indeed in trouble that would require his help, while intentionally ambiguous enough that the Special Force Commander would not believe he had declared himself an enemy and therefore feel compelled to attack him through the Public Security bureaucracy.

Before he went upstairs Commissioner Zhou called the Public Security Minister's aide once again and related what had just happened. Once your version of events reached the very top it mattered little what other stories were making their way through the lower levels.

When the elevator did deliver him to the 7th floor the hallway was still filled with a light fog of smoke. Some of the Special Force were packing their equipment while others lined up to take the elevator down. And grumbling that with rush hour beginning they would never reach their headquarters in time for dinner.

The bomb technicians were just leaving the apartment.

"Is it clear?" Commissioner Zhou demanded.

He was in civilian clothes, and they had no idea who he was. But ordinary Chinese, let alone police, had an unerring instinct about anyone who had the face to speak with authority.

The senior man was a grizzled inspector, obviously with many years of service. He said respectfully, "Yes, it is."

Commissioner Zhou found it difficult to believe they had not discovered any explosive material. "Do not leave with the others. You may be needed."

He could see their confusion and uncertainty. "Notify your commander. He will endorse these orders." He knew as soon as they left his sight, they would ask one of his men who he was.

And with that he stepped into the apartment. "Allow no one inside who is not wearing gloves," he said to Inspector He. Chinese policemen were notoriously sloppy about such things, used to suspects who confessed. Or were beaten until they confessed.

He stood in the center of the living room in order to gain an impression. Such a mass of Western *things* crammed into the space, so alien to the Chinese eye. The difficulty was that this was not the apartment of his quarry, only his temporary lair. So, he must first look for what belonged there, then what might have been taken. And what might have been left.

While he was surveying the room one of his policemen stepped past him and picked up a magazine from the coffee table. Commissioner Zhou stared at him until the man finally looked over and met his eye. And turned pale, hurriedly dropping the magazine and beating a retreat. Harsh whispers from behind as the man was chastised.

Commissioner Zhou sighed and shook his head.

Nothing in the living room struck his interest, so he motioned for his men to begin their examination. But the kitchen unit just off the living room was another matter. A kitchen table always had a cloth or a place set, or a vase or a centerpiece. Condiment dishes. Anything. But this one was totally bare, and so stood out.

He never liked to look down at what he was examining. Always across, because something that might otherwise blend into the surface became apparent. And even more so at eye level. As he bent down, he picked up an unusual smell. Cleanser and something else he could not place. And a burned spot on the tabletop. Very small, much too small for a hot pan or dish to have made.

He could not banish the smell from his mind. "Inspector He."

He hurried in from the living room. "Yes, Comrade Commissioner?"

"Are you able to identify this smell? Not the cleanser, the other."

Inspector He sniffed cautiously. "Comrade Commissioner, my daughter has an electric iron for burning designs into wood. This is what it smells like when she uses it."

"Yes! Exactly. Excellent, He." Now Commissioner Zhou was down at floor level. And there was something the same color as the surface but resting upon it. He picked up a small piece of white plastic wire insulation and showed it to Inspector He. "A soldering iron, perhaps? Left on the table while hot?"

"Yes, Comrade Commissioner."

"If the laboratory teams ever make their way through the traffic, I want swabs taken of the table, floor, and counters to identify any chemical traces. Until then no one is to be allowed near this table."

Colonel Shen walked into the kitchen area.

"No one," Commissioner Zhou repeated, with emphasis.

An anxious glance over at Colonel Shen, then, "As you order, Comrade Commissioner."

Commissioner Zhou opened all the cupboards and then stood back and surveyed them as a whole like portraits in a museum. Something was wrong here, also. "He, tell me what you see."

"A bowl unlike the others, Comrade Commissioner. The rest are not glass. Or so large. And it is forced into the space it occupies. It does not belong there."

"Very good."

Colonel Shen opened the refrigerator on the other side of the kitchen.

Which made Commissioner Zhou furious. But Shen would welcome an argument and attempt to portray him as an obstructionist. So, he swallowed his anger. At least Shen was still wearing the latex gloves.

Colonel Shen leaned into the open refrigerator. It was on, but there was very little inside. Some jars of pickles and mustard. A few bottles of beer. And a glass bowl filled with what looked like paper. He poked it with his finger. Like most Chinese he was totally unfamiliar with the concept of a coffee filter. He smelled his gloved finger. An astringent chemical odor.

He picked up one of the filters, holding it before the light. Only an American would keep paper in a refrigerator. Inexplicable. With a flick of the wrist, he tossed it back into the bowl.

Commissioner Zhou was enveloped by the sound and felt himself leave his feet. A hard blow knocked the breath from his body. He opened his eyes and saw nothing but smoke. It was only when he tried to turn that he realized he was on the floor. The living room floor. Nothing had struck him. He had been thrown from the kitchen to the living room.

Feet crashed down directly in front of his face, nearly trampling him. It was firemen carrying large extinguishers. He tried to roll over onto his stomach in order to regain his feet, but in doing so collided with another body and fell again. It was Inspector He, who had been attempting to do the very same thing.

They each grabbed onto each other and stood up, coughing from the smoke. A loud sound of shattering glass. The firefighters were breaking the windows to let the smoke out. Commissioner Zhou wondered why they did not simply open them.

The smoke began to drift away. Commissioner Zhou tried to speak, but there was no moisture in his mouth. One of the investigators took his arm and led him over to what had been a glass door to the balcony. The broken shards crunched under his feet.

Even though he had done all this, it took the first

breath of fresh air to make him realize what had happened. And spur him into action.

"Out!" he shouted, nearly frightening the investigator at his arm half to death. "Everyone! Out of the apartment instantly!"

They all rushed for the door. Commissioner Zhou noted that all were able to walk, some with assistance. Except the firemen carrying a limp Colonel Shen. He walked around the apartment to satisfy himself that no one was injured and left behind. And that there was no fire. It was clear that the explosion had taken place in the refrigerator. It was blackened, and the sides and top completely separated. Not a large explosion. Designed to kill whoever opened the refrigerator? What could be the reasoning behind that?

The hall outside was utter confusion. Everyone rushing about and either babbling to each other or shouting into radios. Commissioner Zhou shouted again. "Silence!" The noise level dropped but did not cease. "Silence, everyone!" That had an effect. "Get control of yourselves! Cease using your radios and do not call anyone else up here. Send any wounded down in the elevator. If you are unhurt, stand by for orders and be quiet. Where are the bomb technicians?"

They were slow to appear, knowing what was in store. "Here, Comrade Commissioner."

Commissioner Zhou left them standing before him and turned to the firemen. "Is there any further danger of fire?"

"No, Comrade Commissioner. As long as there are no more explosions, of course."

"Stand by in case you are needed." Then he turned back to the bomb technicians. "Return to the apartment and find the other booby traps you missed."

Chapter Sixteen

"WHAT ARE YOU SMILING ABOUT?" Judy asked, smiling herself as she traced the line of his pectoral muscles with her finger.

She was laying beside him in the crook of his arm, and Avakian pulled her a little closer. "I was just thinking it would have been doubly awkward if someone showed up to look at the apartment."

She started giggling. "I know you had a plan for that, and I do *not* want to know what it was."

"More's the pity," said Avakian. "It was one of my best schemes. Though it was dependent on whether the agent and prospective tenants were good looking women."

She poked him under the ribcage.

"I hate to be a killjoy," he said. "But we really should get some sleep."

"But I'm not tired," she purred into his neck.

"Maybe not, but you are definitely naughty. Myself, I think I might be permanently disabled."

"As your doctor, I assure you you're in excellent condition."

"That's reassuring to hear. Nevertheless, after we roll this afternoon there won't be much sleep for the next couple of days. Or more, if things don't go according to plan."

"So, we're going to slip out of the city in the midst of all the confusion?"

"Something like that. But we need to do one more thing before we skip town."

"What's that?"

"Rob a bank."

"*What*?"

"When I was out buying supplies, I used my credit card whenever I could, but there's still a lot of places in modern China that don't take plastic. And that used up all my cash. I don't expect American cards to be honored in light of the current hostilities, and we're going to need traveling money."

"So, we're robbing a *bank*?"

"That's how urban guerrillas finance their operations."

"You're really getting off on this, aren't you?"

Avakian nuzzled her ear. "You'd better believe it."

She giggled again. "I mean being an urban guerrilla."

"Well, I spent my working life studying these guys. And the essential calculus is that it's easier to be one than it is to try and catch one. Until you get killed in a hail of gunfire, that is."

"Why do you persist in bringing that up all the time?"

"Just trying to bring a note of reality to the proceedings. Otherwise, it's easy to get wrapped up in the game."

"And we're really going to rob a bank?"

"Unless you've a got a couple grand in loose yuan secreted away on your person." He lifted the sheet to check. "Or happen to have a better idea where to lay our hands on some cash. Because we're broke."

She gave the matter some thought and drew a blank. "Who said that's where the money is?"

"Willie Sutton, famous bank robber."

"That's right. And now you're going to tell me he said that from prison."

"I hate it when you step on my lines."

"Sorry. But we're actually robbing a bank."

"I'm not going to rob some poor guy's candy store. We've got to stick it to The Man."

"Very urban guerrilla of you."

"Thanks for noticing. But you don't have to rob the bank. You can stay with the getaway car."

That brought her up on one elbow. "Pete, we are *not* going through that again. I'm not sitting outside some bank waiting for the sound of gunfire. I went down manholes. I held the flashlight on the railroad tracks. I'm going in the bank."

"Okay."

"Okay?" She'd been ready for a fight.

"I said okay."

Now she was feeling a little defensive about being ready for a fight. "I just didn't want you getting all protective on me now that we've become intimate."

"Become intimate," Avakian said, rolling it around on his tongue. "I like that. Fine choice of words. No, I couldn't protect you even if I rolled you around the country inside a safe. If anything, it's going to get even more dangerous."

"I was going to say 'fine' to that, but somehow it sounds kind of stupid. Like danger is my middle name or something."

"When we're done with this it will be. Do you know how to ride a motorcycle?"

"That was kind of off the wall, wasn't it?"

"Only because I failed to segue smoothly between thoughts. I repeat: do you know how to ride a motorcycle?"

"Of course."

"And do you ride well?"

"I like to think so."

"Good, because it's an essential element of my plan."

"How so?" Judy asked.

"Because we're going to steal a motorcycle."

"I figured that part out already. I was inquiring about the plan."

"Oh. Well, you've seen rush hour traffic around here. A motorcycle's the only way to get through it. Otherwise, we'd move faster on skateboards."

"But why did you ask me if I know how to drive one? I'm going in the bank with you. Anyone can sit on the back of a motorcycle."

"That's good to hear. I asked because I don't know how to drive a motorcycle."

She came up on her elbow again. "You don't know how to drive a motorcycle?"

"I'm pretty sure I just said that."

"You steal cars. You pick locks. You shoot guns. But you can't drive a motorcycle?"

"Now you're making me feel inadequate. Motorcycles always scared me to death."

"*What*? You were a paratrooper."

"What does that have to do with it?"

"Scuba diver?"

"Correct."

"Mountain climber?"

"Did the German Army Alpine Guide course. Great school."

"And you're afraid of motorcycles?"

"They're not safe," Avakian said flatly. "Need I remind you of the kid on the scooter, the first day we met? Sooner or later, your fault or not, something bad will happen to you on a motorcycle. I'd have thought an orthopedist would know this."

"Actually, motorcyclists make up a large chunk of my gross income. But I still know how to ride one."

"Then that makes one of us."

"But you'd have to ride on the back while I drive."

"It's not a phobia," Avakian explained. "If we had more time, I'm sure I could learn how to work one of the stupid things. As far as riding on the back, I don't have to like it. I just have to do it."

She rubbed her hands together gleefully. "So, I get to ride a motorcycle through traffic, no speed limit."

"Don't make me second-guess my decision."

"You know how to steal a motorcycle, don't you?"

"That I know."

"Do I get to carry a gun while we're robbing the bank?"

Avakian eyed her skeptically. "Have you ever fired a handgun?"

"No."

"Then the answer to that is also no."

"You could teach me."

"And ordinarily I'd be happy to," he said, stroking her. "Maybe we can make an even trade."

She answered that by groping him. "It's a deal."

"Easy, now. I said ordinarily. But in order to learn you would actually have to fire a pistol. And I don't think the neighbors here would appreciate that."

"All right, if you're going to be that way about it. What do we do after we rob the bank and I elude the police during the high-speed chase?"

"Let's just leave out the high-speed chase part, shall we? We'll stage the car off the beaten track while we do the heist. Then come back to it. But we'll make the journey in another vehicle I've had my eye on."

"Why do I think it's going to be just a bit more complicated than that?"

"Probably the triumph of experience over hope. Let's get some sleep and then I'll walk you through the basic principles of bank robbery."

"I've got tell you, Pete, this is the weirdest pillow talk I've ever had."

Chapter Seventeen

THE BOMB DISPOSAL technicians were leaving the apartment for the second time. Commissioner Zhou was waiting for them at the door.

The bomb inspector in his coveralls and flak jacket was sweating profusely, not surprising considering the nature of his job and that the air conditioning was off and the windows smashed. "Comrade Commissioner, there are no explosive devices in the apartment."

"So you said before," Commissioner Zhou replied.

The inspector took a step back but did not retreat. "Comrade Commissioner, we have examined the refrigerator carefully. There was no bomb-triggering mechanism. Peroxide-based improvised explosive is very unstable, especially at higher temperatures. So, it is commonly kept in a cool place. It is possible that this material was left in the refrigerator and the State Security officer somehow disturbed it."

Commissioner Zhou admired the inspector's courage in attempting to save his face, but let his own face say that he did not fully believe the story. "And this explosive is that unstable?"

"Yes, Comrade Commissioner. It could easily detonate if not handled carefully."

"How much of it would cause this damage?"

"Only a few grams, Comrade Commissioner."

"Be serious."

"It is very powerful. Any more would have completely destroyed the apartment."

"So, you theorize that this was residue left from a much larger batch of explosive?"

"Yes, Comrade Commissioner."

"Then which of you checked the refrigerator the last time?"

The inspector hesitated. "Comrade Commissioner, the man is a 1st Grade Officer who has just graduated from bomb school. He saw the bowl in the refrigerator, with paper in it, and did not realize what he was seeing. The explosive is not common in our country and is not taught in our basic school. The paper is used to filter the explosive from a liquid solution."

"This is how you know it was only a few grams?" The story always emerged in small pieces, and always under pressure.

"Yes, Comrade Commissioner."

"And the type of explosive?"

"Yes, Comrade Commissioner. The chemical analysis will prove it."

"Can you determine how much was made?"

"It depends upon the number of batches, Comrade Commissioner. Based on the size of the bowl, less than 150 grams in one batch. It is much safer to make many small batches."

"It is easy to make?"

"Easy but hazardous, Comrade Commissioner. But it is possible that only a small amount was made in order to ignite another type of explosive, due to its sensitivity."

Commissioner Zhou opened his notebook and removed the list of purchases traced to Avakian. "Tell me what you see here."

The inspector examined the list carefully. "Comrade

Commissioner, the hair bleach would be the source of the peroxide. The other ingredients are not here."

"What ingredients?"

"Either acetone and sulfuric acid, or citric acid and hexamine."

"Easy to obtain, then."

"Very easy, Comrade Commissioner. This large amount of swimming pool cleaner indicates another explosive. But the other ingredients are also not listed."

"And they are?"

"Nitromethane fuel used to power model cars. Or common naphtha."

"So, this would bear out your theory of two different explosives."

The inspector was experiencing both relief and newfound confidence. "Yes, Comrade Commissioner. Using the peroxide explosive would make the swimming pool bleach easier to detonate, and also increase its velocity. The pipe listed here would contain the explosive material."

"Why would the suspect purchase a large amount of flashlights?"

"To construct firing mechanisms, Comrade Commissioner."

"What kind?"

"Any kind. Timer, impact, pressure, trip wire, anti-disturbance."

The inspector fell silent as Commissioner Zhou paused to think. "You have redeemed yourself, Inspector. Look again at the list and tell me of any additional impressions."

"The amount of explosive could make one large bomb or many smaller ones, Comrade Commissioner. But based on the amount and diameter of this pipe, I would say many smaller ones. Unless his intent was to deceive us with the quantities."

"Why would anyone carry so much pipe about when they did not have to?"

This served to remind the inspector that his field was explosives, not investigation. "You are right, of course, Comrade Commissioner."

"How many bombs?"

"It would depend on how he cuts the pipe, Comrade Commissioner. If the same general size as the dummy device he left here, then possibly between 25 and 40."

This gave Commissioner Zhou a sinking feeling. But the inspector had been invaluable despite his mistakes. Because all this information was new to him. The explosives section of the Ministry Department of Science and Technology had not yet delivered their report on the list. Finding the explosive in the refrigerator intact would have been just as valuable. And what might they have been able to recover from the carpet before the explosion? That fool Shen. Which reminded him. "What is Colonel Shen's condition?" he asked Inspector Cheng, who waited at his side like a watchdog.

"Very poor. He did not regain consciousness, and it will take time for the ambulance to reach the hospital at this time of day."

A reminder that Chinese drivers did not yield for ambulances. What an interesting twist of fate, to have Shen incapacitated and General Liang disgraced by cowardice. He would certainly not be heartbroken if Shen died, but a description of the contents of that refrigerator would have been useful. No matter. "Inspector He, take your men inside again. The crime scene is most likely ruined but do your best."

"Yes, Comrade Commissioner."

This left Commissioner Zhou with something else to ponder. Avakian obviously believed that the police would find this place. Quite possibly he left the explosive in the refrigerator because he had no easy way to dispose of it.

But he could have booby-trapped the apartment to kill any number of investigators. Instead, he left a joke.

He had known from their first meeting that the American was totally unpredictable. Which had unsettled everyone during the conference security negotiations, because Chinese were very predictable. Doubly unsettling was that Avakian knew just how predictable they were.

Now he would have to begin again to locate Avakian's new hiding place. And if those bombs began to explode the pressure would shift from Avakian to himself. Planting many bombs, he would have to be seen by someone. He would have to. Unfortunately, the Chinese people were eager witnesses but just as eager not to come forward and expose themselves to the authorities. That left a new sinking feeling. Perhaps Avakian had been seen by the two missing police officers. Their vehicle could not have been moved far...

No, he told himself. Not the search for a new hiding place. He had been thinking predictably, and therefore incorrectly. So many bombs meant Avakian had decided to fight them on behalf of his country. He should have foreseen this. Such a man, a career soldier. Commissioner Zhou was filled with admiration, imaging himself attempting to do the same in Washington, unable to speak English.

Two possibilities remained. Had Avakian decided to fight them in Beijing until he was killed, or would he fight and then attempt to flee? And did he still have the woman doctor with him?

Now there would have to be television, radio, and newspaper appeals so he would not be able to purchase more explosive materials. This would also saddle them with thousands of worthless clues. Checkpoints throughout the city, to curtail his movements. And then slowly and surely run him to ground. Not the elegant hunt he had envisioned, but the Center would demand results. And authorize any resources he demanded. If he were in command of the equivalent of a brigade of police, then they would have to make him a commissioner 1st grade. With a favorable result, a deputy-general commissioner's stars would be his. Or he reminded himself, they would remove him and appoint a commissioner 1st grade in his place.

The security checkpoints on all the roads leaving the city would have to be strengthened. And the trafficable areas between them patrolled.

Commissioner Zhou could hardly believe it. One man challenging them all to combat.

"Comrade Commissioner?"

Commissioner Zhou had been leaning against the wall with his eyes closed. "What?"

Inspector Cheng said, "The Central Dispatcher is reporting explosions all over the city."

That woke Commissioner Zhou up. So quickly. "Where? How many?"

"The radio traffic is incredible, and there is much confusion. Trains have run over bombs. Other explosions have been underground. At first it was thought that these were gas leaks, but there are too many in too many different places."

He could understand the rail lines. But underground? To what purpose? Bombs randomly placed on the streets would create more havoc. "Inspector, send someone to their vehicle for a city map. Assign two men to monitor the radio and record the locations of the explosions."

The firemen, who were waiting in case they were needed again, were crowded around their own radio. "What news?" Commissioner Zhou asked.

"Explosions in manholes, Comrade Commissioner," one of them said.

"Gas lines on fire?" said Commissioner Zhou.

"Some," said the fireman. "But more streets flooded."

"Flooded?"

"Water and sewer lines broken, Comrade Commissioner."

"Nothing makes people angrier than water shut off to make repairs," another added.

"Nothing," they all confirmed.

The realization arrived on the tail of the firemen's last words. Commissioner Zhou dashed into the apartment. He went straight for the bathroom and twisted both taps open. Water gushed out. Then sputtered, hissing air. Then stopped completely. The magnitude of it staggered him. Whole sections of the city without water. The people rushing out of their homes to buy any available liquids. And with the day ending, the necessary officials and workers on their way home. Less than three hours before darkness. The panic if this lasted more than a day. The effort required to bring in and distribute water to the city. Trains halted. Roads jammed, especially at the highway checkpoints. One man. And he must have done it in one night. Incredible. He must have a plan.

Holding on to the sides of the sink, Commissioner Zhou looked at himself in the mirror. And said out loud, "He will run."

Chapter Eighteen

"JUDY, we're getting a little pressed for time," Avakian said, not quite at the point of pleading but getting close to it.

"You know you're taking all the fun out of shopping for a new vehicle," she replied.

"And it pains me more than I can tell you, but…"

"Okay, the next motorcycle we see. Even if I don't like the color. But no scooters. I could never enjoy fleeing from the law on a scooter."

"I don't think you *can* flee from the law on a scooter," he said.

They were walking the streets near the SAS Royal Hotel in northeast Beijing, having stashed the car nearby.

There were a lot of motorcycles in Beijing, but not as many as there could have been. The city had stopped issuing license plates for new bikes in 1998. You had to buy someone's old plate, and the price was up to nearly 200 dollars American. A cheaper plate restricted you to the area inside the 4th Ring Road.

As they turned at the next block, she said, "You see what I see across the street?"

Avakian wasn't so much looking at the bike as checking to make sure it wasn't parked in front of a restaurant or a shop with glass front windows. "You down with the color?"

"Not my first choice, but I can make do with red."

As they crossed the street a man stuck his head out his car window and shouted something at them.

"What was that all about?" Judy asked.

"Couldn't quite make out what he said, but I'm pretty sure it wasn't complimentary."

"Yeah, I got that impression too."

"Anti-Western feelings seem to be running a bit high. But it's like I've always said: if you want to know what it's like to be black man in America, be a white man on an Asian subway car."

"Just as well we're leaving," she said.

The bike was a Lifan, one of the biggest Chinese firms. The vast majority of the motorcycles on the road were Chinese, because those manufacturers had been the trailblazers for the national business model. They had entered into production agreements with Honda, Yamaha, and Kawasaki, stole their technology, knocked off cheaper quality parts, and sold the counterfeit models at prices the Japanese couldn't match if they didn't want to lose their reputation for quality. This particular model, the LF125-7F, was gold with red and black detailing. And 125cc was mid-range power for a Chinese bike, the vast majority on the street being between 100 to 150cc.

"Wait," Judy said. "There's a padlock on the disc brake."

Avakian reached into his pocket and, after a bit of feeling around, found one of the T-shaped pieces of metal he'd cut from an empty soda can in an idle moment. The top of the T was two squared-off wings, and the shaft tapered down into a rounded point. He grabbed the padlock and bent the wings around the shackle until the metal was tightly molded to it. Holding the wings together, he worked the shim down the shaft of the shackle until the rounded point slid into the hole where the shackle inserted into the lock body. There was just enough space there for a piece of soft metal the thickness of a soda can. When the shim was pushed all the way down, he gave it a twist and wiggled it to lever the lock latch off the groove in the end of the shackle. He handed Judy the open padlock. It had taken about ten seconds. "Let me know if you see anyone who looks like an irate motorcycle owner."

"What happens then?"

"The dispute gets resolved to no one's satisfaction."

He sat on the bike and removed the dent puller from his duffel bag, leaning over the ignition/steering lock to hide his work from view. Just like the car, the screw went in the keyhole, and it only took one bang with the slide hammer before the lock popped out. He slipped that and the tool into the bag and handed her the screwdriver, shinnying back on the seat to make room for the driver.

Straddling the bike, Judy handed him back the padlock. Avakian dropped it on the ground. If there had been a helmet the owner had taken it along.

Judy turned the ignition switch with the screwdriver. She pushed the starter button and the engine shrieked to life. It sounded like a cat being thrown into a blender. "Hold on," she shouted.

Avakian got his feet up, leaned into her back, and wrapped his arms around her waist. It felt worse than his first parachute jump, and he'd actually been looking forward to that.

She pulled out into traffic.

They were soon heading back into the center of the city but keeping to the less traveled streets. It was illegal to drive a motorcycle on any of the Ring Roads, and the police were always on the lookout for them. They made pretty good time, though. It was always better to be traveling into a city during evening rush hour.

As he'd strongly urged, Judy obeyed the traffic laws on this leg of their journey. Which meant that all

Avakian had to worry about was her weaving in and out of traffic and Chinese drivers running up close enough for him to kick dents in their cars. As anticipated, he hated every minute. The speed limit felt like running Daytona with nothing but two tires and a hunk of wobbling metal between the hard rough asphalt and his precious limbs.

But at least riding on the damned thing wasn't all that hard. Though his body was about as relaxed as a crescent wrench. He couldn't even close his eyes and wait for either the trip or his life to be over. He had to keep an eye on the road ahead and shout directions ever the banshee howl of that single cylinder engine. Pointing was a non-starter, since he was not about to release his grip on her waist.

Finally, they turned down the Yonghegong Daije in north-central Beijing. Judy made the last two turns he indicated and parked the bike. Even after she shut down the engine, he could still hear it in his head.

"How was it?" she asked.

"Oh, simply marvelous," said Avakian. "I'm going to have to buy one of these for myself one of these days."

"Really?"

"No." He looked at his watch. "If I did everything right the bombs are going off right about now and the authorities will be busy answering calls. You ready?"

"I guess so. I can't think of any excuse to get myself out of it."

"You can still stay with the bike."

"I can, but I won't."

"Suit yourself. Just forget about watching DeNiro in *Heat*. We're not going to try to give orders, move everyone around, or manage the chaos. We like chaos. We know what we're going to do—no one else does. That gives us a big advantage. So let them scream, let them go ape. If they're doing that, they're not doing anything else. How do we win?"

"With surprise, speed, and violence of action," she said in an intentionally bored monotone.

"Way to motivate me. And if you see a gun?"

"I yell gun, point, and drop to the floor."

"Outstanding. Here's your stuff." From that all-purpose duffel bag, he handed her a nylon shoulder bag and a sun hat.

"I hate that hat," she said.

"Put it on and cover those golden locks, blondie." He stuck the ignition lock cylinder back into its hole to make everything look kosher. And pulled the spark plug cable to keep any other criminals from driving off with the bike while they were inside. "Let's go."

"You know what we look like, don't you?" she said.

They were both wearing warm-up suits with the logo of an American company that had definitely not been paid a royalty for its use. Hers blue, his red. "No," he said, his mind on other things.

"We look like we're on our way to the early bird dinner in Boca."

Avakian chuckled. "Yeah, but you're not wearing heels and heavy jewelry with yours."

That made her laugh so hard she had to grab onto him. "Oh, you know your Boca retirees, don't you?"

They had a bit of a walk to the bank, and on the way, Judy said, "It seems a little late to be bringing this up, but shouldn't we be wearing ski masks?"

"While we're walking down the street?"

"No. While we're robbing the bank."

"Judy, if the Chinese get their hands on us, trying to beat a bank robbery rap in court is not going to be an issue."

"Serves me right for asking."

"The initial description that goes out on the radio is going to be a man and a woman wearing red and blue warm-up suits. Then while the cops are looking for that we won't be wearing warm-up suits any more."

"That was going to be my next question. Is there a reason we're robbing this particular bank?"

"The location is right. And if you'd ever tried to change money here, you'd want to rob it, too."

"I'm being the compulsive questioner again. In case you couldn't tell I'm nervous."

He put his arm around her and gave her a squeeze. "It's just your body trying to postpone what it doesn't want to do. You probably have to go to the bathroom again."

"As a matter of fact, I do."

"You'll be fine once the starting gun goes off."

"Poor choice of words."

"Sorry."

"You certainly wouldn't think this was your first bank robbery."

"I'm just numb from the motorcycle ride."

And there was the circular red logo and the sign for the Industrial and Commercial Bank of China over the building entrance. Avakian unzipped the duffel bag so it hung open under his armpit again, the rifle safety off and his finger resting against the side of the trigger guard.

Judy went through the glass door first. Using her body as a screen he slid the rifle out of the bag and pressed it against the back of his leg.

Chinese banks were always packed. If they didn't run the customers through that serpentine rodent maze in the lobby the line would have been out the door. Credit and debit cards hadn't gained a lot of traction with the majority of the public yet.

As instructed, Judy went by the guard close enough to brush him, turning her head and smiling as she passed. As predicted, he turned his head to check her out from behind. And while it was turned Avakian smashed the rifle butt into the back of his head. As he hit the floor Avakian bent down to add the guard's pistol to his duffel bag, and the screaming began.

As Avakian rose back up he had the rifle on his shoulder, scanning for targets. No immediate threats. He ripped off a burst on full auto right over everyone's head, shouting, "*Dao, dao, dao!*" Down, down, down.

A couple of people were still frozen upright but a couple of bullets sailing even closer by their ears put them on the floor.

Judy ran to the counter, vaulted herself up on it, and swung her legs over. She almost landed on a teller who was crouched under her station with her finger jammed on the alarm button. Judy froze, as if she couldn't believe what the woman was doing. Then grabbed her hair and yanked her out of the way, kicking her a couple of times for good measure. The teller shrieked, scuttling out of the way and curling up into a ball. The cash drawer was open, and Judy started grabbing handfuls of currency.

Following Avakian's nagging directions, any wrapped packages of money were ripped open, and the bills sifted through her fingers into the bag. Which she thought was silly until one of the stacks turned out to be hollow with a metal box inside. Her hands were shaking but that didn't really hinder the sorting. Ironically, it was easier when she had something to do. Except every time he shot that rifle it felt like her heart was going to explode.

Whenever the volume of the screams began to die down Avakian fired another burst into the ceiling. He paralleled Judy as she made her way down the line, constantly twirling to keep an eye on both the entrance and the offices on the other side. The floor was carpeted with Chinese, but a clear path magically parted in front of him before every step. He watched the body language for any heroes who might think about tackling his legs.

She was just about at the last station, and they'd been there long enough. He stuck two fingers in his mouth and blew a piercing whistle. Then rocked a fresh magazine into the rifle.

Judy looked up at the whistle and saw Pete waving at

her. She zipped up her bag and jumped from a chair up to the counter like crossing a stream from rock to rock, leaping over to the other side.

Avakian fired four rounds and blew the lock out of the door that separated the bank lobby from the rest of the building. A kick opened it up because even armored doors didn't have armored locks. He had no idea why bank robbers always left the way they'd come in, with the police usually waiting outside, when every bank in the world had a back door.

You were always most vulnerable when you were pulling out. Avakian reached in the duffel bag and got his hands on one of the tear gas grenades he'd liberated from the police car. He yanked out the pin and rolled it into the lobby. A mild pop, the loud hissing sound as the white chemical smoke came billowing up, and he could hear the stampede out the front door begin.

Making sure Judy was with him, he fired a round down the hallway to announce himself. A couple of employees who hadn't been able to resist sticking their heads out dove back into their offices and slammed the doors.

"Watch our back," he said to her as he trotted down the hall. They passed a pair of elevators. The gunfire had in fact properly announced them and the hallway was empty. There was no doorway at the end, only a stairway up and down. He began to turn his mind to that problem.

Judy saw a head appear in the doorway they'd come through, then vanish back. But then something else came around the corner. She screamed, "Gun!"

Avakian whirled about. She was already on the floor to give him a clear field of fire. Some rapid-fire pistol shots cracked by and he could see a hand holding a pistol, just sticking it around the corner, unaimed. But he aimed, not for the pistol but the corner the shooter was behind.

He gave it a 10-round burst and watched the splinters fly into the air. The pistol dropped to the floor.

"Go!" he yelled to Judy. "Get out in front!"

She bounced up and sprinted down the hall.

Dammit, Avakian thought. He shouldn't have done that. He had to look both ways and be ready to fire, and she was almost in the next county. He abandoned his plan and ran after her.

Giving none of that any thought, Judy ran flat-out to the end of the hallway but skidded to a stop before the stairs, stymied by the choice of whether to go up or down.

Avakian caught up and ordered, "Back behind me," as he started down the stairs.

One short flight and there was a fire door. Avakian kicked it open. No one took a shot. He bobbed his head out. If there were any jumpy cops out there, they wouldn't be able to resist. No gunfire.

Out the door and another sprint across an employee parking lot. He covered her while she climbed the fence at the edge, then replaced the rifle in the duffel bag and followed. There was a face looking out from just about every window in the bank building, and without a doubt most of them were on the phone.

A twenty-yard run down a side street and they hit the intersection to Xiang'er Hutong, an un-*hutong*-like Beijing back road in that it was actually a relatively straight line to the next north-south main drag. They'd parked the bike on it and walked all the way around to the bank.

"Warm-ups," said Avakian.

They stripped them off and left them in a pile, revealing jeans and shirts. Judy had forgotten all about her hated sun hat, so he plucked it off her head for her.

He had baseball caps for them both, and white surgical masks. Common riding attire in Beijing pollution, and just the thing to conceal those Caucasian features. As did the sunglasses, which were a necessity for driving anyway.

Yes, the bike was still there. He took her shoulder bag and jammed it under the rifle in his duffel.

Avakian was reattaching the spark plug cable when she patted her pockets and turned to him helplessly. "I left the screwdriver in my warm-ups."

Without a word he flicked open his pocketknife and pried out the loose lock cylinder. Sticking the blade in the hole he found the ignition switch cavity and twisted his wrist. "Kick it."

She pushed the electric starter, and just before the bike roared to life, he heard sirens. He slapped her on the rump in the universal signal to get the hell going.

Judy opened the bike up, but perhaps a *hutong* road was not the best place for that. Between cars, bicycles, and pedestrians there wasn't much room to spare. Barely enough for him to stretch out his arms. If he'd been inclined to do so, which he wasn't. "Take it easy!" he yelled.

A cycle emerged from a lane and Judy swerved to avoid it, nearly scraping Avakian off onto an oncoming car. Or so it seemed to him. "EASY!" he yelled, a little louder this time.

There were three cars ahead of them waiting to pull out into the next intersection. And Avakian watched with horrified disbelief as Judy passed them not on the inside but the outside, where one would normally expect to greet approaching traffic. Then barely braked as she bombed out into the main avenue, Jiaodaokou Nandajie.

Judy leaned the bike on its side as she went into the hard right turn. Something she hadn't done until now. And Avakian, in his usual tense upright posture, experienced G-forces he had not experienced before and felt himself being pulled right off his seat.

His first instinct was to press his thighs together like he would riding a horse. Except he immediately realized that inserting his trousers into the spinning rear wheel of a motorcycle was not a solution but rather the start of a whole new problem. Feeling himself being sucked off the back of the bike unleashed a blast of pure terror, and he frantically grabbed at her waist. "I'm falling off the fucking bike!"

Judy couldn't see what was going on, but she felt it as she tried to come out of the turn. They were going to dump. "Lean to your left!" she screamed, throwing her own weight that way. The bike was on its side, barely hanging onto the road. She gunned the throttle. Only speed was going to save them.

It was a complete accident of physics that Avakian, who had passed beyond the ability to follow simple directions at that point, saw the road coming up to greet him and instinctively threw himself away from it.

Their combined weight and the property of inertia righted the bike, almost miraculously.

Judy throttled back, the near miss having supplied her own bracing blast of adrenaline. "You've got to relax and lean into the turns!" she shouted.

Avakian was trying to rearrange the duffel bag, whose strap was strangling him, without releasing his grip from her waist. "What?"

Now he was twitching all over the place, and she was bouncing back and forth in the seat trying to counterbalance his moves. The bike was shimmying all over the road. "Relax, goddammit!"

"What?" It was easier for her to hear him, since he was yelling right in her ear.

"RELAX!" she screamed at the top of her lungs.

"Are you kidding?" came the reply.

"You've…got…to…relax…and…lean…into…the…turns! Turn…with…the…bike! OR YOU'LL DUMP US!"

Well, no shit, Avakian thought. Nice to know that now. Evidently everyone else in the world just had that information imprinted on their fucking DNA, so they didn't need to be told about it. Okay Pete, you can do this. Deep breath. Loosen up. You're going to die on this fucking thing anyway—you might as well die relaxed.

And that took both conscious thought and considerable effort, since every muscle in his body was currently as hard as tempered steel.

Just as he was getting the hang of it, the traffic ahead stopped. Judy weaved through until it settled into a solid unmoving mass, all the cars out of their lanes and packed together, not even enough room for a motorcycle to get through.

This temporary respite from the sheer terror of motorcycle riding gave Avakian a chance to check out his surroundings. There seemed to be a lot of people milling around in front of the businesses on the street, as if they were waiting to get in. And then there were a couple of shop owners pulling their shutters down. He checked his watch. Way too early to be closing. Could it be no water? Oh, yeah.

Judy revved the engine a couple of times. Just as he was about to say it was okay, they could wait, she gave it the gas. As he went back to hanging onto her waist for dear life, she went up over the right-hand curb, through a line of low border bushes, and down into the bicycle only lane. And then speeded back up, flying down the lane with all the bicyclists shaking their fists at them.

Oh shit, Avakian thought. This was definitely not the way to keep from attracting attention to themselves.

Sure enough, a siren started wailing behind them. Avakian looked over his shoulder. A white police motorcycle, lights flashing, was coming up fast in the bike lane.

"Stop!" he shouted to Judy, before she could speed up and start a chase.

As she stopped so did a few bicyclists who were looking forward to seeing them get their comeuppance.

Avakian unbuttoned the front of his shirt. It was both

a little too big for him and not tucked in. He'd cut and modified one of the police holsters to fit inside the waistband of his jeans, and the pistol was riding at an angle right above his groin. He took a firm grip and tugged to loosen it in the holster. His left hand was on Judy's shoulder, and he gave her a reassuring pat.

The cop pulled up right behind them. Once again Avakian was struck by Chinese incongruities. The cop was in the standard blue police uniform, complete with tie, that must have been a bitch on a motorcycle. The only difference from a regular patrolman was a white crash helmet and white pistol belt. The radio microphone was dangling from his shoulder epaulet.

As soon as the cop put the kickstand down Avakian swung his leg over the seat so both feet were planted on firm ground, settled the pistol front sight on center mass, and shot the startled cop right off his bike. A shriek rose from the stopped bicyclists, and they began to scatter.

"Go," he told her, re-mounting the seat. He flicked the safety to de-cock the pistol and replaced it back under his shirt.

Judy peeled out so fast she nearly left him standing bowlegged in the street. He regained his grip on her waist but could barely keep up with the side to side leaning as she tore through the bicycles.

"Next left, next left!" he yelled. Never run in a straight line.

As usual for Beijing the cars were stacked up in the middle of the intersection and refusing to relinquish even an inch of the right of way. What made it hard for a commuter made it easier for a motorcyclist. Avakian remembered to lean this time.

As they turned, he caught a glimpse farther up the road of two white panel trucks of the Water Resources Ministry, lights flashing, stuck in traffic. It was the only pleasing part of the whole drive.

Now they were on another reasonably straight *hutong*

road that was so jammed with cars Judy was forced to slow down to negotiate her way through. Small favors, Avakian thought. They were very near Houhai Lake and the scene of their original crime.

One, two, three, four intersections. "Next right!" he yelled in her ear. "Stick to the speed limit and stay in the car lanes!" There were no cops behind them, but the next avenue would tell the tale.

Judy turned onto Jiugulou Daije. No roadblocks, just traffic. In less than a quarter of a mile they passed under the 2nd Ring Road and over the Andingmenxibin River. The inviting green space of the North River Bank Park flashed by on their left.

After that short trip north they headed east, cutting across the top of Beijing and through the lake parks of Rendingshu and Liuyin. Avakian kept them off the main roads that were usually well covered by traffic cops this time of day. He was finally seeing some benefit from all those months in Beijing and all Kangmei's traffic avoidance tricks.

Four more miles of slicing through bumper-to-bumper traffic and they were once again within sight of the SAS Royal Hotel. But Avakian approached it from the opposite direction this time, not wanting to bump into a motorcycle owner searching the streets for a missing ride. The poor schnook was going to have troubles enough once the cops ran the license down.

He pointed under Judy's arm to a space between two cars. Nothing like finally gaining some confidence now that the motorcycle ride was over.

As soon as the engine was off, he had her arm, and they were walking away as if they'd never seen that motorcycle before. The hats and surgical masks went in the next trashcan they passed. The sunglasses stayed on.

The Xiali was where they'd left it, but with a parking ticket stuck to the windshield. "Keep walking," Avakian said under his breath.

He had to give that some thought. Did Chinese meter maids just write tickets, or did they run numbers looking for stolen cars?

Still, he made a large circle within visual range all around the car, looking for anyone who might be staking it out. The coast was clear, but there was no sense in being careless. Beijing was an easy place to be paranoid in. There was always a crowd everywhere you went, and someone was always watching you.

With the car door unlocked, since he did not have the key, someone had taken the opportunity to remove the radio and rifle the glove box. They were welcome to it. As long as the car ran, that is. He patted himself on the back for disconnecting the trunk latch.

He dumped the duffel bag between the front seats and sat down. It felt so good to be sitting in a car again he almost got a little misty over it. Now all it had to do was run. He plucked the ignition cylinder out with his fingers and turned his knife in the socket. The engine caught.

Avakian leaned forward and planted a heartfelt kiss on the steering wheel.

Chapter Nineteen

SOON IT TOOK ALL of Commissioner Zhou's investigators and all their radios to keep track of what was happening in the city. So much effort that the hallway no longer offered enough space to work. The apartment, of course, was still smoldering from the explosion. Rather than commandeer someone else's apartment, the commissioner had the makeshift command post moved down to the building lobby.

Where the apartment manager watched mournfully as they tacked sheets of paper to a wall to use as an improvised chalkboard. He supposed he should be grateful they were not writing directly on the wall.

Commissioner Zhou was once again standing before a map tacked up alongside the paper, lost in thought. Nine underground explosions or water main breakages. Explosions on two trains and one subway car. All the rail systems shut down until the remaining tracks and trains could be checked, which meant tens of thousands of commuters stranded. Between the normal rush hour and the detours around flooded streets traffic had come to a halt. The incidents marked on the map formed an almost complete oval around the city. Only the upper left part of the oval hung open. Why was that? Then he leaned forward and put his finger on the place where the abandoned police car had been discovered. The open part of the oval. You were interrupted, he thought. But was that an important clue, or only an intriguing dead end?

He would never have thought of water. Or that it could be accomplished without one person, one police officer making a report. None who survived a meeting with Avakian, he reminded himself.

Inspector Cheng said, "Comrade Commissioner, the Industrial and Commercial Bank on Dungsi north has been robbed by two white foreigners, a man and a woman. The man carrying a Type 95 rifle. Many shots were fired, all by the robbers. None hurt by gunfire, but a guard clubbed unconscious. A tear gas grenade was used in the escape."

Commissioner Zhou did not imagine that there were many other foreigners with infantry rifles robbing banks in the city. And it seemed that Avakian still had the Doctor with him. "Tear gas? Is that confirmed?"

"Yes, Comrade Commissioner."

Where could he have obtained tear gas? Of course. From the abandoned police car. So that question was definitely resolved. Commissioner Zhou thought about other standard equipment Avakian might have taken from the car. Did he kill the missing policemen just to obtain their weapons and equipment? The man was as ruthless as he was daring. "Physical description?"

"Red training suit, short beard, bald."

"The nose?"

"Not mentioned, Comrade Commissioner. But estimated height 165-167 centimeters."

That settled it. "How much money was taken?"

"Approximately 220,000 yuan."

A tidy sum to finance an escape. "GPS tracking?"

"No, Comrade Commissioner. The tellers were ordered to the floor, and the robbers chose the money themselves. None of the bundles with the trackers was taken."

"I assume they escaped with no pursuit."

"That is correct. A motorcycle policeman on Andingmen Neidaije was shot dead after stopping a motorcycle speeding in the bicycle lane. Two riders. It was not reported if they were foreigners, but they were not wearing training suits."

They would have changed. "The training suits were for us to concentrate our minds on, as we have," said Commissioner Zhou. "Any sign of the motorcycle?"

"No, Comrade Commissioner. The area traffic cameras and traffic units were concerned with the road problems. But all units have been alerted to the motorcycle license and description."

Commissioner Zhou interlaced his fingers together. "This is all one plan. The motorcycle was chosen to surmount the traffic jams. It has almost certainly been abandoned. How much of the city is without water?"

"Only sections, Comrade Commissioner. The latest estimate is 30% of the city with full water service."

Commissioner Zhou turned to look up at his towering assistant once again. "So, you are saying that 70% of Beijing is without water."

Inspector Cheng knew what was coming. "Yes, Comrade Commissioner."

"Once again please refrain from attempting to put a fine face on bad news. At least with me."

"Yes, Comrade Commissioner."

Commissioner Zhou had hopes that one day Cheng would learn. He said, "How do we proceed? Inspector Cheng, Inspector He?"

Cheng was still smarting from his rebuke, so He answered, "Track down the motorcycle, Comrade Commissioner. Even if stolen, where it was stolen is valuable information. Have our own people review the traffic and bank video cameras. Assemble the evidence from both crime scenes."

Commissioner Zhou nodded. Textbook investigative procedure. And doubly attractive since no one could ever be faulted for following procedure. And the right answer if they had been dealing with a common bank robber. "You are not incorrect, Inspector. But imagine for a moment that you are not investigating a bank robber, but a saboteur who is fighting you with terrorist methods. Put yourself in his place. You have planned this strike where all the damage has occurred within the span of an hour. Do you continue with another series of attacks now?"

They both looked confused. Commissioner Zhou knew he was most likely asking too much of them. More the pity. "I will pose the question another way. What is *our* response likely to be? I am speaking of our national response to this crisis."

Inspector Cheng said, "As you know, Comrade Commissioner, two additional army divisions have been sent into the city to maintain order, man identification screening checkpoints on the streets, and guard vital areas."

"And knowing this," said Commissioner Zhou, "how would you calculate your chances to accomplish additional attacks of this kind?"

"Ordinarily I would say zero," Inspector Cheng replied. "But I will say slim only because I am surprised by this man's skills so far."

"Suicidal," said Inspector He.

"I agree," said Commissioner Zhou. Now he could see them thinking. Good.

Inspector He said, "Comrade Commissioner, could it be that this bank robbery was to obtain funds to pay Taiwan sympathizers, traitorous elements, or perhaps a criminal gang to smuggle them out of the country?"

They knew that nearly all the leaders of the 1989

Tiananmen student revolt had escaped the country, even in the face of a massive national manhunt.

"Now you are thinking along the correct lines," said Commissioner Zhou. "I might say yes, but I have met this man. He would not trust any Chinese, not under the current circumstances. And I do not feel that Avakian has access to American spy networks. He will attempt to escape but will do so without help. So we must ask ourselves another question. How does a foreigner escape first from Beijing, and then from China?"

Inspector Cheng spoke first. "I could not use air, rail, bus, or ship as a normal passenger. Only if I had confederates who could somehow conceal me within cargo. Or hidden inside the transport in some other way."

"I agree with your reasoning," said Commissioner Zhou. "Continue."

"Then by vehicle to a national border is the only solution," said Inspector Cheng. "But there will be some unique element. This man strikes me as an unusual combination of clever calculation and bold recklessness."

Commissioner Zhou was feeling the grip of a strong excitement. What had been scattered elements of his thinking were now coming together. "And where do you go?"

"Vietnam and India are both long and difficult journeys by road," said Inspector Cheng. He did not mention Laos or Myanmar, which would not welcome an American trying to cross a border. North Korea of course was out of the question.

"But perhaps being difficult makes them unexpected," said Commissioner Zhou. "And therefore worthwhile."

Inspector He shook his head doggedly, perhaps forgetting himself. "No, Comrade Commissioner. Fuel, food, shelter, time—all enormous problems. Not with the countryside alerted against foreigners."

There had been a report that morning of two American tourists beaten to death by a group of patriotic workers in Jian. Though this information would of course not be released to the media. Not that anyone cared about American tourists, but public disorders must not be encouraged.

Inspector Cheng was emboldened by He's support. "The man would almost certainly seek to escape to either Russia or Mongolia."

"If I were an American," said Inspector He. "I would not choose Russia. Not with the liberation of Taiwan progressing and Russia courting our favor."

"Yes, I agree," said Commissioner Zhou. "Mongolia. By vehicle."

Guessing what he intended, and concerned for the fate those who would follow him in this course of action, Inspector Cheng said, "Perhaps we should continue with the investigation and wait for the situation to become clearer, Comrade Commissioner?"

"By that time, he will be in Mongolia and out of our reach," said Commissioner Zhou. "Which will happen if we conduct a standard investigation."

Inspector Cheng persisted. "But undertaking such a step with no clear evidence to support it is a bold gamble, Comrade Commissioner. If we are wrong, there will be strong consequences."

Commissioner Zhou was not blind to those fears. His answer was a popular saying about great rewards requiring great risk. "How can we retrieve the baby tiger without going into the tiger's nest?"

Chapter Twenty

"I'M ASHAMED OF MYSELF," said Judy.

Pete Avakian resisted the temptation to look over at her. Which he wouldn't anyway because people who kept turning their heads to talk face to face when they were supposed to be driving drove him crazy. He also had no immediate plans to jump into the conversation. Any that began with a statement like that had danger written all over it—no matter what a guy said, it was going to be the wrong thing.

But she called his silence and raised with one of her own.

Checkmated, Avakian steeled himself for the worse. He hadn't thought the bank was much different from what they'd done before. But he was also aware that women felt differently about most things. "Ashamed of what?"

"There was a teller in the bank. When I jumped over the counter, she was sitting there with her finger just stuck on the alarm button." Judy jabbed her finger furiously in the air. "And that made me so mad I grabbed her hair and kicked her until she cried out. I have never done anything like that in my life."

Avakian didn't say anything.

"And then I was feeling like a real hot shit on the bike," she went on. "I was in control, for the first time in a while." She turned to watch his face. "And I was loving it. Especially the fact that you weren't in control."

Avakian concentrated on the road, because he didn't think smiling at that would be such a good idea.

"I went into the bike lane as if I had to live up to all the smack I'd been talking," she said. "We might have been caught. That policeman didn't need to die. I killed him. And none of it had to happen."

She stopped then, near tears.

"That's why you're ashamed of yourself?" Avakian said.

"I am."

"Good for you."

"What?"

"For feeling ashamed."

"Why should that be good?"

"In our heart of hearts, we all want to rob banks and blow things up instead of going to the office from 9 to 5. Which is why every functioning society makes all that fun stuff, what everyone really wants to do, illegal. Why do you think bored young men become terrorists? And more people know who Jesse James was than Jonas Salk? And why we flock to the movies to watch violence presented as a cartoon where all our fantasies are fulfilled and only the characters we don't identify with suffer any consequences? We're drawn to violence and destruction like bugs to one of those blue light zappers on the back porch. But in the real world every action has consequences. I'd like to comfort you, but I think you'd see right through that. So, I'll just say, as a friend: welcome to the real world."

More silence. Then she said, "You know, Pete, you're a really good guy."

"Likewise, I'm sure. Except for the guy part."

"When am I going to start listening to you?"

"You can always tell a real combat veteran from a wannabe because the vets never talk about it. Everyone wants to hear a good war story, but you can't really understand one if you haven't experienced it. You loved doing it, didn't you?"

She hesitated before answering, "Yes, I did."

"And you're also sickened by what you did."

"Yes, I am."

"Welcome to the club. Only a sociopath doesn't carry a combat mistake around like a rock in their chest."

She leaned over and kissed him very tenderly on the cheek. He took a hand off the wheel and stroked her hair. She sat back in her seat and said, "What was your combat mistake?"

"Oh, there's a whole fistful of them. Biggest one? Once in El Salvador we had decent intelligence that our training base was going to get hit by about a thousand guerrillas. The Salvo officer was a worthless thug who stole babies from guerrilla areas and sold them off for adoption in the U.S. The irony is that all the atrocities the American left complained about would have stopped if we'd been allowed to go out on combat operations with them, but there was this post-Vietnam hypocrisy that we were only trainers. Well, my counterpart wouldn't listen to me. He sent half the base home on leave because he was an idiot in addition to being a thug. And I'd let him know how I felt about him—totally wrong move—and he was going to show me that my advice was crap. The advisory group at the embassy wouldn't listen to me because I was self-righteous about everything in those days, and they didn't want to hear it. So, we got hit one night. We hung onto the base, but a lot of good Salvadoran soldiers got killed who wouldn't have if I'd been as smart as I was loud and immature."

"They stole babies?"

"They looked at it as one less guerrilla to grow up and shoot at them, and childless Yankee couples pay big money for pretty foreign babies. Poor people always get trapped in the middle of every dirty war. The guerrillas would steal their kids too, to be soldiers."

Judy could see the tendons standing out in his neck. "And it's still a rock in your chest."

"Twenty-three years later. Dawn breaks, and there are all the dead bodies. You can't cut to the next scene. You have to go pick them up and put them in coffins."

Okay, Judy, you started it again. Now find a way to change the subject. "You know, the first time I ever heard you use serious profanity was on that bike."

"It's also the first time I learned what my own heart tastes like."

"Welcome to my world of the last few days. But we were speaking of profanity."

"I try not to drop the F-bomb under normal circumstances."

"Any particular reason?"

"I was probably the most profane guy in the U.S. Army, which is saying something. When I moved out into the civilian world, I realized I had to modify that behavior."

She said it slowly, "The most profane man in the Army."

"Well, officer at least."

"Excuse me, but men are not supposed to be capable of change."

"I am not men," Avakian told her. "I am DEVO."

More than anything else, it was the voice he used that made her giggle uncontrollably. "Of course. How could I be so blind?"

"I don't reveal myself to many, Doctor."

I'll bet you don't, she thought, feeling the pull from him letting her in.

A nagging sensation that he'd forgotten something

had been eating at Avakian for a while, and at that moment the insight jabbed its way into his brain. "By the way, did you happen to find any GPS trackers in the bills you grabbed?"

"Were those the metal things hidden inside stacks of money?"

"That's right," he said, trying to keep the anxiety out of his voice. "You did leave them behind, didn't you?"

"I did."

That was a relief. "Wonderful." He really hated it when he let things slip by him.

"GPS trackers?"

"The Chinese version of the exploding dye pack. A cop told me once they haven't had a successful bank robbery since they started hiding them in stacks of cash."

"And the police just show up at your hide-out?"

"Correct."

"I guess you learn these things when you're one of the good guys who goes bad."

"Correct again." He saw the turn coming up. "Okay, here we are."

"Nice place." A modern slab of an apartment building that looked close to twenty stories. "Is that a lake over there?"

"Shuidui Lake. We're really just across the Ring Road and the Airport Expressway from the SAS Royal. And what you're looking at is the Dongyuan Apartments."

"Another hide-out?"

"No. This is where we pick up our ride. So, let's keep a good thought that all our mischief hasn't knocked him off schedule."

"Him?"

"Major General Dong. Not related to the apartments. Army military intelligence type. And, as his name might imply, the biggest tool you'd ever want to meet. He keeps his mistress in an apartment here, and every day he waits out rush hour with her before returning home to the family. I'm told you can set your watch by him. And he's just the kind of creep who'd blow off a national emergency to get laid."

As he'd figured, her female face was set in total disapproval. "And you know this how?"

"I needed to get in touch with him one afternoon and all the Chinese started tittering. Official minders are only human after all. The longer they hang around with you the more torn they get between official circumspection and a natural desire to be informative. Eventually you end up hearing all the gossip."

"And this general is going to be our hostage?"

"Perish the thought. You wouldn't be able to stand him for fifteen minutes, let along a long drive. We're just going to borrow his official vehicle for the trip." While explaining this Avakian had been slowly cruising through the parking lot.

"I assume you know what his car looks like."

Now Avakian did turn and look at her.

"Okay, stupid question. I must be getting nervous again."

Avakian was beginning to despair that they'd kept the general at work. Then he realized the car wouldn't necessarily be near the building. The general would call his driver while he was on the way down and be met at the front door.

Slightly encouraged by that thought, he made a wider circuit of the lot. "There we go. That's my boy."

"Which one?"

"The black Mercedes 350 SUV with the tinted windows."

"It's nice, I guess. Did we want an SUV?"

"What we really want is the license plate."

"Judy's confused again."

"Look closely at the other cars, Doctor. A regular

Chinese registration is a blue plate with white letters and numbers. While this one is…?"

"White with a red-letter prefix and black letters and numbers."

"It's a special military plate. The number also indicates the occupant's rank. Military vehicles do not have to stop and pay road tolls. More importantly, no cop who values his career is going to pull over a major general's car for any reason whatsoever. Likewise, any military checkpoints. Hopefully."

"And you've been planning this for how long?"

"Ah, I see what you're getting at. You've got to understand that the countries I work in usually have some pretty serious governance problems. So, whenever I take a job, I always like to think about how I'm going to get out if, say, the insurgents overrun the capital and the airport gets closed. Or shelled. This actually happens more often than you'd think. Gets to be a habit."

"You always think about what could go wrong in surgery, too."

"Wouldn't doubt it."

"It's certainly turned out to be a big help lately, hasn't it?"

"We'll see."

"You know, Pete, I just realized who you are."

"Why am I not sure I want to hear this?"

"You're Eeyore as a criminal mastermind."

Avakian's mind was on the task at hand. "Eeyore?"

"Winnie the Pooh?" She did the Eeyore voice: "It'll never work. We'll die in a hail of bullets."

Avakian laughed loudly. "Recognizing you have a problem is always the first step, isn't it?"

"Maybe. But not doing it anymore is always the final step."

"I'll take it under advisement until I have reason to be optimistic. Now, when I get out you hop behind the wheel and keep the engine running. Then follow me—we won't go far. Any questions?"

"What are we going to do about the driver?"

He just looked at her again.

"Oh," she said. "All right. I'll shut up now."

Avakian parked two rows back and off to the side of the Mercedes so they wouldn't be visible in any mirrors.

He drew the pistol as he exited the car but kept it out of view behind his back. The attraction of the Mercedes was now a definite disadvantage. With the tinted windows he had no idea what the driver might be doing. Maybe in the back seat taking a nap.

As he turned into the narrow space between the driver's side of the Mercedes and the car parked next to it, he ducked down below the side mirror. Most people didn't lock the driver's door while they were in the car, which was how carjackers made their money.

He reached up, grabbed the door handle, and yanked it open. The driver's startled face twisted around to meet his. Late twenties, senior sergeant's epaulets, phone buds in his ears as he rocked out to his MP3 player. Avakian swung the pistol across his body like a backhand tennis shot, catching the sergeant on the side of the temple.

He fell back against the seat and Avakian pistol-whipped him again just to be sure.

Judy lifted herself over the center console and settled in behind the wheel. She could just imagine the phone conversation. Mom, I met a great guy. Well educated, great sense of humor, incredibly sensitive, and a stone-cold killer and criminal genius. And she could just hear her mother's voice in her head telling not to be so picky —it was a little thing she should overlook.

And her girlfriends? They'd tell her to let him kill anyone he wanted to as long he had a job, was good in bed, and didn't leave wet towels on the bathroom floor. No problems there. He even refused to leave dirty dishes in the sink in a hideout, for heaven's sake.

She chuckled out loud—something that under the circumstances probably would have appalled her a week ago. But she was certainly getting the most from her travel dollar. If any adventure tour company offered the trapped in Beijing in the middle of a war package the price would definitely be in the six figures. Only cheap compared to visiting the International Space Station.

Avakian rolled the driver onto the passenger side floorboard. It was kind of strange using a key to start a car. Three quarters of a tank of gas. Outstanding. He backed out of the parking space and checked the mirror to be sure Judy was behind him.

Less than half a mile south was Chaoyang Park, one of northeastern Beijing's largest green spaces. Avakian found a quiet lane. They parked the two vehicles back-to-back, and after he jimmied the trunk of the Xiali they transferred everything into the Mercedes.

"Now I know why we've been carrying around all this gasoline and water," Judy said. "I got the water part, and it's nice to be the only people around who have some, but I admit I thought you might be contemplating arson."

"Two foreign devils in enemy country aren't going to be driving into a rural service station and telling the attendant to fill 'er up and check the tires. When they make the movie of this, they won't have to worry about stopping for gas or running out of ammo, but for us my best-laid plans mean nothing if I didn't pre-stage the right supplies. As it is, we're going to be on the water and energy bar diet for a while."

"No more instant noodles?"

"I know it's hard."

"I'll try and be strong for both of us."

Avakian went to the front of the Mercedes. He lifted the driver onto his shoulder and carried him over to the now-empty trunk of the car. "You might want to take a quick walk around the block."

Standing next to him and looking down into the trunk, the doctor made her diagnosis with clinical detachment. Depressed skull fracture, right side subdural hemorrhage indicated by the unequal pupil, bloody cerebrospinal fluid drainage from the nostrils. Comatose and expectant. "What are you going to do?" she asked.

"Strip off his uniform and ID so he can't be identified."

"Go ahead," she said. "It doesn't bother me anymore. The fact that it doesn't maybe bothers me, but nothing else does."

Avakian took out his knife and cut off the pale green uniform shirt and darker trousers. He balled the clothing up under his arm and Judy slammed the trunk shut.

They left the Xiali in the park. The afternoon shadows were lengthening into dusk. Avakian drove until they were clear of the car and then stopped. He disappeared underneath the Mercedes with a flashlight and pliers.

"Engine sounded fine to me," Judy said.

"I'm looking for a GPS," came the muffled voice. "The Chinese had a rash of official vehicle thefts, which annoyed the generals to no end. So, they had anti-theft GPS transmitters installed. You know, like LoJack or OnStar? In their cars first, of course."

"How are you going to find something like that without a lift and power tools?"

"Same way I found the burglar alarm. All these widgets have to have power. Nobody ever thinks to hide the power cable."

He traced the wire bundles from the battery on back, and quickly found the lonely pair that seemed to be going not to the taillights but the rear wheel well. "Judy, can you hand me the crowbar?"

She passed it underneath, and soon there was a sound of bending metal. The SUV rocked a bit. Some more protesting metal. And a sharper bang. Then something being beaten back into place.

Avakian reappeared and hurled a small metal box into the trees. "Okay," he said, tossing the pliers and crowbar into the back. "Now where did we put the hand sanitizer?"

"I thought you might attach that to something interesting."

"I considered it," he said, wiping his hands in a towel. "But one of those calls to the driver's cellphone was probably the general. And generals aren't patient." He folded the towel neatly and paused, holding the open door, his head slightly bowed.

"Are you *praying*?" she asked.

"I probably should," he said, looking at her under his arm. "But I was just trying to think if I'd forgotten anything. Nope, don't have that feeling."

He jumped into the seat and started the engine.

"Can I ask you something?" she said.

"Just as long as it's not theological."

"It's not. What are these two switches underneath the center dashboard console here?"

"Are you telling me a doctor doesn't know Mercedes?"

"Very funny. Okay, I drive one. But mine doesn't have two add-on switches on the dash."

"You're talking about one of my major buying points," said Avakian. He flipped the first switch and a siren came alive, nearly levitating Judy off her seat.

"Holy shit!" she exclaimed.

Avakian immediately shut it off and flipped the other one. Blue flashing lights began popping just above the headlights.

"We were getting a security walk-through," he said, shutting them off. "And we're all standing around outside The Great Hall of the People. Chinese and most of the countries' security liaisons. And then there's a siren and

flashing lights and this Mercedes pulls up and General
Dong steps out like he was ready to sign autographs. And
everyone goes: what a tool." He grinned at her. "For
some reason it stuck in my mind."

"I feel better about stealing the car of someone who's
a tool."

"Don't even get me started on the guy." As he pulled
out, he noticed that she'd emptied the ashtrays. "Sorry
about not stealing a non-smoking car."

"I'm not going to complain about the color, either.
You've got enough on your mind." She stroked her seat.
"Leather's nice, though."

"I think we've got everything. Need to go to the
bathroom?"

"No, dad."

"Okay then. Road trip?"

"Road trip," she said.

Avakian made his way slowly north along back roads
while Judy backed up his navigation with a map and a
flashlight.

He actually had the gall to drive right through the
Olympic Park. They wound up on a low hill a few miles
farther north, near the Xisanqi High-Tech Industrial
Park and overlooking the Badaling Expressway. Which
was a solid mass of unmoving headlights.

"This is what I was hoping to see," said Avakian.

"A traffic jam?"

"You're as smart as you are beautiful, Doctor, but you
are not observing two rows of headlights going each way
on a double three-lane highway. Any good civil defense
plan always leaves one highway lane open for emergency
vehicles, military convoys, that sort of thing."

"I guess we have to hope it stays open then."

"Who's Eeyore now, Doctor?"

"My God, it's contagious."

"Actually, you've just voiced my one real concern.
The Chinese military would bulldoze cars right out of the

lane to keep it open. But our friends the Chinese public, whose devotion to rules and regulations is marginal at best, may still have completely jammed everything up in their usual attempt to get over. If that's the case, we go to Plan B. Now you'll ask me what Plan B is."

"It's like I don't even have to be here to have this conversation."

"And I would tell you Plan B, I really would. But we've had a fair amount of success so far with me not giving you a whole lot of time to dwell on what you're going to have to do. Do we really want to break that winning formula?"

She dwelled on that a bit. "No, probably not." Though Plan B couldn't be any worse than her imagination was making it out to be.

"Okay, then. Let's do it."

The highway on-ramp was completely blocked. Avakian hit the flashing lights and went up in the breakdown lane. There was an old Russian UAZ jeep with military police markings sitting there at the end, just waiting for someone to try it. Avakian goosed the siren. A helmeted figure with a flashlight hopped out of the jeep and blinded him by shining the beam at the windshield.

Avakian reached back over the seat and drew the rifle out of the duffel bag, laying it across his lap.

Judy was reevaluating her previous statement about not needing to go to the bathroom.

The flashlight beam dropped down to check out their plate. The soldier shouted something.

Avakian had one hand on the door latch and the other on the rifle.

The jeep pulled out of the way, and the MP beckoned them on with his torch.

Avakian didn't give anyone a chance to change their mind. The right-hand lane was sealed off from the other two with traffic cones and stretched out before them, empty and inviting.

"What do you know," said Doctor Rose. "How far is it to Mongolia?"

"Little over 300 miles," Avakian replied.

"Then out of China by morning."

"This is probably the wrong time to tempt fortune," said Avakian.

Chapter Twenty-One

COMMISSIONER ZHOU WAS ARGUING on the phone with the Public Security Minister's aide.

"Do you have any idea what is happening?" the Deputy Commissioner's voice bellowed over the cellphone static. "There are lines at every store in the city, and every time one runs out of bottled water there is a riot. We have our hands full trying to put these down and clear the roads and bring in more water. The Army sends in tanker trucks and the people refuse it because there is a rumor that the water has been shut off because Taiwan agents have poisoned the reservoirs. So, they want only bottled water. Even the areas that have full water service are out buying bottled water because they are afraid it is poisoned. And with all this you want a helicopter?"

"Do you want the man who caused all this?" Commissioner Zhou countered. "Or do you want him to escape? That is your choice."

The answer came like lightning. "You must speak to the minister."

Which is what Commissioner Zhou wanted all along. And had made possible by using the word choice. No bureaucrat would ever take responsibility for making any decision if he could possibly avoid it.

The connection clicked and the minister came on. "Be brief, Commissioner."

Commissioner Zhou already knew what he wanted to say. "Comrade Minister, I have reason to believe that the foreigner responsible for this crisis is currently fleeing north."

"Fleeing the city? Impossible. Even if there were no checkpoints, no transport is leaving the city."

"One might just as well ask how a single man could create a crisis of this magnitude, Comrade Minister."

There was silence on the other end. "What do you require?"

"One helicopter, Comrade Minister. To transport myself and my investigators to Zhangjiakou."

"You will apprehend him there?"

"With the help of the Zhangjiakou Bureau, that is my hope."

"Listen, Zhou," the minister said, the hard tones of authority cracking a bit and the desperation coming through in his voice. "You must bring this man to People's Justice. He cannot escape and say what he has done. Do you understand? Word of this must not leak out. Gangs of saboteurs, yes. Enemies of the people. Bombing from the air. We can alert the masses to these. We can *use* these. But not one white devil."

"I understand, Comrade Minister. Your aide knows my location. I must stress that speed is of the essence if I am to accomplish this task."

"Accomplish the task, Commissioner," the minister said coldly. The connection clicked dead.

Commissioner Zhou was somewhat rattled by the apparent failure of his attempt to leave himself a way out and ensure the safety of his career. And even more so by the failure to undertake more detailed arrangements for the helicopter. But there was not time to dwell on that. He motioned Inspector Cheng and Inspector He over to him. "A helicopter is on the way here. What is the roof like?"

"Impossible, Comrade Commissioner," said Inspector He. "Crowded with antennas and satellite dishes."

"Very well. Have your men monitor two radios. One on the aviation frequency and the other on our own in case the helicopter tries to contact us there. We must clear a landing space in the parking lot. Then, Inspector He, prepare your men to go. Vests, rifles, ammunition, gas masks. I do not know what type of helicopter will arrive, or how many it will carry. But all must be ready. Quickly now."

Inspector He dashed off, but Cheng remained. "Comrade Commissioner, you will be leaving on the helicopter?"

"Of course," Commissioner Zhou snapped.

"Perhaps I should remain to supervise the remaining investigators."

With this arriving on the heels of the attempt to persuade him to remain in Beijing, Commissioner Zhou knew exactly what Cheng was up to. Trying to distance himself from the effort, for safety. If he captured Avakian, Cheng would remain his faithful deputy, diligently tying up loose ends in Beijing. And if he failed, Cheng would have carefully laid the groundwork for not being a part of it.

Clever, but if it had been truly clever Zhou would never have realized it. Cheng had moved his piece precipitously. "If you wish to be left behind, I will leave you behind," he said. "Conduct a thorough investigation."

Inspector Cheng's face was expressionless. "Exactly as you would order, Comrade Commissioner."

"Comrade Commissioner," one of the sergeants monitoring the radio interrupted. "The helicopter is on its way."

"How many passengers will it take?" said Commissioner Zhou.

The sergeant spoke into the radio. "They say it depends on where you are going."

Of course, no one had told them anything, thought Commissioner Zhou. Then he reminded himself it was a miracle he had received the helicopter at all. And only because the minister had ordered it personally. The default response of any Chinese official to any situation was no, in order to avoid blame. "Zhangjiakou," he said. Two hundred kilometers away.

"Six," the sergeant reported after a brief radio conversation. "Six is the maximum capacity, Comrade Commissioner."

"Very well," said Commissioner Zhou. "Are they aware of our location?"

"Yes, Comrade Commissioner."

"Still, be sure you guide them in."

He walked outside. Inspector He was waiting. "I have your equipment, Comrade Commissioner."

"Good, He." It seemed there was an opening for a new deputy. "The helicopter is near. You and I, and your four best men."

"I am honored, Comrade Commissioner."

"You will be if we do not fail."

Commissioner Zhou used the time to make some phone calls. First, to a fellow commissioner in the Public Security *Zhengzhibu*, or personnel department. He spent a favor he was owed and arranged for Inspector Cheng's transfer to Tibet. The cold high-altitude air would do him good. Being done now would ensure the transfer would take place even if he failed and was disgraced. Next, he called the most reliable of the other team leaders and ordered him to provide daily briefings on Cheng's progress in the investigation. The inspector understood. And he would be able to tell after the first report whether the inspector was Cheng's man or his. He followed that up with calls to two other team leaders, issuing the same orders. Even if they talked about it amongst themselves, they would think the remaining team leaders who denied it were also reporting to him.

Inspector He brought up his four investigators. "Comrade Commissioner, I present Sergeants Guo, Kong, Fan, and Meng."

They saluted. Preoccupied, Commissioner Zhou nodded to them and turned back to his phone.

But the sound of rotors beating in the distance forestalled any more calls. An Italian Agusta A109 wearing the markings of the Beijing Public Security Bureau appeared over the rooftops and cautiously circled the parking lot before descending.

As soon as the wheels settled onto the pavement the six ran up and slid the side door open. The copilot was leaning over his seat, holding out an intercom headset. Commissioner Zhou put the headset on, but it did not work. He slapped at the earphones, to no avail. The copilot kept gesturing something he could not comprehend, and he was about to rip them off his head in frustration when the sergeant sitting next to him reached over and flipped the lever switch on the side of one earphone. He received a withering look in exchange for his kindness, but the pilot's voice crackled through.

"Commissioner Zhou?"

"I am Commissioner Zhou."

"Comrade Commissioner, we are to take you to Zhangjiakou. Is that correct?"

"It is."

"Where in the city?"

"The Public Security Bureau headquarters. And as quickly as possible. This is a state emergency."

"As you order, Comrade Commissioner. Please make sure the door is secured and you and your men are strapped in."

Feeling hands touch him, Commissioner Zhou twisted about angrily, but it was just the policemen on either side reaching over and buckling his seatbelt for him. What were their names again? "Take off," he ordered.

The pilot pulled back on the collective and the helicopter lurched straight up between the buildings, the rotors shuddering.

Commissioner Zhou did not enjoy helicopter travel. It was a matter of considerable relief when they finally cleared the buildings and could begin forward flight.

A violent orange sun was setting to their left. And from this giant's perch the city streets were hopelessly snarled, the traffic unmoving. As it was on the ring roads spreading concentrically out from the center, the headlights like beadwork in a necklace.

The pilot came up in the earphones. "Comrade Commissioner, I have radioed the Zhangjiakou Bureau to expect you. They wish to know the reason for your trip."

Doubtless the leadership of the local bureau wanted to know whether they were in trouble with the Ministry. Or if an unannounced inspection was in the offing. But no reassurance would be provided. He did not want anything done unless he organized it personally. Mention an American spy and even before they landed there would be a massive roadblock on the highway before the city. Something Avakian would be able to see from a kilometer away and avoid even easier. But all that was secondary, of course. Now he had placed his career at risk, no one would take Avakian but him. "Tell them it is a state emergency of the highest priority," he said. "Nothing more."

Once they left the bright environs of Beijing and its suburbs the landscape was mostly black, with only occasional dotted clusters of cities and villages. As they continued northeast the terrain rose into low mountains.

The investigators in the cabin dozed, but Commissioner Zhou kept consulting his watch. The crew had estimated fifty minutes of flight time. They must be close.

Over the intercom the pilot said, "Comrade Commissioner, there is some sort of emergency situation in Zhangjiakou."

"What do you mean?"

"I have been on the radio with the city bureau, and they have advised me not to fly low over the southern part of the city."

"For what reason?"

"Gunfire, Comrade Commissioner."

"Gunfire? What gunfire?"

"I asked this question, but they said nothing except to give me approach directions and that warning. It seemed they did not want to discuss it over the radio."

Gunfire. Incredible. "How long before we land?"

"Five minutes. We will begin our descent as soon as we pass over the peak of Hengshan Mountain ahead."

Commissioner Zhou kept watching for the distinctive shape of Zhangjiakou. It was a long, narrow city wedged into a long, narrow river valley between three mountain ranges.

But as they plunged down the slope there was nothing below. At first Commissioner Zhou thought a low mist must be obscuring the valley.

"Do you see, Commissioner?" the pilot asked.

"I see nothing," Commissioner Zhou snapped.

"This is what I mean. The city power is out. There are no lights. Except the fires. Do you see the fires?"

Now as they drew closer Commissioner Zhou did. That low hanging mist was smoke. The city was black, but there were at least ten different fires burning brightly enough to see from the air. What could be happening? A blackout? Zhangjiakou was a regional power center. All he could think of was an American air attack.

Passing over the river two strings of green balls erupted out of the darkness and floated over the rooftops.

"Did you see that, Commissioner?" the pilot said excitedly.

"Yes," Commissioner Zhou replied. Tracer bullets.

"Do you still wish to land?"

"Yes. Just make sure it is the right location."

The pilot came in fast over the rooftops and only turned on his spotlight as they circled to check for obstructions in the landing zone. "My orders are to drop you and not remain," he said. "I will find somewhere else to refuel. This is your last chance to return to Beijing with us."

"Follow your orders," said Commissioner Zhou. The spotlight was locked on the concrete pad beside the bureau headquarters on Weiyi Road. Which was the only building in the area that had lights showing. He took off the headset and shouted over the rotor noise, "It seems that there is some social disorder in progress. Be prepared for anything."

As the helicopter was settling down someone flashed a powerful light in their direction and blinded the crew. The pilot lost his frame of reference and in desperation tried to bring it down fast. The helicopter lurched like a fast-falling elevator and everyone's stomach slammed into their chest. They almost landed sideways. The port side wheel hit hard and bounced them back into the air, but on the second trip down the machine settled onto all three wheels.

This was added incentive for the passengers to leave quickly. The inspector had barely slammed the cabin door shut when the aircraft rose again.

With no real idea where he was going, Commissioner Zhou halted on the lawn beside the headquarters. If it could be called a lawn. The grass was so dead it crunched underfoot. A good time to take stock of first impressions. The first was a strong smell of fire in the air. Which was cooler than Beijing, perhaps over ten degrees. The streetlights were all out, and what illumination there was came from the headlights of parked vehicles and emergency lighting mounted on trucks. The headquarters building was fenced all around, of course, but propped up against that were shiny coils of new barbed wire. And inside the perimeter freshly made sandbag bunkers like mounds on the grass, manned by armed policemen.

Now the helicopter was gone and the tap-tap-tap of small arms fire could be heard clearly in the distance. At that, Commissioner Zhou heard his investigators cocking their own rifles. He could not find fault with this. The periodic gunfire only punctuated the continuous hammering of diesel generators. That was the source of the building lighting. An armored anti-riot vehicle was filling the tank for its water cannon from a hydrant in the street.

It was strange to be in the midst of all this activity yet have everyone ignoring them as if a helicopter had not just landed. A moment later they were caught in the beam of a flashlight held by an armed policeman, who approached quickly with someone who displayed some authority.

A man in late middle age, wearing a suit, which only made the bulletproof vest and the old-style steel helmet look that much more unusual. He held a walkie-talkie radio in one hand and a cellphone in the other. His face was streaked with grime, drawn and exhausted. And haunted, Commissioner Zhou thought instantly.

Thinking he should make an introduction, he said, "Commissioner Zhou, from the Ministry."

A quick bow. "Commissioner Lu. How many helicopters are following?"

"What do you mean?" said Commissioner Zhou.

"I see. You have been sent to make an appreciation of the situation. It is grave. You must inform Beijing that we need as many forces as possible, as quickly as possible."

Commissioner Zhou knew this could not continue. He had to bring some sense to the situation. "Commissioner, what has happened here?"

Lu was shocked. "You do not know? Beijing does not know?"

He was so upset that Commissioner Zhou said gently, "Comrade, please brief me on the situation. From the beginning."

Lu dragged his forearm across his eyes. "Yesterday there was a meeting of the city factory owners. Not mining or energy, just manufacturing. And only exporters at that. Since the war began all container ship traffic has halted. No ships, no factory export orders. And by this morning all the factory owners and managers had disappeared."

Commissioner Zhou had expected to be invited inside the headquarters for the briefing, not receive it outside in the darkness. But forgetting that for a moment, he blurted out, "Disappeared? Disappeared where?"

"I assume somewhere with a more favorable climate, Comrade. We shall certainly investigate where the owners fled once we have put down the riots they caused. This morning half the city discovered they were out of work."

Commissioner Zhou still could not understand it. "How could a riot occur so quickly?"

Commissioner Lu was practically spitting the words. "This morning there was a march on the mayor's office, demanding explanations and relief." He shook his head, holding up the hand with the radio as if to signal himself to stop.

"I assume the masses left unsatisfied," said Commissioner Zhou.

"We have been dealing with riot and fire all day long. And with every plea for help to Beijing we have received nothing but words of solidarity. Excuse me, Comrade. Nothing except six policemen who arrive by helicopter, a helicopter which we could have put to good use, with absolutely no idea what is going on."

"There is no doubt Beijing knows, Comrade. You are not aware that at this moment Beijing is also in the grip of an emergency situation. We were not informed of your plight because we have come on a different mission."

"What has happened in Beijing?"

"Major sabotage to transport and the water system. The city is virtually shut down."

"Son of a bitch!" Commissioner Lu blurted out.

"Have you employed strong measures?" Commissioner Zhou asked, using the euphemism for live ammunition.

"Of course. Gas and rubber bullets and water cannon were proven useless this morning."

"And you have not been able to wipe out these nests?"

"Are you serious? Two militia armories were ransacked. We are completely on the defensive. There are close to 100,000 men out of work—more than an army corps. And we have but one division of armed police left in the entire province—a drop of water in the river. We've been able to confine the worst to the southern districts only because the city center is so narrow and easy to defend. And because the streets are blocked. But our men are growing exhausted while the rioters are emboldened. This is why we cry for help."

The more he heard, the less sense it made to Commissioner Zhou. "But what of the local army units?" The Zhangjiakou region was known as "Beijing's northern door." From Mongol times to the present, it was the traditional invasion corridor to Beijing. When the Russians controlled Mongolia during the Cold War and the world's two largest communist powers had been at each other's throats massive underground military installations were constructed in the Zhangjiakou area. It was still a major military training ground.

"What Army units?" Commissioner Lu shouted. "They are gone. To Korea. And now I suspect to Beijing. The Public Security Director and Armed Police commander are endeavoring to hold the situation together. Beijing is deaf to our pleas. One helicopter gunship is all we need. That would break their backs."

In his agitation Lu took a step forward, almost seeming to touch Commissioner Zhou. And this totally un-Chinese action seemed to startle them both. "Do you realize what this means for China? The West will simply buy their goods from some other nations. But we will be left to deal with millions of jobless citizens throughout the country."

Even in the almost nonexistent light Commissioner Zhou could see the fear on his face. All heard it in his voice. And he was sure Lu could see the same on his face, because now he had the same vision of chaos sweeping across China. As Chairman Mao had said: a single spark can start a prairie fire.

They were interrupted by shouting from the adjacent vehicle lot. It was fenced with barbed wire and faced a large garage. Two armored trucks had rolled in and policemen were driving bound men from the backs at bayonet point. The men were run over to the side of the concrete garage, and three sets of headlights snapped on to illuminate the scene. They were forced to their knees facing the wall and two policemen walked down the line, shooting them in the back of the head. They had to pause once to reload. The headlights went off and left the row of fresh corpses in darkness.

The execution seemed to have shifted Commissioner Lu's mood. "Why are you here?" he demanded, as if it had just occurred to him.

"An important American spy is attempting to escape to Mongolia," Commissioner Zhou replied. "We have come to intercept him as he passes through your city."

Commissioner Lu's laughter had the pitch of hysteria to it. "An American spy? *One* spy? Are you serious?"

"This is the highest national priority, Comrade."

"Really? Our highest priority is restoring order to this city, Comrade. And then possibly we will begin to deal with the problem of how the masses will earn their daily rice."

Starvation was the age-old Chinese horror, whose real memory was less than a generation old.

A string of cracks split the air as bullets fired from some distance away passed overhead. Everyone instinctively ducked.

"At least give me a few men," Commissioner Zhou pleaded, aware of how hollow that sounded.

"What, to catch a spy?"

"That is my mission."

"After all I have told you, you will not assist *us*?"

"What can six men do for you? I have my orders. A handful of men."

"Impossible."

"At least a vehicle or two."

"We have none to spare. If you do not wish to join us and offer assistance, then I suggest you fuck off." Commissioner Lu used the term, *qu ni made*, which meant, literally: go to your mother.

With the gunfire from the executions still ringing in his ears and Lu and his men unmistakably close to the edge Commissioner Zhou thought better of any retaliatory language. Nothing gave him better insight into the desperation of the situation than that a provincial would dare to talk to a Beijing official that way.

Lu was halfway down the stone walk back to the headquarters building when he turned on his heels and called out, "Do not worry, Comrade. Your spy will never make it through the rioters."

Commissioner Zhou stood where he was, thinking. He turned to his investigators, who had remained protectively near him. "We seem to have encountered more than the usual difficulties."

There was total silence for a long uncomfortable moment. Then Inspector He laughed very loudly, and all the sergeants felt free to join in.

"Shut up!" some anonymous voice screamed out of the darkness.

Commissioner Zhou ignored it. "I must think. All of you make your way around the building. Have comradely talks with the men here and see if you can get a better idea of the situation. As we know, sergeants always have more information than commissioners."

He could see the sergeants grinning at that. What were their names again? "Spend a few minutes and return to me here. Oh, and take care not to be pressed into any service. I need you."

Inspector He gave his sergeants some additional instructions in a low voice, and they all split up.

Commissioner Zhou took a seat on the dead grass. Zhangjiakou air was nothing but coal smoke in the best of times, so the demise of the grass was not a complete surprise.

Three roads led out of the city, but only one to Mongolia. And that was in the northern part of the city. He flipped open his phone. No cellular service. Either the authorities or the rioters had shut off the electricity. There seemed to be only one solution. But he would wait and see what his investigators were able to discover.

They returned to him together, which meant Inspector He had arranged to debrief them beforehand. Which was merely good initiative. When he was an inspector, he would have done the same thing.

They brought nightmarish tales of disorder. Policemen burned alive by firebombs. Others taken prisoner in the early hours and then, after the rioters had been fired upon, found nailed to the sides of buildings. Moving in to clear areas and being met by accurate automatic fire and even anti-tank grenades.

"The armed police are calling it Iraq," a sergeant reported.

No one knew how many weapons and how much ammunition had been taken from the southern public security sub-stations and the militia armories. Terror tales were told of huge Army weapons stockpiles in unguarded bunkers under the city.

But as far as detailed information the local police knew nothing more than what they had seen with their eyes in the street fighting and the wild rumors passed along with the usual blinding speed.

Commissioner Zhou listened carefully, and said, "It seems clear what we must do. We are trapped here by events—there is no knowing how long. That being the case, there is nothing to do but continue our mission. Inspector He, how do you see it?" The Commissioner knew the sergeants would carry out any plan but volunteer nothing.

"The man..." Captain He stopped. "Forgive me, Comrade Commissioner, but I cannot pronounce his name."

"No matter. The man will be sufficient."

"Thank you. I see it as this. The man will encounter the disorder and return to Beijing. That buys us more time to track him. Or he will attempt to travel through the city regardless. He will succeed, or he will not. If not, we will find some trace of him or his transport eventually. If he does, the highway to Mongolia is where we will find him."

Commissioner Zhou was pleased to hear his own thoughts. "Excellent, Inspector."

One of the sergeants said, "Your pardon, Comrade Commissioner, Comrade Inspector. I was told there is a small police unit stationed on the highway northeast to turn all traffic around, so the coal and ore trucks do not reach the city and become immobilized and a burden on resources."

Commissioner Zhou was just as pleased to hear that. "Well done, Sergeant. Then somewhere between the city and this unit is where we must be. Let us not delay."

"On foot, Comrade Commissioner?" one of the more senior sergeants asked hesitantly.

Commissioner Zhou tried but could not recall his name. And having been informed once, to keep his face he could not ask again. In any case, the plaintive tone amused him. "Thank you for your concern for my feet, Sergeant. But have no fear. As we walk, remain vigilant for available transport."

He pointed the way north and Inspector He organized the formation so they would be spread out and able to react to danger. Not necessarily police tactics, but they had all served the Army as conscripts.

The streets were totally empty. Everyone who owned any kind of vehicle: bicycle, scooter, or car, had somehow removed it from both sight and possible damage. It was eerie.

After they had walked perhaps a half kilometer, Commissioner Zhou told two of the sergeants, "Check that alley."

They carefully stalked down it while the rest covered the street.

When they trotted back the leader reported, "Comrade Commissioner, the mystery is solved. The private vehicles have been driven down the alleys and hidden behind the buildings."

"Excellent," Commissioner Zhou replied. "Did you see two in reasonable condition that can be commandeered in the name of the people?"

Smiling, the sergeant nodded.

There were in fact three cars hidden in a stone courtyard off the alley. The only problem was that it was not clear which buildings the owners lived in. They could spend half the night pounding on doors looking for keys.

Something Commissioner Zhou had no intention of doing. "Inspector He?"

A sergeant smashed a side window with his rifle butt,

then used the same blunt instrument to hammer away at the steering column until the ignition cylinder gave way.

At the sound of the glass shattering faces appeared in nearby windows. But disappeared as soon as they saw the silhouettes of men with rifles.

One car would not start, so they smashed the window on the third.

Commissioner Zhou went in one car with two sergeants, Inspector He the other. In the commissioner's car was the sergeant who had voiced his misgivings about walking. As they drove out of the alley he asked the man, "Better?"

"Much better, Comrade Commissioner," the sergeant replied.

Chapter Twenty-Two

"I KNOW BEING anal has paid off for you so far," Judy Rose said from the back seat as she passed him tear gas grenades. "But as your doctor I'd like to advise you that even the most successful personality traits can easily become pathological."

"Remind me to consult a psychiatrist the next time I tweak my knee," Avakian replied, placing the soda can–sized grenades in the Mercedes cup holders.

"Touché," she replied.

"If for some reason we need to change vehicles there may not be time to pack a leisurely bag. So each of us having one ready to go with food, water, and money isn't such a bad idea, is it?"

"It'll never work," she said in her Eeyore voice.

Once again, Avakian had to grin in spite of himself.

She climbed back over the seat and thumped her bank heist bag down on the floor. "You want to cut up the loot now, Clyde?"

"That's okay, Bonnie. You hang onto it. If I have to get the rifle out of my bag in a hurry, I'd just as soon a shower of loose bills didn't come flying out along with it. By the way, buckle up. Safety first."

"Yeah, that's one rule we've been following religiously," she snorted, clicking her seatbelt. "You know, just to totally change the subject, I keep thinking I'm still carrying around a sense memory of those Beijing manholes. But it's your bag."

"Which is disturbing," Avakian conceded. "But it's the only thing my rifle fits in."

"You always run into that with accessories."

Every exit they passed had a military police jeep sitting on it. Which kept the right lane mostly clear. Occasionally they ran up behind a scofflaw trying to get over on the system. Avakian enjoyed driving up close, hitting the lights and siren, and watching them swerve into the breakdown lane trying to get out of the way. Once when they were in a section of expressway without a breakdown lane the violator sent up sparks scraping the guardrail.

After they cleared the far suburbs the traffic jam largely disappeared. Few seemed to be traveling north tonight, though the lanes on the other side heading into Beijing were still packed. And the open emergency lane was full of military trucks.

A bit farther on they did come up on a military convoy that couldn't match their speed. But Avakian gladly settled in behind them, pleased to have the camouflage. The trucks turned off at the Changping exit right after the Ming Tombs.

The expressway went from three lanes to two as they climbed into mountains.

At Badaling, 60 kilometers from Beijing, the road went right through a gate in the Great Wall of China.

"Never got a chance to see it," Judy said sadly. "I was going to wait until after the competition. And now it's dark."

"Don't think of it as a missed opportunity," Avakian urged. "Think of it as a big honking stone wall you don't have to climb now."

"You always know the right thing to say."

"I have my moments."

Once through the wall the road turned more sharply northwest and became the Jingzhang Expressway. At the changeover there was the Beijing City Limits Toll Gate. Plenty of police checking vehicles, and MPs backing them up. Avakian turned on the flashing blues, cut through the backed-up line of traffic, moved into the open lane, and switched the lights off. Two cops in reflective vests were on either side of the toll lane. They had a military van stopped and were checking the driver's papers.

That wasn't good. Avakian took out the pistol and laid it on his lap. "Remember," he said. "If we have to bail out don't forget your bag. And if there's any shooting duck down below the window."

Judy didn't say anything, but he could hear her breathing hard.

He pulled in behind the van. One cop looked up, saw the plate, and said something across the hood. His partner handed back the driver's papers and impatiently waved him along. The van driver, probably nervous, took his time getting it into gear and the cop pounded on the roof with his fist.

The van shuddered through the gears and Avakian moved up. Both cops waved him through.

As they cleared the gate, Judy let out a breath she didn't know she'd been holding. "Are you sure I can't write the general a thank you note, even if he is a tool?"

"We'll send him a postcard," Avakian said, trying to steady out his own breathing.

After they passed the first exit, at Donghuayuan, a bridge rose out of the darkness ahead. On the way up it they were enclosed in mist. Faced with the problem of the proposed expressway being blocked by the large expanse of Guanting Reservoir, along with an ever-increasing onslaught of traffic and the deadline for the 2008 Olympics, the Chinese had pragmatically decided to put up a bridge right across the water. All that extra economic boom cash didn't hurt.

Avakian turned on his high beams, but they couldn't cut the night mist coming off the water.

"Very creepy," Judy said.

Avakian was thinking of a witty quip to that when lights loomed up out of the fog right in front of him. He yanked the wheel hard left to avoid the car lying on its side and felt his right wheels leaving the ground.

A little yelp from Judy. Easy now, Avakian told himself. He got off the gas, fought the impulse to step on the brake, and eased the wheel back right.

The tires squealed but he made it because there was no other traffic to contest his little journey across the lanes. More deep breaths to try and quiet that pounding in his chest. "Sorry, buddy, no good Samaritan tonight," he muttered.

"Jeez," Judy exclaimed.

"I was probably going too fast for conditions," he said.

"Hey, I thought it was some kind of sign," she said. "You don't often see taillights stacked up on top of each other. Did you notice the other wreck next to it?"

"No, I think I missed it in all the excitement."

"I think that was the first, and the guy who flipped did what you did."

"I'm not used to SUV's. These things really will roll on you, won't they?"

"That was two," Judy said. "My mom always used to say bad stuff comes in threes."

"Just what I needed to hear. Thanks."

Despite the bad joss, things calmed down after that. At every change of jurisdiction there was a toll booth, but they were waved right through.

However, when they approached Exit 5, the interchange with the Xuanda Expressway, a blinking arrow directed traffic to the right. And a mile farther a line of stopped traffic in the right lane.

Avakian stayed in the left. "We'll keep portraying the arrogant general," he said, to forestall any debate.

Now traffic cones showed up in the lane divide. And more arrows.

Police lights flashing up ahead. Avakian turned his on. Two cruisers were parked on the highway, directing all traffic onto the exit. There was just enough room for him to get by on the left. He turned on the siren. As he reached the cruisers a cop came running across the highway, waving his flashlight.

Avakian, still at speed, blew past them onto the empty highway. He kept one eye on the rearview mirror, but neither of the cruisers gave chase.

"Ah…?" Judy said.

"Go ahead."

"What if the road's out, or there's an accident?"

"I'll go 4-wheeling overland if I have to. Or I'll turn around and come back. But I'm not getting stuck in a traffic jam on some detour I know nothing about with signs I can't read. No way."

"Fair enough," Judy said. "Those cops seemed pretty excited."

"Cops are always like that when you break the rules."

"That must have been our number three," she said.

"We're almost in Zhangjiakou, which is the biggest city around. If we can just get into the city, even if there is some kind of construction tie-up, we'll be able to make it around. Better be ready with the map."

Judy began thumbing through his English-Chinese road atlas. "How do you spell that?"

"Z…h…a…n…g…j…i…a…k…o…u."

"Okay, found it." She checked the distance scale on the map. "A million people in that? It's about the size of my hometown."

"A million people live in the area around it," said

Avakian. "I seem to recall that the actual downtown has less than twenty thousand."

Mountains were looming up on all sides of them. And city signs now made regular appearances.

The road's in pretty good shape," Judy said. "Why haven't we seen any accidents or construction?"

"You're reading my mind," Avakian replied.

The highway was now paralleling railroad tracks on the left. It was kind of creepy being the only car on the road. Avakian had to keep reminding himself not to let the old imagination run wild, but those bad feelings just kept coming.

They went over a little rise and at the top gained a good view of the area up ahead. Everything was black. It was like a line drawn right down the middle of the land-scape, light on one side and dark on the other. No street-lights, no lights in windows.

"Power failure?" said Judy. "Maybe that's why they closed the highway?"

"Could be."

Then the breakdown lane was filled with vehicles. Showing no lights at all, and apparently no occupants. They seemed to be abandoned. This was really getting weird. He didn't say that out loud, of course. No sense in making Judy nervous.

Judy was thinking it was even creepier than the foggy bridge. An abandoned vehicle or two wasn't an unusual sight on a highway, but she'd counted over twenty of them so far. Something wasn't right. She didn't want to mention it to Pete, though. He had enough on his hands driving. Great, look at that. "More fog up ahead," she said.

Avakian leaned his head closer to the windshield. That wasn't fog. He brought his window down and the blast of cool night air provided the answer. "That's smoke. There's a fire around here somewhere. Pretty big one, too."

"That must be why the power's out and everything's shut down."

"Maybe," he said noncommittally.

But he did slow down. They were now getting the usual view of a city's outskirts. Warehouses, more development, a greater building density every mile. Superficially everything *looked* right, except for the power outage, but it wasn't the China he knew. Where unless you locked yourself in a room you were never alone, always surrounded by masses of people. He didn't think a blackout would make that any different. Driving down that highway was like being in one of those 1950's nuclear war movies, where the wind blew papers on deserted streets in a totally empty city.

"This just isn't right," he said.

"Thank God someone said that out loud," said Judy. "What do you think is going on?"

"If I had the faintest idea, believe me, I'd share it with you."

"You think we should keep going?"

"I don't see any alternative. But I hate doing something because I can't think of anything better."

Now the breakdown lane was a solid mass of abandoned vehicles. And they were right at the edge of the city proper.

Judy said, "Pete, there's a whole bunch of people off to the side of the road."

Avakian speeded up. The highway narrowed a bit and curved as they came around the bank there was a crowd of people right in the middle of the road.

Avakian wasn't stopping to see what was going on. He turned on the flashing blue lights.

It was like setting off an explosion.

A barrage of rocks came raining down on the Mercedes, one skipping across the windshield and cracking it lengthwise.

Flinching and involuntarily shutting his eyes at the

impact, Avakian just as instinctively floored the gas pedal and locked his elbows tight against his body to keep the wheel straight no matter what.

The engine roared and the SUV lurched forward. His next move was to kill the headlights. He could do that without taking a hand off the wheel, but he didn't want to reach down. "Shut off the flashing lights!" he yelled to Judy.

He didn't see her do it, but the lights went off and road went black. The cargo window on his side exploded, and a flash of light appeared on the right.

The Molotov cocktail hit Judy's side with a crack of glass and a whoosh of flame.

Judy yelled, "Oh shit! Shit, SHIT, SHIT!"

Avakian grabbed the back of her head and pushed her down.

The crowd parted as they sped through, but it was wishful thinking to imagine everyone hadn't bent down to pick up a rock reload.

Avakian had his head so low he could just see over the dash, which saved his life when his window blew out in a shower of glass and the projectile skimmed over his head. Then one young *bravo* darted out in front of them and something very large punched through the center of the windshield and passed between them into the back seat. A second after the rock the shuddering boom of a frontal impact as the thrower didn't get clear in time.

When Avakian got his eyes open again and his head up, he had to lean over because the windshield was so cracked it was opaque and he could only see through the open hole. His death grip on the steering wheel had kept them more or less in a straight line. There was hardly a piece of glass left on the vehicle. The wind was whipping in from everywhere, but no fire followed it inside—the Molotov cocktail had burned itself out. A metal car body wasn't easy to set fire to, and whoever made the cocktail had used only gas and added nothing to thicken it and make it stick to the target.

Now they were past the mob and still moving Avakian allowed himself some faint hope that they might make it.

Until he saw more people up ahead, and a roadblock made from a couple of vehicle hulks piled up with furniture and who knew what other junk.

All this happened in a span of literally seconds because his right foot was still on the floorboard, and they were approaching 90 miles per hour.

Off to his left the unmistakable white blossom of an AK-47 muzzle blast, and the equally unmistakable sound of bullets breaking the sound barrier. All he could do was steer for the junction of the two hulks and hope German engineering was up to the challenge. He grabbed Judy's shoulder and yanked her back upright against the seat in preparation for the impact. As the roadblock came up, he tried but failed to keep his eyes open.

The Mercedes hit the barricade like a cannonball, and that was exactly what it looked, sounded, and felt like. Roadblocks generally worked because most people balked at driving their cars into them, but unless they were made out of concrete or steel rails, they weren't going to stop an SUV going flat out. But it wasn't going to do the SUV any good either. Force equals mass times acceleration squared.

Pieces of everything from the roadblock blew out like fragmentation. The airbags all deployed, and there were a lot of airbags in a Mercedes. The front end buckled but it punched through the block and kept going.

When the Mercedes finally came to rest and Avakian opened his eyes they were nearly 200 yards farther down the road. And as a rebuke to the man who didn't believe in luck the SUV was sitting sideways in the street pointing directly at a very narrow alley.

Stunned and deafened, Avakian had absolutely no

idea whether the engine was running or not but put his foot back on the gas anyway.

Incredibly, the Mercedes shuddered forward. But there were no longer any tires, and shudder was all the wounded SUV did, the rims screaming on the road and throwing up showers of sparks. This only slightly masked the sound of an engine that was not long for the world. The axle was definitely dead, and it took nearly a complete turn of the wheel to keep it lurching in a relatively straight line.

Avakian got it into the alley entrance only because that happened to be the direction the vehicle was moving anyway. The body scraped against the wall.

They were not going any farther and he was thinking about how long it took to run 200 yards. He twirled the wheel three full revolutions and managed to wedge the Mercedes sideways against the walls of both buildings.

He popped his seatbelt and hopped up with both knees on his seat, ramming his shoulder against the windshield. It came out in flapping pieces that he punched onto the hood.

Releasing Judy's seatbelt and without checking her physical condition in any way he lifted her up and threw her through the open windshield. Followed by his bag.

As he bent down to grab hers, he noticed the bizarre sight of the tear gas grenades still retained securely in the cup holders. He yanked out his pistol, leaned between the seats, and fired four rounds into the gas cans in the back. On his way out through the windshield opening he grabbed two grenades.

Rolling off the hood there was Judy standing in the alley, holding both bags, apparently in traveling condition. He pulled the pin on a grenade and whipped it into the back of the Mercedes.

A tear gas grenade was nothing more than a container filled with CS chemical powder, the irritant agent, mixed with a pyrotechnic that when burned produced an aerosol. And CS burned hot. So when the ignition charge in the grenade set fire to the CS powder, it also set fire to the gasoline Avakian had released to be vaporized.

When the two-second delay went off there was a loud whoosh and the alley lit up.

Avakian grabbed his bag from Judy and Judy by the arm and they ran. He'd heard shouting on the other side of the Mercedes just before one of the gas cans inside blew up and drowned out every other sound.

They ran down the alley until stopped by a crumbling old brick wall. Slinging the duffel bag over his back, Avakian bent down and slapped Judy's knee. She lifted her leg up. He got his cupped hands under her foot and launched her over the wall. His best jump got one hand over the top but that was enough with adrenaline giving him the strength of many.

Once again Judy was waiting for him on the other side. "You okay?" he whispered, putting a finger to his lips.

She nodded and turned toward the opening into the next street.

Avakian grabbed her arm. He didn't think running out that end would be such a great idea. On this part of the alley there was a break in the building walls on one side, covered by a short section of rickety wooden fence. He pulled himself up for a look. Another smaller alley along the back of a row of houses. Not bad. He dropped back down and gave her another boost up.

Staying put wasn't an option. Your perfect hiding place was a joke to someone who knew every rock and junk pile in the neighborhood. On the other side, he paused only to draw the rifle from his bag.

"Watch where you step and stay right behind me," he whispered in her ear. She nodded again. Scared shitless but still standing tall. Quite a woman.

Nothing was blacker than an urban landscape with all

the lights out. Avakian picked his way carefully along the alley. This was not the time to kick a garbage can. A couple of gunshots rang out nearby, and someone was running down the alley they'd just left. The shouting all around them made him wish he'd studied Mandarin a little harder.

A substantial explosion from the direction of the Mercedes caused him to instinctively drop to the ground. It took a second before he realized it was the leftover bombs in his toolbox. More running feet on the street on the other side of the house.

At the end of that alley a narrow little walkway led out to the street. Avakian crept down it cautiously. He could hear people talking inside the house and didn't need to speak Chinese to recognize terrified when he heard it. Join the club, folks.

He dropped to his stomach to peek out into the street. No moon, no stars, no lights—he could barely see a thing. But if he couldn't, they couldn't either. He could hear, though. Young men and teenagers running up and down, yelling like it was Halloween. Whooping it up because they could do whatever they wanted and no one seemed about to stop them. A few hundred yards down was another roadblock, which he could see only because someone had thrown some tires on it and set them afire.

It would be nice to know what was going on. Not a cop in sight. Definitely not the China he knew. Normally anybody who pulled this kind of shit had the whole weight of authority drop down and carpet-bomb them. Maybe it was the power blackout. Those had a way of bringing out the beast.

Well, they'd just act like part of the mob. He turned to Judy lying next to him and pointed to the alley across the street. "We're going to run," he whispered. "Stop only if I do. Run on the balls of your feet—makes less noise."

She nodded.

They got up on their feet. Avakian touched her arm

and they sprinted across the street. Ducking into the cover of the alley entrance he stopped so he could listen for pursuing feet. Nothing that seemed to be coming in their direction.

There wasn't even the glow of a candle from a single window. Avakian wondered, then realized why. Showing any light or sign of life was like inviting someone to kick down your door to see what you had worth taking.

This alley was open all the way to the next street over, so they were able to go a little faster. As they neared the end there seemed to be a shape moving across the opening. And maybe another along with it. It was so damned dark. Avakian slowed his pace and held out an arm so Judy wouldn't get past him. Okay, the glow of someone's cigarette. There were a few of them.

He kept walking toward them. They knew someone was there—they all turned his way. He smelled the cigarette smoke in the breeze. He could only make out the face of the one that was smoking, which meant they couldn't see his features.

Somebody asked a question in Chinese and Avakian fired the whole 30-round magazine across the width of the alley. Before the sound even stopped echoing off the walls he was in his bag for a fresh magazine, reloaded, and charged right at them.

A move totally unexpected by Judy, who had been ready to retreat and now had to sprint flat out to keep up, high stepping over the groaning bodies littered across the alley like running through the tires in high school gym class.

When Avakian got out into the street someone was running away in the other direction. He didn't fire.

That pause allowed Judy to catch up, and they crossed the street and dashed along the line of houses until they reached the next alley.

More shouting and pounding footsteps, but those were all headed toward the sound of the shooting. It was no place to hang around, but Avakian did go a little slower down that alley to forestall any more surprises.

At the end he paused to take stock. Replaying all their moves in his head from the crash on, he was fairly sure they'd moved in a rough westerly direction. Trying to visualize the map, he remembered that the long avenues seemed to go north-south.

So, he decided to go up this street instead of across, to see if it really was north. These neighborhoods were like someone had grabbed every size and shape of house and shop from a one-room shack to a two-story family, all made out of different varieties of dirty brick, and like a jigsaw puzzle had randomly shoehorned them together within a city block with barely an inch of space in between. He and Judy stayed on the narrow uneven walkways as close to the buildings as possible. No lights meant no shadows, but the darkness was even darker there. And because of that everyone else seemed to prefer running down the middle of the street.

Shop windows broken, doors hanging open, and unwanted goods scattered across the street. Quite a bit of the woodpecker tapping of gunfire in the distance, in the direction they were moving. What the *hell* was going on? Maybe the cops were trying to reestablish control. And maybe it wasn't that easy. It dawned on him that they hadn't just been throwing rocks at the Mercedes, there had been people shooting at them, too. Didn't hit anything, but they were definitely shooting.

Avakian thought he saw another roadblock down the street. And where there was a roadblock there would be people. Wandering around aimlessly all night long wasn't going to cut it. He had to find out what was going on. Preferably without getting killed in the process.

The only solution seemed to be to find some high ground with a view to the north. Not the highest ground, though. That was bound to have someone already on it.

Since a hill or patch of open ground apparently did

not exist in that urban landscape, it would have to be a building. No office or apartment buildings, at least in this part of town. Four stories was a skyscraper.

Finding one wasn't the problem. Getting up it was. The Chinese were not big on safety equipment like fire escapes. And knocking on doors during the current state of emergency didn't promise a warm welcome.

Standing next to him in the darkness, watching his face, Judy realized she'd never appreciated the incredible strain he'd been under these past few days. All she'd had to do was play follow the leader and be scared to death while he made a continuous series of split-second life or death decisions that made surgery pale by comparison. Easy to overlook because he rarely showed it, cracking jokes instead of lashing out the way anyone else would have. At least life or death surgical decisions were made in a clean cool operating theater with plenty of help and consultation. The surgical team wasn't wondering if they'd live through the next minute.

And the man moved like a leopard. If it had been up to her, she'd still be curled up in the bottom of the Mercedes back in that street, waiting for the angry mob to pry them out and tear them to pieces. And if Pete had been anyone else, he might have left her there while he saved himself.

Well, if she couldn't shoot people at least she'd do what she could for him. She cupped her hand under his chin, and he jumped a little in surprise. But he let her turn his head and she leaned over and kissed him.

Startled, Avakian put his free arm around her and kissed her back. That really punched through his crust and made him very emotional. He kissed her again and whispered in her ear, "Thank you." But before he got too maudlin, he dropped his hand down and gave her ass a squeeze.

In return she gave him an affectionate grope, and if

she hadn't been kissing him at the same time, he might have made a noise.

"There's no crying in baseball," he whispered in her ear. "And there's no making out in combat."

In response to that she groped him a little more lasciviously.

"Actually, it's more of a recommendation than a rule," he whispered. "But we have to keep moving. I'm going to find the top of a building where we can look things over."

They continued down the street, turning in at the next alley because Avakian did not want to get anywhere near that roadblock.

The problem was that this alley turned into a labyrinth of four different zigzag turns as it followed the walls of four different houses, none built in anything resembling a straight line. Avakian even had to retrace his steps once when they ran into a dead end. He emerged onto the next street frustrated and pissed off and had to remind himself to take a few deep breaths and not let it make him careless.

Maybe a mile to the north—it was hard to judge distance at night—three parachute flares popped over the rooftops. Followed by a furious exchange of gunfire. Someone was making a move, Avakian thought.

More running feet on the pavement and he pulled Judy into a doorway, squeezing her into the corner behind him. He kept the rifle across his body so as not to show any silhouette. Shit, it sounded like a lot of people coming. He turned his head so his eyes wouldn't shine if they had lights. The feet grew louder, and about twenty ran by, panting loudly, heading in the direction of the flares.

Avakian didn't want to go in the same direction they were, but also didn't feel he had any choice.

Just as well, because on the next block it seemed he'd found what he needed. A little shack that was some kind of garage or workshop, butted up against a single-story house that was just a little higher. And next door two- and three-story buildings right down the line, just like a stairway.

He checked around the back to make sure he wasn't walking into anything. Someone had been busting up wood crates for firewood, and there were a couple of intact ones next to the pile of pieces. He took the sturdiest and set it against the wall of the shack.

Handing Judy his duffel bag, he gingerly put a little weight in the box to test both its stability and the noise factor. Stepping up on it he carefully placed the rifle on the roof and made sure it wouldn't slide before releasing it.

With his back to the wall, he got a good grip on the overhang. Pulling himself up, he bent at the waist, kicking his legs up over his head while letting his head swing down until his feet were pointing up at the sky and he was looking at the ground. The momentum of the swing put him stomach-down on the roof.

He wiggled back a bit, so a little less body was dangling over the eave. He reached down, and Judy handed him the duffel bag and her shoulder bag. Grabbing her wrists, he lifted her up until her upper body was draped over the edge of the roof, grabbed her belt with one hand, and pulled her over.

Slinging the rifle and duffel bag he walked across the roof peak, which sagged alarmingly under his weight. Yes, the next one was within reach and had a very shallow peak. He didn't even have to drop the duffel bag.

But he did on the one after that. He took a little run at it and caught the overhang, dangling in mid-air until he swung his leg up and hooked a heel over the edge.

When he rolled onto it and looked down there was Judy eyeing him dubiously. But she held up her arms again.

He was amazed that someone in at least one of the

houses didn't at least yell at them to beat it. But then again it probably wasn't such a great idea to yell at someone walking across your roof during a blackout and riot. Better to hope they just went away.

The highest building had a flat roof, and as they walked across it to find a good vantage point something occurred to him. He leaned over to put his mouth next to her ear. "I just remembered you once told me you didn't like heights. Sorry about that."

She turned her head to look at him and he offered her his ear. "Only trapezes," she whispered back.

Avakian just gave her butt another pat. She was something.

He was pleased to discover that the view was perfect. With only a few taller buildings in the way he could see at least a couple of miles. More when the flares went up.

At least his navigation was correct. They had been heading west and then north. It was too far away to hear, but he could clearly see the tracers going back and forth from at least five pretty good firefights. This displeased him because they followed a jagged line right across the width of the city. The front line of this little conflict. It didn't take a military genius to figure out that the combatants were the citizens of Zhangjiakou on their side and the government on the other. The public reaction to their flashing blue lights more than confirmed that. And where anyone else would just see green tracer bullets flying back and forth, Avakian's more experienced eye told him that the ones going out from their side were all rifle rounds while some of the stuff coming in from the north, judging from the size and spacing between them, was medium and heavy machine-gun. All the flares were being fired from that direction, too.

They were well and truly screwed. Because the 110 Highway was the only way to get to Mongolia. And that left the city in only one place, at the very north. There was no other way to reach it other than somehow making their way through the entire length of the city. But they weren't going to be slipping through the front lines of two sides loaded for bear and shooting anything that moved. Maybe they could find a quiet sector to infiltrate?

Don't be an idiot, he told himself. Even where there wasn't shooting there would be roadblocks and people in the houses on both sides watching like hawks.

It sure would be interesting to know what started this. And whether it was happening elsewhere. Once dictatorships showed a crack in their armor anything could happen.

Get your head off that, he told himself. Start thinking about how to get your ass out of there. If their round eyes and white skin were visible when the sun came up, they were in a world of trouble. How was he going to manage that in what was left of the night?

Break into someone's house and be their uninvited guest until sundown tomorrow? Sure. With all the kids and grandparents and brothers and sisters in the typical Chinese household you were going to control them all for a whole day? Without the neighbors getting wise? No way.

He took some more deep breaths to help himself relax and think clearly. Break it down into manageable pieces. First, he needed an avenue of approach. Then maybe he could figure out *how* to do it.

Judy tapped his arm and passed him a bottle of water. He drank gratefully, having pushed his thirst out of his mind. She offered an energy bar, but he shook his head. He took another drink and sloshed the water around in his mouth to cut the sensation of thirst without having to drink more than they could spare. Wait a minute. He looked from the water bottle in his hand to the landscape across the rooftops to their left. Oh, you saw, Avakian, but you did not *observe*.

Okay, don't get excited now and go off half-cocked. Think it through. Make sure it's doable.

Yeah, it was crazy. And probably suicidal. But it wasn't like there were a ton of other options.

What he'd been looking at was the dark outline of the Sanggan River, that flowed right along the valley floor and therefore right through the entire length of the city.

Very carefully, he committed the terrain to memory. It would be too easy to get turned around in this warren of buildings and alleys. On a whim, he stuck his head over the edge of the roof to see if there might be another way down rather than retracing their steps. Well, that was embarrassing. A metal escape ladder was bolted to the side of the building. So much for a thorough reconnaissance. Good thing Judy didn't have a weapon. She might be tempted to kneecap the guide.

He pointed down at it and opened his hands in the form of a question. She looked down, saw it, gave him a look, and finally nodded.

The ladder passed covered windows with no one looking out and ended about fifteen feet above the ground. They dropped the rest of the way.

There were more people on the streets than before. Some zipping by on scooters with rifles slung across their backs. The rifles were mostly old semi-automatic SKS carbines. Which explained a few things to Avakian, knowing how the Russian and Chinese armies worked. Whenever new equipment came into service, like his Type 95 rifle, it went right to a first-line unit. They in turn passed their old stuff, like the Type 81 modernized AK-47, on to the second line. And so on. Finally, the remaining junk went into storage for wartime reserve or militia use. So, these Korean War-era rifles must have come from militia stockpiles. Interesting.

The ones on foot were traveling back and forth from the front line. Some pushing wheelbarrows or carts filled with stores up and returning with yelling wounded. Unlike the younger kids he'd run into farther back, who mostly carried rocks or Molotov cocktails and only about one in ten had a weapon, nearly all of these were armed.

It meant moving carefully and stopping to hide often as they made their way toward the river. At one point they happened upon a small park that Avakian made a wide detour around. Too open for his taste.

He did some scavenging along the way. Cheap plastic sheeting was ubiquitous in the Third World, used for a million different things. The trick turned out to be finding a good-sized piece that wasn't ripped or full of holes. Clothesline was even easier since dryers were unimaginable luxuries in most of the world. Wire was a little harder but not impossible. Poor people's houses looked like junkyards because if you couldn't afford to buy things you couldn't afford to throw anything out.

They hit the railroad tracks long before Avakian thought they would. Just stuck their heads out of an alley and there they were. City land was too precious to allow for much right of way, and the Western concept of noise mitigation as an urban planning consideration was laughable in China. Recalling the map, he was sure the tracks paralleled the river. And at some points ran right next to it.

His problem was that it was all open area. A street, a fence, a short gravel slope up to the tracks, the railway line, and another slope down. No cover at all. Known in the trade as a linear danger area. A perfect field of fire to shoot at someone.

They said tactics were like opinions—everyone had a different one. His was that you always crossed a danger area at full speed. No creeping around. That also meant running full speed into whatever might be on the opposite side, but so be it.

"Okay," he whispered to Judy. "We're going across as fast as we can. Stick right behind me and don't stop unless I do. If we get shot at just keep running. Your instinct will be to hit the dirt. Do not. Just keep running.

Stay low going over the tracks. And don't get in front of me in case I need to shoot. Questions?"

Judy shook her head. That was the longest lecture of the evening, which meant they were about to do something particularly dangerous. Okay, Judy. Run. Don't stop. Stay behind him. Stay low. Don't hit the dirt. That shouldn't be too hard for a doctor of medicine to remember. Then why did it feel like there were goldfish swimming around inside her cranium? Well, that was probably what happened when you became a blonde.

Avakian held up three fingers. One, two, three, go.

They ran out of the alley, crossed the road, and leaped onto the fence. Avakian dropped down and turned his head to make sure Judy was all right. She landed beside him.

The gravel slope was like running on ball bearings, only noisier, and they even used their hands to claw their way up.

As they gained the top, Judy's legs felt like lead. She tried to step over, but her foot caught on the outside rail and she went down hard. Only her outstretched hands kept her from cracking her head open on the opposite rail.

Avakian heard her fall and turned back. As he bent down to pick her up a bullet broke the sound barrier right above his head. He dropped on top of her, wrapping his arms around her waist. A second shot sounded right between his shoulder and ear with an even louder crack.

With Judy in his arms, he rolled them both over the rail. A clang and a vicious whine as the next bullet hit the rail and ricocheted off. Now they were rolling down the slope, and a final frustrated shot sailed high overhead as they slipped into defilade.

Their downhill roll was halted by the fence on the other side. Avakian kicked up the bottom so Judy could crawl under, digging herself a groove in the dirt like a badger.

They were practically on the bank of the river, and Judy followed as he crawled into a row of stunted riverside trees and brush.

Once inside cover Avakian grabbed her and ran his hands over her body, feeling for wounds because he couldn't see anything in the darkness. No blood. "Are you okay?" he whispered.

"I'm going to have a mother of a bone bruise on my shin," was her whispered reply.

His teeth shone in the dark. "You can check another block on your list of experiences. That was being shot at. Enjoy it?"

"No. I don't want to tell you your business, but shouldn't you have been shooting back at them?"

"That was a sniper with a night scope. No idea where he was."

"Never mind, then."

"You just catch your breath," he whispered.

It was an absolutely perfect spot. Even though it was littered with empty booze bottles and trash of every description. Avakian took the Chinese Army equipment harness from his duffel bag and put it on, filling the pouches with all the remaining rifle magazines. And a few handfuls of cash from her bag that he stuffed into his pockets.

Judy rolled over to watch and almost put her hand on a pile of used hypodermic syringes. Someone's shooting gallery. Eeew.

Laying a sheet of plastic out on the ground, Avakian placed both their bags in the center, folded the plastic over, and rolled everything up like a cigar. One end was twisted shut, folded over, and cinched tightly with clothesline. Gathering the other open end in his fist, he blew into it to fill the package with air. Judging the buoyancy to be correct, he cinched that end also. Then duplicated the process with a second sheet of plastic, though without inflating it with air.

Judy watched fascinated as he wrapped the outside of the plastic roll with more clothesline in diamond hitches, yanking up brush and stuffing it into the rope until it looked like a big pile of brush instead of a tied-up roll of plastic.

He wasn't done. He literally yanked a six-foot sapling with a full spread of leaves right out of the ground and laid it across the camouflaged plastic roll so the leaves hung over one end and the root ball the other. That was when the wire came out and lashed everything together.

"We get underneath the leaves," he whispered, demonstrating. "Hang onto the rope underneath the water and float right down the river and through the city like a piece of debris."

Her first thought was that it actually might work if the summertime depth of the river wasn't too shallow. But there was another factor. "I don't want to be a killjoy, but I'm getting the chemical smell of that river all the way up here."

"Let's look at it this way," Avakian whispered back. "Jumping into the river might take ten years off your life. Not jumping into the river will take all the years off your life."

"Okay, I'm sold. If I said no you were going to leave me here, right?"

"Time's wasting. You ready?"

"Ready as I'll ever be."

"We'll probably get shot at somewhere along the line."

"I'm sorry, but I already checked that block."

"Just remember that a foot of water will stop any bullet. If we do take fire hang onto the raft and go underwater. Do not let go for any reason. Stay bent at the waist and keep your feet pointed downstream so they hit any rocks first. Don't let them dangle down—your foot gets snagged on the bottom rocks and you're in trouble. Other than that, we'll just have to play it by ear."

Judy knew it was even more serious when he deliberately tried to sound casual and optimistic. Well, she'd never been rafting like this before, either. "Let's go."

He held up one finger and crawled to the edge of the bank, spending a few minutes eyeing every inch of the area. Could be another sniper out there. This really sucked. But he couldn't afford to listen to his gut unless his gut gave him some other alternative.

He crawled back to her. They picked up the raft and went over the bank.

The water did smell like a chemical plant. With an added bouquet of sewer for good measure. Judy made a mental note to herself to not swallow a single drop of it.

Four steps into the water and the bottom dropped away, surprising them both. The weight of the tree put the raft almost entirely underwater, with only the twigs from the brush camouflage sticking out.

The water was a little cooler than Avakian had anticipated. A steady current, though not whitewater by any stretch of the imagination. The average width of the river was about three times that of a city avenue.

He could barely see through the leaves, which was exactly what he wanted. If you couldn't see them, they couldn't see you. He had one arm around Judy's waist, grasping her belt, and the other was hanging onto the raft. As long as it didn't start leaking, they were okay.

The water was foul, but not to the extent of his fears. His fears had been formed by tales of the Schuylkill River in Philadelphia back in the 70s, when it was so polluted it occasionally caught fire. It was said that people who fell in would puke for the next three days. The smell was giving him a little headache, but he didn't feel sick.

Judy had managed to concentrate hard and shut her nostrils to the odor. Other than that, the cool water was actually refreshing. She was starting to relax a bit when the tree's root ball, which was leading the way downriver, hit something and the whole raft began to turn around.

They both kicked in the opposite direction and got it straightened out. But the raft was dragging on something. Avakian grabbed the sapling trunk and gave it a hard shake. They were moving faster now so something must have come loose.

Judy sensed the pressure in the water and swung her feet toward it. Her sneaker hit something soft, and she poked her foot at it until she realized it was a human body and kicked it away. God.

Avakian had been oblivious to this, and she did not share the story of her experience. He was just relieved they'd cleared the obstruction.

The railroad tracks disappeared from the right bank and were replaced by a street. Streets ran alongside both banks now. A bridge spanned the river up ahead. The gunfire was really loud, almost immediate. Through the leaves they could see as well as hear the tracers darting overhead. They were getting right into it.

One of the concrete bridge arches loomed up over them. People shouting up on top.

An automatic rifle opened up from there. Avakian and Judy went underwater under the raft, pulling down on it to get it even deeper.

The sound of the bullets punching into the water could be heard just as clearly underwater. Avakian felt a spent round drop against his leg. He was running out of air. The impacts stopped. They must be under the bridge. He still had his arm around Judy's waist, and they came up together.

Under the bridge was as dark as a locked closet. The splashing of the water against the concrete sounded like an echo chamber. Then a vehicle drove overhead and that vibration drowned out everything else.

Their underwater dive had turned the raft to one side. They kicked it back into position.

"Get ready for more when we come out the other end," Avakian whispered.

The only indication was the change in the echo of the splashing, and the darkness becoming a little lighter. And the sound of more laughter from up on the bridge. Weapon actions being cocked. Avakian prepared to take a deep breath.

But an authoritative voice screamed something and there was no more shooting. Probably some lieutenant yelling about wasting ammo, Avakian thought.

There wasn't much time to appreciate the open water. Another bridge was coming up soon. This one was for the railroad.

A flare popped and floated over the water. Right behind it came a stream of slugs that boomed instead of cracked. Heavy machine-gun, Avakian thought, sliding down so only his face was sticking out of the water. Either 12.7mm or 14.5mm. The tracers floated from the right bank to the left and hit something, maybe a building, close enough that they could hear the impacts. Tracers always seemed to be floating slow enough to reach up and catch, until they came close, and the shocking violence of their arrival immediately changed your mind.

By the time they reached the next roadway bridge the mass of the firing was behind them. They sailed under and were within sight of the opening on the other side when they hit something and stopped dead in the water, the impact nearly knocking them off the raft. Hung up. They shook the raft and kicked but it wouldn't budge.

"Got to go forward and take a look," Avakian whispered.

They went hand over hand to the front of the raft. A big pile of debris, brush, and wood was wedged all the way across. They kicked at it, exhausting themselves, but it wouldn't move. No way could they pull the raft over it.

"Don't let go," Avakian whispered. And disappeared.

Judy was left hanging onto the raft with a jet of ice in her stomach. Even if she wanted to follow, she had no idea where he was in the darkness. God.

Avakian paddled down the length of the obstruction until he reached the concrete wall of the bridge arch. It felt like a full-size tree was wedged in there, with every other bit of junk that had floated down the river piled up on it.

Holding onto the tree, he braced his feet against the concrete bridge wall and pushed. It moved a little bit. Coiling himself up tighter, he pushed off with all his power. Barely moving. He got a better angle and did it again. It felt like his gut was going to burst. Maybe rocking it back and forth would work. He didn't have a lot left.

He took a good grip on the trunk, driving himself forward and yanking back. Something cracked and the pile moved. Encouraged, he bounced back and forth without stopping.

Another crack and the logjam broke. The pressure of the water swept everything forward with a rush, and he got pulled along with it. Except where was the raft now that all this crap was moving? More than a little panicked, he let go and swam hard to his left.

Judy felt everything begin to move but there was no Pete. The raft floated out from under the bridge. With her on it alone. God.

One lump of brush looked pretty much like another in total darkness. Avakian kept swimming at a diagonal across the debris field. Now he was out in the open on the river.

Someone on the bridge saw the enormous pile of debris float out and opened up on it.

Judy hunched under the branches and held on to the rope so tightly she lost feeling in her hands. God, God, God.

Avakian dove under as the rounds came in. The current carried him, but he had to come up for air. Pushing up against the surface, he only exposed enough of his face to take a breath. He'd lost her.

The fire was being aimed at the big tree off to this right, so he brought his head up out of the water. He couldn't see a thing.

A flare ignited far upriver and cast just the faintest glow on the water. Sticks, lumber, brush, plastic jugs. Were those leaves? He swam hard at it, a silent side stroke. As he strained in the water it occurred to him that going for a little swim fully clothed with an extra twenty pounds of rifle, pistol, and ammo harness wasn't the swiftest move he'd ever made.

He was getting close, but there was a real question whether he was going to conk out before he reached it because he was swimming slower by the second. It had better be the raft, because otherwise even staying afloat without ditching all his gear was going to be an issue.

The shooters on the bridge walked another few bursts much closer. It was fun to watch the spray as the bullets hit the water.

Avakian dove again, kicking hard but blindly. His head hit wood. He reached out and touched plastic.

Something hit the raft and it swung around. In the grip of the blackest depression of her life, Judy barely felt like moving. Then a hand grabbed her, and she almost screamed in mortal terror before Pete's beautiful bald head bobbed up out of the water beside her.

Avakian tried to get a breath, but her arm was around his neck squeezing like a python and her legs were wrapped in a scissors around his waist. He nearly went under before, thrashing around wildly, he managed to grab the raft. Eyes burning from whatever chemicals were in the water, sputtering for air, and Judy saying in his ear, "Never, ever, EVER do ANYTHING like that again. I swear, I'll kill you with my own hands."

"I believe you," Avakian gasped. "But unless you want to do it now, let me get a little air."

She loosened her grip but continued to whisper, "Never. I mean it…"

Just as relieved, and trembling just as hard as she was, all he could do was hug her back.

It took a while, but he caught his breath and things settled down again.

Avakian had completely lost track of the distance they'd traveled. But he didn't want to take any chances. "Nice and easy," he whispered. "Start kicking this thing toward the left bank. The river branches off to the left somewhere up ahead, and if I remember the map that smaller branch eventually flows alongside the 110 Highway that's our route to Mongolia."

He didn't want anyone who might be watching the river through a night scope to suddenly see a tree start moving diagonally across the water under its own power. So, they kicked periodically and let the current do the rest of the work. Just as well as they were both exhausted. Even though the water wasn't cold it was still enough to pull the heat from their bodies after enough exposure.

They almost missed even seeing it. The road that ran along the left bank ran right over the entrance to the branch in the river, and in the darkness the bridge arch looked like just a continuation of the bank.

Their hiding place under the leaves didn't offer much of a view, so the opening came as a complete surprise. Judy saw it first and signaled him by kicking hard. But a raft made from a tree and bushes didn't exhibit dazzling maneuverability in the water. They were almost past it when one more kick took them into the right line of the current and the water did the rest.

They both hung off the raft, spent. Please, no more logjams, Avakian thought. But they cleared the bridge without any problems.

This new branch was much narrower than the main river channel, about the width of a single city street. And for some reason didn't smell as bad, though Judy thought that was because her senses were now permanently damaged.

They let the current drive them, with only an occasional kick to keep the raft straight. They didn't have the strength for anything else.

The branch flowed under three more bridges. Avakian kept checking his watch. They were going to have to get out of the water soon, destination or not. At least they'd have an extra half hour or so of darkness after sunrise. It would take the sun that long to pop up over the mountains.

The highway they should have been driving on went through the entire length of the city and then hooked left, heading directly west. China National Highway 110. So, this water also had to make a substantial bend to the left. That would be their spot, right after the bend. Hopefully it would be the right one. And hopefully they'd reach it in time.

Chapter Twenty-Three

"EXCUSE ME, COMRADE COMMISSIONER," said the sergeant behind the wheel. "They say they have control over the northern part of the city. But control can mean many things in such a complex situation."

"Yes, I also assumed they were lying," said Commissioner Zhou. "And I share your concern. We must be on our guard. But at the moment I am more concerned about being shot by our own nervous forces than by bad elements. I will be surprised if there is not a roadblock on the bridge ahead, so proceed cautiously."

There were actually two anti-riot vehicles blocking the bridge. Land Rover-type vehicles but with armored bodies. As they drove up, they were caught in the beams of two searchlights. An amplified voice ordered, "Halt!"

The sergeant stopped the car.

Commissioner Zhou said, "Do not show your weapons." He opened his door and stepped out with his hands over his head, holding his credentials. Walking forward he kept his head turned to one side against the blinding light.

Armed police guards with rifles trained upon him were in the top hatches of each vehicle. Commissioner

Zhou hoped that the sight of his armored vest reassured them.

A voice commanded, "Step forward."

An armed police lieutenant appeared from between the vehicles. "Identify yourself."

"Commissioner Zhou Deming of the Ministry of Public Security."

The lieutenant tightened up a bit and said, in a much more respectful tone, "Show your credentials."

Commissioner Zhou passed them over.

The lieutenant held them up to the searchlight and then saluted. "My apologies, Comrade Commissioner. Lieutenant Mao of the People's Armed Police."

"What is the situation ahead?" Commissioner Zhou asked.

"What is your destination, Comrade Commissioner?"

"The 110 Highway."

"You will find one more checkpoint, Comrade Commissioner. And the Public Security station just before you leave the city."

"Radio ahead and inform both of our arrival."

"As you order, Comrade Commissioner."

"Will we encounter trouble on the road?"

"More thieves and criminal opportunists than rioters, Comrade Commissioner. But be cautious. Since you are not traveling in an official vehicle, they may attempt to stop you and steal it. I assume you are well armed?"

"Thank you for your concern, Lieutenant. Is there anything else we should know?"

"Continue straight ahead as you cross the bridge, Comrade Commissioner. A right turn would lead you to the city and party offices. There are many troops there, and they have orders to shoot on sight."

Of course, they did. "The vehicle behind is also with me."

"Yes, Comrade Commissioner." The lieutenant

dropped his voice. "Comrade Commissioner, is it permissible to tell me what is happening?"

Commissioner Zhou did not wish to spread alarm. "All is well, Lieutenant. Be resolute before your men, perform your duties, and all will continue to be well."

The lieutenant saluted. "Yes, Comrade Commissioner."

Commissioner Zhou returned to his car.

The lieutenant gave a hand signal and the two riot vehicles backed up to open a space. The cars passed through, and he signaled the searchlights off and the block restored.

The platoon sergeant sidled up to his officer. "Comrade Lieutenant, what did he say?"

"It is very bad," Lieutenant Mao replied.

Once over the bridge they followed the lieutenant's directions.

"Comrade Commissioner?" said the sergeant driver, the one who had been so concerned earlier about the possibility of walking. What was his name?

"Yes?"

"We may be out on the highway for some time?"

"It is possible."

"Perhaps we should stop for provisions?"

Commissioner Zhou smiled. He had given this matter no thought at all. Trust a sergeant to deal in practicalities. "If you are able to find a shop open for business you have my permission to stop."

The lieutenant had called ahead, because they were waved right through the next checkpoint. Nearing the city outskirts they saw a light up ahead, an oasis in the darkness, with a column of trucks parked on each side of the road.

"It seems someone is open for business," said Commissioner Zhou.

A small store with a large clientele. Men were sitting on the steps and all across the ground in front, drinking beer and playing cards by the light shining through the windows.

The sergeants took their rifles.

Commissioner Zhou replied to Inspector He's questioning look with, "The sergeants felt we needed provisions."

Inspector He nodded. And did not sling his rifle. Even outside there was a sullen drunken atmosphere that the policemen picked up on instantly.

At least four small generators were hammering away at the side of the building. The electric cables ran in through a window.

The inside was even more crowded. Between the shelves and the drinkers there was hardly a clear space on the floor to place one's foot. The loud talk all shut off as soon as the policemen stepped inside. A fan spun furiously without making any headway against the cigarette smoke and body heat. Jangling pop music was being played too loudly from a too-small speaker.

At Commissioner Zhou's nod two of the sergeants began shopping. The rest spread out and watched the crowd.

The proprietor was a mousy little man who seemed torn between abject terror of his customers and the windfall he was experiencing.

"Good business?" said Commissioner Zhou.

The man shrugged.

A door opened and a middle-aged woman, obviously his wife, appeared from the back room carrying a crate of beer. A chubby dynamo, all smiles and perpetual motion. Every store seemed to have one. "Good evening, good evening!" she shouted at Commissioner Zhou.

"Good evening, Mother," he replied, bowing. "You are busy tonight."

"Busy?" she exclaimed happily. "We have never seen such business." She walked the crate around the room to see who might need a fresh bottle.

Commissioner Zhou did not doubt it, from the way her husband was glaring at her. With power and refrigeration and traffic unable to enter the city their fortune seemed at least temporarily assured.

A man stuck head through the front door, yelling, "Hey, we've got some more!" The words choked off when he saw the policemen.

Commissioner Zhou leaned over to look through the open doorway. A small pickup truck loaded with beer crates and other goods.

The wife took charge of the situation, grabbing the man by the arm and dragging him out. "Take your delivery to the back," she sang, still smiling at Commissioner Zhou. "All deliveries in the back."

"It seems your supply chain is still functioning," Commissioner Zhou said to the proprietor. "I congratulate you." Buy beer from looters at cut rate—sell it at full price or more. A fine business. Though even in normal times, half the stock of any small grocery was stolen goods.

"He's an honest man!" an angry voice shouted, shocking everyone in the store. A young truck driver, barely out of his teens, staggered to his feet while his friends plucked at his trouser legs, trying to stop him. Heedlessly drunk. "He could charge us triple but doesn't!" The boy stopped as if he'd forgotten what he wanted to say next. So, he swayed back and forth in silent defiance.

He would lose consciousness soon, Commissioner's Zhou's experienced eye predicted. Big mouth, no threat.

The sergeants had finished their shopping and he was after bigger game. "How much?" he said to the proprietor.

The reply came as a question. "Two hundred RMB?"

Commissioner Zhou opened his notebook and wrote out a voucher for the amount. Placing it on the counter, he took out his official signature seal and put his chop on the document. The proprietor gazed at it mournfully. "You may redeem this at any Public Security office."

"If there is a Public Security office tomorrow!" the young truck driver shouted, surprising everyone by coming back to life. "Your time is here. All you cheaters, thieves. Hold up our trucks. Make us wait a week in our cabs to be inspected. Steal our money to let us pass. Every day you have your foot on our neck, and now our day is come. How does it feel, eh? How does it feel? *Choubiaozi*!" Stinking whores.

Everyone else in the store was acting like a Chinese: as if they weren't even there yet hanging on every word.

It was one thing to have more pressing business, quite another to permit loss of *mianzi*, authority face. The sergeants had been waiting for his signal, and all he had to do was glance at them. Two sprang across the room and smashed the truck driver with their rifle butts. They beat him down to the floor while the others covered the room.

No one else moved.

They were particularly thorough, stopping only when the truck driver was bloody and moaning unintelligibly.

Commissioner Zhou pointed to two of the driver's friends. "Pick up our goods and carry them outside. The rest of you remain seated."

The music was still playing, the bouncy beat in complete contrast to the mood in the store. And underneath that the whirring of the fan and the truck driver's monotone moaning. The two sergeants who had administered the beating looked to Commissioner Zhou for guidance. He nodded. They snapped handcuffs on the driver and dragged him out the door. Inspector He and the other sergeants backed out with their rifles leveled.

A crowd had been watching through the windows and parted to let them through, muttering angrily.

Commissioner Zhou said to Inspector He, loud

enough to be heard, "If a single rock is thrown, open fire."

Whispers passed that news along, and everyone began melting away into the darkness.

The supplies were loaded, and the truck driver thrown onto the floor of the car. "We will stop for information at the Public Security station," said Commissioner Zhou. "And leave him in custody there."

They drove off into the darkness, leaving that oasis of light on the road behind them.

Commissioner Zhou anticipated that the station would also be lit by a generator, so perhaps he and his driver paid a little less attention to the roadside because of that. Until Inspector He's car beeped its horn and flashed its lights.

The driver pulled over and the trail car drew even with them. "We have passed the station," Inspector He called out.

"Were there no lights?" Commissioner Zhou shouted through the window across the driver's body.

"No, Comrade Commissioner."

"Lead us back, then. And be cautious."

It was a small office right on the side of the road. They did not stop in front, but on either side.

"Circle the building, quietly, and report to me at Inspector He's vehicle," Commissioner Zhou ordered his sergeants.

They exchanged glances, and the metallic snaps of their rifle safeties coming off could be heard.

When they disappeared along the side of the building, Commissioner Zhou walked casually across the front, toward the other car. There was light inside the building, faint light, but the plastic window blinds had been shut tightly.

"What do you make of it?" he said to Inspector He.

"There was movement inside when you passed,

Comrade Commissioner. This is not as a station should be. Perhaps it has been taken over by rioters?"

Commissioner Zhou was furious at all the effrontery he had witnessed. "Then we cannot drive away and leave it in their hands."

"We are few, Comrade Commissioner. Perhaps we should return to the city for assistance?"

"I believe we will receive none. But we will withdraw if the opposition is too great."

The two sergeants returned from their tour around the building. "Everything as usual outside, Comrade Commissioner. The generator is operating. No sign of any officers inside, but the windows are all blocked."

"Vehicles?" said Commissioner Zhou.

"A patrol car."

One of Inspector He's sergeants was carrying a single-shot riot grenade launcher in addition to his rifle. "Stand by to fire a gas grenade through the window," Commissioner Zhou ordered. "You two, go back and cover the rear. If there is any firing from the front, shoot anyone who runs out." And to the others, "Cover me and be ready with the gas."

He walked across the parking area to the front door. With his back to the wall, and only exposing one arm, he tried to open it. Locked. He pounded on the door. "Open up!"

"Go away or we will shoot," said a quavering voice from inside.

Go away or we will shoot? "Are you police or not?" Commissioner Zhou shouted.

"Go away. Go to the city bureau."

No rioter would say that. "This is Commissioner Zhou of the Ministry. Open the door at once or I will fire gas inside the building." He waved Inspector He and his men over.

The door opened slowly and revealed a sergeant 3rd grade attempting to button up his uniform blouse.

Commissioner Zhou stuck his credentials under the man's nose. "What is happening here?"

"Y…your pardon, Comrade Commissioner."

He pushed his way in. Drunk. The man was stinking drunk. An officer 1st grade was asleep on the floor among empty alcohol bottles.

"Drunk!" Commissioner Zhou shouted. "And *hiding*? During an emergency? Who is in charge here?"

"T…the inspector has gone, Comrade Commissioner." The sergeant had developed a nasty stutter.

"What do you mean, gone? Where?"

"I…I do not know, Comrade Commissioner. He left."

"You mean he deserted his post." Commissioner Zhou turned to Inspector He. "Call the men in back and bring in the prisoner." His attention shifted back to the sergeant. "Is there anyone else here?"

"N…no, Comrade Commissioner."

"You have one patrol car in the back. Is it in operating condition?"

"A…as far as I know, Comrade Commissioner."

"I will be taking it. And roadblock barriers, if you have the proper kit here. Now, are you able to fully understand me?"

"Y…yes, Comrade Commissioner."

"I could have you dismissed and sentenced to 10 years in a labor camp for this. But I will allow you to redeem yourself. Pull yourself together, sober up, clean and reopen this station, and perform your duty. Regain your courage and I will forget this. I will have your inspector and the other deserters shot. Brave police officers are fighting hard in the city. Do you understand?"

"Y…yes, Comrade Commissioner. Thank you, Comrade Commissioner."

"Do not forget what I have said."

They dragged the truck driver in.

"Lock him in a cell," Commissioner Zhou ordered. And to the sergeant, "Charge this man with drunkenness, resisting arrest, and assault on officers. Do you understand?"

"Y…yes, Comrade Commissioner."

"Remember my words," Commissioner Zhou warned. As he turned to leave, he nearly stepped on the officer still snoring away on the floor. "And wake up this drunken fool!"

As they waited in front for the patrol car to be brought around, Commissioner Zhou heard one sergeant whisper to another, "Things are falling apart."

The city and the store had not shaken them, but this had. Police cowering behind the locked doors of their station in fear of mobs. "Listen to me," he said loudly. "It will not fall apart if we do not allow it to fall apart."

Chapter Twenty-Four

THE RIVER SEEMED to come to an end up ahead. Avakian knew that meant a bend. He just didn't know if it was the one he wanted.

As they floated around it and continued downriver, he did see something that pleased him. Highway guardrails. The bank was too high to see the highway, but the metal rails were enough. Still no stars or moon through the smoke overcast, but the sky was beginning to lighten near the horizon. It was time to get out of the river.

"Start kicking for the right bank," he whispered to Judy.

"Are we there yet?" she whispered in a little girl voice.

If she hadn't been there, he knew for sure he wouldn't have felt like smiling at that point in the evening. "I honestly don't know."

It took time to kick the raft out of the main channel and near the bank. Though the feel of finally standing on the solid rocks of the riverbed was incredible. They beached the raft just far enough inland to keep it from moving.

Avakian had his rifle pointed up at the bank, drawing the cocking handle back an inch to retract the bolt, breaking any suction in the chamber and allowing the water to drain from the barrel. Otherwise, it might blow up if he pulled the trigger. Which would be awkward. "I have to see if the coast is clear," he whispered in her ear. "And you have to make sure the raft doesn't float away."

That was absolutely the last thing Judy wanted to hear. The logic might be unassailable, but that wasn't her concern. Being abandoned again was. She shook her head violently.

He opened his hands as if to say: no choice.

She pointed at him: I'm warning you.

He blew her a kiss and disappeared.

She punched the raft in frustration. And the impact caused it to slide back into the water. And she had to grab it and drag it back. And then felt like punching something else.

Avakian glided up the bank, trying not to dislodge any rocks. He poked his head over the top and, as expected, there was a hard surface road. No signs in sight, though. Dammit. Across the road was one building with lights on in the midst of a darkened neighborhood. What could that be? He looked at it from the side, since the rods and cones of the peripheral vision were much more acute at night. Still too far to make out. Maybe he ought to cross the road for a better look.

Firmly in the grip of every worst-case scenario her imagination could come up with, Judy was well on her way to panic. Sitting half out of the river and getting a full appreciation for how much she stank. Literally stank. And just waiting for the sound of gunfire. She wasn't sure if it was the anxiety or the stink that was making her sick to her stomach.

She nearly launched out of the river like a rocket when Pete suddenly appeared right next to her without having made a sound.

He grabbed the raft and pulled it back into the water. A moment later, they were continuing their journey down the river.

"A frigging police station," he whispered. "Would you believe we came out of the water right across the street from a frigging police station?"

She was just glad he hadn't dealt with the frustration by going in there and shooting them all. And was so relieved to see him that the list of grievances she'd been preparing to address evaporated. "So, what now?" As soon as those words came out of her mouth it occurred to her that it would be really embarrassing to know how many times those words had come out of her mouth that night.

"Keep going for another mile or so and try again."

It was probably well under a mile. But he was impatient. "Be right back," he whispered.

She pointed her finger at him again. And once again he shrugged and disappeared.

Judy decided to look at her watch this time. Because his last business trip had seemed like an hour and probably lasted ten minutes. Her watch was dead. So much for waterproof. Maybe all the pollution in the water had eaten it away.

Shit! There he was again. She wished he'd stop doing that. But he'd probably say something about not making noise or whatever. She didn't know how many more frights she could take but was pretty sure there were a few more in store for her down the road.

"We're in business," Avakian whispered. He dragged the raft all the way up onto the bank. With the few slashes of his knife, he removed the rope and opened up the plastic, tossing it all back into the river. No guilt about polluting China. Their bags were a little damp but not soaked. Outstanding.

He went to grab his duffel bag and Judy grabbed his arm. She tilted his head back and flushed out his eyes with a bottle of water from her bag. "Blink," she ordered.

That did feel a little better. He was ready to reciprocate but she took care of herself. She handed him another bottle and two energy bars, sternly pointing both at his mouth and not to touch the bars with his contaminated hands.

Avakian chugged the bottle down and, holding them by the foil wrapping, rammed both bars into his mouth in about twenty seconds. He brushed his hands off on his pants as Judy shook her head.

While she ate, much more slowly, he whispered, "There's a park just a little way down and across the road. Full of trucks. Maybe a hundred. I think they're waiting out whatever's going on. Looks like they had a bonfire and tied one on last night, and a lot of them are sleeping on the grass instead of in their cabs. I found one truck that's ready to be borrowed. Whenever you finish nibbling on that thing."

"Okay, okay," she whispered back.

He got his duffel bag ready to go. Thirty years and trying to get the troops to saddle up and move out hadn't changed one bit. t had taken those two trips up and down the bank to make him realize just how worn out he was.

Though the park was packed with trucks, most of them run up onto the grass, a few latecomers had only been able to find space on the road. Not wanting to miss the party, they'd locked up and left their rides. Something Chinese truck drivers didn't ordinarily do.

Avakian had taken a little extra time to choose his mark because, although Judy had been fantastic so far, he wasn't sure if she was ready for advanced sneaking and peeking.

It was a FAW—all the commercial trucks on the roads were Chinese brands. A six-ton freight carrier, about midsize between an American tractor trailer and a large delivery truck. Wood slats up the sides of the cargo bed and an open top covered by a plastic tarp. It was loaded with scrap steel. The driver must have tried to get into Zhangjiakou and turned back because it was parked

facing west and halfway down a gently sloping
downgrade.

The sun hadn't appeared yet, but it was getting much
too bright for Avakian's taste. "Just walk regular," he
whispered. "Less suspicious."

So, they walked right across the road like regular
pedestrians. Loud snoring was coming from some of the
other trucks. Avakian jumped up on the running board to
check the cab once more. his was not the time for any
surprises.

The auto theft kit was still in the duffel bag with his
rifle, more by oversight than anything else. The door was
easy. The locks were those long up and down latches with
the mushroom heads just like in the good old days.

He opened the door gingerly and ushered Judy in.
She bounced across into the passenger seat, sighing at the
incredible luxury. It was just a dirty fabric-covered foam
seat, but luxury was all a matter of perspective.

Avakian placed his pistol on the dash. If you were
going to fight from a phone booth a pistol was a lot better
than a rifle. "Things might start happening real fast," he
warned her.

The dent puller went into the ignition, but to his utter
frustration took five bangs on the side hammer before the
lock cylinder came out. Shit. Someone had to have heard
that.

Inserting his knife to unlock the steering column, he
cut the wheel to the left, shifted into neutral, and released
the brakes. Nothing. They were parked on a downhill
slope and the frigging truck refused to move. What the
hell? Avakian checked to see if there was another brake
he'd neglected to release. God-dammit. C'mon, c'mon,
he was shouting his internal monologue. Haven't you ever
heard of fucking gravity? Unbelievable. He imagined a
mob of angry truckers closing in on them even then. He
cycled the brakes and was even rocking back and forth in
his seat in an effort get it moving.

The truck moved an inch. Let's go, let's go, Avakian was screaming inside his head, still bouncing in the seat. The truck picked up a little steam and swung to the left, barely missing the bumper of the one parked in front.

"Clear on the right," Judy said helpfully. Except she was still whispering out of habit.

He cut the wheel back over and they were heading down the road, picking up a little speed. The owner hadn't been his height and he couldn't see squat through the side mirrors—a little detail he'd overlooked. "Anyone running after us?" he asked.

Judy stuck her head out the window. "No. And no trucks starting up, either."

"You don't have to whisper anymore."

She was embarrassed. "Sorry."

"Hard habit to break." Deciding not to tempt fate by trying to pop the clutch, he stuck his knife back in the steering column and started the ignition. It roared to life. "How about that?"

Judy was emptying the ashtray out the window. "There are no non-smoking vehicles in China."

"But are you okay with the color?" he asked.

"I'm okay with the color."

It was green. Which was a big color for Chinese trucks, for whatever reason.

"How are you feeling?" he asked.

"A little better since I had some food and water." She was examining her fingertips. "But I'm all pruned up."

"I can't imagine why," he said. "But you're still beautiful."

Hair wet and matted down, clothes soaked, sneakers squishing, smelling like she'd swum through a vat of petrochemicals and then rinsed off in an open sewer. And her smile lit up that dingy truck cab. "What about you?"

"I'm definitely still beautiful."

His droll tone cracked her up. "I mean how do you feel?"

"I've been better. That was the longest night of my life."

"Always nice to know I'm not the only one who feels a certain way. You mean you never did anything like that before?"

He broke his cardinal driving rule by turning his head to stare at her.

She cracked up again, pounding on the dashboard. "Oh, I wish I had a picture of your face just then. But hey, a series of hairbreadth escapes from certain death count as new and interesting experiences, don't they?"

"I'm going to have to say yes on that."

"And that's what's really important. And we're driving instead of floating down a polluted river."

"You know I hate to be negative, but it's still not clear whether we're on the right highway. Or even going in the right direction."

"Where else could we be?"

"In the absence of a road atlas, I'd have to say anywhere in China."

"I forgive your negativity. But you're missing the crucial point here."

"Which is?"

"We're not floating down a polluted river with people shooting at us."

"I concede that point."

Judy immediately started rummaging around the cab. Avakian was always amused by female curiosity. She found a plastic bag that she thought might contain clothing, opened it up and peered in. "Whoa!" she exclaimed, shutting it up and throwing it out the window.

"Do I even want to know?" said Avakian.

"Somebody's dirty clothes that smelled worse than what we have on."

"That's pretty bad."

"Cleared out my sinuses."

But that didn't stop her. A second later, she found a

bottle under the seat. No label, clear liquid. She uncapped it and sniffed cautiously. "It's alcohol, all right. Must not have wanted to share."

"As your spiritual advisor," Avakian said. "I recommend you not try that homebrew unless you want to risk blindness."

"I appreciate your concern for my spiritual needs. But have no fear."

"Don't throw it away, though. We might need to start a fire."

"It's definitely volatile." She tucked the bottle back under the seat.

Her only other discovery was four cartons of domestic cigarettes and a small bag containing an extra pair of shoes with a hole in one sole and a toilet kit with a grubby towel, an encrusted razor with a blade that looked like it was hosting tetanus, and a bar of soap that had originally been white before being smeared with black grease.

Two miles down the road a sign appeared. A highway marker with a 110 in the center. And in Chinese and English, as had been customary so far, it read: *Hohhot 270 km*.

"Well?" Judy demanded.

Avakian shook his head. "Of all the crazy dead reckoning navigation I've ever pulled out of my ass, this has to win the prize." The sense of relief was so profound it felt like every muscle in his body, which had been tensed up for so long he no longer noticed, relaxed all at once.

"I'm going to assume that's good. Are we going to Hohhot?"

"No. About halfway there we take the 206 Highway north. Through Chinese Inner Mongolia and right up to the Mongolian border."

"How long before we get there?"

"Oh, no," said Avakian. "I'm not doing that again.

You remember what happened when I angered the gods the last time."

"Okay," she said. "Then how far?"

"Ballpark estimate? Little over 200 miles."

"Okay, I see what you mean. The last hundred did take us a little longer than we expected."

Chapter Twenty-Five

SUNRISE ONLY MADE the investigators sluggish after the long day in Beijing and a sleepless night in Zhangjiakou.

The road zigzagged as it followed the river and the path of the valley floor. Commissioner Zhou positioned the roadblock directly after a turn so there would be no early warning of its presence. With the river on one side and a grove of substantial trees on the other it would be impossible to drive around.

He had thought about using the vehicles to create a hidden roadblock—only springing out from concealment at the last moment. But he remembered the warning of the lieutenant on the bridge. They were in plainclothes, after all. If someone mistook them for thieves, who had been known to use counterfeit police cars, it might well result in two groups of police shooting at each other. No matter that the sergeant who collected the patrol car had also shown the foresight to obtain a list of the local Public Security and Armed Police radio frequencies. Commissioner Zhou wished he could remember his name.

They set up the block with the marked patrol car across one lane and the plastic police barriers in the other to force approaching vehicles to reduce speed. They had left one of their confiscated civilian vehicles at the station. The other was parked inside the trees.

It was still dark when they did this, and they were prepared for anything. But vigilance relaxed with the passing of the hours. There was no traffic coming from the west into the city. The news had made its way quickly, as it always did in China. No cars leaving the city, but about two trucks every hour. Those with cargos destined beyond Zhangjiakou. Tired of waiting to pass and heading back to begin the very, very long drive to circle around the city.

The first truck had everyone swarming over it. But after the fourth load of coal or dirty sheepskins interest flagged. Commissioner Zhou allowed Inspector He to post two men at a time and allow the others to rest. Though he would not. He spoke with every driver, seeking any sign or rumor of Avakian.

He knew the sergeants, and most likely He, regarded it as a fool's errand. And Commissioner Zhou himself had absolutely no idea how Avakian could possibly make his way through Zhangjiakou. Only that he would.

Once the riots died down and order was restored, he could arrange to have the appropriate forces placed on the road to relieve them of this task. Perhaps a day, no more than two.

He had felt more alert in the darkness. The rising sun was like grit in his eyes. The sergeants had made a fire to brew tea. Perhaps that was what he needed.

———

"I CAN TAKE the wheel if you'd like a break," Judy said.

"I'm just droning along on adrenaline right now," said Avakian. "When we get on the 206 Highway you can spell me for a while. Why don't you take a nap until then?"

"I couldn't sleep right now if you threatened to shoot me."

"How did you know that was going to be my next move?"

"Just an educated guess."

"That's right, you doctors are used to staying up for days at a time, aren't you?"

"When we're young doctors, Pete. And then later we make the young doctors stay up for days at a time. Except when we get the shit scared out of ourselves repeatedly."

"Okay, now which one is this?"

"The third part."

"Scared shitless?"

"Right."

They came around a turn and Avakian saw the white police barriers. "Take the wheel," he said, springing over to her side, continuing to steer with one hand, before she'd fully comprehended what he'd said.

Judy slipped underneath him and grabbed the wheel.

Avakian had the rifle out and was jamming magazines into the crevice in his seat. "Get down low so you can just see over the wheel," he instructed her calmly. "Steer so the wheel is centered in the front tire of that police car. Lock your elbows against your body so the wheel doesn't move. You're going to ram them and continue on down the road." Then he added, "You can step on the gas now."

Judy followed his instructions to the letter.

Avakian leaned his shoulder against the door and braced his left foot against the dash to give himself a solid shooting platform.

The two sergeants held up their hands to signal the truck to stop.

Commissioner Zhou had just been handed a mug of hot black tea and was blowing to cool it.

"Hit the horn," Avakian said.

"Where the hell's the horn?" Judy shouted after a frantic but fruitless search.

"Never mind," he said.

One of the sergeants raised his rifle to fire a warning shot over the top of the truck.

Avakian leaned out the window.

The sergeant did not see him in the glare of the rising sun and fired the warning shot.

Inspector He was dozing in the confiscated civilian car parked amid the trees. The sound of a gunshot woke him with a start.

No precision shooting from a moving truck. Avakian had the selector switch on full auto and, noting the vests, dropped his aim point to the policeman's knees. He held a breath and squeezed the trigger.

Commissioner Zhou dropped his tea and fumbled for his pistol.

The sergeant who fired the warning shot went down under the first burst. His partner ran for cover as bullets kicked up dirt all around him.

Avakian leaned farther out the window and fired three fast six-round bursts at the fleeing target, emptying the magazine. He ducked back into the cab and grabbed a fresh one.

Commissioner Zhou could not believe it. Avakian. Finally confronted by the object of his search, he stared transfixed and forgot he had a pistol in his hand.

Inspector He snatched up his rifle and leaped from the back seat of the car.

Avakian rocked in the full plastic magazine and yanked the charging handle back. He aimed over the hood and put a burst through the windshield of the police car, the only other target he could see. The impact moments away, he pulled himself back into the cab.

Inspector He took up a good kneeling position and aimed for the truck door.

Still following her instructions, Judy had the truck

lined up on the front of the police car. She prepared herself for the collision.

Inspector He opened fire.

The side mirror exploded right in front of Avakian's face, and his thigh felt like he'd gotten the world's worst white-hot bee sting. He yelled in pain and twisted around to see where it had come from. The shooter was kneeling out in the open. Avakian emptied the magazine at him one-handed before the collision threw him up against the dashboard.

The truck hit the front of the police car and spun it like a top. Commissioner Zhou had to dive out of the way to keep from being hit.

Speeding down the road with no apparent mechanical problems, Judy yelled, "How about that?" Receiving no answer, she looked over and saw Pete with a bloody hand clamped to his thigh. She swung the wheel to pull over.

"No, no, no," Avakian yelled. "Keep going!"

He started thrashing around, and Judy wondered how she was ever going to restrain him. Then he settled down, and she saw he had cinched his belt around his thigh above the wound. Quite a feat, doing first aid on yourself after being shot. But she realized, with another jab of ice to her stomach, that he'd probably seen people bleed out before.

"Switch over again," said Avakian. "And you can take a look at this."

He pulled himself back into the driver's seat and she jumped over again. With his right leg extended across the passenger's seat, he was steering with his left hand and working the pedals with his left foot. His right fist was up in the air, grasping the free end of the constricted belt. "The knife is in my right pants pocket."

She pulled it out and opened the blade, and carefully sliced open the seam of his jeans. Definitely a gunshot.

No exit wound. "Give the belt some slack, just a bit," she said.

He followed her instructions, and there was no arterial bleeding. "Okay, tighten it back up."

"There's a first aid kit in that Chinese equipment harness," he mentioned helpfully.

She had to open every pouch until she found the two plastic-wrapped five by seven compresses with the gauze wrappings. But Pete had been swimming through sewage all night long and the wound field was totally contaminated. Who knew when they were going to reach somewhere she could treat him properly? Infection was a certainty. Better to risk tissue damage. She furiously rooted through her bag and then reached under the seat. It was going to be a total insult to orthodoxy. "This is going to hurt."

"It already hurts," he said through gritted teeth.

She poured Chinese moonshine into the wound and over his leg.

"FUUUUCK!" Avakian yelled.

While he was yelling Judy inserted one of her tampons into the bullet hole. placed the battle dressing over that and secured it with the dangling gauze. The femur wasn't broken and thank God no major vessels had been compromised. "Okay, release the belt."

The tampon and dressings were containing the bleeding. He'd lost a bit of blood, but not like some gunshots she'd seen. It would have been much worse if he hadn't stopped it himself so quickly. "There's nothing here to splint it with. Let me back behind the wheel, and don't move too much."

Avakian pulled himself over again, wincing at every bounce. He picked the rifle up off the floorboard and checked the magazine. "I suggest you drive as fast as you can."

Chapter Twenty-Six

COMMISSIONER ZHOU RAN out into the road. The truck had disappeared around the next bend. He burned with shame that he had not even fired his pistol.

One of the sergeants at the roadblock was dead and the other was wounded in the legs and groin. The other pair was attending to him with the patrol car first aid kit.

One glance at this and Commissioner Zhou was running for the patrol car. The front was crushed, and the windshield peppered with bullet holes. Ducking into the front seat, he snatched up the radio handset. Dead.

Furious with himself for not thinking of it before, he flipped his cellphone open. No signal.

Inspector He came panting up. "Comrade Commissioner, I shot at him but do not know if I hit him. It was a white man."

"It was him," said Commissioner Zhou. "Get the car, He."

"Yes, we must get Sergeant Fan to medical attention. He is badly wounded."

"No. Leave one man and tell him to flag down the next passing vehicle."

Inspector He could not believe his ears. "But who knows when that may be? If we take Fan back to the city, we can call forward to arrange for blocks on the highway ahead."

"Who knows what disorders are on the road ahead to prevent this?" Commissioner Zhou shouted. "The man is a demon! If he can get through Zhangjiakou last night, he can get through some halfhearted roadblocks. We must pursue him. Carry out your orders."

Inspector He doggedly stayed put for a moment or two, then turned and ran for the road. He stopped and bent over his wounded sergeant, exchanging a few words before he and one of the surviving investigators headed for the car.

Commissioner Zhou stood out on the road to spur them to action. They left a cloud of dust pulling out of the trees. He got in the back seat, saying, "There is no way that truck can outrun a car. Do not worry. This will be finished soon."

———

"BETTER EASE up on the gas a bit," Avakian said. "Don't want to blow the engine with this heavy load." He was kneeling on the seat with his good leg, keeping an eye on the road behind them through the window.

"We're not going to outrun anything in this," Judy said.

"This is true," he said. "Let's hope that police car isn't in any condition to run until we pick up a new and faster ride."

"But they must have radioed ahead."

"Hey, easy there," he said. "Never expect unfailing efficiency from any bureaucracy. Mountains block radio waves. Riots happen. Shit happens."

"I appreciate you trying and make me feel better. Even though I don't necessarily buy it."

"By the way, you looked real good back there. Didn't Bogart say that to Bacall one time?"

"*The Big Sleep*," Judy said automatically. "Thanks, but after all this time I finally got a chance to work inside my own skill set." She smiled. "I'm only sorry you didn't get shot sooner."

"I'm going to try and take that in the spirit you intended."

"It's probably not the first time it happened to you."

"Actually, it is. It's something I've always worked hard to avoid."

"Hurt bad?"

"Doesn't hurt good. But I'm still here, so it's all good."

"I wish you wouldn't do that."

"Hey, you're always okay as long as you've still got your sense of humor." Oh, shit. He leaned farther out the window to be sure. "We've got company. Looks like they had a plainclothes car we didn't see." He turned around to check the road ahead. "Okay, when we go over the next hill slow down and let me out. Then park down at the bottom. When I wave come back and get me. If anything unfortunate should happen, remember 110 to 206 right to the border. You've been watching me steal cars. The tools are in my bag."

"Are you kidding?" Judy shouted. "I'm not letting you out. You can't hop around on that leg. You shift that bullet you could cut a major vessel and bleed to death."

"Like you said," Avakian pointed out calmly. "We're not outrunning anyone in this truck. You stick to the driving and the medicine, and I'll do the shooting. Let me out on the reverse slope of the hill so they can't see you do it."

She really, really hated when he was logical and reasonable.

As they crested the hill, he opened the door and hopped onto the running board on his good leg. Every movement was like sticking his finger in an electric socket.

He watched the top of the truck to make sure it was out of sight. "Okay, stop."

Judy wasn't used to truck brakes, and almost threw him off. Dangling from the handrail for a moment, he let himself down amid red flashes of pain every time he blinked his eyes. "Go!"

She pulled out, and he hopped all the way across the road, so he'd have a better angle on the driver. Every hop was like an ice pick being stuck into his brain. Reaching the dirt on the other side he dropped to his stomach and crawled to the top.

The pain left him trembling and bathed in cold sweat. Not the best state in which to do some precision shooting. He pulled the last two 30-round magazines from the equipment belt and laid them on the ground close to his hand. Now that he wasn't moving, the pain had subsided. He wiped the sweat off his face with his shirt and concentrated on steadying his breathing. The roadside weeds were high enough for good concealment. They'd be looking for the truck, anyway. He looped the sling around his arm for a good tight firing position, peering through the rear sight aperture at the front sight post and shifting a bit for a better sight picture. When he was moving, he'd been afraid he was going to pass out. But now was as ready as he was ever going to be. A good ambush was like cold-blooded murder. One that went bad meant the ambusher got murdered.

"We will have them on the next hill," said Commissioner Zhou. He was holding the driver's rifle. It had been a long time since he fired one, but it felt comfortable in his hands. They would shoot out the truck tires, surround them, and wait. Perhaps to take Avakian alive once he realized it was hopeless. What an achievement that would be.

———

AVAKIAN REMEMBERED a sergeant major at the Special Warfare School, who had run recon into Cambodia during the Vietnam War, telling them to never get anxious and open fire too soon. If the enemy was going to oblige by running right up onto your front sight post, let them. And all the better since he was low on ammo anyway. He moved the selector switch to single shot.

They were almost to the top of the hill now. Commissioner Zhou leaned over the seat partition in order to see better. With the ground they had gained the truck should be in sight.

The sound was exactly like a rock hitting the windshield. The driver's head snapped back and Commissioner Zhou recoiled as he was sprayed with blood.

Inspector He reached over and grabbed the steering wheel as another round came through the glass and hit him in the breastplate of his vest. The vest stopped the bullet but the force of the impact threw him back and he lost his grip on the wheel. With the driver's foot still on the gas pedal, the car began to swerve off the road. All Inspector He could do was grab the shift lever and throw it into park. The car shuddered and lost speed to the shrill accompaniment of grinding metal. Inspector He pulled the emergency brake.

Commissioner Zhou bent over to pick up his dropped rifle and more bullets came through the windshield.

With the car stopped and the engine still roaring, Inspector He pushed his door open and laid his rifle across the top of the frame to fire.

There he was, Avakian thought. The guy who liked to shoot from out in the open. Hope you have *your* own doctor, motherfucker. The car was less than 30 yards away. Anyone could make that shot.

The bullet caught Inspector He under the chin and blew out the back of his neck, severing his spinal cord and killing him instantly.

Commissioner Zhou spilled out his door onto the ground and scrambled around the back of the car, trying to determine where the gunfire was coming from. Heart pounding, hands shaking. Both his men wounded, perhaps dead.

Avakian wasn't about to hang around all day waiting for a clear shot. He blew out the front tires and the left rear, only the angle of the car preserving the last one, followed by four more rounds through the radiator. Those dinky little 5.7mm bullets weren't going through any engine blocks.

Thinking he was under fire and Avakian advancing on him, Commissioner Zhou leaned his rifle around the bumper and fired rapid bursts to hold him back.

Avakian remained untouched. If they didn't hit you or come close enough to make you duck it was just noise. Only rookies thought everything they heard was going to hit them. The trouble with these sprayers and prayers was that nobody ever told them full auto didn't guarantee anything. You could miss just as easily with ten as one if you didn't sight carefully and concentrate on your shooting. It offended his professionalism. Anyway, it was time to move on.

Commissioner Zhou yanked the charging handle back three times before realizing his magazine was empty. And the rest of the ammunition was with the dead men. But there had not been any more firing. Perhaps he had killed Avakian? He cautiously raised his head above the trunk for a look before pulling it back down.

Too fast for Avakian to make the shot. But he couldn't believe it. Commissioner Zhou. How the hell? They'd been waiting there for him. And that brought with it a whole avalanche of new worries. Well, if he didn't have time to kill him, there was still a little matter of face. "Hey, Commissioner!" he shouted. "You better hitchhike back to Beijing. You're a smart guy but you're no gunfighter."

He turned around and waved to Judy.

Commissioner Zhou had once put his hand on a hot stove as a child. This humiliation burned like that. Avakian waving farewell to him. He pounded his fist on the trunk. Wait. What was that? He stopped pounding. The sound of a truck.

Handling the truck more confidently, Judy swung it around inside the span of the road. Avakian grabbed the handrail and pulled himself in.

"I'm assuming that went well," she said.

"You're not going to believe it," said Avakian.

Commissioner Zhou bolted over to Inspector He's body, pulled a magazine from his pouch, and ran for the top of the hill.

"What am I not going to believe?" said Judy.

Commissioner Zhou reached the top of the hill just as the truck reached the bottom. He fired the whole magazine at it.

Judy automatically hunched down. "Someone's shooting at us."

"Don't worry," Avakian said. "We're out of effective range, with about four tons of steel between us."

"What if they hit a tire?"

"Then we have a flat. Nothing we can do about it right now. He's just trying to get some face back."

"He?"

"I told you you wouldn't believe it," said Avakian. "You know who was on that roadblock? Commissioner Zhou."

"Get out."

"I kid you not."

"But that means…?"

"Yeah, he tracked us all the way from Beijing. And, believe me, at first, I was sweating the load over that. But then I thought about it. A commissioner of police on a roadblock with a handful of cops? Doesn't add up. But so close to the city I'm thinking maybe he had a lot of the same Zhangjiakou problems we did, and this was the best he could do. Not to say he can't call up ahead for more help. Which is all the more reason for us not to dawdle."

"You didn't shoot him." She said it as a statement, not a question.

"Would have, but I didn't get the chance. His car isn't going anywhere. And maybe it's better this way instead of us at each other's throats atop Reichenbach Falls."

"I just totally missed that allusion."

"Sherlock Holmes and Professor Moriarty."

"Ah. But who is which?"

"I've got the doctor as my partner. I think that settles it."

"Yeah, well, we are talking about The Napoleon of Crime, after all. So, I may have some different ideas on that."

Commissioner Zhou threw the rifle onto the road and slumped down beside it. He put his hands over his face as tears came to his eyes.

Chapter Twenty-Seven

SITTING STILL in the truck reduced the pain in Avakian's leg to a dull throb. His exertions had left the battle dressing soaked in blood. Although dazed by fatigue he focused his attention on potential trouble on the road ahead. But soon the absence of stimulation and the droning of the engine put his head back against the seat.

Judy kept glancing over to check on him. He was sound asleep. He needed it. And she was loving driving the truck. Having something to do energized her.

She drove through sunburned brown hills and occasional belts of green trees beside the highway. If you could call it that. It was two lanes, and the other was full of coal trucks. Stopped, in the middle of nowhere, as if they'd somehow heard what was up ahead. The drivers kept sticking their heads out their windows, as if they'd never seen a blonde driving a truck before.

The river swung off, and now the bottom of the slope below the highway held small brown riverbeds, long dried-up.

The road straightened out, but a new problem presented itself. The road signs were exclusively Chinese. It was nerve-wracking to see a blue sign indicating a branch in the highway, and at the end of both arrows were two or three Chinese characters. There was nothing to do but follow the principle of staying on the road you were on.

But Judy experienced yet more panic as a whole succession of signs kept popping up to announce…something. She thought about waking Pete up, for consultation if nothing else. Then over a low rise a sign with the beautiful Arabic numerals 206. It had to be north to Mongolia so she picked the turn after consulting the path of the sun.

That stomach-churning tension of wondering whether you'd taken the right exit reminded her of trips with her family. Her dad always had her read the map, and if she ever had a stroke one day that was going to be the cause. The tension lasted more than a few miles until she was rewarded with a billboard image of smiling industrious Chinese amid waving grass and heavy machinery that read, in small print at the bottom: *Welcome the Inner Mongolia Autonomous Region.* Oh yeah. Thank you, thank you very much. She relaxed and enjoyed the ride for the first time in a long while.

The countryside rolled out to the horizon. Greenish brown grasslands intercut with solid brown trails and, hauntingly alone out in the middle of all the space, single green trees. As if they'd been put there just to make you wonder how the hell that happened.

At first breathtaking but soon monotonous. But the highway had in store one of the strangest things she had ever seen. So strange that at first Judy thought it might be a fatigue-related hallucination. An undulating landscape of nut-brown sand dunes. More dirt dunes than sand dunes, actually. But not dunes in a sea of sand. Dunes in a sea of grass. Lush green grass but lifeless dunes. As if, like the lonely trees before, they'd been plopped down to provide some striking artistic contrast.

She felt a physical pang of sadness as the grasslands became browner and browner as she drove north, finally disappearing altogether. Overgrazing and desertification. A herder's choice was always between many animals and fewer but higher-quality ones. But high-quality animals were too expensive for poor people to capitalize, and where was the high-quality forage they needed going to come from? So, the grass burned away, and the deserts expanded.

At first Judy didn't realize what was approaching. Thinking it had to be incredibly low cloud cover. Then she realized, rolling her window up tight. As soon as she stretched her arm across Pete he awoke with an electric jolt and had the pistol halfway out his holster.

"Whoa. Easy, easy, easy," she said.

Avakian took stock of his surroundings, not to mention the jab of pain whenever he moved.

"Don't shoot the driver," Judy said.

He holstered the pistol. "Sorry." He yawned and stretched his arms. "How long have I been out?"

"We've gone about 150 miles." She reached over again and felt his forehead and face. No fever. Yet.

Avakian's first reaction was anger. They should have ditched this truck by now. That transitioned to deep embarrassment. She'd been taking care of him. "You shouldn't have let me sleep that long."

"Roll your windows up," she said. "There's a sand-storm coming toward us."

Getting his bearings, he saw the desert and the billowing dust cloud. "Are we okay?" Sort of an all-inclusive question.

"We're on the 206 Highway in the Autonomous Region of Inner Mongolia."

"Who says women can't navigate? Not I."

"We were lucky," she said. "The signs were all in Chinese."

He didn't talk about luck. "You must be shattered. Let me take over."

"That's okay. I'm actually less nervous driving. And you may need to shoot someone."

Avakian shook his head. "This close to the border there can't be any more shooting. If it is, it's us being shot."

"That was nice to know. Thanks."

The sandstorm enveloped them. The truck rocked and fine dust blew through gaps in the windows. Judy couldn't even see the surface of the road right beneath the hood. She had to stop.

———

INSPECTOR HE and the driver were dead. The car was ruined. Commissioner Zhou picked He up off the road and placed him in the car. Shifting into neutral, he let it roll down the slope until it was off the road.

Commissioner Zhou could not stay there and look at them. He threw off his vest and began walking back.

Two kilometers down the road a truck appeared around a bend. Commissioner Zhou held up his hand, but the driver gave no sign of slowing down. So, he held up the rifle instead. They stopped for that.

A coal truck. Empty. As always in Chinese trucks, a driver and a co-driver. Both plainly terrified.

He stepped up on the running board and flashed his credentials at the driver. "Ministry of Public Security. I must have a ride to the next town."

"Back to Zhangjiakou?" the driver asked.

Commissioner Zhou had to stop and think. Go back after having not only failed, but lost his men? "No. Take me to Huade."

He walked around the front and opened the door. The co-driver pulled in his feet, as if to make room for him to go behind the seats. Commissioner Zhou stared at him until he got up and went behind the seats himself.

There was no small talk. Chinese did not make small

talk with the police. It could only bring trouble. They drove in silence, Commissioner Zhou watching his cellphone for a signal.

When they passed the shot-up police car the driver looked over at Commissioner Zhou but said nothing. The co-driver cleared his throat as if to speak. The driver grunted loudly. A clear warning, and enough to keep his partner quiet.

When the highway rose and crested a low ridge Commissioner Zhou got a cellphone signal. "Stop the truck." He climbed out so as not to share his business with the two yokels.

He called the Ministry in Beijing, at first having the switchboard connect him with a fellow commissioner in the Bureau of Border Controls and Frontier Inspection. He gave the description of Avakian and his companion Doctor Rose and told them to alert the border post at Erenhot.

Back to the switchboard and the Regional Bureau for the telephone number of that north Zhangjiakou police station. The lines must have been working in that direction, because the same sergeant answered the phone.

"This is Commissioner Zhou. From last night."

The sergeant had sobered up and lost his stammer. "The station is open and alert, Comrade Commissioner!"

"I have an urgent mission for you. Use the vehicle we left in your car park and proceed immediately west on 110 Highway to retrieve an officer wounded by bandits. Approximately ten kilometers from your location. After you have taken this officer for medical treatment return to the highway, twenty kilometers further west. You will find your patrol car with two officers who have been killed. Recover their remains with all honor. Their weapons are in the trunk. Do you understand?"

"At once, Comrade Commissioner."

"Do not fail me. Now give the number of the Bureau at Huade."

A thrashing of papers and the sergeant read out the number. Commissioner Zhou wrote it onto his hand. He broke the connection and dialed it, reaching the Deputy Director at Huade. Providing the description of the two Americans and the truck, he requested that an alert be issued, and a car and driver be placed at his disposal when he arrived. They rarely received requests from Beijing Ministry officials, so he knew there would be a sense of emergency.

Finished for now, he got back on the truck. "Take me to the Public Security Bureau headquarters in Huade as quickly as possible," he told the driver. "And I will no longer trouble you."

There was still a chance. He could not tell the Ministry about his failure and his dead until he had something to balance them.

———

IT WAS an hour before the sandstorm passed through and they were able to continue. Sand had drifted across the highway, in some places an inch or more thick. Avakian opened the door and brushed out as much of the dust as he could. It was in their eyes and mouths and felt like a layer of fine sandpaper on their skin.

Now there were signs for Erenhot.

"That's the border town," Avakian said. "Maybe 30 miles."

"Have you given any thought to how we're going to get across?" Judy asked.

"Only how we're not going to cross. We're not going to present our passports and ask to leave. Other than that, as you know by now, I'm a firm proponent of Occam's Razor."

"The simplest solution is the best."

"Correct."

The only problem with that, which she didn't

mention out loud, was that the simplest solution seemed to involve things like crawling into manholes and floating down rivers that hadn't been the beneficiaries of a clean water act.

———

COMMISSIONER ZHOU FELT himself being shaken. He had fallen asleep.

"Sir," said the driver. "We are at Huade Public Security."

Commissioner Zhou checked his wristwatch. Time kept slipping from his grasp. He started out the door but held up. Taking out his card case, he jotted a few lines on the back of two of his business cards before passing them to the driver and his helper. "If you should ever find yourselves in trouble with the authorities, show this card. If that does not suffice, call the number and I will assist you."

"Thank you, sir," said the driver, bowing deeply. Such a thing was like gold to a Chinese truck driver.

The commissioner entered the headquarters waving his credentials, so the there would be no consternation over his rifle. "I am Commissioner Zhou, from the Ministry," he told the desk sergeant. "Are you aware of the alert I issued?"

"Yes, Comrade Commissioner. The deputy director has ordered it enforced. Inspector Yan of the Criminal Bureau is expecting you."

"Take me to him quickly."

An officer rushed him through the building to the desk of an Inspector 1st Grade who came to attention.

Commissioner Zhou blasted through the preliminaries. "I am Commissioner Zhou from Beijing. Any word on the American spy I am hunting?"

The inspector was slightly rattled by his manner, as most Chinese would be. "Nothing as yet, Comrade

Commissioner. All stations and highway units have been alerted."

All this time wasted to tell him nothing. Avakian was almost certainly long gone. "I require a car and driver to take me to Erenhot. Immediately."

"This is very difficult, Comrade Commissioner. Our resources are limited, and all our units committed."

Always a no before a yes. "This American spy has murdered six Ministry officers. Perhaps more as we waste time here. This is a state emergency, and my mission comes from the Minister of Public Security himself. I will now walk outside to the front of this building. If a car to take me to Erenhot does not appear within five minutes I will telephone the minister personally with a report of this bureau's obstructionism."

The car was there in four minutes.

"PULL over to the other side of the road and park in front of that truck," said Avakian. "I want to talk to the guy."

"If you don't mind me asking," said Judy. "Out of a hundred truck drivers taking a leak by the side of the road, why do you want to talk to him?"

"Because my mother always used to say that when you saw a truck full of hay you should make a wish."

"Of course. I should have known."

"And also, because he's a Mongol driving a truck with Chinese plates. Because he's my age, which means he might speak some Russian. And because he's carrying hay, which means he came from Mongolia."

"I'll understand later, won't I?"

"You will if this works."

Avakian grabbed her bag and let himself down gingerly. The Mongol was zipping himself up, more than a little concerned about the bearded bedraggled foreigner with one leg of his bloodstained jeans flapping open. His hand dropped into his pocket, and Avakian figured there was a knife in there.

He opened both hands in a peaceful gesture. "Speak Russian?" he asked in his very bad Russian.

The Mongol nodded warily and replied in that language. "A little. American?"

Avakian did not confirm or deny. "You—me. Talk. Do business?"

Another wary nod told him to continue.

"You. Take over border." Avakian pointed to the truck. "I. Back. Secret. No tell border guard." He knew how to say border guard, at least. "No tell none. You take other side—safe—I give you 150,000 yuan." He unzipped Judy's bag to show him the color of his money. "Understand?"

During this little chat the Mongol's expression had shifted from outright skepticism, to impending dismissal, to holy shit.

"Think," said Avakian. "You work one hour. Big money. Border guard, you tell Zhangjiakou fighting. Afraid. Go back. But." At that he held up a warning finger. "You tell border guard I," a wave of the hand toward the truck, "truck—you die number 1." He showed him the pistol. "Understand? Tell me."

The Mongol replied in much better Russian. "I hide you in back of my truck. Take you across the border. You pay me 150,000 yuan." And at that point he stopped. "Yes?"

"Yes," Avakian said, relived he'd gotten through.

"I tell border guard I scared of fighting in Zhangjiakou. Go back home. I tell border guard about you, you kill me."

"First thing," said Avakian, having dug up the right words in the interim.

"150,000 yuan?" said the Mongol.

Avakian nodded. He knew that had to be a couple years pay, if not more. He was counting on the nearly universal Asian belief in fortune and luck.

The Mongol gestured toward their truck.

"You want?" said Avakian.

The Mongol nodded.

"You take," said Avakian. "After border."

The Mongol grinned. "Okay," he said in English, holding out his hand.

Avakian shook it. An ancient human custom that may have originated with the Mongols. Done in order to confirm that your weapon hands were empty. "Money after."

"Money after," the Mongol confirmed, still grinning.

While he conferred with his assistant, Avakian hobbled back to Judy. "Grab my bag, darlin'. We're leaving."

"What's up?" she asked.

"They're going to give us a ride across the border."

"Just like that?"

"I venerate human nobility," said Avakian. "But I rely on human greed."

By the time they packed up and made the way over, the Mongols were hard at work in the back of the truck. The driver stuck his head out the top and waved them up.

It was another open-topped FAW. Red. There was a ladder on the front of the cargo bed just behind the cab.

"I'll take both bags," Judy said, in a tone that brooked no discussion. "You just get yourself up, nice and easy."

"Yes, Doc." Avakian used both hands and one leg, rolling over the top onto the hay. The Mongols had pulled bales out like building blocks to create a hollow pocket near the bottom. It sure looked like they'd done this before. Maybe he hadn't needed to be all that persuasive.

The Mongol pointed the way down. He made a gun with his finger, aimed it at the cab, and mimicked the sound of a gunshot. Smiling all the time.

"What's that all about?" said Judy.

"Promised I'd kill him if he hosed me," said Avakian.

They even arranged a bale to make a comfortable seat. For 150,000 Avakian would have expected no less. They sat down and the Mongols set the bales on top of them. Lights out. They could hear and feel the bales thumping down, and the tarp being pulled back over the top.

"Are you sure you can trust these guys?" Judy whispered in his ear. "Wait a minute. Forget it. That had to be the stupidest question I ever asked in my entire life. And at the worst possible time." She kissed his cheek. Still no temperature.

"Comes down to this," Avakian whispered back as the truck started moving. "You go to Vegas, you bet your life on black, and you watch while they spin the roulette wheel."

COMMISSIONER ZHOU'S driver was a young officer 2nd grade who seemed overjoyed to have the opportunity to drive a hundred miles down a highway at top speed. He was also a terrifyingly bad driver, a rural boy who had probably never even set foot in a car until he joined Public Security.

To keep his mind off that Commissioner Zhou worked his phone the entire trip, hounding both the border post and the Erenhot Bureau. The bureau promised to begin sweeping both the highway and the town for the truck.

The car swerving caused him to look up from his phone just in time to watch the driver move into the oncoming lane in order to pass a truck. The boy was following his orders, he thought, dropping his head to dial again. The car shook, which made him look back up to see a car coming head on, disregarding the police car and the flashing lights his own driver seemed serenely confident in. "Get over!"

The driver swerved back into the right lance, missing both the truck and the oncoming car by centimeters. "Be careful, you fool!" Commissioner Zhou snapped, as the phone in his hand rang. "Commissioner Zhou," he said into it.

"Comrade Commissioner, Inspector Kuang of Erenhot. We have found your truck. Ten kilometers outside the city limits on 206 Highway."

Commissioner Zhou cut him off with, "What of the Americans?"

"The truck is abandoned. There are gunshot holes in it and signs of blood. We have alerted all hospitals and medical stations."

He must have wounded one of them. "Good work, Inspector. I am very close. Look for them on stolen motorcycles. They have done this before."

"We will alert our units, Comrade Commissioner."

Despite his words Commissioner Zhou was not encouraged. For Avakian to have left the truck without being chased meant he had found something else. Now the vehicle description was worthless to the border post.

"Lights ahead, Comrade Commissioner," the driver reported.

"Stop at the truck."

Officers were dusting it for fingerprints. A sergeant was in charge.

"Commissioner Zhou, Beijing."

The sergeant saluted. "Sergeant He, Erenhot city bureau, Comrade Commissioner."

"What did you say your name was?"

"Sergeant He."

A common enough name, but it had given him a start. "Report, Sergeant."

"Ten bullet holes in the truck, Comrade Commissioner. Observe this one in the door." The sergeant opened it. "And the blood on the inside, floor, and passenger seat. A substantial wound caused by the bullet through the door. Expended 5.7mm rifle casings inside the cab. No other evidence so far."

"Witnesses?"

"None yet, Comrade Commissioner."

Without another word to the sergeant, Commissioner Zhou walked slowly around the truck. On the south-bound side of the road yet facing north. Why not park on the normal side of the road?

The Erenhot patrol cars had parked both in front and behind the truck, in the soft sand beyond the highway pavement. And the vehicles in front were parked directly over the tire prints of another truck. The wind had barely blown sand into the tread marks. "Sergeant!"

He came running. "Yes, Comrade Commissioner?"

"Make a plaster impression of these truck tire marks before your fools drive over them again."

"Yes, Comrade Commissioner. My apologies."

Commissioner Zhou was already running for his car. Yokels. "Quickly, to the border," he told his driver.

Who left his own sandstorm speeding away?

Would Avakian try the crossing, or would he brave the fences and mines? It was difficult to believe he would try to bluff his way across. Every westerner was taken aside for intensive examination, and all Americans automatically detained. This was not common knowledge, but Avakian would of course suspect it. As for himself, he had no choice. He would have to stake everything on the border crossing. Deep in thought he chanced to glance out his side window. "Pull over," he ordered.

Two bicyclists. Mongols. Pedaling for the border with their bicycles piled high with shopping bags. Everything was cheaper in China.

No other witnesses on the highway. Only vehicles that had long since passed by. But these two were just slow enough that they might have seen something.

Commissioner Zhou had risen when so many had not because he knew that nothing happened in China, nothing, without being seen by someone. The trick was always to find them and make them talk.

The bicycles halted before his outstretched hand. "Speak Chinese?" Commissioner Zhou asked. With the police car behind him he did not bother with credentials.

One Mongol shook his head. The other said, "Yes, sir."

"Did you see the green truck back on the highway? Abandoned?"

The Mongol gave a negative shrug.

"Papers," said Commissioner Zhou.

Two Mongolian passports were handed over. They seemed to be in order. "What can you tell me about the people in the truck?"

"Nothing, sir. We saw nothing."

The other trick was to know when you were being lied to. "Maybe you remember something at the station," Commissioner Zhou said. "Get in the car."

"What of our bikes, sir?"

"We have no room for bikes. Leave them here. Unless you remember seeing something." Their bicycles and goods would most certainly be gone when they returned.

A brief conversation in guttural Mongol. "We saw two people with the truck, sir. A man and a woman."

Despite his swelling excitement, Commissioner Zhou was careful not to react to that. "What did they look like?"

"Foreigners, sir."

"Mongols?"

"No, sir. White foreigners. Both of them. The woman was blonde. The man limping."

"Where did they go?"

"Into the back of a red truck, sir. Filled with hay."

"License number?"

"We did not see it, sir."

"The driver?"

"Just a truck driver, sir."

"Which way did the truck go?"

"North."

Commissioner Zhou threw the passports at them and frantically dialed the number of the border post. As it rang, he shouted to his driver. "The border crossing. Use the siren."

———

KNUCKLES RAPPED on the back of the cab.

Avakian put his arm around Judy. "We're at the crossing. Not a sound."

Right after he said that Judy was seized with an irresistible impulse to start drumming her feet on the floor. She actually felt like she had to grab ahold of her knees to stop herself.

The truck stopped, and those brakes really squealed. The hay shifted, rocking back and forth around them as if threatening to come crashing down. Avakian had always loved the smell of hay, but couldn't help wondering if Judy had allergies.

He could hear the driver speaking Chinese to someone. It sounded cordial. He only caught the word Zhangjiakou.

The engine started up, and they were moving again. The truck seemed to make a bit of a turn. Shit, they weren't getting sent over for inspection, were they?

The truck stopped again. More talking. He couldn't make out anything on either side this time.

Moving again. He didn't know how much more of this he could take. A siren behind them, getting louder. They came to a sudden stop. Both cab doors slammed. Son of a bitch! Getting out of the line of fire.

Feet clomping on the ladder and the tarp being pulled back.

Avakian turned Judy toward him so he could kiss her in the darkness. And took his arm from her so he could draw the pistol. Time for that last stand around the flag. The hay above them began to move.

———

COMMISSIONER ZHOU'S driver came up the emergency lane of the 4-lane border highway. When he jammed on the brake, they went off the pavement and skidded into the soft sand, nearly knocking down a lamp pole.

An arch stretched across the width of the highway. It was painted like a rainbow. There was a white guard-house with a red roof, and a metal accordion fence that could be pulled all the way across the highway if neces-sary. Two Army light tanks were posted on either side.

He ran up to the guard on the northbound side. "Commissioner Zhou."

A salute. "Yes, Commissioner, we are expecting you."

"Have you seen the red truck?"

"Was it not a green truck, Comrade Commissioner?"

"Red. Red, I say. Filled with hay. You were not told?"

"No, Comrade Commissioner."

At that precise moment an officer stuck his head out from the guardhouse and shouted, "Alert for any red truck filled with hay, trying to leave. Must be stopped."

The guard turned to Commissioner Zhou with his mouth open. "Comrade Commissioner, one just went across."

Commissioner Zhou gave no sign that he had heard. He was standing before his countrymen, his subordinates. He could not lose face.

They would not let him resign. No, they would send him to Tibet. The freezing cold. The altitude sickness. Not Lhasa, but some forsaken town with yak butter tea and yokels who did not wash. They would not let him keep his rank. It would be years of standing in the snow on anti-riot duty. Beating up locals for having pictures of the Dalai Lama. That would be his fate.

Chapter Twenty-Eight

AS THE HAY bale was pulled up over their heads and the sunlight washed in Avakian's arms were extended and his finger on the trigger. Just waiting for a target. Even though they'd probably toss a grenade in first.

The Mongol's smiling face appeared in the opening. He gave the thumbs up. "Okay."

Avakian blinked. What?

Judy was already climbing up. She stuck her head out, looked around, and said, "Hand me up the bags."

Shaking from the adrenaline dump, Avakian re-holstered the pistol. He tossed her bag up and started climbing.

"What about yours?" she said.

"Present for the boys." He did not want to be toting an automatic rifle around Mongolia. Reaching the top, he sat down on the hay and looked around. It was the most beautiful ratty border town he'd ever seen in his life.

The Mongol said, "Zamen Uud."

"Zamen Uud," Avakian repeated.

The Mongol pointed down at his bag.

Avakian pointed to the Mongol.

The Mongol nodded and grinned again.

While Judy climbed down, he had a few words with

the driver, passing him some money. Borrowing a pencil, he wrote some numbers on one bill. The driver handed the cash to his assistant, who jumped from the back and ran off.

His leg kept zapping him all the way down the ladder. The pain was becoming as familiar as a toothache. Two more zaps as he took the bag from Judy and climbed into the cab to settle up.

The bank had given them a lot of small bills, which was just fine with the Mongol. Avakian carefully counted out 150,000 and the Mongol just as carefully re-counted that.

"Okay?" Avakian asked.

"Okay." The Mongol said something in his language that sounded like a blessing. They solemnly shook hands.

The reckoning had taken a while. The assistant driver was already back with a bag. Avakian gestured for him to give it to Judy. He tried to hand Avakian the change. Avakian gestured again for him to keep it. The assistant insisted on shaking hands, too.

The truck drove off with hands waving out the windows.

They'd been dropped right in front of the Zamen Uud railroad station. Now that was service.

"There go two honest thieves," Avakian said admiringly.

They were both looking around as if checking for new threats. Both realized it at the same time, looked at each other, laughed, and embraced.

They held each other for a good long time.

"Thank you, Pete."

"Thank *you*, Judy."

She wiped her eyes. "If there was ever a situation where thanks weren't enough. Don't worry, I'll show you the full extent of my appreciation later."

"Believe me when I tell you I've never looked forward to anything more."

He was white from the stress and the pain. She held his face in both hands, part affection and part checking for fever again.

"I feel like I should steal something and keep running," said Avakian, laughing. "We don't need to, but it's like eating potato chips. Once you get started it's hard to stop."

"We'll try to break you of that," Judy said. "Maybe there's a twelve-step program." She realized she'd been holding the Mongol's bag and peered into it. "What's in here?"

Avakian grinned. Feminine curiosity overruled everything. "Should be a pair of pants for me. Soap, towels, and a comb. Though based on the speed I'm not holding out much hope. I thought if we went in a store in our present condition people would be diving out the windows. Shall we repair to the station lavatories?"

"Why, are they broken?"

"Oh, that was just wrong."

Twenty minutes later, Avakian was sitting on a station bench, watching the world go by. The Mongol kid had actually gone a little crazy. He was wearing a new white shirt and black trousers. With the sleeves and legs rolled up they even halfway fit. Anyway, he didn't smell completely like shit anymore. But it was going to take a lot more scrubbing later.

He was still all keyed up and knew he would be that way for a while. But it was not only an utter pleasure to be alive, it was a pleasure to be sitting around waiting for a woman to get out of the bathroom.

When Judy turned up, he about fell off the bench laughing. She was wearing the same white shirt and black slacks. "This is great," he said. "Promise me we'll always dress alike from now on."

She was giggling uncontrollably. "We look like Mormon missionaries, don't we?"

"I love it."

"The underwear wasn't working. I had to go commando."

"I don't know if that information is important now, but it may be in the future."

"What's going on the world? I assume you found out while I was in the ladies' room."

"Unfortunately, the newspapers are all in Mongolian Cyrillic, and international TV news has yet to reach the Zamen Uud railway station. But I talked to a few people who spoke some English and German." He laughed. "They wanted to know where *I'd* been."

"Really," said Judy.

"Taiwan hasn't given up yet, but everyone seems to think it's only a matter of time. It seems that China and the U.S. are kind of like a couple of heavyweight boxers shuffling around each other without throwing a punch. Each one knows they can knock the other out, but they don't want to get knocked out trying to do it. The U.S. imposed a sea blockade, without calling it that, on the entire region. Which is a major hit to the Chinese economy. Riots popping out around the country, which seems to be what we ran into back in Zhangjiakou. Big buildup in North Korea, but they haven't come across the border. And the Chinese haven't let any Americans out of the country since the shooting started. There's rumors of prison camps."

Judy sighed and shook her head, feeling very emotional. "I obviously picked the right guy to travel with," she said, looking down at him fondly.

Avakian had no response to that. "That's all the news I was able to get."

"Well, let's get the hell out of here before the Chinese decide to invade Mongolia."

"The next train to Ulan Bator is in two hours, so you can get yourself some better threads. The sleepers were all booked, so we'll probably have people snoring on our shoulders the whole way."

"I don't care if someone's sitting on my lap the whole way. Two hours, you say? Give me some money. I'm going shopping."

He started to get up.

"You're not moving an inch on that leg," she said. "That's final."

"Judy, this is a border town."

"I've been to Tijuana. I'll be fine."

"I'll worry myself sick."

"Well, welcome to *that* club. I'll show you the secret handshake later."

He'd already changed a bunch of yuan to Mongolian tugruk at the railway station bank. Handing it over, he said, "Stay on the main drags, don't go down any alleys, don't listen to any guides, and don't flash too much of this around."

"I'm sorry," she said. "Did you say something?"

He sweated out every minute of the hour she was gone.

Eyeing the bags she dropped at his feet, he said, "You didn't engage any servants?"

Judy handed him a bottle of water. Producing a pill bottle from her new knock-off Prada bag, she shook out two pills. "Are you allergic to any antibiotics?"

"No." He looked the tablets in his hand. "What are they?"

"Antibiotics."

"I walked right into that, didn't I?" He popped them down.

"These are brutes. So, if you start feeling weird, let me know."

"Judy, I don't know what weird is anymore."

"Really. There's a lot of that going around." She gave him another, larger pill. "Painkiller."

"Now we're talking." Then it occurred to him. "Are you licensed to prescribe drugs in Mongolia?"

"No, but I am licensed to bribe pharmacists."

"I won't squeal on you to the AMA."

"I've got everything I need to dress your wound properly."

"Hey, the tampon was great. A real combat medic trick. But I'm sure we can get the bullet out in Ulan Bator."

"We are not," she informed him. "I'm chartering a medevac flight and getting you back to the U.S. Where I will operate on you personally."

"Isn't that some kind of professional conflict of interest?" he inquired.

"*You're* getting concerned about rules now?"

"It's not that," he said. "This is going to be payback for everything I put you through, isn't it?"

"I'm not going to put another bullet in your leg, if that's what you're worried about."

"But I will wake up with hair plugs and a new nose, right?"

Now she almost fell off the bench laughing. "I like your nose just fine, thank you. And I prefer your head shaved."

"I like you better as a brunette," he said.

They both smiled at each other lovingly.

"I'm serious about the flight," she said. "The lesson I've learned from all this is that I don't want to stay in Asia one minute longer than I have to."

"We've learned many lessons, Judy," he said gravely. "But aren't they all secondary to what we've learned about each other, and ourselves, over the course of this journey?"

Her laughter rang through the terminal. Everyone was looking at them. She laughed so hard she fell over him onto the bench and ended up with her head in his lap. "Oh, I almost threw up," she said weakly.

"I assume I'm doing my rehab in Denver," he said, stroking her hair.

"Of course," she said, looking up at him. "But this doesn't mean we're dating."

"What are you talking about?"

"You know how this all started."

"Yeah. There was an assassination. Which caused a war. And then everything kind of went downhill from there."

"This happened," she said firmly, "when I went out to dinner with you. I'm sorry, but I've learned my lesson. I'm never going out to dinner with you again."

Avakian thought that one over. "Do you cook?" he asked.

A Look at: Bargain with the Devil

Retired U.S. Army Special Forces Colonel Peter Avakian is now in Africa. Having accepted a contract to protect an abrasive South African oil executive in Nigeria, he foils a kidnapping plot and neatly extracts the man from the country.

Summoned to a meeting in Cape Town that he imagines is a thank-you and a payoff, he is instead invited to join a group of British and South African mercenaries intent on staging a political coup in the West African country of Benin that—it later becomes clear—is being financed by Nigerian drug runners, Russian gun smugglers, and South African oil interests.

Now that he's heard the proposal, Avakian needs to both protect and cover his behind. So, he turns to the CIA. And, as he could have predicted, he's pressured to become their mole inside the coup plot.

How far is Avakian willing to go? And how far can he go and *still stay alive*? In the end, Avakian's survival may depend on two women: a CIA officer and a South African reporter. Whether they will save him or betray him is anyone's guess.

AVAILABLE MAY 2022

About the Author

William Christie was born in Massachusetts. He graduated from the University of Pennsylvania with a Bachelor of Arts degree in Political Science. He then joined the United States Marine Corps and served as an infantry officer.

After leaving the Marine Corps he began writing. His first novel, *The Warriors of God*, was published in January 1992. He has published nine novels.